THE CEO, THE PUPPY AND ME

JENNIFER FAYE

THE TEXAN'S BABY BOMBSHELL

ALLISON LEIGH

MILLS & BOON

First Published in Great Britain 2020
by Mills & Boon, an imprint of HarperCollinsPublishers,
1 London Bridge Street, London, SE1 9GF

The CEO, the Puppy and Me © 2020 Jennifer F. Stroka
The Texan's Baby Bombshell © 2020 Harlequin Books S.A.

Special thanks and acknowledgement are given to Allison Leigh for her contribution to *The Fortunes of Texas: Rambling Rose* series.

ISBN: 978-0-263-27882-8

0620

MIX
Paper from responsible sources
FSC www.fsc.org
FSC® C007454

This book is produced from independently certified FSC™ paper to ensure responsible forest management.

For more information visit: www.harpercollins.co.uk/green

Printed and bound in Spain
by CPI, Barcelona

THE CEO, THE PUPPY AND ME

JENNIFER FAYE

CHAPTER ONE

THIS WAS IT.

The moment Gia Bartolini and her two siblings, Enzo and Bianca, had been waiting for.

And yet this was also the moment they'd been dreading.

On this sunny June day, their lives were about to be once more upended. And worst of all, it could be any one of them who received the devastating news—that they were not a Bartolini.

After their parents had unexpectedly died in an auto accident a few months earlier, their lives had never been the same. Her older sister, Bianca, had found their mother's journal, which contained a secret—a big secret, a *huge* secret. Their mother had had an affair years ago, and one of the siblings wasn't a true Bartolini.

And to make matters worse, their parents had spelled out in their will that only one of them would inherit their childhood home—a vast estate and vineyard in Tuscany. The two remaining siblings would inherit an equal fortune in cash and investments. But all three of them wanted their home—well, that was until Bianca had literally found her Prince Charming. Now she was about to become a princess, and that left Enzo and Gia in the contest to figure out who would lay claim to their childhood home and the family business. Talk about a complicated situation.

Within the Tuscan villa, Gia wrung her hands as her gaze moved around what had until recently been her father's study. While the rest of the house had been remodeled into a boutique hotel, she'd strived to keep this room as her father had left it—warm and cozy. The place where she'd spent countless hours as a child getting help with her homework. Now it was the boutique hotel's office—her office.

The Barto Villa had had a slow start. However, when Bianca agreed to be the wedding planner for the prince of Patazonia in exchange for a media campaign for her wedding business based here at the villa, the hotel business had boomed practically overnight.

The increased business meant Gia had to hire a couple of assistants to help manage the place. Michael, her manager, had moved there from Florence with his young family. Rosa, her assistant manager, was an older local woman with an incredible ability to keep everything organized. Together, they kept the hotel running smoothly.

Upon Bianca's acceptance of the prince of Patazonia's marriage proposal, they all knew things would have to change once more. Bianca had to let go of her wedding planning business in order to assume her new responsibilities—first as a princess and a short time later as the queen.

Not wanting the wedding business that meant so much to her to die, she'd put her assistant, Sylvie, in charge of upcoming weddings, and Bianca flew between the vineyard and the palace on a regular basis, making sure everything in both places was running smoothly.

And then there was Enzo. He'd given up his work in France, where he'd married some of the world's finest grapes to create the most amazing wines, in order to return home and take over the Barto Vineyard. Would he regret that decision if he were not a Bartolini?

Gia's gaze moved around the room. Each sibling had consciously or unconsciously taken a seat on a different side of the room from the others. Their parents' deaths had divided the family. And Gia didn't know if they'd ever be close again.

Even though it was a summer morning, a distinct chill hung over the room. Gia folded her arms across her chest. She'd never felt so worried and—and scared. Yes, she was scared of what the DNA results would reveal. Would her family—the only family she'd ever known—be able to navigate past this?

She had absolutely no idea. Her mind was reeling with all the possible scenarios. None of them were good. All of them had heartache and pain. It wasn't right. And it was her parents' fault. They'd done this to their own children. What kind of parent held on to such an important secret for so long?

What if she wasn't a Bartolini? She quickly dismissed the idea. That couldn't be the case. Even Bianca had pointed out that Gia had been her father's favorite. It wasn't something that she would ever admit to anyone, but her father used to spend extra time with her, teaching her how to ride a horse, how to pick a grape at just the right time. When she was little, he would carry her around the vineyard on his shoulders. No matter how busy he was, he made time for her.

But that knowledge and those memories didn't lessen the significance of this moment. No matter what, three lives were about to change. And Gia didn't like change. She liked routine. She liked the reassurance of knowing what to expect. And right now, she had no idea what to expect. Would it be Bianca? Or Enzo?

Her heart went out to them. She couldn't imagine what it must be like to be facing such a great unknown. She would be there for them, doing what she could to lessen the blow. She loved her siblings with all her heart—even if things had turned turbulent lately.

But if Aldo Bartolini wasn't the biological father of one of them, who was? And why had their parents kept it a deep dark secret? The questions nagged at her.

Gia clenched her hands together, noticing a slight tremble. She wanted to stand up and tell the attorney to burn the unread DNA results—let everything go back to the way it used to be. Back to when her overprotective brother gave her dates a stern warning about dealing with him if they did anything to upset his little sister. Back to the times when she and her sister could spend hours on the phone talking about absolutely nothing in particular and yet ended up talking about everything.

"Thank you all for coming," said the attorney, Mr. Lando Caruso. The older gentleman sat behind what had been her father's desk as though it were his. "I know waiting for these results hasn't been easy. So I'll dispense with any advice except to tell you that these results in no way change the will that your parents left behind."

Gia's insides shivered with nerves. This was it. This was the last moment all three of them would be a full-fledged family. Her gaze watched the attorney as he used her letter opener to slice open the white envelope.

It was as though time slowed down and her heart pounded louder. She rubbed her moist palms together, squeezing her laced fingers. She didn't know what to wish for when he read the results. She didn't want either of her siblings to feel as though they were any less a Bartolini.

The attorney unfolded the sheet of paper. He adjusted his reading glasses, and then his gaze skimmed over the page. "There's a bunch of legalese and scientific lingo that I'm sure none of you are interested in at this moment." He was quiet for a few seconds "Ah, here we go. The lab has confirmed that two of you are indeed the biological children of Aldo and Carla Bartolini—"

"Who is the unlucky soul?" Bianca pressed.

"Yes," Enzo interjected. "Let's get this over with."

Gia remained quiet. After all, this wasn't her crisis. Not really. She was an observer.

The attorney folded the paper, took off his reading glasses as his gaze met with each of them. There was regret and sympathy emanating from his eyes. Then he cleared his throat. "I'm sorry to say that the Bartolini sibling who is not Aldo's biological child is… Gia."

She gasped.

This can't be right. There has to be a mistake.

The attorney looked at her with pity. "I'm sorry, Gia."

No. No. No. This isn't happening.

And yet it was happening. To her.

She sprang out of her chair, which toppled over. She backed up, stumbling into it.

I am the outsider.

It was at that precise moment that her world came to a screeching halt. She wasn't even sure she was still breathing because the attorney's words sucked the oxygen from the room.

I'm not a Bartolini. I'm not a Bartolini.

The words swam around in her mind at a dizzying pace. Her stomach churned. She didn't move. She didn't speak. Was it possible this was just some horrific nightmare? Her gaze moved around the room. They all looked at her with pity in their eyes.

It's true. She inhaled a sob. *I'm the outsider.*

Each admittance was like a dagger to her heart. The scene before her blurred. She blinked repeatedly. How did this happen? Why her? Not that she'd wanted it to be her brother or sister either. Why did it have to happen to any of them?

The next thing she knew, Enzo and Bianca were beside

her. Bianca enveloped her unmoving body in a big hug. She wasn't sure what Enzo did because she just couldn't process anything. She vaguely heard the deep timbre of his voice. It was the words he spoke that eluded her.

I am not a Bartolini.

Her world had gotten smaller and smaller until she was caught up in her own thoughts—disturbing thoughts. Painful thoughts. Anguished thoughts.

I am not a Bartolini.

CHAPTER TWO

SHE WASN'T A BARTOLINI.

Not a true Bartolini.

Not like her brother and sister.

Each time she thought of it, Gia felt betrayed. The knife of pain would sink further into her heart. How could they have kept this from her all of this time?

And who was she if she wasn't a Bartolini?

She recalled what her sister had said once about possibly not being a Bartolini, the fear she'd expressed that her father—if not Aldo—might be a criminal. Anything was possible at this point. And that made the agony that much worse.

Though her siblings tried to comfort her, she closed them out. They didn't understand this level of uncertainty—about herself, about the past and about the future.

Betrayed by the two people she thought she could trust most in the world—her parents—Gia threw up barriers around her shattered heart. After all, who was going to care about her—to love her—when she had absolutely no idea about her true identity, her heritage?

Gia had barely slept or eaten since the DNA results had been revealed. And each day the walls of the villa felt as though they were closing in around her. She didn't belong here. But where did she belong?

Thankfully she had assistants to pick up the slack with the hotel. Right now, it took all her willpower just to take care of herself. She felt like a fraud. She wasn't Gia Bartolini any longer. But she didn't know who she was. She was a woman who'd been lied to all of her life. How could her parents have done this to her?

Anger roared through her veins. It wasn't fair that this life-altering news was tossed in her lap—destroying everything she thought she knew about herself—and her parents weren't here to explain it to her, to fill in the details.

Bianca had stuck around a couple of days, but last night she had to return to Patazonia as Prince Leo was waiting for her. Their engagement was to be made formal and their wedding date announced for December of that year. It seemed her sister was becoming the queen of planning quick weddings.

Already the mad rush to have a wedding planned by a future princess was dying off now that word was out that Bianca was no longer running the day-to-day operations, but rather overseeing things from a distance. Gia knew as time went by and her sister's calendar filled in with royal obligations that Bianca's visits to the villa would grow farther apart.

Gia was happy for her sister, but sad for herself.

It was though the rug had been pulled out from under her. And she was struggling to regain her balance, because she had nothing to grasp on to. She had no idea who her biological father was or even how to contact him.

Frustration and anger balled up in her gut. The poignant emotions clawed at the back of her throat. And then they erupted in an anguished groan.

She had taken three days to wallow in her pain, but now it was time to do something. Something good must come of this heartbreaking disaster. She refused to think this wasn't some sort of journey she was meant to go on.

That was it! She was meant to find her biological father. It would be an adventure for both of them. Because surely he didn't know about her. If he did, she imagined he would have fought to be in her life. That's what fathers did—looked out for their children. No matter what.

She had to find him. Now. This very moment. Too much time had already passed.

She jumped out of bed. Gia rushed to the shower for the first time in forty-eight hours. She wasn't going to just let this unknown past swallow her up. She would find the answers she wanted—the answers she needed.

After a quick shower and a moment to run her fingers through her short hair, fixing her pixie hairstyle, she was headed out the door of the guest house where she resided. She was a lady on a mission. She entered the main house and successfully avoided everyone as she took the back stairs to the second floor.

In her parents' room—the only bedroom she'd yet to convert to a guest room—she began her search. Sure, she and her siblings had been through this room before looking for clues, but she was certain they'd overlooked something. And she wasn't going to stop until she'd found it.

She started in one corner of the spacious room. No piece of furniture was overlooked. Every nook and cranny was examined. She had no idea how long she'd been searching by the time she'd reached halfway around the room. So far she'd uncovered absolutely nothing…

Creak.

It was the door. Gia inwardly groaned, realizing she'd forgotten to turn the lock.

"Gia?" It was her brother's voice. "What have you done?"

There was astonishment, surprise and disapproval in his voice. Like he had room to judge her. He had his life just as he'd always known it. He knew who his mother and father were. No one had lied about his birth. He knew that he'd gained his passion for growing grapes from his father.

But what did she have? A bunch of questions? An unknown—unnamed—father? No. Enzo didn't get to judge what she said and did now.

She straightened, leveled her shoulders and turned to her brother. "I'm looking for answers."

He stepped farther into the room. "But this?"

So she'd made a little mess. She'd clean it up. She turned to see what he was complaining about. And then she realized it was more than a little mess.

She'd removed every drawer from the dresser and flipped it over to see if there were any pages, documents or scraps of paper taped to the bottom that might point her in the right direction. She'd moved furniture, looking beneath each piece with the flashlight app on her phone as well as searching for loose floorboards where things might be stashed.

So far all she'd succeeded in doing was making a mess. But it wouldn't stop her. If it took pulling up each and every floorboard or chipping away at any uneven surface on the wall or ceiling, she'd do that too. She wasn't leaving here without something to point her in the direction of her biological father.

"If you've come here to stop me," she said, "you can just turn around and leave."

Enzo didn't say a word at first. "I didn't come to stop you. I came to help you."

Disbelief quickly followed by a rush of love flooded her system. "You did?"

He nodded. "I'd be doing the exact same thing if I were you. Just tell me where to start."

She turned all around, looking for a clean space for him to start in. And then she pointed to the vanity—the place where her mother would powder her nose and apply her eye shadow each morning. "Try searching there."

Enzo nodded and set to work.

Together they worked side by side just like they always had. But did Enzo still consider her as much his sister as he did before the test results? She didn't know. And she didn't have the courage to ask. Some things were better left unsaid.

"I've got something!" Enzo held up a black leather-bound journal.

"Where was it?"

"There was a secret compartment in the back of one of the drawers. I'm afraid that since I didn't have the key, I had to break the drawer."

"Who cares?" She rushed forward and took the journal from him.

She flipped opened the book to a random page, immediately recognizing her mother's handwriting. At last she would learn the truth.

But would she like what she'd learn?

CHAPTER THREE

IN HIS OFFICE on the small Italian island of Lapri, Riccardo Moretti pressed enter on the computer keyboard. Then he typed the last lines of coding for a cutting-edge predictive algorithm. It would streamline transportation, pointing out inefficiencies as well as suggesting alternatives.

He smiled. If this worked out the way he'd planned, not only would he make a nice tidy profit, but more importantly it would also help reroute food and supplies to those in need. Shipping costs would be minimized and absorbed by transportation companies instead of charitable organizations and private donors. This program could make a fundamental difference in people's lives.

Buzz. Buzz.

He pressed the intercom button to speak with his assistant. "Yes, Marta."

"Sir, there's a woman on the other line. She's calling about your uncle's house."

"My uncle?" Uncle Giuseppe had passed close to a year ago, leaving his entire estate to Ric.

"Yes, sir. It sounds serious."

Alarm shot through him. He knew possessing a now vacant house might cause some security issues, but he wasn't ready to part with it. For some reason he wasn't willing to examine too closely, he had an attachment to the place.

Ric checked his cell phone. There hadn't been any alerts from the alarm system. How could that be?

Still, he didn't have time for problems. There were only

a couple of hours before his very important business dinner—a meeting that had taken months to arrange. But he couldn't just ignore this call. "Put her through."

He'd speak to the woman. Surely it was nothing important. And then he'd be back on track. Everything would work out.

In no time, an older woman came on the phone. "Ric, is that you?"

He smiled, remembering his uncle's neighbor, the kindly woman who'd offered him cookies still warm from the oven when he was young. "Mrs. Russo?"

"Yes. It's me. Pardon me for bothering you at the office, but I thought you'd want to know there's a young woman snooping around your uncle's house."

"Is she trying to break in?"

"I don't think so. But I can't be sure. She's moved to the back, and I can't see her now."

His office wasn't far away. "I'll be right there."

And with that he ended the call. He rushed to his car, anxious to catch this intruder. He wanted to stop them from doing any damage to his uncle's estate.

He went to call the police but then hesitated. Calling them would draw media attention, and he'd had more than his share in recent weeks. He'd check out the situation and then decide if the authorities needed to be called in.

In no time, his midnight blue sporty coupe rolled to a stop in front of the house. From the front, nothing looked disturbed.

However, Mrs. Russo had indicated the person was making her way around the house. Being that it was quite a large place, he would need to make the rounds in order to surmise if the intruder was still there.

He stepped out of his car. Immediately, Mrs. Russo came

rushing out of her house. He waved her off, signaling for her to go back inside until he had the situation under control.

It could be as simple as a salesperson, but then why would they have ventured around the house? Ric moved carefully and quietly. He wasn't about to engage the intruder if they were armed. But that didn't mean he couldn't witness what they were up to so he could report it to the police.

As he neared the back of the house, he noticed a young woman in a flowy white-and-aqua top. White capris clung to her curves and a coordinating purse completed the summer outfit. As his gaze lowered, he noticed she only wore one high heel. As she hopped around on one foot, he noticed the other aqua heel, which appeared to be stuck between two cobblestones.

Her face was turned away from him. She had short, dark, spiky hair. If she was a burglar, she was an awful one. First, that summer outfit was bright and eye-catching. And those shoes, wow, how could anyone walk in them? Well, obviously she couldn't, or she wouldn't be hopping around on one foot. Whoever this woman was, she certainly seemed quite harmless.

Ric stepped into the backyard. "What are you doing here?"

The woman's head turned. Her eyes rounded. Her mouth opened, and for a moment nothing came out. "I…uh, heard something back here."

"Heard what?" He crossed his arms over his chest as he waited for her to explain herself.

He'd been down this road before. Beautiful women made up every excuse possible to access his home or the office. One had even posed as his sister to get past his assistant. The problem was, he didn't have a sister.

The movie release had been just the other week. His very

brief movie debut had been the result of losing a bet to the star of the film—an old friend from school. The press coverage over his nonspeaking appearance hadn't died down at all. In fact, it appeared to be getting worse as time went on. If this kept up, he was going to have to hire a security detail. He didn't relish the idea. He valued his freedom to come and go as he pleased without checking in with anyone.

The fact that his privacy had been invaded to such lengths infuriated him. So if this woman thought he was going to fall for some concocted story, she had another think coming.

Before either could speak, a sorrowful whine filled the air.

"Please help it." Her big blue eyes begged him.

Regret for jumping to conclusions assailed him. Her dog had gotten loose, and she'd followed it into this overgrown garden. When Uncle Giuseppe had grown sick, he wasn't able to continue working in his beloved garden. Ric had offered to hire a gardener, but his uncle wouldn't hear of it. His uncle never lost hope that he would win his battle with cancer, and he would one day be back in the garden. That day had never come.

The woman balanced on one foot while hunched down, trying to free her other shoe. Seriously, how did he end up in these situations?

The whine sounded again.

He moved to help the woman first.

"No." She shook her head. "I'll get this. Go help him."

Ric found a new appreciation for the woman, more worried about her pet than herself. He looked around but couldn't see the animal. He wasn't even sure about the size of the dog, but it couldn't be very big or he would have spotted it by now.

Still, it would just take a moment for him to help the

woman. He bent over and pulled on the heel. To his surprise, it was thoroughly wedged in there. She really was in a bit of a bind.

He pulled on one of the stones with one hand while working the shoe free with the other. And then it pulled loose. When he handed it over, he waited for her to have a meltdown about the mangled shoe, but she quietly slipped it back on her foot.

He felt compelled to say something. "Sorry about the shoe."

"It's okay. It's kind of the way my life has been going lately." When she put weight on her foot, her face scrunched up into a look of discomfort. She immediately raised her foot again.

"What's the matter?" he asked.

"I twisted my ankle when my shoe got stuck. It's not a big deal. Just help the puppy."

"You're sure?"

"Positive."

He did as she asked. However, his light gray loafers weren't the best shoes to venture through this overgrown jungle either. Limbs poked and prodded him.

There went the high-pitched whine again.

"Do you see it?" the woman asked.

He shushed her as he backtracked a bit. And then he followed the scratching sound to the back corner of the garden. There were shrubs and other overgrown vegetation blocking his view.

He worked his way through the vines, ignoring how the thorns dug at his arms. As the dog whimpered, Ric grew more determined to help it, even if he ruined his clothes during the rescue.

And then at last, he spotted a little puppy all caught up

in some old wire. Its big brown eyes turned to him. They showed its panicked state.

"It's okay." Ric spoke in a calm, soothing tone. Every time the puppy got worked up and yanked to get loose, the wire dug farther into its flesh. Ric knelt in front of it. "I'm going to help you."

The puppy stopped wiggling for a moment and studied Ric. The animal watched his every movement but didn't react. It was either so relieved to finally have help or it was too exhausted to put up much of a fight. Either way, it took a bit but Ric was able to untangle the dog. He made a mental note to call a gardener ASAP. This place not only looked bad, but it was also dangerous to anything that meandered in here. He didn't want any other creature getting hurt.

But the deepening red stain on the dog's ginger fur had him concerned. Heedless of the blood and dirt, Ric scooped the pup up and held it against his chest.

"It's okay," he said in a gentle voice. "You're safe now."

He made his way back along the overgrown path to where the woman was standing. He stopped in front of her. "Here's your dog."

All her attention was focused on the animal. However, she made no motion to take it from him. That was strange.

"It's not mine." And then her eyes widened with concern. "It's hurt."

"I know. It got caught up in some wiring. Looked like some old fencing or something." He glanced at the dog wiggling in his arms. It was still bleeding, and it was getting all over his shirt. "Could you hold him?"

"Sure." They moved carefully, trying to avoid aggravating its injury.

Ric pulled off his ruined shirt. In any other context, the surprised look on the woman's pretty face would make him laugh but not now—not under these circumstances.

"It's for the puppy, to help stop the bleeding. I have another shirt in my car."

The woman's glossy lips formed an O.

Once the shirt was securely tied around the dog's midsection, it settled in her arms. "Does he belong to one of your neighbors?" she asked.

"I don't know. It's not my…" He was going to say it wasn't his house, but that was no longer true. It was his house—his great big house. That he had absolutely no idea what to do with.

It was far too big for just him, but he didn't have the heart to get rid of the place where he'd spent so much time with his aunt and uncle when he was little. It was the only real home he'd ever known. The short time he'd lived with his mother, they'd moved from one house to the next. His jaw tightened as he slammed the door on the unhappy memories.

Ric turned his attention back to the villa. He supposed he'd have to work up the nerve to cut the emotional ties and sell it sooner rather than later. There was no point of letting it turn to rubble because he couldn't bear to part with it. After all, he was a businessman. He made tough decisions every day. Why was this one so much harder than the rest?

That he couldn't answer. Maybe it's what he was waiting for—the answer. And then he could move on.

"Your shirt will help for now," she said, drawing him from his thoughts. "But we have to get him to a vet. The cut looks bad. It might need stitches."

We? When had they become a we?

When Ric finished adjusting the makeshift bandage, his gaze met the woman's. She was no longer frowning at him. "I take it you approve?"

Her gaze lowered to his chest before her eyes quickly

rose to meet his. Color bloomed in her cheeks. "I... I do. Now, where's the closest vet?"

"I have no idea. I don't have a pet." For a man used to having all the answers, he felt totally out of his depth here. And he didn't like the feeling—not at all.

"If you hold him again, I can look on my phone."

Noticing that the puppy looked content in her arms, Ric shook his head as he pulled out his own phone. "I'll do it."

In no time, he had the address of the first listed vet. It was across town. He thought of calling for an appointment, but that would just waste time, and by the way the blood was soaking the makeshift bandage, they didn't have time to wait. The puppy needed help now.

He read off the address to her. "I would just show up. I'm sure they'll help you."

"Help me?" Her gaze searched his.

It was then that he really looked at her, taking in her spiky, short hairdo and those vivid blue eyes. He'd never seen eyes of that vibrant color. They were stunning, just like the rest of her.

She frowned at him. Oops. He'd missed something she'd said, but he refused to let on that he'd gotten utterly distracted.

"You want me to go with you?" he asked, hoping he was on the right track.

"Well, this is your home, is it not?"

He thought of his afternoon appointments. His calendar was full. But more importantly, he had that meeting with Giovanni Grosso. This was the man who held the keys to Ric's company expanding into charitable work—a can't-miss opportunity.

But then Ric's gaze moved to the puppy. It needed help, and it did get hurt on his property.

With a resigned sigh, Ric nodded. "We better hurry."

He would call his assistant on the way. Hopefully, his appointment with Mr. Grosso could be moved around. He knew the man was only in town for a short period.

The woman limped along beside him. He felt bad for her. "Do you need some help?" When she sent him a puzzled look, he added, "You know, walking?"

She shook her head. "I'm fine. I just sprained it. It'll be better in no time."

They rounded the house, and he came to a stop next to his car. He reached in the open window for his gym bag. He withdrew a muscle tee and pulled it on.

Ric turned back to the woman. "Do you want to lead? Or follow?"

"I… I don't have a car."

Interesting. But there was no time for questions—even if he had a lot of them. He opened the passenger door. "Hop in."

She did so without argument.

Once they were on the road, he realized he had absolutely no idea what this woman's name was. They'd been thrust into saving the puppy and had dispensed with the pleasantries. But if they were going to help the puppy—together—they should at least exchange names.

"We didn't introduce ourselves," he said. "My name's Riccardo Moretti. You can call me Ric."

"My name's Gia."

No last name. Interesting. He supposed he didn't blame her for being a bit reserved. After all, she didn't know him at all.

When he glanced her way, he found her head turned to the side as she stared out the window. So much for making small talk. Besides, he preferred the silence. He wasn't one to get close to people. After his mother dumped him on his aunt and uncle at the age of seven, he'd learned not to trust people. And the fact his mother never told him who his father was only added to his distrust—distrust that morphed into anger. Not knowing how to deal with such strong emotions at such a young age, it came out at all the wrong times.

It wasn't until he was older that a teacher took him under his wing. Mr. Rinaldi told him that he should take all the energy he put into being mad at everyone and use it to make a difference in the world. He had to admit that his fourteen-year-old mind didn't think the man knew what he was talking about, but when he began applying himself to his classes, just to see if he could do it, he was quite surprised with how easy mathematics and computer sciences came to him. And soon he was at the top of his class—for the first time in his life. When he realized the only thing holding him back was himself, he excelled at most anything he tried.

Ric swore to himself that he was never going to need anyone again. He built his life so that he could be totally autonomous. He lived his life behind a computer screen. He ordered food, clothes and anything else without the need to interact with people. He would never be let down, used or hurt again.

Minutes later they arrived at a very busy veterinarian's office. Thankfully, the staff took notice of the severity of the cut and rushed them back to an exam room.

While Gia was inside, seeing that the dog was properly taken care of, he moved outside. He phoned his assistant, trying to figure out how to reorganize his afternoon.

When Ric ended the call, he heard the office door behind him open. He turned to find Gia limping toward him with the puppy in her arms. It now had a red collar and a matching leash. "How'd it go?"

"They said the cut looked worse than it was. The vet put in stitches and gave me some medicine. And a cone. They also supplied me with a care package of food and toys to tide us over until we get to the pet store." Gia lowered a big white bag from her shoulder and handed it to Ric. "Poor guy. We're good to go."

He was relieved to hear it was nothing more serious than stitches. "I'll just go inside and pay."

"I already took care of it."

"You did?" He could tell by the frown on her face that it was the wrong thing to say. He'd been caught off guard as he was used to always picking up the bill.

"I did."

"They also checked him for a chip," she said. "He doesn't have one. They took his photo and said they'd post a notice for a lost dog."

"That's a good idea. I'll post a notice online when I get home."

Once Ric got Gia and her bundle situated in the passenger seat, he closed the door. He rounded the car, hopped in and started the engine. At last he could get some answers that had been nagging him since he'd found the woman in the garden.

But first there was something he had to know. "Where can I drop you?"

She mentioned a trendy little hotel in the heart of Palmas. "But I don't think it allows pets."

He grabbed his phone and checked. She was right. He smothered a sigh. Whatever could go wrong with this day had gone wrong.

"We'll just have to find a place for the puppy," he said.

"You could take him." Her eyes held a hopeful gleam.

Ric shook his head. "I'm never home. And I know next to nothing about animals."

"It isn't that hard. And we can't just drop him anywhere. We have to see that he gets his medicine and make sure he doesn't rip out his stitches. The vet also said we had to watch for signs of an infection."

It looked like it was up to one of them to look after the puppy until they could find its owner. But with the future of his company in the balance, it couldn't be him.

Ric shifted the car into drive. "We'll stop and pick up your things. Then we'll find you a pet-friendly place to stay."

He waited for her to argue. But instead, she nodded.

As he made his way into traffic, the questions that had been nagging him returned. Keeping his eyes on the road, he asked, "What were you doing at the house?"

She didn't say anything at first. He was beginning to think she wasn't going to answer the question. Did she have something to hide? Was she in fact one of those women who sought him out because of his five minutes of fame?

He halted that thought. Sure, he hadn't known Gia for more than an hour or so, but in that time, he'd learned a lot about her. She loved animals. She was more concerned about the puppy than her sprained ankle. And he sensed she was a good person.

She didn't strike him as the type to track him down…for what? A photo? To ask him out? He never was sure what women wanted from him. Whatever it was, they weren't going to get it. He had his priorities aligned. And they didn't allow room for him to get distracted.

Then Gia's soft voice filled the car. "I'm not really sure why I was there."

That was not the response he was expecting. "Are you lost?"

"No. Not exactly."

She wasn't making a whole lot of sense. "There had to be some reason you were at that particular house and not somewhere else."

"The address was on a slip of paper I found in my mother's journal."

If he was confused before, he was even more so now. "So you were searching for your mother?"

"No." When he pulled to a stop at an intersection, he chanced a glance at her. She once more had her head turned away. "I was searching for my father."

That answer startled him. It took him by surprise to the point where he sat motionless until a car honked behind them, spurring him into pressing the accelerator once more. His thoughts raced as he tried to put what she'd said into perspective.

He swallowed hard. "You think your father lived in that house?" She didn't answer, so he looked her way again. She nodded and he continued. "I take it that it's been a while since you've seen your father."

"I... I, uh, never met him."

Alarm bells were going off in Ric's head. Was it possible this gorgeous woman sitting next to him was his cousin? He shifted in his seat, leaving a little more space between them. This day had definitely taken some unexpected twists and turns. None of which he'd seen coming. Not at all.

CHAPTER FOUR

WHAT WAS WRONG with her?

Why was she telling this perfect stranger about the most painful secret in her life?

Gia leaned her head back against the black leather headrest, holding the puppy that was still groggy from the sedative the vet had given it in order to put in the stitches. Her fingers brushed gently over its downy soft fur. The action gave her some sort of comfort, but not enough to keep her from dwelling over the disappointment of not finding the answers she'd been seeking. If her father had ever been in that house, he was long gone now.

How was she going to find him? Was she even on the right track? The questions swirled in her mind at a nauseous pace. Maybe some people would say it didn't matter. But to her, it mattered very much.

She wanted to know, did the smattering of freckles over her nose came from him? Did he love snack food as much as her? Did he sing in the shower? They would have such a good time answering each other's questions. In no time, they'd be the best of friends. If only she could track him down.

And in the next breath, she had to ask herself if this mission would be so important if she hadn't just lost her mother and the man whom she'd always thought of as her father in a sudden and horrific car accident. No, she didn't have to stew over it or debate the matter. She knew finding her biological father would be important no matter what.

But her mother hadn't left many clues. She rarely mentioned the man in her journal, and never by name. Gia wondered if it had something to do with her father... No, the man who'd raised her. Aldo never struck her as the jealous type, but she supposed if your wife had an affair and a baby from said affair, that might make a person jealous—very jealous. Still, Aldo never let on—at least not in front of her.

So who was her biological father? And when she did find him, what if he wanted nothing to do with her? The breath hitched in her throat. It was nice to dream of him welcoming her with open arms, but what if he refused to acknowledge her?

Her pulse raced. Her throat tightened.

That won't happen. Just think positive. It will all work out. It has to.

She needed it to.

She swallowed hard. This subject was so difficult for her, but she couldn't give up now. "Have you owned the house long?"

Ric continued to stare straight ahead at the thickening traffic. "No."

That was it? A one-word answer. Not good enough. "Did you know the previous owner? Maybe he's who I'm looking for."

Ric was quiet for a moment as though debating his answer. "The house belonged to my aunt and uncle."

"Oh." Her mind ran with the idea. If the house belonged to his aunt and uncle. And if his uncle was her father—

Her thoughts screeched to a halt. No wonder he was acting strangely around her.

"Do you think— I mean, is it possible...could it be—"

"That we're cousins? I don't think so." His tone was firm.

"But we could be..."

Ric wheeled off into a parking spot and turned to her. "Did you hear about my uncle's death? Are you here for the inheritance because if you are—"

"I'm not!" She glared at him. He had absolutely no idea what she'd been going through ever since her parents died and left their family totally upended. "I swear. I have money of my own. Enough that I never have to work again if I choose not to."

"But you work now?" His tone had changed to something less hostile.

"I do. I started a boutique hotel." She didn't offer him more details than that. At this point, he hadn't earned her openness about her parents' will or the contest to gain control over the Bartolini estate.

Surprise and…was that respect flickered in his eyes? "So if I check, I'll find that you aren't some scam artist or anything nefarious?"

There he went again, ruining their semi-truce. "Check if you must, but you won't find any of those things." And then turning the tables on him, even though she knew exactly who he was from all the media hype, she asked, "And if I were to check on you, what would I find?"

"That's a good question. I'm not sure either of us would like what the media's printing about me these days." And with that he made his way back into traffic. "I guess we have things to learn about each other."

"And whether we're cousins. Or not?"

The words hung in the air between them like some ominous cloud. The potential for it to be true bothered Gia. Her cousin should not be so dashingly good-looking. The memory of his tanned, toned abs came to mind. She definitely shouldn't notice his good looks. But it was impossible not to.

Without another word, he made his way to her hotel.

When he pulled up in front, he turned to her. "I don't have time to care for an injured puppy. And you can't take him into the hotel, so it looks like we're going to have to work together. Do you think we can do that, you know, for the good of the dog?"

"I don't see why not." Her gaze met his. Every time he stared into her eyes, like he was doing now, her heart raced. She swallowed hard, trying to maintain her composure. "I don't mind doing my part, but you should know I can't take care of an injured dog full-time. I'm only here for a brief amount of time. And I have things to do."

He looked as though he was going to say something, but he paused as though rethinking what he'd been about to say. "Understood."

Using the utmost care, she handed him the puppy. And then she got out. She headed into the hotel to see if they would make an exception to their no pets policy and, as expected, they refused. And so she checked out early. She wasn't sure where she was going to stay that night, but she couldn't just abandon the puppy, and Ric didn't seem comfortable caring for him.

As she made her way to her room to gather her things, she couldn't stop thinking about Ric. She'd recognized him right away in the garden. Someone would have to live under a rock not to recognize the man after all the media coverage he'd garnered for his part in that movie—this year's smash hit.

The funny thing was that he didn't have an actual part— at least not a speaking part. It was more like he came walking out of the ocean with waves breaking behind him as rivulets of water raced down from his short dark hair to his broad shoulders to his muscled chest, and then there were those six-pack abs. She could now testify that those close-ups were most assuredly real and not airbrushed.

But the fact there was a possibility he was her cousin utterly blew up all of those totally inappropriate thoughts. She'd been eager to learn about her other family, but she hadn't thought she'd end up with Ric Moretti for a cousin.

This day had started so promising.

And with each passing hour, his optimism had faded away.

A frown pulled at Ric's mouth. The fact Gia could be his cousin shouldn't bother him. After all, it wasn't like he would be upset about losing the inheritance. To be honest, he'd amassed his own fortune with his innovations. And now he wanted to pay it forward—to leave this world a little better than he'd found it.

The dog whined, drawing Ric from his thoughts. He adjusted his hold. His thumb stroked the pup's fur, feeling its little ribs in the process. This little guy had been on his own for a while now. Ric knew how that felt, but it didn't make it better. In fact, it made it worse.

"Don't worry fella. We'll make sure you end up in a good home where you'll always have plenty to eat, a warm bed and you'll never get hurt again."

The puppy turned its head and rested it on Ric's forearm. He seemed quite content on his lap. And though Ric would not admit it to anyone, he was content holding the little guy. He could see why people had pets. Although he wasn't changing his mind about walking through this life alone. No matter how cute the puppy was or how appealing it would be to share life's burdens, he knew relying on someone—trusting someone—came with risks. And he'd already paid dearly. It was a lesson he'd never repeat.

So while the puppy closed its eyes, seemingly content to fall asleep, Ric used his free hand to start searching for a hotel in the city that accepted pets. His first three tries failed.

But the more he thought about it, the more he realized the answer was right under his nose. Or in this case, the answer was right under his roof. His apartment had a spare room that had never been used. And he didn't mind having the dog there—on a temporary basis.

And it would help to have Gia under the same roof until he unraveled the real story about her. Was she really his cousin? Or was she scheming for the inheritance?

He didn't want her to disappear until he knew the absolute truth. And so the decision was made. He would offer her a place to stay.

The car door opened. Gia leaned inside. "I think we have a problem."

He smothered a sigh. "What is it?"

"It's my luggage. It's not going to fit in your car."

Why hadn't he thought of that?

The puppy sat up. He lifted his head and licked Ric's cheek. That was why he hadn't been thinking clearly. This dog had upended his entire day.

"Leave your luggage with the valet. I'll send a car to pick it up."

She hesitated, not moving. The look on her face said she wasn't sure about this arrangement.

"It'll be fine," he said. "Just give them my name."

"Okay."

A few minutes later, she returned to the car. "You were right. Once I mentioned your name, there was no problem. You must have a lot of pull in this town."

"I don't know about a lot, but enough." He went to hand over the puppy, but its little paws went into overdrive as it fought to stay on Ric's lap.

"I think he likes you." Gia smiled.

Her face glowed bright like the sun. The way her lush lips lifted at the corners to the way her cheeks puffed up and her eyes sparkled, it chased away the dark clouds that had been dogging him all day. In fact, her sunny disposition warmed a spot in his chest. He was inclined to smile back, which wasn't like him, but he resisted the urge.

Ric cleared his throat. "Who? The concierge?"

Gia laughed. "No. The puppy. Well, I don't know about the concierge," she said in a teasing manner. "Would you like me to go back and ask?"

"No." Now with the puppy on Gia's lap, Ric checked his side mirror and then stepped on the accelerator.

"Where are we headed?"

"That's what I wanted to talk to you about. I did some searching and tried to find an available hotel on the island that accepts pets, but it wasn't as easy as I would have hoped."

"Oh."

He glanced over, catching the smile slipping from her face. "But I do have a solution."

"I'm listening."

He drew in a deep breath. He knew once he uttered the words, there'd be no taking them back. "You could stay at my place. I have an extra bedroom. And it's right here in the city, so you'd be close to everything." Upon realizing that he was actually trying to talk her into this arrangement, he stopped himself. He would not beg. No way.

"I don't know. You don't exactly seem like the dog type."

He cast a sideways glance at the puppy, who was watching him. "We can manage."

"I... I don't know." She seemed genuinely caught off guard. If this was a performance for his sake, she deserved an award.

She wouldn't be the first person to try to scam him out

of his money—not that his uncle's estate was truly his, at least it didn't feel that way. It felt odd to take what once had been his uncle's.

"It'll make life easier with the dog. And I have a house-keeper who stops in every other day. I'm sure she won't mind helping out with him." He wasn't so sure of that, but he would definitely make it worth her time to puppy-sit.

He could feel Gia giving him a sideways glance. "You're sure about this?"

"It seems rather logical. And I do feel responsible for the puppy winding up hurt."

There was a moment of silence as though she were truly debating her options. He was once again surprised by her. Most women would have thrown themselves at such an arrangement, but Gia seemed really hesitant to take him up on the offer.

"Okay. We'll try it for tonight. By tomorrow, hopefully I can find someplace that takes a dog."

It wasn't much but it was something. "Sounds like a plan. I'll just drop you off at the apartment before I head back to the office—"

"You're leaving?"

Her outburst caught him off guard. This whole time she was acting as though his presence was a bother, but now that he had opened his home to her and needed to get back to work, she wanted him to stay? What was up with that?

He maneuvered his car through the light midmorning traffic. "I have work to do."

"But what about the puppy?"

"I was thinking you could watch him." He slowed and made a right turn. They weren't far from his place.

"And what makes you think my time is any less valu-able than yours?"

She had him there. He couldn't even throw out that he

was on the verge of making a valuable contribution to mankind because he frankly didn't know if his plan was going to work out. Perhaps it was time to get to know his new roommate a little better. He didn't like it, but he could work from home that day—or rather what was left of his day.

"Okay," he said as he wheeled the car into his reserved spot, "I'll stay home too."

"Wait. What?"

"It sounded like you were worried about being home alone with the dog, so I'll work from home today. But this evening I have to go out."

Her fine brows rose in question, but as though she'd caught herself, she glanced down at the pup. "And if I want to go out?"

He shrugged. "I'm not going to stop you." Did she want him to? With most of the women in his past, they would have wanted him to make a fuss. But with Gia, he had the feeling she wasn't the clingy type. She had other priorities on her mind. "You can come and go as you please. I'm just sticking around today to help you out."

"You mean to help the dog."

"Yeah, that too."

She didn't look too pleased with him. He wasn't sure what he was saying wrong, but obviously it was something. The truth was, he wasn't well-versed in making casual conversation with women. Sure, he had his share of dates, but they were usually out in public. And when they were alone, conversation hadn't been foremost on his mind.

So maybe he was a bit rusty with what to say and do. Which was yet another reason he should go to the office. But he'd said he'd stay home today, and that was what he intended to do. Everything he needed to access for his dinner meeting could be done remotely.

Gia's blue gaze met his. "Would you mind getting the

door while I hold on to the puppy? I don't want him jumping out of my arms."

"Sure." He hurried around the front of the car and opened her door for her. "Why don't I show you inside, and then I'll come back for the supplies?"

She nodded. "It has been a long day."

"Did you just arrive in Lapri today?"

"Yes. It's my first visit to the island. After checking in at the hotel, your uncle's villa was my next stop."

"Then you can get the puppy situated and rest while I take care of a few things."

What was wrong with him? He didn't normally play the congenial host—in fact, he didn't play any sort of host. He didn't like people invading his personal space. The only reason he had a housekeeper was because his dislike of cleaning surpassed his dislike of sharing his space.

It had actually worked out for him because Mrs. Rossi was excellent at her job. She cooked for him a couple of times a week, leaving the food in the fridge. And she was always gone before he returned from the office. Of course, that was because he would get lost in his work and forget the time until it was very late.

But having Gia and the puppy here was really going to take some adjusting for him. Still, it would give him a chance to disprove her belief that his uncle might be her father. Because Ric did not believe it. Not a chance.

Or was it that he didn't want to believe it? As she passed him and entered the apartment, he inhaled the gentlest floral scent. It teased him, drawing him in for a closer, much deeper whiff. He resisted the urge. Barely.

CHAPTER FIVE

THIS WAS HIS HOME?

Gia stepped past the double doors into a streamlined modern apartment. It was like something straight out of the glossy pages of an architectural magazine. Everything was in its place. There were no decorations, absolutely nothing on the glass coffee table. White and red couch cushions didn't have a wrinkle or indentation as they sat along the back of the black leather sofa. Trailing the edges of the very high ceiling was exposed ductwork. On one wall hung the biggest flat screen she'd ever seen.

The floors were a gray slate. And the puppy's nails clicked as he danced in a circle, not sure where he should go. He wasn't the only one that felt totally out of his element.

She'd thought her parents' villa was fancy, but compared to this place with its industrial decor and lack of decorations, her parents' home—erm, now her and her siblings' home—was downright warm and cozy.

How did someone live like this? She wasn't exactly a slob, but even her place wasn't this clean and perfectly arranged. Perhaps this wasn't his place. Maybe he was just borrowing it? Maybe it was part of a hotel suite plan. Yes, that sounded like a viable option.

"Make yourself at home," her host said.

"Uh, thank you." She wasn't sure how to be at home when she felt as though the apartment was staged for a photo op. "Do you spend much time here?"

She shouldn't have asked. It was none of her business.

But curiosity was eating at her. She wasn't sure how to make herself at home if he really was some sort of neat freak.

Please say it isn't so.

"I spend a lot of time at the office. But I make it here at some point in the evening."

"Really?" She bit back her bottom lip, hoping to hold in any other unwise comments.

"Yes, really." His dark brows drew together as he studied her. "May I get you a drink?"

She shook her head, not trusting her mouth as it kept betraying her at every turn. There was something about being close to Mr. Tall, Tanned and Toned that disengaged her mind from her mouth. Then remembering the manners her mother instilled in her, she said, "Thank you."

"If you change your mind, help yourself to anything in the kitchen. My housekeeper keeps it well stocked."

"Thanks. But I meant thank you for everything." She knelt next to the dog, who was now sitting beside her. "The puppy and I appreciate you opening up your home to us."

He glanced away and started looking at the teetering stack of unread mail on the console table behind his black leather couch. "It's no big deal."

She had the feeling it was a very big deal. She'd be willing to guess he didn't invite many people into his home. The place definitely didn't look lived in. She'd hazard a guess that this apartment was his housekeeper's favorite place to work as there would never be much that needed to be done.

"I'll just let you get settled. Your room is down the hall to the right."

"Oh." She didn't move.

"Is something wrong?"

"I was just hoping you'd tell me more about your uncle—"

Ric shook his head. "He's not your father."

"How can you be so sure?"

He opened his mouth as though to argue but then word-lessly pressed his lips back together. The frustration glinted in his eyes. But even he couldn't definitively reject the possibility that his uncle was her father.

Ric sighed. "You aren't going to give up on this, are you?"

"No." There was a firmness in her voice. She wanted him to take her seriously. He had no idea how hard this was for her.

Not so long ago, she'd had a family. A mother, father and two siblings. And now it'd all been shattered. She needed to find the truth about herself—about the past. It was the only way she could move forward.

"Why is this so important to you?"

"Really? You don't think it's important to know who your father is?"

"Yes." He drew in a deep breath. "I meant, why now? Why not seek him out years ago? I mean, the timing would make anyone wonder."

"The timing?"

"Yes. You know my uncle passed away and you're looking to challenge his will."

She ground her back teeth together as heated words clogged the back of her throat.

Never speak in the heat of the moment.

Her mother's sage advice filled her mind.

How dare he think she was some gold digger here to steal his money? She liked him much better when he was just a really hunky guy on the big screen with no shirt—ripped abs on display and his mouth closed.

"You might be used to dealing with gold diggers, but I am not one." That was it. She was done with him. She gently picked up the puppy.

"You're leaving?"

"Looks that way. This was a mistake. I'll take care of the dog. Don't worry."

Without waiting for him to say a word, she turned and headed for the door. He was a stranger—a famous stranger but still a stranger. And now she was certain she didn't want to know him. And she certainly didn't want to share her painful secret with him.

"I'm sorry," he said softly. When she didn't stop—when she grasped the door handle—he said louder, "Hey! Did you hear me? I'm sorry."

She paused with one arm around the dog and her other hand on the handle. Apologies were easy. Why should she believe him? It was best they end their brief encounter now.

"I'm not used to having people in my home—in my space," he said. "And I spend most of my time at the office working so my social skills may be a bit rusty. Can we start over?"

He was trying, she'd give him that. But even so, she wasn't willing to open up about how her family had been blown apart by a devastating secret.

But she also sensed how hard that apology was for him. And it deserved a response because those manners her mother taught her at a young age, well, they were still a part of her—even if she didn't know who she truly was.

Gia turned back to him. "Apology accepted."

A small smile pulled at the corners of his lips. He went from being incredibly handsome to incredibly sexy in zero point six seconds. Gia's heart stumbled.

And then she realized she was smiling back at him. How was that possible? One moment, she was furious with him. And then the next, she's smiling at him like some lovesick teenager.

She pressed her lips into a firm line. "I should be going."

"Don't. I mean, stay. I shouldn't have been so blunt."

He at least had the decency to look contrite. She supposed that was something.

"You were being honest." Now that she'd cooled down a little, she could see his perspective. It wasn't like he knew her at all. She was a perfect stranger. A rich man like himself was probably used to people trying to take advantage of him. But she wasn't one of those people.

Just then the puppy whimpered.

"I better take him out." And with that she made a hasty exit.

Luckily, there was a small park just across the street and down the road a little way. She and the puppy were there in minutes. There were a few benches. Nothing fancy, but she wasn't the only one there with her dog. It seemed to be a popular spot.

Now what was she going to do? Return to the apartment and a man who unnerved her with his sexy good looks? Or just head off on her own?

That went wrong.

Completely wrong.

And now he'd run her off. That hadn't been his intent. Well, maybe it had been at first, when he thought she was a con artist. But he saw the pain in her eyes when he'd accused her. That sort of pain couldn't be faked. It was real. And he was the one who had caused it. He felt awful.

He started for the door. When he realized he was chasing after her, it startled him. He didn't chase after women. If anything, it was the other way around, especially lately because of that silly movie. Seriously, it wasn't even fifteen minutes of fame. It was more like sixty seconds. And it was never supposed to amount to anything. And yet it had gained so much media attention.

Ric stopped himself as he reached the door. Maybe it was

best that he let her go. After all, she wasn't going to be related to his uncle. He was as certain of that as he was his name.

And now Gia was one more complication he didn't need—didn't want. He knew the dangers of letting someone into his life. When they found something better, they moved on—no hesitations, no apologies. He refused to let himself be vulnerable again.

She would find her own way—or she wouldn't. He knew something about attempting to track down missing parents. You didn't always get the result you wanted.

He turned and headed for the kitchen. He didn't know why. It wasn't like he was hungry. Still, he opened the fridge and stared inside. Nothing appealed to him.

He wondered what Gia would do for dinner. It wasn't like she could just stroll into a restaurant with a dog. Again, not his worry.

He closed the fridge and then opened a drawer with a stack of takeout menus. Some of them had worn edges. His gaze scanned the first menu. Not even his most indulgent selections could tempt him today—

Buzz. Buzz.

The doorbell drew his attention. He slipped the menus back in the drawer. So she'd changed her mind. Interesting.

His steps were swift. He swung the door open, about to greet her with some glib comment but the words died in the back of his throat. It wasn't Gia and the puppy. He refused to acknowledge the disappointment that settled in his chest.

"Hi." A young man in a black and white suit smiled at him. "I believe you were expecting these." The man moved aside so Ric could see the purple luggage.

Gia's things. They'd totally slipped his mind. He was about to turn the man away, but he had no idea where Gia had gone. It looked like the luggage was his problem.

"Thanks. You can set them inside the door." Ric backed

up, making room for the man and the three pieces of matching luggage.

After Ric tipped the man handsomely, the door shut and he was alone with Gia's things. He rubbed the back of his neck. What was it about this woman? Since she'd entered his life mere hours ago, it had become increasingly complicated.

What he needed to do was head back to the office. When he was at his computer working on his latest project, he felt in control—at peace. Adrenaline rushed through his veins when he was sorting out a new idea. And all his attention was focused on the letters and numbers on his monitor. There were no emotional land mines to avoid. There were facts and figures. Nothing more. Work was clean and for the most part straightforward. Relationships were messy and complicated.

Even when people said they loved you, they ended up hurting you. Not that he loved Gia. He didn't even know her. And that was the whole point—he didn't want to get to know her, to let her into his world. He was better off on his own.

And with that in mind, he reached for his phone. He flipped the leather tag on a piece of luggage and snapped a photo of her name and address. His assistant was good at locating people as well as things. He was certain Marta would be able to reunite Ms. Bartolini with her luggage.

As though his thoughts had summoned her, his phone rang. His assistant's name popped up on the caller ID. She was probably wondering what was keeping him.

"Hello."

"Mr. Moretti, I'm sorry to disturb you, but I've just had a phone call I thought you would want to know about immediately."

Marta was very good at her job and dealing with people. She was used to prioritizing interruptions and only bothering him with the most important items. He had a sinking feeling he wasn't going to like what she had to say.

"What is it?" he asked hesitantly.

"Your dinner meeting with Mr. Grosso has been canceled."

"Canceled?" That couldn't be right. "You mean rescheduled."

"No, sir. His assistant called and canceled the meeting."

Ric's body tensed. This wasn't good—not good at all. He had his entire rollout planned. He was ready to start testing on Mr. Grosso's system.

"What did he say?" Ric's voice came out in a heated rush. "There has to be a reason. I want to know what it is."

Marta was quiet for a moment.

He drew in a deep breath, calming himself. "I'm sorry. I don't mean to take this out on you. I just can't believe after months of going back and forth, trying to arrange this meeting that it has fallen through."

"I'm sorry, sir. I know how much you were counting on this."

"Did they give any hints of what went wrong?"

"The assistant said that Mr. Grosso had looked over the proposal and decided there wasn't enough evidence the program works."

Ric muttered under his breath as he raked his fingers through his hair. "Of course it works. I've been perfecting it for the past year."

He wanted to say that if this man wasn't interested, he would just sell his technology to someone else, but there was no one else with pockets as deep as Grosso Global Transports. And he'd written the algorithm with that company and its needs in mind.

"What shall I do, sir?"

He wished he had a quick answer. He wanted to say to

call them back—to insist on the meeting—but he knew that wouldn't work. Mr. Grosso was a recluse. The fact he'd been granted the meeting in the first place had been a miracle. But Ric wasn't giving up. He just needed a moment to regroup.

"I'll let you know." And with that they concluded their call.

He'd totally lost his appetite now. He headed out the door and straight to his car. He jumped in, fired up the engine and set off toward the office. Soon his fingers would be moving over the keyboard, and then the tense muscles in his neck and shoulders would loosen. His pounding headache would subside and he'd be able to think of a plan B.

He pulled to a stop at the next intersection. As he waited his turn to proceed, he glanced around, taking in the busy storefronts to his right. He'd moved back to the island of Lapri close to four years ago. In all that time, he'd not so much as strolled down the sidewalk. Even though most people walked or rode a moped, he always drove, no matter where he went.

Time was money. And money was power. He didn't have time to waste. He had a life plan—to be the best of the best.

It was one thing he could thank his mother for. She'd shown him what it meant to do whatever it took to reach for your goals—even tossing aside your very young child or leaving him home alone while out on a date. The clincher had been when she'd told him that she was going on vacation while he stayed with his aunt and uncle and she'd be back for him. The truth was, she had no intention of coming back for him—ever. She'd sloughed off his seven-year-old self in order to marry a man who abhorred children. It still left a bitter taste in the back of Ric's mouth.

And then there were other women who used children to get what they wanted—or at least they tried. One girlfriend had even faked a pregnancy, trying to get him to marry her. Until he'd demanded a paternity test.

He'd truly thought his last girlfriend was different. They'd dated for close to two years. Then he'd caught her cheating on him. When he'd confronted her, she claimed the new guy was open, trusting and wanting a family—everything Ric wasn't.

His luck with women was bad—to say the least. It's the reason he'd sworn off relationships. He was better off on his own.

His gaze moved to the driver's side window, zeroing in on a small park. It was really no bigger than a few benches, a swing set and a fountain.

Today it seemed rather busy with people walking their dogs—another thing he didn't have in his life. Sometimes he thought it might be nice to have a pet, a dog loyal to him that would never reject him or use him for its own greedy needs.

And then other days, he enjoyed his freedom to come and go as he pleased. Not to have to worry about anyone else but himself. He realized how selfish that sounded, but he wasn't hurting anyone. It was simply his choice to live alone—

Wait.

A flash of bright aqua caught his attention.

Is that Gia?

He stared over at the park. The woman had her back to him, but it sure looked like her. And then his gaze lowered to the puppy with the plastic cone around his neck. It was definitely her.

Honk! Honk!

The angry horn blast reminded Ric that traffic was stacking up behind him. He proceeded through the intersection. He found a safe place to turn around, and then he backtracked to the park.

He told himself it was the luggage that had him seeking Gia. It couldn't be anything else. After all, her problems were just that—her problems. And he had enough of his own problems at the moment.

Still, that didn't keep him from pulling into a parking spot along the road. He told himself the sooner the luggage was gone, the sooner any thought of Gia would be gone and the sooner his life would return to normal.

He climbed out of his car and headed for Gia, who was talking to an older woman. He found that odd, considering she said she was from the mainland. And she'd acted as though she hadn't been to Lapri before now. Perhaps she hadn't been telling him the truth. It wouldn't be the first time a woman had lied to him.

He cleared his throat. "Excuse me. Gia?"

Both women turned to him. The older woman with short, silver hair smiled at him. A big bright smile lit up her eyes. She adjusted her black-rimmed glasses as though to get a better look. "Aren't you?" She snapped her fingers as though she couldn't quite place the face with a name. "You know, the guy in the movie." Color rushed to her cheeks. "The one who walks out of the ocean with all of that water rushing down over that muscular chest?"

The woman certainly didn't shy away from matters. He could respect that. However, he didn't return the woman's smile. "That would be me."

"Oh, my! Wait until the women in my apartment building hear about this. I'll be the most popular person today."

Hmm…so he was only good for one day's worth of popularity. He stifled a laugh. If he'd have known the notoriety that clip would have given him, he never would have agreed to it. Still, this woman looked mighty pleased with herself—as though she'd discovered him.

Gia tilted her chin upward. There was no sign of a smile on her face. "What are you doing here?"

"I wanted to let you know your luggage has been delivered."

"Oh."

That was it? He stopped to let her know—to let her retrieve her things from his place. "I'm headed to the office, but I can let you in the apartment to get your stuff."

The older woman lightly elbowed Gia. "If I was you, I'd definitely stay." She glanced at Ric and waggled her brows before turning back to Gia. "You'll be okay with this one?"

"I will."

"Then I'll be going. I can't wait to tell Josephine about this. She's always bragging about her nephew's celebrity friends. This will get her." Then a worried look came over the older woman's face, and she turned to Ric. "You don't know Josephine, do you?"

He shook his head. "I don't know any Josephine."

"Good. Good." She turned back to Gia. "I'll see you tomorrow, if you decide to stay." Then she gave the leash in her hand a gentle tug. "Come on, Princess. It's time to go home."

And then they were alone, except for the dozen or so other people in the park. He shifted his weight from one foot to the other, not sure what to say. Still, he couldn't stand here all day. Even the dog agreed as he sat down in front of them and stared up as though asking what they were going to do now.

Ric told himself to make a clean break. He once again reminded himself that her problems weren't his problems. But he knew what it was like to wonder about a missing parent. The only problem was he didn't have a clue who his father might be. Unlike Gia, his mother didn't have a clue. When he'd asked her, she'd told him that his father was a nobody and that she didn't recall his name. Who didn't recall the name of someone they procreated with? Every time he thought of her casual response, his blood pressure shot up at least twenty points.

When he glanced around, he noticed people were pointing in his direction. Oh, no. It appeared Gia's new friend wasn't the only one to recognize him. He inwardly groaned.

"We should go," Ric said.

"Back to your uncle's place?" Hope shone in her eyes.

"You really believe he's your father, don't you?"

She lifted her shoulder before letting it fall back in place. "If he isn't, I have to believe there's some sort of link in the house."

"And if I refuse you access?"

Her pointed stare met his. "I will find out the truth. With or without your help."

He knew she meant it. And he respected her determination. He just hoped it'd be enough for her to find the answers she so desperately needed.

Ric checked the time. It was past lunch, and with his business dinner canceled, he had no pressing appointments. "Why don't you come back to the apartment? Maybe tomorrow I could help you with your search."

Why in the world had he gone and offered to help? To clear his uncle's name, sure. But when she turned to him with excitement and appreciation gleaming in her eyes, he knew there was no way he could take it back.

And yet the smile that followed sent his heart racing. And then without thinking, he smiled back. Once he realized the affect she had over him, he glanced away.

He cleared his suddenly dry throat. "Shall we go?"

"Yes."

As they walked to his car, he assured himself that her stay would be brief. He'd make sure of it—even if he had to spend every waking moment disproving her claim.

CHAPTER SIX

RIC TURNED OUT to be a surprisingly good host.

They'd even gone on a shopping spree at a pet store after leaving the park. Gia told herself accepting his invitation to stay at his apartment was the simplest solution as far as the puppy was concerned. And there was Ric's sincerity when he'd said he would help her search for her father. How could she turn him down?

After all, she didn't have any leads other than the address of his uncle's island villa. There had to be a reason her mother held on to that address. And Gia had to hope it had something to do with her conception. Because if it didn't, she might never find the answers she so desperately needed.

And so the next day, Gia stood behind Ric as he unlocked the massive door to the villa. The puppy continually barked, pulling on the leash to get away. What was up with that? Usually he was quiet—well, as quiet as a puppy could get.

Gia gently pulled on the leash. "Gin, enough."

"Gin?"

She glanced at Ric wearing an amused look. "I couldn't keep calling him puppy, could I? What kind of name is that? And he is a ginger. So I shortened it to Gin." She glanced down at the puppy. "You like your name, huh?"

Gin looked up at her as though trying to tell her something.

"Do you need a little walk?" She turned to Ric. "We'll be right back."

She let Gin lead her to the patch of grass, but instead of stopping to do his business, he pulled hard on the leash trying to get to the backyard. Gia knew the dangerous mess that awaited them back there. Gin barked repeatedly.

"No. We're not going back there." Not in the mood to fight with the dog, she leaned down and picked him up.

Her action startled Gin into silence. As she headed back up the steps to where Ric was waiting for them, Gin licked her cheek. All was well in the world once more. Well, sort of. At least where the puppy was concerned.

But now she had bigger matters on her mind. Her heart raced as she thought how this moment might lead to answers about the past—about her conception. She couldn't wait to track down her biological father.

"Please excuse the condition of the place." Ric opened the door. "I've had it locked up since my uncle's passing. I… I just needed time to deal with it."

"I understand." Not everyone was thrust into action by a contest written into a will, like she and her siblings had been after their parents' unexpected deaths.

Gin wiggled in her arms. With the door shut, she put the little guy down to explore, but she didn't let him off the leash.

Her thoughts turned to her family's villa in the rolling hills of Tuscany. Guilt niggled her for just up and leaving the whole business with her two managers. But she just couldn't stay there and continue to act like nothing had happened.

Finding out she wasn't a Bartolini had been devastating. She'd lost her footing, and she didn't know if she'd ever feel sure and confident again—not until she found out exactly who she was and who her ancestors were. And most of all, she had to learn why her parents had lied to her all her life. Who did something like that?

"Gia?" Ric turned to her from where he now stood across the spacious foyer. "Are you coming?"

The puppy pulled on the leash, anxious to follow Ric. In comparison to her childhood home, this place was colder and a lot more proper. She glanced around, finding what looked to be expensive works of art on the walls.

While the puppy sniffed his way around the room, Gia took in her surroundings. She wasn't sure what she'd been expecting. It was as though the house was just waiting for someone to walk in the door and bring it back to life. There weren't any dust covers, though the place could definitely use them.

"My uncle's study is this way." Ric headed toward the back of the house.

She followed him. All the while, she took in the high ceilings with their ornate plasterwork as well as the collection of artwork. It was like walking through a museum. She couldn't believe Ric had closed up this place instead of moving in.

Though maybe it was the old-world style of the home that kept Ric away. After all, his apartment was state-of-the-art, and the style had a modern industrial flair to it. Very different from this villa that was from another century.

Gia entered the study, noticing all its dark wood and antiques. It was an organized room. Everything appeared to be in its spot, but coated with an inch of dust.

However in a matter of minutes, Ric had undone all the order as he opened drawers and piled papers on the desk and more on the coffee table that sat in front of the brown leather couch beneath the windows.

Gia sneezed.

Gin sneezed.

"Sorry," Ric said. "I guess it's been a while since this place was dusted."

"Can I help you go through the papers?" She wasn't quite sure what he was searching for other than proof she wasn't his uncle's daughter.

She couldn't really blame him. She knew how devastating family secrets could be. They didn't just change the past, but they also changed the here and now. And who knew about the future. Something told Gia that no matter who her biological father turned out to be, her family would never be the same. The thought weighed heavy on her heart.

"Give me a second." He heaved another stack of file folders onto the already crowded desk. "On second thought, give me a few minutes to figure out where to start looking for clues."

She wanted to ignore him and just dive into the files. She was so anxious to find the pieces of the puzzle to complete her life's story, but she had to wait. She was here at Ric's invitation. She didn't doubt if she got pushy, he'd withdraw his help immediately. She just had to be patient. That was easier said than done.

But if Ric's uncle was her father, that meant this villa was a piece of her past. And without anything better to do, why not explore the place? Maybe she would learn more about the man. The thought appealed to her.

"Do you mind if I look around?"

Ric glanced up from an open folder. He looked confused at first, as though he'd forgotten that she was still in the room. "Um, sure. Yeah. I'll be here if you need me."

And so she was off, Gin right at her heels. She hoped while she was gone that Ric would find the answers she so anxiously wanted. The home was quite spacious, with three floors of elaborately decorated rooms.

Gia noticed there were portraits of the same woman on each floor. They must be images of Ric's aunt. She had been a beautiful woman. And as Gia passed through room after room, it was obvious Ric's uncle loved and missed his wife after her passing, because her feminine touch was in each room as though he was just waiting for her to return.

Gia fell in love with the home. Its classic decor was tasteful but not overdone. And sure, it needed some updates, but whoever lived in this house next would be fortunate. She could imagine many happy family moments spent here.

Ric's image flashed in her mind. Would he someday give up his bachelor pad and settle down here? Something told her that he'd only do it once he had a family of his own. The thought dampened her mood.

She told herself the reason it bothered her was that she still had no idea about her other family. And she had no idea why her parents had strived to keep the secret from her. Why do that? It wasn't like her parents were super secretive people. But when it came to her birth, there was a reason they didn't ever let on. Did her very existence threaten their marriage? Did they fear she would bring her biological father into their lives and it would ruin the reconciliation they'd strived to achieve?

And without knowing about the circumstances of her conception, how could she move forward? What would people think when she said she didn't know who her father was? How would anyone truly love her when she didn't truly know herself?

"Gia!" Ric's voice echoed through the wide hallways and up the grand staircase. "Gia, come here."

She left her troubled thoughts behind as she rushed down the wide staircase to the main floor and to the study where Ric was rifling through a large stack of papers. He was certainly intent on finding the answer of her paternity.

* * *

What a mess!

And he was only making it worse. But it had to be done eventually.

Ric leaned back in the old leather office chair that his uncle used to spend most of his day in before his death. When Ric was young, he imagined himself one day sitting in it and working at this very desk.

It was amazing how things had changed. Now, Ric knew he'd never live in this house. And he would never spend his days working behind this desk. It just wasn't in the cards for him.

This sprawling villa was for a family—something he'd never have. To live here, he'd be reminded every day that he was alone. But he also knew too well that people could tell you they loved you in one breath and leave you in the next. Family life was not for him. Gia may want to expand her family but not him. He was fine alone.

Ric frowned as he glanced at the overflowing desk drawers. He shouldn't have put off cleaning out the house. Not only did he have the unruly garden to tend to, but the inside would need a cleaning crew if he was ever going to make it presentable for a buyer. But those were problems for him to deal with another day.

However, he realized if he had taken the time to clean out the house, he would have found this information sooner. Realizing he'd paused, he continued scanning the page before him.

"What is it?" Gia's voice cut through his thoughts. "What did you find?"

There it was again. The hope in her voice. She wanted Uncle Giuseppe to be her father. She wanted this to be her reality. And suddenly Ric felt guilty for being right.

He cleared his throat. "My uncle saved everything. And

when I say everything, I mean it. It's going to take forever to sort through all these papers."

She moved over next to Ric on the couch. In that moment, he was tempted to turn to her—to take her in his arms and kiss her.

He halted his runaway thoughts. What in the world was wrong with him? He barely knew her—though that had never stopped him in the past. And she would probably be leaving town after he confirmed his suspicion—though her imminent departure was more of a reason for him to get involved. He was torn between his rising desires and his common sense.

Stay focused. Tell her the truth. And then walk away.

He focused on the papers in his hands. "What is your birth date?"

She told him.

"So that would mean at the time of your conception my uncle didn't own this house. He was, in fact, working in New York City."

"That can't be right." She frowned.

"It is. I checked three times." He handed her the documents to see for herself. "I'm sorry."

Gia's fine brows drew together as she scanned the very old pay statements from his uncle's employer as well as the sales agreement for the house. There was no way she could claim they were forged. Those papers were so old and aged that they'd fall apart if anyone were to tamper with them.

Maybe his uncle being a bit of a hoarder wasn't such a bad thing. Still, Ric was going to have to go through this stuff page by page. He didn't relish the idea. And he wasn't taking this mess to his apartment. No way. He'd sort through it here with a paper shredder and a very large garbage can—or two.

Gia was quiet for a long time. She must have had her

heart set on finding answers today. He told himself not to get drawn in. It wasn't any of his business.

And then he made the mistake of looking at her. The pain and disappointment in her big blue eyes was like a kick in the gut. He understood her turmoil. He'd tried for years to search for his mysterious biological father. With his mother unable or refusing to help, there were no other leads for him to follow.

Gia glanced down, staring at the pages in her hand. She flipped through the papers. Her gaze quickly scanned for something.

"What's the matter?" he asked.

"The ink is faded on this sheet. I'm trying to figure out who sold your uncle this property." Lines of frustration formed on her beautiful face.

"Here. Let me take a look."

She hesitated as though unwilling to admit defeat but then she handed him the pages. He looked through them and noticed how some of the corners had fallen off or had been torn off. And he couldn't read the faded type print.

"I'm sorry. I can't make it out either," he said.

Gia lifted her head. Her eyes were misty. "I should have known it wouldn't be easy. Nothing about this entire journey has been easy."

The unshed tears shimmering in her eyes tugged at the walls around his heart. He reached out and squeezed her arm. "It's going to be okay. You're going to be okay. Even if you never find him, you are strong and you'll find a way to make peace with it—"

She pulled away from his touch. "How do you know that?" Anger and pain vibrated in her voice. "You have no idea what I'm going through. No one knows."

He didn't know if he should remain quiet or if he should speak up. It wasn't like he ever talked about it, though it was no secret. "I don't know my father either. I have absolutely no idea who he is or anything about him. And trust me, I did everything I could think of to find him."

Her eyes widened. For a moment, she didn't speak. "I... I'm sorry. I had no idea. I shouldn't have said that." She shook her head. Her shoulders drooped. "I'm just so frustrated. I don't know why my parents kept this from me. They should have told me a long time ago."

"My mother didn't tell me either. Well, I obviously grew up without a father, but she refused to tell me his name." He gave himself a mental shake. "But this isn't about me. I hope you're not too disappointed."

She didn't say anything for a moment as though thinking things over. "It's okay. I'll find him another way."

"I guess this means you'll be heading home." The thought should have elated him. It didn't, which made no sense.

Her gaze met his. "No. I'm not done here."

"What else is there?"

"My mother kept this address in her journal. There has to be a reason. And I'm not leaving until I find out who lived here at the time of my conception."

He rubbed the back of his neck. "What happens if you still aren't able to get the answers you want?"

"I don't know. But I'm not giving up. I have to find him." She turned to Ric. "Don't you see? He clearly doesn't know about me."

"How do you know?"

"Because if he did, he'd have come to find me."

Ric wasn't so sure that was the case, but the hope in Gia's eyes kept him from vocalizing his doubts. She'd already had enough disappointment for today. But then again, just because he'd had a disappointing journey searching for a missing parent didn't mean Gia's journey would yield similar results.

Feeling himself being drawn further into Gia's troubles, Ric stood. "I should clean up these papers before we leave."

Gia handed him back the documents, and he returned them to the big wall safe that was crammed full of information. Then he swung the heavy door closed. Safe for another day.

When he turned around, he found Gia had gathered all the folders scattered over the coffee table. He hadn't had a chance to go through them because they hadn't been labeled as anything he thought would reveal information related to the time period surrounding Gia's birth.

He noticed she had opened a folder to replace something that had fallen out. Her eyes widened as she pulled out a drawing. Her gaze turned to him. "Did you draw this?"

He shook his head. "I don't draw."

"But this looks like you might have done it when you were a kid. I think this is your name at the bottom."

He moved to the couch. He took the drawing and stared at it. He didn't recall it. But when he peered at the bottom right corner, he found his name penciled in childlike writing.

He couldn't believe his uncle had kept this. Why would he do that? His uncle never seemed that interested in his schoolwork other than making sure he got his homework done.

"Look," Gia said, "there's more of it. This folder is filled." She checked another. "So is this one. And this one."

Ric was left speechless, and that didn't happen often. After all these years thinking his uncle had been indifferent to him, Ric was deeply touched that his uncle had kept all of this stuff.

He started sorting through the folders, finding all sorts

of things he'd done in school. And then they uncovered a folder with his accomplishments as an adult, including every press release since the launch of his company. It was all there. And Ric had to blink a few times. Stupid dust.

"I had no idea he kept all of this stuff."

"He loved you a lot."

A rebuttal rushed to the tip of Ric's tongue, but then his gaze moved over all the papers in front of him. Art projects to term papers to newspaper clippings. It was like a synopsis of his life. How could he deny his uncle cared for him when the evidence was staring him in the face?

"I had no idea." His voice was so soft it was like a whisper.

Gia rubbed his back as though in comfort. His instinct was to pull away. He wasn't used to anyone comforting him. But he liked her touch. He found himself welcoming her gentle concern as he took in this monumental realization.

"I was so wrong about him," Ric said. "How did I not know any of this? I thought I was a bother—a nuisance. And worst of all, I never got to tell him how much I appreciated him always being there for me—no matter what. I… I never told him that I loved him."

Gia's hand moved to his shoulder and squeezed. "He knew."

Ric wanted to believe her—he really did—but he wasn't so sure.

CHAPTER SEVEN

THINGS HAD WORKED out for Ric.

Gia was happy for him to have proof of his uncle's love.

But what about her? She let out a deep sigh. Where was her rainbow?

The following day, Gia took a moment to feel sorry for herself. Then she straightened her shoulders. Her father, um, Aldo, had taught her not to be a quitter.

Nothing good came to those who quit.

If Ric's uncle wasn't her father, she would find out who lived in the house before him. She was close—very close. She could feel it.

And then there'd be a happy reunion. Reunion? Was that the right word? After all, they hadn't actually ever met. Had they?

No, of course not. Fathers didn't just let go of their children, never to see them again. She imagined a man with the same shade of brown hair as her own, much taller than her and wearing a warm smile as he enveloped her in a big hug. Because he'd be overjoyed to know her. He had to be. Anything else—it was unacceptable. Just the thought of being rejected by her own flesh and blood...

No. It won't happen. Everything is going to work out.

The buzz of her phone halted her thoughts. Gia moved across her spacious bedroom to retrieve it from the bedside table. She glanced at the screen, finding a message from Enzo.

When are you coming home? The hotel reservations have declined dramatically. We're in trouble. You need to fix this.

He'd been trying to reach her since last night, and she'd been dodging his phone calls. The hotel was in trouble. But Gia knew if she took the call that she'd be obligated to return to Tuscany to try to fix the problem, something she couldn't do until she learned the truth about her birth. Usually she put family first, but in this moment, she needed to put herself first.

She knew that made her selfish and she felt awful about it, but if their parents hadn't kept this huge secret, she wouldn't be searching for her biological father. If there was anyone to blame for this mess, it was them. And worst of all, they weren't even here to explain any of this to her.

And right now, she desperately needed her mother. She needed to hear her soft, comforting voice. She needed her to say everything would be all right.

Gia's vision blurred as she stared at the phone. She blinked repeatedly. She would keep it together. She wasn't a crier. She was strong.

Her fingers hovered over the phone. And then she started to type.

Michael and Rosa have this. Don't worry. Everything will work out…

She reread what she'd written. Would everything work out? She wasn't so sure about that anymore. Too much had happened to continue being a Pollyanna.

She knew no matter what she said, it wouldn't be the end of the discussion. Her brother hadn't wanted her to go on this trip. He wouldn't give up until she was on a plane home. And so she deleted the message.

Knock. Knock.

"Gia?"

It was Ric. He'd promised to help her track down the prior owner of the villa. Maybe she would have news for her brother soon.

"Coming."

She took one last glance in the mirror. She ran her fingers over her hair, smoothing a flyaway strand or two. And then she glanced down to find Gin staring up at her as though questioning what she was doing.

She realized she was nervous. She wanted to look her best for Ric. There wasn't anything wrong with that, was there? She applied some lip gloss, and then she was ready.

When she glanced down once more, Gin was still giving her a questioning look, making her feel paranoid that she was trying too hard to impress Ric.

"Stop looking at me like that."

The puppy whined.

"Did you say something?" Ric called through the door.

"Um…" She rushed over and opened it. "I was just telling Gin that we were leaving."

Ric's gaze moved to the dog, who rushed over and propped himself against Ric's leg. He bent down and picked up the dog. "And how's Gin this morning?"

Arff!

Ric laughed. "That good, huh?"

"Someone has you wrapped around his paw," Gia teased.

Ric put the dog down. "I think you must be looking in the mirror."

Her eyes widened with surprise. "Good one. But I think Gin has won us both over."

"Agreed. Are you ready to go?"

She felt bad about him missing work. "You know, I can go to the library and the courthouse by myself."

"And miss the adventure? Never. I'm curious to learn about the history of the house."

A thought hit her. "So you can use it when you go to sell the place?"

"That hadn't occurred to me, but now that you mention it, if the history is interesting, sure, why not?"

She shouldn't have asked. She didn't like the answer. But then again, why should she care what he did with his property?

Maybe it was because it was a piece of his past and right now, she was searching for her past without any luck. Surely things would be different today. Today she would uncover the key to her story—something to lead her in the right direction. She could feel it in her bones.

The library and the courthouse were at the center of town.

Not far from Ric's apartment.

And so they opted to walk. With the housekeeper watching Gin, they set off on the beautiful sunny day. The light sea breeze made the summer day quite comfortable. Plus, Gia wanted a chance to take in more of the old-world city.

The only disappointing part was having to switch from her pretty pink-and-white heels that matched her white skirt and pink top so well to a pair of sneakers. At least her sneakers were white with pink and yellow flowers. She couldn't help it; she like coordinated, colorful outfits. They helped her feel more confident. And today she needed a boost to get through this challenging period.

She turned her thoughts to more serious matters. What would happen after she located her father? Would he invite her to move in with him so they could get to know each other? There was no making up for all the years they'd been robbed of, but they had the here and now. They *would* make the most of it. Excitement and nervousness fought for room in her chest.

As they continued to walk, Ric informed her that there was an ordinance requiring new architecture to be approved by the city council so it didn't conflict with the older structures. Thus, the city looked as though it were from another era. Gia immediately fell in love with it. It was like stepping back in time. That was until you had a look at the pedestrians with their smart phones. It was quite the contrast. Still, she wouldn't change any of it.

She snapped some photos with her phone and then sent them off to her sister. She missed her siblings—even if she wasn't ready to go home. Not yet. Not without answers.

A message dinged on her phone. It was from Bianca.

Thank goodness. We've been wondering if we'd ever hear from you.

Sorry. I just need some time to do this on my own.

Gia's thoughts turned to Ric. Maybe not exactly on her own, but she wasn't ready to tell her sister about Ric.

Everything is good. Tell Enzo not to worry. I just need some space.

Have you found your father?

Not yet.

Gia had to keep glancing up to make sure she didn't run into anyone or walk into a lamppost.

But soon.

Is there anything I can do?

Talk to Enzo. Let him know I'm okay. But I can't come home yet.

I'll try. He's worried about you. We both are.

I love you.

I love you too.

Gia slipped her phone back in her purse.

"Everything okay?" Ric's voice drew her from her thoughts.

"Um…yes. It was just my sister. She hadn't heard from me in a while and was worried."

"I'm surprised she isn't here with you."

Gia shrugged. "It's complicated."

"How so?" When she didn't immediately answer, he said, "Sorry. I shouldn't have asked."

She shook her head. "It's okay. I've certainly insinuated myself into your life."

"You had a reason," he said. "You thought I could help you figure out your past."

"Sadly, we aren't related." She glanced his way. "Or perhaps we're lucky the way things worked out."

What had she gone and said that for? Heat rushed to her cheeks. She was flirting with him? She pressed her lips together before she could say more.

"Maybe you're right. Otherwise it'd be quite inappropriate if I were to, say, kiss you."

"You want to kiss me?" There she went again, saying the wrong things. She should have pretended that she hadn't heard him, but how did you pretend you didn't hear something like that?

They were alone on a side street when Ric stopped and turned to her. "Would you like me to kiss you?"

Yes!

She struggled to hold back her answer.

Their gazes met and held. There was definite interest reflected in his eyes. "It sounds like you're the one with kissing on your mind."

A deep growl rattled in his throat. "I have a whole lot more than kissing on my mind."

She hadn't been expecting him to say that. His words melted her insides into a heated ball of need. Would it be wrong if she were to fall into his arms right now?

She stifled a frustrated sigh. Probably. She couldn't—she wouldn't—be one of those women who threw themselves at him.

But would that be so bad? After all, he was the one who had opened this door. Or had she? Either way, she was more than willing to yank that door wide open and march right through the opening and into his arms—

"You're smiling," he said, cutting right through her daydream. "Must mean you like the idea."

Oh, yes, she did. A car honk from farther down the block startled her back to reality. The voice of reason reminded her that they weren't out and about on this gorgeous sunny morning to fall in love. Wait. Where had that thought come from?

She swallowed hard. She was not falling for him. No way. Admiring his sexy good looks was one thing, but anything beyond that was off-limits. Because no one could truly love her until she knew the truth about herself. She reinforced the walls around her heart with sheer determination.

She wouldn't let herself be vulnerable again. Not even for someone as kind and amazing as Ric. Because whenever she found her father—whoever it might be—she couldn't stand for Ric to look at her differently, to push her away.

In that moment she knew the flirting had to stop. She straightened her shoulders and lifted her chin to look into his dark and mysterious eyes, but then she realized her mistake as her movements had only succeeded in bringing her closer—much closer—to his tempting lips.

If she were to lean forward ever so slightly, their lips would meet. And then she'd lean into his arms. He'd pull her closer. And as his mouth moved over hers, they'd get lost in the moment.

Desire flashed in his eyes. Did he know she was fantasizing about him—wanting him? Her heart hitched in her chest.

No. No. No! Get a grip girl. You are here on a mission. Don't get sidetracked.

She stifled a frustrated sigh. Was it wrong that she wanted both? A summer fling with Ric and to be united with her father. Probably. One couldn't be greedy.

Stay focused.

With great reluctance, she pulled back. "We should keep going."

He hesitated for a moment, but when she moved past him to continue down the sidewalk, he fell in step beside her. All the while, she couldn't help wondering what would have happened if she had given in to her desires and kissed him back there. Where would things have gone between them?

And when it was over, what would happen? Would she just be one more conquest for him? After all, he could practically have his pick of women. There were certainly enough of them willing to be with him.

She didn't like the thought of just being another notch

on his bedpost. And she didn't like the thought of him turning to another woman with that devilish grin that made his eyes twinkle with unspoken promises of passion.

But there was no point dwelling on it. She wasn't in Lapri for fun and romance. She was here to find out who she was and get to know her father—a father who'd been kept from her. She had to right the past before she could contemplate the future.

The old book had been searched.

Every entry regarding his uncle's house had been analyzed for clues.

And they were still no closer to locating Gia's biological father.

"I'm sorry," Ric said. All the while his mind raced, searching for something they'd missed.

Deep sadness filled Gia's eyes. "This isn't supposed to be this hard."

"I don't know what to tell you. It doesn't appear the prior owner has any living relatives."

"But how am I supposed to find my father? I just know he was in that house. It's the only reason my mother would have that address in her journal on the page that speaks of him."

A woman working at the counter gave them dirty looks for making noise. Even though this was a government office, it was much like a library where speaking was frowned upon.

"Come on," he said. "Let's get out of here."

Gia didn't argue. They returned all the research material they'd borrowed and headed out the door. The bright cheery sunshine seemed to mock the dark stormy look on Gia's face. Right about now, he'd be willing to do most anything to put the smile back on her face. But even he couldn't work miracles. He'd already run an exhaustive search on the internet for any reference to a man who might fit the criteria Gia had given him. The problem was she didn't have enough definitive information to narrow down his search enough. Ric had ended up with thousands upon thousands of results. Far too many to weed through.

"Don't worry," he said. "We'll figure something out. This isn't the end."

Although he had serious doubts if she was ever going to find her father. He knew what that frustration felt like. He knew she'd never truly give up hope. He still hadn't. Every now and then he would come across something that would spark a new search, and as usual, it would lead him down a rabbit hole that led nowhere.

He didn't want that for Gia. And then he had a thought.

"Do you have your mother's journal?" he asked as he led her to a nearby coffee shop.

"I do. Why?"

He held up a finger, signaling for her to wait. By then they'd entered the nearly empty coffee shop, as most people were at work at that hour. They placed their order. He wanted to wait until they were seated at a table before he posed his proposal to her. The bistro was quick, and in no time they were holding one steaming espresso for him and a latte for her. They headed over to a table by the window.

"I can't wait any longer," she said. "What do you have in mind?"

"I wonder if you'd be willing to lend me your mother's journal. I have a friend who's good at locating people. I don't know why I didn't think of this sooner." Actually, he had. He knew Gia would resist the idea, but now that they were out of options, she might agree. "But if you were to allow my friend to read your mother's journal, he might be able to unearth some clues that were overlooked."

Gia was already shaking her head before he said the last words. "No. I couldn't do that. It's private."

"I can vouch that he's very discreet."

Gia continued to shake her head. "It wouldn't be right."

"So you're okay with giving up and never finding your father?" He knew the answer before he asked the question, but he doubted Gia had come to terms with what her decision would mean.

Gia finally stopped shaking her head. She stared at him, and he could see in her eyes that she was turning over the idea and weighing her options. "Your friend, he doesn't need the original, does he?"

Ric noticed the hesitant look on her face. It was though there was an internal struggle waging within her. "I don't know."

"I couldn't do that. I couldn't lend someone my mother's last words. I… I couldn't."

"I understand. I'll talk to him. Maybe we can scan the book or make photocopies. Would you be all right with that?"

She stirred her coffee. "I guess so."

That was all the affirmation he needed. He reached for his phone and signaled that he'd be right back. He wanted to make the arrangements before she changed her mind.

He knew if she didn't do absolutely everything within her power to locate her father, she would regret it. Maybe not today. Maybe not tomorrow. But one day she would look back on this moment, wondering why she didn't have the courage to do whatever it took. And Ric didn't want her to have any regrets—not about this.

After a brief phone conversation and promising access to his yacht for a future unnamed date, his friend said he'd look at it. But Nate made it known there were no guarantees. In his line of work, sometimes things worked out and sometimes he would hit a dead end. Ric told him he understood, but Nate wasn't referring to him but rather Gia. She shouldn't get her hopes up, but he would do his best.

"Well, what did he say?" she asked as soon as Ric returned to the table.

"He can't guarantee results, but he'll take the case."

"I understand." Then the worry returned to her face. "And the journal. Does he need the original?"

Ric shook his head. "He said we can scan the pages and send them to him."

Gia visibly exhaled. "Okay. I can do this." And then for the first time since they'd left the courthouse, a smile came over her face. "I have hope again. And it's all thanks to you. I wish there was some way I could pay you back."

"Don't worry about it."

"But I do. You've gone above and beyond for me. I will pay you back."

He knew she meant it, but it wasn't necessary. "I just want you to have a happy ending."

Not everyone got those, but Gia had a big heart for stray puppies and stray CEOs. She deserved her happy ending, and he'd do whatever he could to make sure she got it.

He told himself that it wasn't anything more than he'd do for a friend. Because that's all they were—friends. He couldn't let it be more—even though it was tempting.

In the end, she'd be gone. And he'd once more be alone. He couldn't risk losing someone else he cared about. It was best to keep his beautiful houseguest at arm's length.

CHAPTER EIGHT

A DEAD END.

That was the opposite of what she'd been hoping for.

The next morning, Gia squinted at the bright sunlight streaming through her bedroom window. She yawned and stretched. She had zero motivation to get out of bed. Her lack of sleep might have something to do with it.

After staring into the dark, she'd turned on her light and combed through her mother's journal again, searching for any clue to the identity of her father. If she couldn't find anything, how was Ric's friend going to turn up anything? Still, when they'd returned from the café yesterday, Ric had helped her painstakingly scan the journal and email it to his friend.

Gia had all her hopes and dreams pinned on Ric's friend working miracles. After all she'd been through, her journey just couldn't end like this. There had to be a clue.

By the time she'd showered and spent a little more time than normal applying her makeup, she found Ric sitting out on the terrace, drinking his morning coffee. Well, not so much drinking as holding his coffee while staring blindly off into the clear blue sky. It seemed she wasn't the only one that day with something on their mind.

And she felt guilty. She'd taken up a lot of his time and kept him away from his office. He needed to know that he didn't need to stay here and babysit her. She and the pup would be just fine on their own.

Speaking of Gin, she hadn't seen the little guy all morning. In fact, she hadn't seen him since she'd finally slipped off into a restless sleep last night. As she stepped out onto the terrace, she was surprised to find him lying at Ric's feet. Those two had certainly bonded. Immediately the puppy spotted her and ran over for some cuddle time. She bent over to pick him up.

"I'm sorry."

Ric turned to her. "For what?"

"I fell asleep last night and didn't notice that Gin had wandered off. I hope he wasn't too much bother."

Ric didn't say anything for a moment. "He was fine once I got him out of my shoe closet. He seems to think my leather dress shoes are good chew toys."

"Oh, no!" Gia pressed a hand to her chest. "I'm so sorry. Let me know how much they were and I'll pay for them."

Ric shook his head. "No need. It was my fault for leaving the door open."

Gia frowned at Gin. "Naughty puppy. You have to be a good boy or Ric will toss us to the curb."

When Gin started to wiggle, she put him down. Gia had an idea she wanted to run past Ric, but first, she needed caffeine.

In the kitchen she poured herself a cup of coffee, leaving barely enough room for sweetener and creamer. A swish of the spoon and then she eagerly lifted it to her lips. She drank in the steamy brew and moaned her glee.

With cup in hand, she returned to the terrace. Gin was hot on her heels. Ric was still sitting there, once again staring into space. Whatever he was thinking about definitely had a hundred percent of his attention.

"Mind if I join you?" she asked softly, so as not to startle him.

He lowered his cup to the small table and turned to her. He smiled, but it didn't quite reach his eyes. "Please do."

Gin ran up to him and put his paws on his leg. The pup excitedly barked at Ric. The little guy was doing so well that they'd dispensed with his plastic cone.

Ric laughed and picked up the little dog, settling him on his lap. While those two went through their morning ritual, Gia made herself comfortable in the other chair. All the while, she tried to figure out what to say.

She raised her gaze to find Gin giving Ric a kiss. "I'd like to pay for the investigation. Whatever it is, just let me know."

Ric shook his head. "That won't be necessary."

"But I insist."

"There's nothing to pay. My friend, Nate, and I have a mutually beneficial arrangement, so he's doing it pro bono."

"Oh." Still, she just couldn't take any more charity from this man. She had been raised to carry her own weight. "Then let me pay you."

Ric again shook his head. "That won't be necessary."

He was not making this easy for her. "I appreciate everything you've done for me, but there has to be something I can do for you in return."

"You're serious, aren't you?"

"I am. My parents raised me to be independent and not to rely on the generosity of others." And then the thought about his uncle's villa came back to her. She still wasn't sure how Ric would feel about it, but it was worth mentioning. "I could work on cleaning up your uncle's place, you know, so it's ready for you to sell."

Ric arched a brow as he studied her. "And you feel you're up to the challenge?"

She nodded. "I did a good job with my hotel. I can show you pictures."

"Actually, I've seen the pictures online. Your hotel is beautiful. But my uncle's house would need a whole lot of updates to come close to looking that good. Surely you can't do it by yourself."

"Oh. Sorry. I didn't mean to imply I would. I'll work on the design, with your approval of course, and then I'll hire contractors or we can do it together, if you desire."

Ric's lips pressed together as though he were mulling it over. "And how long do you think it will take?"

"If the contractors are available, I wouldn't think too terribly long." And then a thought came to her. "You aren't planning on tearing down walls or anything drastic, are you?"

"The walls stay. The kitchen and bathrooms need to be gutted."

"I agree."

"But will you be around that long?" His gaze searched hers.

"Probably not. When we find my father, I'll want to spend time with him." When Ric frowned, she added, "But if we get started right away, the design should be in place. You'll be able to oversee the finishing touches. And then you won't have to worry about it sitting around being neglected."

He was quiet for a moment. "I like the idea. I'll make sure you have whatever funds you need. You know you really don't have to do this."

"But I want to do it." She truly did. It would be a much welcome distraction from the search for her father. "I went to design school, but with my parents passing, I never really got to put my education to use, aside from internships and working on the hotel."

"If you're an interior designer, why are you running a hotel?" He looked genuinely confused.

She shrugged. "It just worked out that way." But that answer didn't seem to appease him. And so she decided to tell him about her parents' very unusual will. "When my parents died, they left the estate to the sibling who could generate the biggest profit with the villa and vineyard."

"But what about the other two siblings?"

"They'll inherit an equal fortune."

"Do you want the estate?"

She shrugged. "I did at first, but now, I don't know."

"Why would you change your mind?"

"Because now I know I'm not a Bartolini. Not by blood. It seems the estate should go to a true Bartolini." It made her sad to admit it. She felt different now. She couldn't explain it to anyone, but until she found her father, she'd never truly know who she was.

Sympathy showed in Ric's eyes. "But you were raised a Bartolini. If your parents didn't feel you were a Bartolini, don't you think they'd have told you?"

Gia shrugged. "It doesn't change the fact that I need to find my biological father. Once I find him, I'll be able to figure out what comes next."

"And if you don't find him?"

His pointed questions poked and prodded her, making her consider things she'd put off until now. "I can't think about it because…because it would mean I'll never know the answers to my past. I just know that if I can find my father that…that…"

"That you won't feel so alone anymore? That it will lessen the pain of losing both of your parents?"

How dare he say those things to her? She jumped to her feet. "You don't know what you're saying. You don't understand."

And with that, she turned and forced herself to walk in slow steady steps with her spine straight and her head held high. Gin trailed behind her. She wouldn't let Ric see how deeply his words had hurt her.

Had they hurt her? Or was it just that he was right? No.

She wasn't trying to find a replacement for her parents. She would never do that.

All she wanted were answers, and there was nothing wrong with that. She needed to know about the part of her life that was missing. Who was her father? Had he known about her? And where did they go from here?

He'd utterly mucked that up.

Royally.

The next day, Ric was still worried about Gia. She was getting her hopes up for a happy reunion with her biological father, and Ric was worried that might not happen. Sure, his PI friend was good but sometimes good wasn't enough. His friend had searched for Ric's own father and come up with nothing. Absolutely nothing.

Maybe his mother had been right. Maybe it really had been a bad time in her life and she'd lost control. Ric didn't understand losing control like that because he always made sure he was in charge of everything from his business to his personal life. He had definite plans for both—none of which included a beautiful woman or a stray dog.

Speaking of the pup, no one had claimed Gin. It was looking more and more like the little guy was permanently theirs—correction, Gia's.

Mrs. Rossi had offered to take Gin for a walk to the park after the little guy was caught ripping a pair of Ric's socks to shreds. Why exactly had he said the dog could stay? The recollection was becoming fuzzier with each item of Ric's that the puppy turned into some sort of chew toy. He reminded himself that soon they'd be gone, and he'd resume his quiet existence. However, that idea didn't sound as appealing as it once had.

Not wanting to examine his feelings for Gia, he turned his thoughts to getting the reclusive owner of Grosso Global

Transports to sit down with him for a meeting. Ric knew if he were to publicly announce what his program did that bids would come pouring in. But a bidding war wasn't what he had in mind. Money wasn't his goal with this project.

He wanted to test his technology with the biggest global transport company. If he could master their system, he could take what he'd done and duplicate it into something to help those in need. It would be a supply corridor using the goodwill of commercial transporters. That was his ultimate goal, but for companies to sign on to the emerging plan, he had to show them that he knew what he was doing and could make it work.

Tap. Tap.

Ric glanced up to find Gia standing in the doorway of his study. The sadness in her eyes was like a jab to his gut. He wanted more than anything to replace that sadness with a smile, but he didn't know how to find her father for her.

"Do you have a minute?" she asked.

"Sure. Come in. I've been meaning to speak with you, but I wasn't sure you wanted to hear anything I have to say—"

"It's my fault. I shouldn't have gotten so defensive."

"And I'm sorry for being such a pessimist."

"No, you were being a realist—something I'm not ready to deal with." She sat down in the chair off to the side of his desk. She wrung her hands, letting him know she was still upset. "I just need to believe out of something so horrible happening that something good will come of it."

"I understand." He truly did. And just because it hadn't worked out like that for him didn't mean it wouldn't work out for her.

"I also wanted to know if you changed your mind about me working on the villa?"

A voice in his head told him she was giving him an

easy out. Cutting ties with her was best for both of them. But what came out of his mouth was quite the opposite. "I haven't."

What did I go and say that for?

"Good. Very good." A tentative smile lifted the corners of her lips, but it didn't reach her eyes. "I… I should go now. I'm sure you're busy."

He didn't want her to leave. He told himself it was because he wanted to cheer her up, but deep down he knew he craved her companionship for more selfish reasons— reasons he wasn't ready to acknowledge.

When he glanced up, she was already at the doorway. "Wait. I need your help."

He didn't have a clue what he needed her help with, but this wasn't the first time he'd been stuck in a position where he had to think on his feet.

She immediately turned back. "You do?"

Was that a flicker of interest in her eyes? Or was he only seeing what he wanted to see? It didn't matter; he'd started down this path and now he had to keep going.

He glanced down at his desk, and the only things on it were related to his current project. "Yes, I do." He had to go with what he had, though he wasn't sure how she would be able to help him. "I'm having a problem getting a reclusive businessman to meet with me. And it's really important." As he spoke, she ventured back into the office. "Everyone in the business knows he only signs on with the best of the best."

"So his working agreement is like the gold standard?"

"Exactly." He smiled, hoping she'd do the same. She didn't. But that didn't stop him from trying. "And I just have to get him to buy my technology."

Instead of smiling, she frowned. "Is this the meeting I interrupted on that first day at your uncle's villa."

"Yes. Well, no, you had nothing to do with it being canceled. I just need to figure out a way to lure him to a face-to-face meeting. I know if we can meet, I can convince him to buy into my technology."

"So what's the problem?"

"He's claiming there's no proof my program works."

"Didn't you test it?"

"Of course I did." The words rushed out of his mouth with a rumble of frustration. When Gia's eyes widened, he realized his error. In a friendlier tone, he said, "But it was in a closed system with a simulated world."

"So you need something in the real world?"

He nodded before rubbing the stiff muscles in his neck. His head started to throb.

"You seem like a man who knows everyone. Just pick someone out and try your program on their business."

"If only it were that easy, but I don't have anyone I trust in that line of business. And I can't afford for news of my development to get out into the public. I can't have another company steal the concept before I have a chance to use it to help others."

"Help others?"

He nodded again. And then he told her about his quest to provide an efficient and free mode of transportation for goods to those in need. It was when he finished his pitch that she smiled. Not a little smile but a big beautiful smile that lit up her eyes.

"That's an amazing endeavor. And it's so big. I mean, it would provide a transportation route to anywhere in the world. And people who never considered donating goods could do so without any real cost to them."

He nodded. "And the best part is that it wouldn't cost the transportation companies much money because my program would streamline everything, and no one company would take on the burden of delivering all of the packages. It would be a shared effort. But those companies, both big and small, would have to trust me with their vital information—the backbone of their business. To gain their trust would take something major."

"Hence the need to convince Mr. Grosso to buy your technology."

"Exactly."

"What exactly does your program do?" Genuine interest was written all over her beautiful face.

He normally didn't tell people about his work, most especially the things that were still being developed or that hadn't been sold yet, but Gia wasn't just anyone. He wanted to share this with her. Her stamp of approval meant a lot to him.

"You have to promise not to share any of this with anyone. In my world, it's all about who comes up with the idea first."

"Don't worry. I won't tell a soul. Your secret is safe with me because honestly, I'm lucky I know how to turn on a computer and enter reservation information. But that doesn't mean I don't want to hear about your work."

That was all the encouragement he needed. He started talking, laying out the generalities of what his algorithm could do for the transportation industry and how it could help charitable causes.

"That's amazing. And you did all of that by yourself?"

He nodded. He wasn't used to people praising him.

"You're a genius. But don't you have a company to run?"

He nodded again. "I quickly grow bored with paperwork. I need to keep myself in touch with technology, and I start my own personal projects. Sometimes they don't work out, and other times they explode into something bigger than I ever imagined." Not wanting the whole conversation to revolve around him, he said, "I'm sure that's how you felt when you started your own hotel."

She shrugged. "Not exactly."

"But you must have been excited to take on such a big venture."

"I like dealing with people. They are the best part of the business. And I had a lot of fun turning the villa into a boutique hotel. But I didn't go into the venture because it was a dream of mine."

"What is your dream?"

She shook her head. "It doesn't matter."

"Sure, it matters. Life is short. You need to be passionate about the time you spend on this earth."

She arched a brow. "I didn't figure you for a philosopher."

"It's something my uncle used to tell me. At the time, I didn't think he was serious. I thought he was just trying to get me to go do things and leave him alone."

"But now you know different?"

Ric nodded. "He was trying to help me, but I was too young and too angry with my mother to notice."

"But you remembered and that counts. And you listened to him. Because if anyone is passionate about their work, it's you."

He smiled. She was right. He hadn't thought of it that way, but in a sense, he'd honored his uncle's memory. He just wished his uncle was here so he could tell him thank you for always being there for him—even when he wasn't the easiest to deal with. And…and that he loved him. He was the father that he'd never had.

"Thanks," he said. When Gia sent him a puzzled look, he added, "For helping me realize that my uncle cared."

"I didn't do anything. You would have stumbled over those papers eventually."

"Would I have? I don't know. I was so determined that he didn't care to the point I might have thrown all that stuff out without paying much attention. But you made sure that didn't happen. So thank you."

"You're welcome, though I still don't think I did much."

He glanced down at his desk. "It seems we got off topic."

"Oh, yes. You need to figure out how to show Mr. Grosso that your program works in the real world but without telling anyone." She frowned as though giving it some serious consideration. "I'm not sure you can do that unless you were to try it on my business. But I don't transport anything."

Ric shook his head, dismissing the idea.

"Which is a shame because now that my sister has pulled out of the wedding business to marry the prince of Patazonia, the business at the hotel is spiraling."

"Wait. Your sister is marrying a prince?" When she nodded, he asked, "How is it that we've been sharing this apartment and puppy all of this time and you've failed to share this most interesting bit of your life?"

Gia laughed. "Like you're interested in fairy tales."

"I am when they concern you. So your sister…she's really going to become a princess?"

Gia nodded. "The royal wedding is set for Christmas."

"Next year."

Gia shook her head. "This year. The prince is going to be crowned king on New Year's."

"Wow. Your sister isn't just going to be a princess but a queen. And you're good with all of this?"

"Why wouldn't I be? I love my sister and want her to be happy."

"But you haven't found your father."

"One thing doesn't have anything to do with the other."

Ric nodded in understanding. "So your hotel, it isn't

doing well because your sister isn't offering wedding packages?"

"Actually, her assistant, Sylvie, has taken over the wedding business. My sister still oversees it but mostly from a distance. Apparently, there's a lot to do before a royal wedding."

Ric was concerned for Gia. If she didn't find her biological father, she was going to need the hotel to focus on, and the last thing she'd need was to deal with a failing business. There had to be a way of turning things around.

He had to give it some thought. His algorithm was geared toward a lot larger, complex system. Still, there were components of it that dealt with bringing in business from individuals as well as other businesses. Would it be possible to rework the algorithm to scale it down to bringing in customers to a hotel? It was a stretch. A big stretch. But he was up for the challenge.

CHAPTER NINE

THINGS WERE LOOKING UP.

At least where the villa was concerned. The search for Gia's father was still a wait and see scenario.

More than a week had passed since Ric had agreed to let Gia work on his uncle's villa. She hadn't wasted one single moment. It felt so good to be productive. Sitting around just wasn't for her.

Ric had spent a lot of time in his study. Gia wasn't sure how much time he spent at his office, as she had the go-ahead to hire a construction crew and to start work on his uncle's villa. Not just a couple of men but a whole army of them, tackling different rooms at once. Ric wanted this job done as quickly as possible, and he was willing to pay whatever it cost.

Gia was so excited about taking this run-down home and turning it into something magical that the wait for news about locating her biological father wasn't nearly as excruciating. She'd even started taking calls from her siblings, who were so relieved to speak directly to her instead of getting by with sporadic text messages.

And Gin went with her every day to the villa. Though the pup was interested in making it to the garden in back, Gia was having none of it. He was hurt back there once; they weren't having a repeat episode. Though the garden was on her list of things to do, it had moved down in the order of priority because the gardener couldn't fit her in for a couple of weeks.

Gia wasn't one to bark out orders and stand back; she was the type who liked to get her hands dirty. She blamed it on her— She paused. She blamed it on Aldo. Even though they weren't biologically connected, she couldn't ignore how much they had in common. Aldo had enjoyed getting his hands dirty at the vineyard, testing the soil, sampling the grapes and fixing the irrigation system.

And so she'd spent the day patching walls and prepping them for fresh paint. In all honesty, the villa's bones were in awesome shape. And with Ric wanting to keep the layout as it was, this job was going to go quickly. It was more a touch-up than a remodel. Still, she enjoyed it. The villa had a rich history and warmth to it that drew her in.

There was a marble floor in the spacious foyer, with a crystal chandelier. Both were staying. They just needed to be cleaned until they gleamed. Each room had tall windows, and when the old drapes were removed, the Mediterranean sun lit up the place. What wasn't there to like?

The walls had ornate trim that was unique but not over-the-top. Gia made sure to tell the crew it was to remain. Any trim that was damaged by a leak in the roof was to be repaired or if worse came to worst, it was to be re-created. She knew plasterwork could be a painstaking job, but it added so much character to the house. It was like this villa had its own personality. Some family was going to be very lucky to live there.

She thought of Ric living in the villa. It was a lot of house for one person to live in alone. But would he always be alone? She could easily imagine him with a baby in his arms. The child would be laughing because Ric had just tickled them. Gia found herself smiling at the image.

Then a beautiful woman entered Gia's image. The woman was tall, slender and gorgeous. She was smiling as she came to lean into Ric. They both fussed over the child. She would be his wife.

Gia blinked away the troubling image. It was best she focused on the here and now. And right now, she had to hurry and get to the villa. The kitchen floor had been put in, and the cabinets were being delivered today.

She glanced in the mirror, taking in her newly bought navy-blue T-shirt, which hugged her curves, and the new jeans with the perfectly placed worn holes near the front pockets and her hips. She smiled. If her mother knew how much she'd paid for jeans that already had holes in them, she would lecture her about wasting her money. As her mother's voice filled her mind, Gia's smile broadened.

She missed her mother. She may be mad at her for keeping such an important part of her life from her, but she really missed her. She missed being able to talk to her as they cooked in the kitchen together.

Gia wanted to tell her mother about Gin and his boundless energy. But more importantly, she wanted to tell her about Ric and how amazing she found him. She knew her mother would take things out of context and suggest she date Ric. At which point she would tell her mother she couldn't. He was a workaholic and she, well, she was still figuring herself out. It was bad timing among other reasons…

Tap. Tap.

"Yes?" Gia called out.

The door opened, and Gin barked before running over to Ric. He smiled and bent to pet the puppy. It gave Gia a moment to study him. Wasn't that the same shirt he'd had on the night before? And his hair, it was unusually scattered. What was up with that?

When Ric straightened, there were shadows beneath

his eyes. "I was wondering if you had a couple of minutes to talk."

That sounded serious. "Should I be worried?"

He shook his head. "Nothing for you to worry about. I just have a proposal for you."

Proposal? Suddenly her thoughts went in the wrong direction. Flowers. Candlelight. Ric down on one knee—

She screeched her thoughts to a halt. Where in the world had that come from? She wasn't ready to settle down. Not with Ric. Not with anyone.

She swallowed hard, trying to calm her nervousness. "A proposal?"

He nodded. "It'd be easier if we did this in my study."

Without waiting for her response, he turned to walk away. Gin was hot on his heels. Gia stood there for a moment, wondering what was up with him. And then curiosity had her following.

When she reached his study, she came to a complete halt. Her gaze took in the scene before her. Ric's usually clean study, where everything was in its place, was in complete disarray. There were papers scattered across the desktop with his oversize monitor and keyboard in the center. There were coffee mugs, not just one or two but many of them here and there. Empty dinner dishes were stacked on an end table. And the curtains were drawn. There was no indication that it was a beautiful sunny day outside.

"What in the world happened in here?" Gia moved to the windows and drew back the heavy curtains to let the sunshine stream in. It didn't help the state of the office. "Have you been living in here?"

"Sort of."

"Aren't those the same clothes you had on yesterday?"

He glanced down and then ran a hand over the wrinkled

shirt as though it might actually improve his appearance in some small way. "They might be."

She arched a brow. "Might be?"

"Okay. They are." He sat down behind the desk in a red-and-white gaming chair. "But you have to understand, this is the way I get when I'm involved in a project."

"So nothing is wrong?"

He shook his head. "For once, I think something is right."

Her heart seemed to pause. She'd been working so hard to keep herself distracted, but with each day that passed, she grew more anxious.

"Is it my biological father? Is there news?"

Ric shook his head. "I'm sorry for being so cryptic. There's no news yet, but don't give up hope. These things take time."

Her heart sunk down to her new work boots. She didn't want Ric to see how disappointed she was, so she sucked down her disappointment. "What's had you so preoccupied?"

"That's what I wanted to talk to you about. I've been working on modifications and scaling down the program. It's taken a lot of work, but I think it was worth it—"

"Whoa! Slow down. You lost me."

He visibly drew in a breath and blew it out. "Sorry. I think I need some sleep. You gave me the idea the other day when we were talking. And I thought we could help each other. My program needs a practical application and your hotel business needs people directed to it, so I've been working to marry the two."

"You have?" She hadn't been expecting this. She sank down on the armchair near his desk.

"Well, not exactly. I've been working on modifications to my program to see if it was even possible. And now I think it is. I need your permission so I can access your hotel files."

"Wait. But I thought your program was to streamline transportation of goods?"

"It is. But I modified it so that instead of goods, it's moving people to your hotel. So it will access public transportation, airlines, boats, whatever to make the trip to your hotel expedient and economical."

"I... I don't know what to say."

"Say yes. I think it can help both of us." He paused. His gaze searching hers. "Will you let me access your system?"

"I... I don't know." She seemed to be saying that a lot lately. "What are you going to do?"

"I'm going to fine-tune things. I'll guarantee that your business won't decline when I'm done."

"You can't promise something like that."

He sent her a self-assured smile. "Sure, I can. Trust me."

She wanted to trust him. It'd be so easy to trust him. But she had the feeling they were talking about totally different things. While he wanted her to trust him with her business, she was daydreaming about something a lot more personal.

How could she turn him down when he was pleading with his eyes? He wanted this. He needed this to prove that his program worked in the real world. And her hotel really needed more business now that her sister—the almost-princess of Patazonia—was no longer running the wedding portion of the business.

"Okay. But on one condition—make that two conditions."

"Which would be?"

"You take a shower and get some sleep. And I want to be a part of this. I want to know what you're changing."

He frowned at her. "That's three conditions."

She thought about it. "So it is. What do you say?"

"Sleep is overrated."

She pressed her hands to her hips. "But showers aren't."

"Point taken. And I suppose a nap wouldn't hurt. Coffee only goes so far."

"Good. We can start when I get back. We're starting to put the kitchen together." She checked the time. "And I'm late. Get some rest."

"Yes, ma'am." He sent her a tired smile.

"I knew there was something I liked about you—you listen to me. Unlike someone else." Her gaze moved to the puppy. "Come, Gin."

The puppy didn't move from Ric's side.

"Gin." She tried again to get the puppy to come to her, but she was having no luck. She definitely saw some puppy obedience classes in Gin's future.

"Don't worry," Ric said. "He can stay with me."

"Are you sure? He might keep you awake."

"Between you and me, I'm so tired right now that I don't think anything could wake me once I'm out." His gaze moved to the puppy. He ran his hand over the pup's back. "And he's a good snuggler."

"Aw… I was wondering where he snuck off to at night."

"He climbs in my bed and steals a pillow."

She smiled. So Mr. Independent, Mr. I-Don't-Need-Anyone was hooked on the puppy. "Okay. You two be good. I've got to go."

And out the door she went, anxious to see the beginning of her vision for the villa's kitchen. But as excited as she was about the remodel, she couldn't help thinking of Ric. Every day she saw a little more of the man behind the CEO persona, and she was drawn in a little more.

She told herself not to get attached because soon she'd be leaving.

But what would it hurt to enjoy the time she had left here in Lapri? And to enjoy the time she spent with Ric as they worked on marrying his program with her business?

This wasn't good.

He couldn't concentrate.

Ric told himself that his inability to focus was because he hadn't taken a long enough nap like Gia had insisted upon. But the truth was, he was distracted by her closeness as they huddled around his computer.

She'd showered as soon as she'd returned from the villa. And now, as she leaned in close to read something on the screen, he inhaled the gentle floral scent of her perfume. Her short hair was still damp, and she hadn't slowed down to put on any makeup. Even without primping, she was the most beautiful woman that he'd ever seen. In fact, he preferred the natural look on her.

He'd caught himself more than once staring at her and thinking he wanted nothing more than to pull her into his arms and kiss her. Thankfully, she hadn't seemed to notice he was distracted or that he'd hit the wrong key repeatedly, which wasn't like him at all.

He told himself to think of her as a client he was working with on a way to help her boutique hotel. And it worked for a little, but then she'd tucked a strand of hair behind her ear and now he was thinking about combing his fingers through the short, silky strands that accentuated her heart-shaped face.

His fingers paused on the keyboard, having lost his train of thought. "What's your password?"

"Sunflower01."

"That's it? No special characters?"

She shook her head. "I only added the numbers because the system insisted on it."

Concern filled him. "Do you know how easily hackers could crack such a simple password?"

She shrugged. "Who would want to break into our reservations system?"

"It's more than reserving rooms. There's payments and identities."

Gia frowned. "Okay. I get it. I have to be more careful."

Together they came up with a more elaborate password. And then she phoned Michael to inform him about the changes.

"And you need to set up a three-factor authentication," he said.

"Now you're being over the top with security."

"Actually, I'm not. Hackers are good. Very good. They just haven't found you yet, but when they do find your site, you'll have big problems. It could ruin the hotel's reputation."

"Are you serious?" When he nodded, she added, "Hackers really need to get a life instead of making everyone else's so difficult."

They went about setting up the three-factor authentication. He could tell Gia wasn't happy about all of the extra steps, but he assured her that in the end, she would appreciate her business being secure. She merely nodded and continued to frown. He couldn't help but smile. The little frown lines between her brows were adorable.

And he knew the more adorable she became, the more hooked on her he became. That was dangerous. Once her biological father was located, she'd be gone. He'd once more be alone.

The evening flew by.

Gia did her best to walk Ric through her online system, but she didn't always know what he was asking. It seemed he knew more about the program without having to work on it than she did after using it for months. But then again, computer programs were his thing, not hers.

She ordered a pizza and insisted Ric take a break to eat. She even persuaded him to join her on the couch with Gin taking his usual spot between them, waiting for a scrap of food to fall so he could scarf it up.

"You know, you don't have to go to all of the extra trouble with my website," Gia said, feeling guilty that he was spending time fixing her security and search engine optimization.

"I don't mind. In fact, I enjoy this type of work."

"Have you always been good at computers?" She'd seen another side of him while they'd been working on her website—a side that was nothing like the man in the movie or the headlines posted about him on the internet. A wickedly smart, funny and caring man—a man any woman would be foolish not to fall for.

He finished his last bite of pizza, wiped his mouth and then set aside the empty plate. "I started messing around with computers when my uncle gave me one for my eighth birthday."

"Your uncle? Not your mother?"

He was quiet for a moment. "My mother wasn't in my life much as a kid."

"Oh, I'm sorry. I didn't know."

"Nobody knows because I don't talk about it."

"I shouldn't have said anything. Sometimes my mouth gets ahead of me."

"It's okay. It'd be natural to assume I'd have grown up with my mother, but she wasn't the maternal kind most people have. I'm sure your mother baked you cookies, helped with your homework and tucked you in at night."

It was true. She'd always thought she'd had the best

mother in the entire world. And then she and her siblings had read their mother's journal. Those cherished memories grew tarnished. Sometimes she wished they'd just burned her journal and let the fire consume her mother's secret. And other times, she was excited about the future and meeting this mystery man who was her biological father.

"But you have to remember," Gia said, "my mother lied to me my entire life. So she wasn't perfect."

Ric reached out and took her hand in his. He gave it a squeeze. "No one is perfect. But your mother loved you."

"I'm sure your mother loves you too."

He shook his head. "I was always a bother—a mistake."

This time Gia squeezed his hand and leaned her head against his shoulder. "I'm sorry. Looks like both of our mothers let us down."

"I guess."

"At least you had your uncle. Was he always there for you?"

"He was. I took his quietness for aloofness, but thanks to you finding all those papers he'd saved from my youth, I realize that I misjudged him. And for that I'm really sorry. I remember one time he threw me a surprise birthday party. It wasn't really my thing, but he made sure all of my classmates were there—"

As Ric regaled her with stories of his childhood, she felt the walls between them coming down. Beneath his cool, business exterior there was a really warm, passionate man. And she was utterly falling for him—falling for his deep soothing voice; falling for the gentle rumble of his laugh; falling for *him*.

"I really should get back to work," Ric said.

That was her cue to release his hand even though it felt so natural to have his fingers laced with hers. And it was time to sit upright, instead of letting her shoulder lean into his. It was with great reluctance that she did those things. Once they were no longer touching, she missed the warmth of his touch—the coziness they'd shared.

She turned to him to say how much this time had meant to her at the same moment he turned to her. Their faces were so close. If she were just to lean forward ever so slightly, her lips would press to his. And what would be the problem with that? After all they'd shared this evening, a kiss was the perfect way to end it. Or would it just be the beginning?

Without thinking of the consequences, Gia leaned forward. Her lips pressed to his. He didn't move at first, as though unsure what to do about this new situation. Gia was more than willing to show him what she had in mind.

He continued to sit perfectly still. Was he shocked by her actions? How was that possible? She was certain plenty of women had thrown themselves at him. Not that she was throwing herself at him.

She was—she thought for a moment—sampling him. Her lips moved over his smooth ones. Definitely sampling—like he was the finest, most decadent tiramisu dessert. And she loved desserts!

Then there was a groan—or was it a moan? Had the sound come from him? Or her? But then it didn't matter because he'd reached out to her, stroking her cheek. He met her kiss for kiss. She was getting lost in the moment.

Why exactly had she waited all this time? Kissing Ric was something that should be done often—as in twice in the morning, at least three times at lunch and definitely all evening long.

His tongue touched her lips, seeking access. She opened herself up to him, anxious to take this to the next level. She couldn't get enough of him. He was so addictive.

As his tongue probed and stroked her, a moan swelled

in the back of her throat. No kiss had ever been quite like this one—

Buzz. Buzz.

No. No. No. Just ignore it. It'll stop.

Not the kissing. Definitely not the kissing. She never wanted it to end. Apparently Ric felt the same way as he reached out and pulled her closer—her soft curves aligning with his hard planes. At some unknown point Gin had discreetly disappeared, leaving the couch all theirs. Mmm...

Buzz. Buzz.

It was Ric who pulled back. "You should get that. It might be important."

"Me? Isn't it your phone?"

They both reached for their phones on their respective end tables. Ric was right. It was her phone. And it was the contractor.

"I'm sorry," she said. "It's work."

Ric nodded in understanding. While she pressed the phone to her ear, Ric returned to his desk and started running his fingers over the keyboard once more.

Upon answering the phone, she heard shouting in the background. She dispensed with pleasantries. "What's wrong?"

"We have a water leak in the kitchen," the contractor said.

"The kitchen?" She didn't even want to think of what the water would ruin. "I'll be right there." Once she ended the call, she looked at Ric. He was already absorbed in marrying his algorithm with her business's website. "I've got to run out."

"No problem. I'll be here when you get back."

Gia got to her feet. She couldn't leave quite yet. She stepped up to the desk. Not sure what to say or how to say it. Still, she had to know where they stood. His fingers stopped typing, and his gaze lifted to meet hers.

Her heart pounded in her chest. "About what happened—"

"Don't worry. We can talk about it later. Go deal with your problem."

"You're sure?" She felt weird kissing him one moment and running out the door the next.

"Positive. We're good. Now go."

So she did as he said. But she couldn't help but wonder where it would have led them if they hadn't been interrupted. Was Ric falling for her too?

CHAPTER TEN

THINGS WERE DEFINITELY coming along.

The walls were painted.

The counters were in.

The floor was finished.

Three days later, Gia stood in the center of the spacious kitchen and turned around. They still had a lot of details to work on, like the backsplash, the fixtures and the cabinet pulls. Things that would make this house a home. Lucky for them, the leaking pipe had been caught before it caused any major damage.

A smiled lifted her lips. This place had an old-world feel but with all the modern conveniences. Though the long center island did give the room a more modern vibe, she'd weighed need over authenticity. But they'd made sure the island matched the look and feel of the cabinetry. All in all, anyone would be lucky to have this kitchen. She'd certainly feel that way if it were hers.

She couldn't help but wonder if Ric would change his mind about the place and move in once it was completed. After all, he'd grown up here. It was a part of his past—

"There you are." The sound of Ric's voice came from behind her.

She turned to him. "You were looking for me?"

"I've been calling you and texting you. Didn't you get my messages?"

"Sorry. My phone is in the other room." She couldn't help but worry that something was wrong. It wasn't usual for Ric to track her down in person. "Is something wrong with Gin?"

"No." He shook his head. "He's fine. He's at home with Mrs. Rossi."

"Then what's wrong?"

"Nothing is wrong. Not exactly."

"You aren't making any sense." And her anxiety was climbing with each passing moment.

"It's about your father—your biological father. Nate called—"

"He figured it out?" Excitement flooded her veins. "He knows the man's name?"

"No. I'm sorry. He wasn't able to uncover any additional information from the pages we scanned to him. But he has an idea that might lead to more information about him. However, it's going to take your agreement."

"What is it?" She was getting desperate. She couldn't stop now. She felt as though they were very close to finding out his name.

"Nate needs the actual journal to run some tests on. He might need to remove a page or two."

For the briefest moment, Gia hesitated. She worried her bottom lip. It was her mother's final words. If anything happened to it, she'd be miserable. But her siblings had given their blessings for her to do with the journal what was necessary to locate her biological father. Maybe the risk was worth it.

"Okay. Do it," she said in a rushed breath before she could take it back.

Ric arched a brow. "I know how protective you are of your mother's journal. Are you sure? I don't know exactly what he's going to do with it."

"I'm sure." She wasn't. Not really. But her mother used

to say, nothing ventured, nothing gained. "It's back at your place."

"Can you leave now? Nate has some time this afternoon."

"I…uh, yes. Just let me have a word with the contractor."

"I'll meet you at the car."

"Sounds like a plan."

Gia thought of the scratched-out lines in her mother's journal. She'd always wondered if her mother regretted what she'd written. Or had she been afraid that someone else would read it?

Either way, this was it. She was certain they were going to get some answers now.

No matter the results…

Everything was about to change.

Ric wanted Gia to find her biological father and learn the answers to all her questions. And yet there was another part of him that didn't want her journey to end—not yet.

He was just getting used to sharing his apartment with her. And then there was the puppy. Who'd have thought he was a dog person, but he was. If it hadn't been for Gia, he'd have never figured that out.

He'd also learned that he enjoyed having someone to share morning coffee with. Not just anyone, Gia. She was talkative at all the right times. And when he just needed some companionable silence, she seemed to recognize that and leave him to his thoughts.

After stopping by the apartment for Gia to clean up and grab the journal, they headed off to the other side of the island. The trip was quiet as each was lost in their own thoughts.

What would happen when she learned the true identity of her father? She would leave. There would be no reason for her to stay. Sure, there was the villa to finish remodeling, but her plans were already written down. There was no reason someone else couldn't follow them. There would be no pressing reason for her to remain. And that thought dampened Ric's mood.

He parked at a research facility and followed his friend's instructions to the fifth floor where they were to meet Nate in the lobby. Ric checked the time. They were a few minutes early.

He told himself it would be good to get back to his solitary life. He could work as late as he liked. He could get up whenever he liked, but then again, he never slept in, no matter how late he worked. He wouldn't have to eat on a schedule. He could walk around his apartment in as little clothing as he liked—

"Are you sure Nate said to meet him here?" Gia's voice interrupted his thoughts.

"Um, yes, he did."

Just then Nate, a tall lanky man with sandy blond hair, rounded the corner. His gaze met Ric's. "Sorry to keep you waiting." He kept moving until he stopped in front of Gia. He held his hand out to her. "Gia, at last we meet. I'm Nate, and it's a pleasure to finally meet you in person."

"It's nice to meet you too." She flashed him a brilliant smile.

Was it Ric's imagination or did Nate hold Gia's hand longer than necessary? And the way he was smiling at her, it was like he was flirting with her. Who could blame him? Gia was a knockout. But they were here to get some work done.

Ric cleared his throat and stepped closer. Gia pulled her hand back, but her face was flushed and she was still smiling. Why didn't she act like that around him?

"We should get to work," Ric said, wanting to move this along.

"Right. This way." Nate led them down a hallway and up a flight of steps. "I have a friend with a lab and some special equipment that should help us uncover what's crossed out in your mother's journal." Just outside the lab, Nate turned to her. "You do realize this might be a futile effort. This might not lead to any clues about your biological father."

"I understand." Gia had a certainty in her eyes. "But I have to do whatever is necessary."

"Even if it means removing the pages in question from the journal?"

Gia momentarily hesitated. "Even then."

Nate nodded in understanding. "Then let's do this."

Inside the lab, they shook hands with a shorter, older man. Gia was very quiet. Her hands tightly gripped the journal. And the smile had disappeared from her face.

"May I have the journal?" Nate asked.

Gia handed it over and then wrung her hands.

Nate quickly located a page with some crossed out writing. "I'm going to see if I can hold it up to a very bright light to see if we can make out the original writing."

They struggled to hold the journal up to the light. It quickly became evident that this process would work better if the page was removed from the journal. With a sharp knife, Nate sliced the page from the book near the spine.

And so they worked through a process starting with a bright light and then applying a blue light. Neither was able to distinguish the handwriting from the scratch-out marks.

Next, they tried applying some heat to warm the paper to see if it would make a difference with the ink. Again, it didn't work.

Finally they ran the page through a high-resolution scanner that was equipped with image editing software that was able to discern the different inks by applying a contrast. As the two men worked to get the contrast just right to display the text, Gia rubbed her hands together.

One look at her rigid shoulders and clenched hands let Ric know her whole body was tense. This just had to work. He wasn't sure how much more she was up for. She'd already endured so much when she lost her parents.

He moved close to her and draped his arm over her shoulders, drawing her to his side. He wasn't sure how she'd react, but the next thing he knew, she was leaning into him. He welcomed the warmth of her body. Her head landed against his shoulder. He leaned his head to the side, resting his cheek against her silky hair. He breathed in its floral scent from her shampoo.

He wasn't sure how long they stood there quietly waiting and watching. Gia didn't move. Neither did he. He wanted to be there for her—to be the pillar of strength she'd need if this experiment didn't yield the desired results.

"We got it!" Nate projected the image on the large monitor.

Gia let go of Ric as she rushed forward. "I can't believe it. It worked!"

"It did," Nate said. "It really helped that your mother used two different colored pens."

Ric moved to stand with them. His gaze focused on the words now revealed.

I'm so mad at Aldo. Why does he have to be such a jerk about the inheritance? His stupid pride. It always comes back to the money. I wish I'd never inherited it.

Ric wasn't exactly sure what that meant, but he was certain it was of no help in finding Gia's biological father. He turned his attention to her. Her momentary excitement had deteriorated into a frown.

"I'm sorry it's not what you were hoping for," Ric said.

"Do it again." There was determination tinged with desperation in Gia's voice. "Whatever it costs, I'll pay it."

And so they did it again with another page.

And again, they uncovered her mother being upset with Aldo—for forcing a separation.

But it was on the third try that they uncovered something useful. Gia stood front and center, staring up at the screen.

Ric positioned himself behind her. His height enabled him to look over her to the words on the screen.

Stupid. Stupid. How could I have let this happen? Too much anger—too much wine—and a sweet-talking man. Now I'm pregnant with Berto Gallo's baby.

When I went to tell him, he never gave me a chance. He turned me away without letting me say a word. He said if I came back, he'd have me arrested. Arrested!

Oh, what a colossal mess.

The last words were blurred even with the high diagnostic equipment. It looked as if water had been spilled on the page, but just a couple of drops. Tears?

This man didn't sound like a good guy. Far from it. Ric felt really bad for Gia. He knew that she'd imagined a happy meeting with her biological father, and now it wasn't to be. He was ready to do anything to console her when she turned to him with a smile. A smile?

"This is it. We have his name." Her eyes shimmered with unshed tears. "Now I can track him down."

He couldn't tell if those were tears of sadness, relief or was it possibly she was truly happy about this discovery?

"Are you sure you still want to go through with—"

"Of course I am."

Ric opened his mouth, then, thinking better of it, he wordlessly closed it. At the very least, she was in shock. He couldn't let her continue on this journey alone.

He would be there to cheer with her if it worked out with her biological father. To dry her tears if it went awry. No matter what, she wasn't getting rid of him.

CHAPTER ELEVEN

ANY DAY NOW...

Any moment...

A couple of days had passed since the discovery of her father's name. Nate had promised to call when he had information about her father. Her gaze moved to the phone in her hand. Nothing. But soon.

She glanced over at Ric as he sat behind the wheel of his sporty coupe. "Ric, where are we going?"

A smile played the corners of his sexy mouth. "It's a surprise."

Hope bubbled up within her. "Did you find my father?"

The smile fell from his face. "Not yet. I'm sorry, Gia. I have people working on it." He reached out and took her hands in his. "It's a common name. And so far, he doesn't appear to be on the island. But we'll keep looking. But in the meantime, I have something to take your mind off the search."

He was so supportive and thoughtful. She wanted to smile—to be excited—but she was struggling. "What is it?"

"I can't tell you. Remember?"

"I know. It's a surprise."

"Right." There was a twinkle in his eyes, and she noticed that twinkle only appeared when he was up to something—something unexpected.

So what was he up to? She had no clues. All she knew was that it was a surprise. That's all he'd told her since that morning when he'd mentioned he had plans for them. He'd asked her to get all dressed up in her finest clothes.

It was a little black number because a black dress worked anywhere. It dipped low in the front, giving a hint of her cleavage and it left most of her back bare. She'd paired it with diamond earrings and a diamond pendant that her parents had given her on her twentieth birthday. For her feet, she'd selected a pair of silver- and crystal-studded heals.

When she'd packed for the trip, she hadn't any idea what clothes would be needed once she met her father. She certainly hadn't expected to meet someone like Ric, so she was glad she'd had the foresight to pack an outfit like this. Life certainly worked in mysterious ways.

Gia glanced around as the city faded into the background.

Ric's luxurious midnight blue sports car glided over the roadway. He was in a particularly good mood. They'd both been working so hard that they hadn't been able to spend much time together. And when the evenings rolled around, they'd both collapse on the couch with Gin between them. Just like one big happy family.

Not that they were a family by any stretch of the imagination. Okay, maybe the thought crept into her imagination now and then. Was that so wrong? After all, once you got past Ric's prickly exterior, he was warm, thoughtful and fun. Any woman would be lucky to have him for a husband—

Not that she was thinking of him in that way. Suddenly the air grew warm. Gia's mouth grew dry as she chanced a quick glance in Ric's direction. His attention was focused on traffic instead of paying attention to her self-imposed discomfort. Thankfully.

The farther they got from downtown, the more she wondered what he was up to. "You do know that most of the restaurants are behind us?"

"Don't you trust me?"

"I do." The automatic admission surprised not only him, with his raised brows, but also herself.

When did they change from being strangers to pleasant acquaintances to trusted friends? She didn't know, but she knew without a doubt that it was true. She trusted him.

"Good." He reached over and squeezed her hand. "I trust you too."

His response warmed a spot in her chest, but she refused to dwell on it. "Good. Now that we've established that, tell me where we're going."

"I can't."

She sighed. "Why not?"

"Because it'd ruin the surprise."

"What surprise? It's not my birthday." And then a thought came to her. "Is it your birthday?"

"No. And that's all I'm telling you."

She huffed and crossed her arms. She wanted to be mad at him but she couldn't. He was too sweet and thoughtful. He'd been spending every free moment to help her track down her father. He'd used his technology to help her hotel. And in turn, he'd given her a way to help pay him back by letting her help fix up his uncle's estate.

Her experience with remodeling her parents' villa and changing it into a boutique hotel had definitely come in handy. She'd learned so much the first time around, and she was learning more through this process. She was starting to wonder if the hotel business was really what she wanted to do with her life. She liked working with her hands, getting dirty and designing beautiful homes.

"Hey," Ric said, "you didn't have to go all quiet on me."

"Sorry. I was just thinking about your uncle's, or rather

your, villa. It's come a long way. You should be able to put it on the market soon."

"The more you work on it, the harder it's going to be for me to part with it."

"Really?" She narrowed her gaze on him. "Or are you just saying that to make me feel good?"

He cast her a quick glance. "Would I do that?"

She didn't hesitate. "Yes, you would. You might fool other people with that occasional growl of yours, but not me. I've seen your soft side."

He laughed. "You have, huh?"

"I have. You're a softy."

He nodded. "I wonder if my assistant would agree with you."

"She would."

"You sound confident. Have you been discussing me with Marta?"

"Perhaps." She hadn't, but she'd let him wonder about that one.

"We're here."

She glanced around at the marina. This wasn't just any marina. The boats docked here weren't "just a boat." These beauties were big and expensive yachts. She'd never seen so many in the same spot.

She was confused. "What are we doing here?"

"Having dinner."

"Dinner? Here?"

He got out of the car without an answer, not that she was expecting one. She was still sitting there taking in the impressive view when her car door swung open. And there stood Ric in his black tux with a black tie and white shirt.

He held his hand out to Gia and helped her to her feet. As she placed her hand in his, his fingers wrapped around hers, sending a wave of energy up her arm. It set her heart pounding.

She told herself to calm down. This was probably another business dinner. No big deal. She would do her best to help him sell his technology. It was the least she could do after all he'd done to help her find her father.

As he guided her down to the docks, she asked, "Who are we meeting tonight? Is there anything I can say to help you?"

"Help me?"

"You know, to make a deal." She rambled on because she was nervous and he was still holding her hand, which was making thinking a challenge. "You can count on me to back you up. If you want me to tell them how your technology is helping my hotel, I can do that." Because ever since Ric had helped her strengthen her passwords, he'd also strengthened her hotel's online presence. Reservations were steadily climbing. "Just let me know what you want me to say."

A smiled played at the corners of his lips. "And that's what you think we're here for? Business?"

"Aren't we?" Her stomach shivered with nerves.

Ric stopped walking and turned to her. He gazed into her eyes. "No. We're here for something far more important."

She wanted to say something. But the pounding of her heart drowned out her thoughts. And instead she stood there quietly, as though by staring into his eyes he'd cast a spell over her. Her gaze momentarily lowered to his lips before she caught herself and raised her gaze to meet his once more.

He stepped closer to her and lowered his voice. "I wanted to do something special for you."

"You...you did?" She struggled to string two words together.

He smiled at her, and it was like a hundred butterflies took flight within her. He turned and they continued walking. What exactly had he planned for this evening? And what did it mean? Was this just a friendly gesture? Or was it something more?

When he came to a stop next to a huge white yacht with navy trim, her mouth gaped. They were going to board this? She'd never been on a boat before, let alone one so fancy.

Her family had money, but it was old money and her parents liked to live simply. Though they could have owned something like this beautiful vessel, they wouldn't have. The man she'd always thought of as her father hadn't liked the water, and her mother was happy with their life at the vineyard—at least that's what Gia and her siblings had thought until they'd uncovered their mother's journal and the circumstances surrounding Gia's conception.

She wondered what else they'd assumed about their parents and been wrong about. How could people be so close and yet not know as much about each other as they'd thought?

"Gia? What's wrong?" The concern in Ric's voice startled her from her troubling thoughts.

"Um, nothing."

The look on his face said that he didn't believe her. "Are you sure?"

"Positive." She forced a smile to her lips. "What are we doing here? I thought we were going out for dinner."

"We are." And then he led her aboard.

She looked around. The boat looked brand-new. Everything sparkled and gleamed. "How did you manage this?"

"It wasn't hard. The truth is that I don't use it much. When I purchased the yacht, I thought I'd use it for business meetings and to entertain business acquaintances, but

I quickly found out they were just as busy as me. No one these days has time for long, leisurely outings."

Her mouth gaped as she looked around again with the knowledge that this huge boat was all his. "This is bigger than the guest house on my parents' estate."

It wasn't until the words were out of her mouth that she realized the estate was no longer her parents'. It was still so hard to comprehend that they were gone, and now she was searching for where she fit in this world. What once was, was no longer.

"I should probably sell it, but I'm glad I didn't." He stepped up close to her.

"Why not?"

"Because then we wouldn't be able to have dinner out on the sea."

And with that the yacht pulled away from the dock, and they headed off into the sunset. Gia felt as though she were Cinderella, but this definitely wasn't a ball. It was better.

Once they were away from the shore, it was like they were the only ones on earth. Well, except for the staff that served them the most delightful dinner. And the captain who navigated the peaceful seas. However, they made themselves scarce, leaving her and Ric alone.

Ric had her full attention. He was sweet and attentive. She'd noticed that he hadn't checked his phone once since they'd left the dock. His attention was fully on her. And she had no idea what that meant. Was this the beginning of something? A follow-up to that steamy kiss they'd shared? Her heart quickened at the thought.

Thoughts of her business, the villa remodel and the search for her biological father slipped to the back of her mind. This evening, with classic ballads playing in the background, she found herself getting swept up in their words of love.

With the dinner dishes cleared and the tiramisu finished, Ric stood and held his hand out to her. "Would you care to dance?"

She glanced around. There was plenty of room on the outer deck. And then her gaze met his. The crooning ballad called to her. Ric had gone to a lot of effort. Why not enjoy every moment of this evening? Her problems would be waiting for her tomorrow. For tonight, she would enjoy the evening Ric had gone to such bother to plan for her.

He held his arms out to her, and she happily stepped into them. Her body fit next to his as though they'd been made for each other. As they moved about the floor, she leaned her head on his muscular shoulder and let her eyes drift shut. Instead of all the questions and worries that plagued her at night when she closed her eyes, right now, all she could think about was the strong, reliable man holding her so close.

She inhaled his spicy cologne. It mixed with his manly scent and made quite an intoxicating mixture. She breathed in deeper. A murmur of pleasure vibrated in her throat.

The truth was, they'd been dancing around each other since they'd met. The chemistry had arced between them since that first day in the garden of his uncle's villa. The first time he'd touched her, the tingles of awareness had zinged through her body. Since then she'd been fighting it. And right now, she couldn't remember why she'd been resisting him.

Ric was a good guy—strike that—he was a great guy. And she was so tired of fighting the magnetic pull that he had over her heart. Because with each morning coffee they'd shared, with each soul-searching conversation, with each heated glance, piece by piece he'd broken through the wall around her heart.

She stood there in his arms feeling utterly exposed and

vulnerable. And at the same time, she felt liberated and excited to find out what would come next.

She once more breathed in his heady scent. Deeper. Longer. It must be going to her head because all she could think about was kissing him. Right here. Right now. And not just a peck on the cheek or lips. No. She longed for a deep soul-stirring, feet-floating-above-the-ground kiss.

But maybe she'd start with an appetizer. She moved her head ever so slightly and pressed her lips to the smooth skin of his neck. Immediately she heard the swift intake of his breath. She smiled. She wasn't the only one caught up in this evening of a dazzling sunset and twinkle of candlelight.

They stopped dancing. Experience had taught her that life could be short—much too short. And each moment had to be lived to its fullest. Gia decided to live daringly. She trailed kisses up his neck. She lifted up on her tiptoes. When she pulled back, their gazes met. There was passion ignited in his eyes.

And then she pressed her lips to his.

There was no hesitancy. There was need. Hunger. And desire. Oh, yes, lots of desire.

Her hands slid up, taking in the lines of his muscular chest. And then they slid over his broad shoulders. She tried to remember every feeling—every sensation—but every nerve ending of her body had been stimulated and her mind was on overload.

Her hands wrapped around the back of his neck. All the while, her lips were moving over his. His tongue delved inside her mouth. He tasted sweet like dessert wine. She didn't know if she'd ever drink that wine without being swept back in time to this delicious moment.

And then Ric swept her up in his arms. He took long, swift strides over to the navy-blue spacious deck lounge.

Their lips parted as he gently set her down. And then he joined her.

Suddenly she turned shy. "Ric, we can't. Not here."

"Look around. There's no one to see us."

She glanced out at the black sea with just the moonlight dancing upon the water. "But what about the staff?"

"Trust me. We won't be disturbed." He leaned over and pressed his mouth to hers.

What was it about this man that had her doing things that she would never consider otherwise? Still, the thought of her and him beneath the stars seemed so fitting.

She wrapped her arms around his neck and drew him to her. She didn't need to dream tonight because no dream could be better than this moment with this amazing man, who had sneaked past her defenses and into her heart.

CHAPTER TWELVE

HAD THAT REALLY HAPPENED?

Oh, yes. It definitely had.

Ric smiled. The next day, he was still trying to wrap his head around the direction dinner had taken. Sure, it had been a quiet, intimate dinner, but he never imagined things would go that far. Okay. That was a lie. He'd definitely thought of it, but never really believed Gia would go for it.

Until now, Gia had been holding him at arm's length. Sure, they'd shared a kiss or two. But where they'd gone had been so much further than that. And now he had no idea where they went from here.

Before, they'd been two people helping each other get what they wanted—what they needed. She was helping him prove the merits of his program. And he was helping her locate her father. It was a clean, unentangled relationship. It was safe.

But now this thing between them was anything but safe. In one evening, she'd pulled back all the protective layers that he'd spent years wrapping around himself—to never be as vulnerable as he had been when his mother rejected him.

Now Gia had him thinking about life with her in it. When he thought of lunch, he wondered if she was free to have it with him. When he went home, he anticipated seeing her. She even had him bonding with Gin. That dog was an equal opportunity lover, who tucked Gia in at night but gravitated to Ric's bed sometime during the night.

Gia had stumbled into his life not so long ago and somehow in that short period of time, she'd managed to change everything. He felt off balance and not sure what to do next—with regards to his relationship with Gia—

Wait. Did they have a relationship? Was she expecting a commitment from him? His heart stilled. Did he want to make a commitment? His palms grew damp. In the past, the question wouldn't have materialized.

The questions without answers swirled in his mind, distracting him from work. Now he was pondering it. He was supposed to be answering an abundance of neglected and waiting emails. He had to do something while he avoided Gia—while he figured out what to say to her. Somehow, he couldn't imagine *Wow. The other night was awesome. We'll have to do it again sometime* going over very well.

No. Gia was much deeper than that. Relationships meant a lot to her. She took them seriously. If she didn't, she wouldn't be searching so hard for a biological father she'd never met. And she sure wouldn't be pinning all her hopes and dreams on it being a happy union—no matter that the man's past history said otherwise.

Gia was the type of person who couldn't help but walk around with her heart on her sleeve. She might try to hide it, but she wasn't very successful. And that's why when she'd looked at him in the morning light, after they'd made love, that he'd known he'd made a very big mistake.

Gia wanted a relationship. A real relationship with entanglements and emotions—all the things he'd been avoiding. And he had no idea what to do about it.

And now, when everything was so complicated, he'd gotten the phone call that he'd been waiting for—hoping for. Mr. Grosso wanted to meet with him that evening. And Mr. Grosso wanted him to bring along Gia to tell him how the program had helped her company.

Ric stared in the full-length mirror in his bedroom. His

dark suit with a white shirt and burgundy tie exuded success and confidence, but he felt like a fraud. Sure, he was successful at business, but his personal life was in shambles. And where he was once quite confident, now he wasn't so sure he could be, or wanted to be, the man Gia wanted or deserved.

He checked the time. They had to leave for the restaurant. The last thing he wanted was to be late and give Mr. Grosso a bad impression of him from the start.

When he stepped into the living room, he was surprised to find Gia sitting on the couch with Gin, waiting for him. When their gazes met, she smiled. Not just a little smile, but a big one that lit up her whole face and warmed a spot in his chest. This wasn't good. Not good at all.

Stay focused on business.

Ha! That's easier said than done.

And then his gaze drifted lower, taking in the dazzling deep red dress that she'd chosen for the evening. His mouth grew dry. How was he supposed to focus on business when she was dressed like that?

When he stopped in front of her, she stood. "You look stunning."

Color bloomed in her cheeks. "Thank you."

Gin barked in agreement. They both laughed. After Mrs. Rossi scooped up Gin and moved to the kitchen, they were alone. An awkwardness descended over Ric. He wasn't sure how to act around her.

"Shall we go?" He presented his arm to her. He told himself the gesture meant nothing.

She placed her hand in the crook of his arm. Her touch made his heart pick up its pace. This was going to be a long evening. Very long.

Everything is all right. It's just a very busy time. That's all.

It was what Gia had been telling herself since they'd

made love and Ric seemed to have pulled away. At first, she told herself she was just imagining things. But as time went on, she noticed when he smiled at her, the smile didn't go the whole way to his eyes. What was up with that?

And she hadn't worked up the nerve to ask him about it. What if she was just seeing things that weren't there? What if she questioned his commitment to this relationship when he was already invested? She didn't want to do anything to rock the boat.

Maybe she was just expecting too much, too soon. After all, Ric was used to being a bachelor. He was used to doing things at his own pace. Now he not only had her in his life, but he also had an incorrigible dog living with him—who chewed on his good shoes if he forgot and left them out.

She just needed to slow down and let things happen naturally—even if it was slower than she'd like. They were fine. After all, if they weren't, would he have taken her on this very important dinner meeting?

What she hadn't anticipated was that they would be in a private room for dinner—just the two of them and Mr. Grosso. They were seated in a room that was obviously normally used for much larger parties than a party of three. When Ric said this man was a bit of a recluse, he hadn't been kidding.

Still, she couldn't dismiss the strange feeling of being in a big restaurant, but so alone. The murmur of voices reached them every time the server went in and out of the door. Gia wished they were out in the main room. Out there would be distractions that would perhaps put her more at ease.

She must not be the only one to feel the tension because Ric had been quieter than normal. He'd barely caught her gaze throughout the meal. He'd tried talking to Mr. Grosso, but the man wasn't talkative. At one point, the older man mumbled something about too much talk ruining a meal.

Okay, then why request a dinner meeting?

But thankfully the meal was almost concluded. She wasn't sure the mostly silent meal had helped Ric's sale. In fact, she was thinking it hadn't. And Ric must have felt the same way as the muscle in his cheek twitched like it did when he worked on his computer and something wasn't going right. Or when the dog wouldn't listen to him.

As the dinner dishes were cleared and their coffee was refilled, Gia decided to try to help Ric. "It was a lovely dinner. Thank you for suggesting we should meet here." Her gaze met the older man's. "We really appreciate you agreeing to meet with us. I'm sure once you hear about Ric's creation, you'll feel the same excitement about it that I do."

The older man's gaze moved between her and Ric. "How long have you two been together?"

Heat rushed to her face. She hadn't anticipated discussing her complicated relationship with Ric. "I haven't known Ric all that long."

"About the program," Ric intervened. "I have the real time results you'd previously requested."

The older man waved off the mention of business. He took a sip of his coffee and then leaned back in his chair. His gaze continued to move between the two of them. His gaze settled on Gia. "My Elizabeth was a lot like you. She was my biggest supporter." He sighed as though the memories were bittersweet. And then his gaze moved to Ric. "I just wish I'd have noticed her sooner—paid more attention to her."

Ric's jaw tightened. It was as though the man was trying to send him a message, and Ric wasn't having any of it.

Gia went for a distraction. "Is Elizabeth your wife?"

Mr. Grosso turned his attention back to Gia. "Yes. She was. Taken from me far too soon. When are you two getting married?"

"We aren't," Ric said. "Now about the program." He reached for his attaché, pulling out a manila folder. "I've brought some printouts that we can go over."

Mr. Grosso frowned and waved away the papers. "You two, are you a couple?"

"Yes," she said.

"No," Ric said.

They looked at each other after giving conflicting answers. Had she heard Ric correctly? After all they shared, it meant nothing to him?

His eyes were dark and filled with a swirl of emotions that she was unable to make out. Still, his answer hung there in her thoughts. Each time she recalled it, it was like a stab to her chest.

Their lovemaking meant nothing?

She meant nothing?

"Aw… See?" said Mr. Grosso. "I was right. There is something between you two." His attention zeroed in on Ric. "You're making a mistake by not marrying her as soon as possible. And trust me, you will regret it—"

"What I regret is not going over these reports," Ric said. "I think if you have a look at what I was able to do with my program to help Gia's business that you'll realize it will streamline and increase business for your company."

"I can't trust a man with my business who can't see what's right in front of him."

Ric raked his fingers through his hair. "Gia is not part of this business agreement."

"But she should be part of your life. When you are old like me, you'll find your business is a cold bed partner and a demanding mistress that never has enough of your time and always wants more, but never gives enough in return."

Ric was quiet.

Gia was still trying to wrap her mind around what

was happening. Mr. Grosso was trying to be some sort of matchmaker. And Ric was denying that there was anything between them. And she was quiet because she didn't trust her voice right now. She didn't know which man she was most upset with.

After a tense moment, Ric said, "Would you like to see the reports?"

"I think I've seen as much as I need to." Mr. Grosso stood. "You get your life straightened out, and then we'll talk."

Ric stood. "My personal life has nothing to do with this." His words reached the man's retreating back. Once the man was gone, Ric turned to her. "Can you believe him?"

"What I can't believe is you." She grabbed her purse and followed in Mr. Grosso's footsteps.

"Gia, wait."

She kept going. She didn't want to have this conversation in the restaurant with witnesses. What she had to say to him, she didn't want overheard. And with the number of people gaping at Ric and pointing him out, she was certain a scene between them would make the headlines. That would just take a painful situation and make it unbearable.

Outside on the sidewalk, she turned the opposite direction of the valet.

"Gia, where are you going?" Ric rushed up to her.

She kept walking, stuffing down the heated words she had for him.

"Gia, please stop. Talk to me."

It was obvious he wasn't just going to let her walk away and find her own way back to the apartment. And so she stopped and turned to him. "What?"

His eyes widened as though he just realized what was going on. "You're mad at me?"

"You're sharp. No wonder you own your own business."

"Listen, about back there. I'm sorry. That man, he was

over the top. I didn't realize he was going to talk about everything but business."

"Not everything."

Ric looked puzzled. "What?"

"Mr. Grosso didn't want to talk about everything, just about us. At which point you corrected him and told him there was nothing between us."

"Oh." Ric forked his fingers through his hair, scattering the short curls. "That's why you're mad."

"You bet it is." Her pride stopped her from admitting how deeply his words cut. "You didn't have the decency to tell me privately that our lovemaking was a mistake. Instead, you've been avoiding me. And then you blurt out to a stranger that it meant nothing to you."

"It's not like that."

She narrowed her gaze on him. "Then how is it?"

"I don't know."

"Don't know what?" She wasn't going to let him off that easy.

"I don't know anything. I wasn't expecting this, you, me and what's going on between us."

"Are you saying you want out? Or are you saying you were never into this thing between us?"

"What I'm saying is that I need time to process this. I need to figure things out. You are amazing." He reached out for her hand, taking it in his. His thumb rubbed over her skin. "Can you just give me a little time?"

She let out a pent-up breath. It wasn't the gushing admission of love she'd daydreamed about, but then again, it wasn't a big push-off either. It was actually a realistic approach to whatever this was between them. And maybe they both could use a little time to consider things.

She gazed deep into his eyes, finding nothing but honesty. "Time is a good idea."

His gaze searched hers. "You're sure? We're okay?"

She nodded. "We're okay."

He didn't release her hand; instead, he laced his fingers with hers as they walked back to get the car. She wasn't sure where they went from here.

It seemed like her life was becoming one big question mark. Would they find her father? Would things work out with her siblings? Would this thing with Ric lead somewhere?

Dinner had gone worse than he'd ever imagined.

And the ride home was quiet and strained.

Ric's grip tightened on the steering wheel. Everything he'd worked for—everything he'd planned—was falling apart. How dare that man judge him and his work by his lack of a committed relationship? What kind of archaic thinking was that?

The only saving grace had been Gia's calm presence. Through it all she'd remained pleasant, kept her cool and exuded a friendly demeanor. It was more than he could muster. Obviously that man had spent too much time alone, holed up in his mansion.

And then a worrisome thought came to him. Was he going to end up like Mr. Grosso? Old, alone and miserable?

He banished the thought. He liked his life. He was happy being a bachelor—not allowing anyone close enough to hurt him. He had nothing to worry about.

"I'm sorry about dinner," he said as they neared his apartment.

"The food was good."

"I meant the company." He wheeled into his parking spot.

"I'm sorry your deal fell through."

"I'm not." He never thought he'd say those words and mean them, but he did mean it. "I won't do business with someone so stuck in his ways." Ric's gaze met hers. "Thank you for being so good about everything."

"What will you do?"

"I don't know. I didn't have a backup plan because I thought I'd come up with the best pairing, his company and my program. I obviously thought he would be professional. I was wrong."

"You aren't giving up, are you?"

He raked his fingers through his hair. "You think I should try to work with that man?"

"Not necessarily him, but I'm sure your program can help another company."

She was right, even if he wasn't in the mood to hear it right now. At the moment, he just wanted to wallow in his disdain and anger. Sure, come tomorrow he'd see things in a different light. But for now, he just wanted to leave the subject alone.

Ric climbed out of the car and before he could round the car to get Gia's door, she let herself out. She was unlike the other women he'd dated. Gia wasn't helpless, but she could ask for help when she needed to. He admired her strength.

The more time he spent with her, the more he liked her. And he knew that was dangerous. Because when she tracked down her father, she would leave the island—leave him.

Unless he was to keep her at a friendly distance. He could do that. After all, it wasn't like he was falling in love with her. He could do the friends with benefits thing. He prided himself on being able to accomplish most anything he set his mind on. This wouldn't be any different.

CHAPTER THIRTEEN

SHE FELT BAD for Ric.

The meeting had been a total bust.

Gia wished there was something she could do to help him. But she knew absolutely nothing about computers, other than the basics. Programming was way beyond her abilities.

Still, she could tell Ric was going to be in a funk the rest of the evening if she didn't come up with a way to distract him. But what could she suggest that would keep him from heading back to his study where he'd grow even more melancholy?

When they entered Ric's apartment, the puppy came running up to them.

Arff. Arff.

"Does somebody need to go out?" Gia knelt and petted the little guy.

His tail rapidly swished back and forth.

"Okay. We'll go." She straightened and reached for the red leash on the black stand near the front door. It was then that she noticed Ric was lingering nearby and a thought came to her. "Would you like to join us for a walk?"

Ric shook his head. "That's okay."

It wasn't a direct no. In fact, it wasn't a no at all. And so she tried again. "It's a lovely evening. We could walk to the little gelato shop I spotted. I've been dying to try it. And then we could—"

She stopped herself before saying they could watch the

sunset together. She was pretty certain that would sound like she was crossing the line between their arrangement to care for Gin and romance.

She told herself she had no room in her life for romance. She didn't even know who she was. Putting the brakes on this relationship was for the best. But she knew it was a lie. She'd fallen for Ric. Hard.

His dark brows lifted as though in question. "Could what?"

Heat rushed to her cheeks. The more she willed herself not to blush, the warmer her face became. "I don't know."

"Ah, but you do know."

If her face grew any warmer, she was quite certain her hair would spontaneously combust. "If you don't want to go—"

"Oh, I definitely want to go now. I just need to grab something."

Of course he would.

Without waiting for Ric, she attached the leash and was out the door in a jiffy. What was it about that man that could rattle her so much? Luckily, there was a light breeze. She welcomed the rush of air, even if it was warm.

"Hey, slow up," Ric called from behind them.

She supposed she couldn't act like she hadn't heard him, not after inviting him to join her. She pulled on the puppy's leash, getting him to slow down. Gia came to a stop. She refused to let Ric get to her. After all, he was just a guy—a sexy movie star sort of hunky man. And when he stared into her eyes, like he was doing right now, her knees went weak.

She waited for him to catch up to her. "Sorry. Gin is in a rush."

"Is it the puppy who's in the rush? Or is it you?"

She chanced a glance at Ric to find him smiling at her from under a navy-blue ball cap. So that's what he had to grab. Didn't he know that no hat could hide his good looks? And that sexy smile—was he flirting with her? Her heart picked up its pace as did her footsteps.

But she wasn't going to let him know he was getting to her. "Why would I be in a rush to get away from you? After all, I was the one who invited you on this walk, remember?"

"Oh, I remember. I also remember you blushing."

"Oh, you. You're insufferable."

At this point, he broke out in a deep, hearty laugh. This only made Gia blush more. She picked up her pace, not wanting him to see the affect he had on her.

At last they reached the park. As the puppy stretched its legs, Gia pretended to be intently interested in a red flowering plant. She would do anything to avoid Ric's inquisitive gaze.

"Are you going to ignore me after inviting me on this walk?" His words echoed her thoughts.

She stifled a groan and then proceeded to plaster on a friendly smile. "I was just intrigued by this flower. I don't think we have it in Tuscany."

He held out his phone and snapped a photo of the flower. "There. All taken care of. I'll have my assistant track down the plant for you."

She wasn't sure that was necessary. Still, she said, "Thank you."

She glanced at him before quickly turning away. Something had happened tonight. Maybe it was that man assuming they were a couple. Or maybe it was going to dinner with Ric as though it were natural for her to accompany him to important business meetings. Whatever it was, the delicate balance in their relationship was tipping over into the heart-pounding, staring-into-each-other's-eyes, kissing-like-there's-no-tomorrow area. And she'd just promised him time to figure things out. Why did this all have to be so complicated?

"Gia, wait." He reached out for her hand.

Her heart lodged in her throat. She stopped and turned to him. Her gaze met his once more. Did he know what she was thinking?

Ric reached out to her. His thumb gently caressed her cheek. A sigh whispered across her lips. All the while, their gazes connected.

She wanted to ask him what was happening. Where were they going to go from here? The words hovered in the back of her mouth, but her lips refused to cooperate. The words faded away.

When Ric's gaze lowered to her lips, she knew his thoughts had strayed to the same idea she'd had. He was going to kiss her. And in that moment, she wanted him more than she wanted anything else in the world—

"Hey, aren't you the guy from the movie?"

The voice was like a bucket of cold water thrown in the face. Both she and Ric pulled back as though they were doing something wrong. Were they doing something wrong? Had they been saved from making another mistake?

Her mind said one thing while her heart said something quite different. And right now, she didn't know which one to listen to because the pounding of her heart was too distracting.

Ric plastered on a smile, like the one he'd worn at dinner when Mr. Grosso had started going on about how a man who could invest in a long-term relationship was a reliable sort of man. Yeah, it was that smile.

"Can I help you?" Ric asked the young woman.

"Can I get a selfie with you? My friends are going to be so envious."

And so Ric granted the young woman one photo together. When it was over, Ric pulled his hat lower and added a pair of dark sunglasses.

"I don't think that's going to help," Gia said as they walked away.

He shrugged. "I don't know why I agreed to do that movie."

"Sure, you do. You thought it would be fun." At least she hoped that's the reason he'd done it.

"In truth, it was a bet and I lost. My friend starred in it and had producing rights. It was just supposed to be a small clip, no big deal. And then I don't know what happened."

She knew exactly what had happened. Most every woman on the planet who had seen the clip was now part of the Ric's fan club. Secretly she was a member too. Not that she'd ever admit it to him.

"Most men would die to be in the position of having women throw themselves at them."

"I'm not most men." Any hint of the smile that had been on his face was now gone, and in its place was a distinct frown.

"Why is that?" She shouldn't have asked. It was none of her business. And yet her mouth just kept doing its own thing. "Did someone break your heart?"

At first, he didn't respond. "It was something like that, but it's in the past. And now I have my career to focus on."

And here she thought she was the only one hiding behind a wall in order to keep from getting hurt. She sensed his wall was much thicker than hers and had been reinforced over years. How did one break down such a wall?

Deciding she needed to lighten the mood, Gia asked, "Would that be your acting career?"

He frowned and then shook his head. "A guy takes a sixty-second spot in a movie and everyone blows it out of proportion."

"Oh, but those sixty seconds were quite something." And then, because she couldn't resist teasing him, she asked, "So was that a body double? You know for those washboard abs?"

His lips pressed into a firm line as his brows drew together. "You know that was all genuine. No stunt doubles were involved in the shooting of that scene."

Then, because she was having fun, she said, "I don't know if I believe you. You might have to prove it." When he reached for his shirt as though to rip it off and prove himself, she hurriedly reached out and grabbed his forearm, holding it in place. "Not that I wouldn't mind the show, but weren't you trying to stay under the radar?"

He glanced around, as though for a moment forgetting they were in public. "Yeah, right. But I was serious. It was me. All me."

She couldn't help but laugh as he stressed the point.

His dark brows drew together. "I'm serious."

"I know you are. That's what's so amusing." She couldn't stop smiling.

"I don't understand."

"It's okay. You don't have to." Men and their egos.

When they reached the gelato shop, it appeared they weren't the only ones to have the idea on this perfect summer evening. As they stood in a long line that stretched out the door, Gin drew people's attention. Passersby stopped to fuss over him, and the pup ate up all of the attention. There was no shyness when it came to Gin.

"Wait. Aren't you Ric Moretti from *Into the Sunset*?" a young woman asked.

"It is him," another young woman agreed.

"Hey, everyone!" the first woman shouted. "It's the hottie from *Into the Sunset*."

It all happened so fast that it caught both Gia and Ric off

guard. One second they were standing beside each other, and the next there was a crowd forming around him.

Gia was shoved out of the way with such force that her foot landed on the edge of the sidewalk. She lost her balance. She flung her hands out to break her fall as she tumbled back.

She'd managed to turn herself midair and land on her hip. The air was knocked from her lungs. It took her a second to collect herself. Limb by limb she made sure everything was still working properly. Thankfully she could move everything.

When she went to stand up, Ric appeared in front of her. He knelt next to her. Concern etched across his handsome face. "Are you all right?"

"I think so. I just lost my balance." She struggled to get up.

Ric placed a hand on her shoulder, holding her in place. "Maybe you shouldn't move. I can call for help."

"Don't be ridiculous. I'm fine." She lifted a hand to him to help her up. It was then that she noticed the ugly red scrape on her elbow. "Just a couple of scrapes."

He took her hand in his. His grip was warm and steady. In no time she was back on her feet and feeling like a total klutz.

Ric lifted her arm and frowned at the oozing scrape and the cut on her palm. "We have to get you looked at."

She glanced around. A sinking feeling came over her. "Gin?" She continued turning in a circle; with each step her heart sunk lower. "Gin, come here. Gin?"

The puppy was nowhere in sight. How could she have let this happen? All she had to do was hold on to the leash. That was it. And yet she hadn't managed to do it.

Guilt pummeled down on her. Poor Gin. The little guy had to be so scared after that rush of people. But where could he have gone? She pulled away from Ric. She had to find the puppy.

"Gia, you need medical attention," Ric said firmly.

"What I need is to find Gin." When Ric didn't move, she turned to him. "Please. I can't go anywhere until we find him. He's scared and lost."

To her surprise, Ric didn't argue with her. He turned and started searching around their immediate vicinity. He walked to the nearby alley, looking behind garbage cans and in discarded boxes. She rushed over to join him. He looked on one side while she searched the other. No sign of the little guy. They retraced their steps to the park. Gin wasn't there either.

"I'll alert Marta," Ric said. "She can get people on social media involved. We'll find him."

Gia turned to Ric. "With his leash still attached, he could get hung up on something and not be able to get loose."

A rush of protective emotions pumped through her veins. She couldn't think of anything else but finding Gin, not even tending to her cuts and scrapes.

They kept moving—kept calling Gin's name. There was no sign of him. How could that be?

"Don't worry," Ric said. "We're not giving up. Maybe we should check the beach."

"I don't know," she said. Tears stung the backs of her eyes. "He wouldn't even know to go there."

"Actually, we go there almost every morning."

She blinked away the moisture gathering in her eyes. "You do?" When he nodded, she asked, "How do I not know this?"

"Because we go very early in the morning."

"While I'm still asleep?"

Ric nodded.

"Then let's go."

They race-walked to the beach. Gia called for Gin until her voice was hoarse. He wasn't here. He wasn't anywhere they'd looked. And she was starting to wonder if she'd ever see him again.

The thought of never seeing that impish, loving puppy again was her total undoing. The world in front of her blurred. A tsunami of emotions engulfed her. Ric wrapped his arms around her. He held her as grief washed over her, leaving her raw and vulnerable.

She didn't know how much time passed when she pulled herself together. "I'm sorry about that. I didn't mean to fall apart."

"It's okay. I understand."

"But I'm not a crier. When my parents died, I didn't cry. When I found out I wasn't a Bartolini, I didn't cry. So why am I crying over a stray puppy that's not even mine?"

"That's a whole lot to hold inside."

"I'm strong. I'm a—" She stopped herself from saying she was a Bartolini like her…her father had taught her to say when she was young.

"Even strong people cry," Ric said.

"You don't."

He arched a brow. "How do you know that?"

She shrugged. "Ah…well, do you?"

They started walking along the beach as the sun set, sending splashes of color over the water. "I've cried," he said. "But I never told anyone because I was a jumble of emotions."

"What happened?"

Ric was quiet for moment. "It was a long time ago." His voice was soft as though his thoughts were caught up in the past. "The reason I'm so protective of my uncle and needed to prove he wasn't your father didn't have anything to do with his estate."

"You wanted to save his reputation?"

He nodded. "But more than that I needed to preserve the image that he wasn't like my mother—that he put other people's feelings ahead of his own."

"I take it you and your mother still aren't close."

Ric shook his head. "I haven't seen her in years. She prefers it that way and so do I."

"Wow. And here I thought I was the only one with parental issues."

"Trust me. You don't corner the market on parent problems."

"I'm here. If you want to talk about it."

He stopped walking and turned to her. "Has anyone ever told you how easy it is to talk to you?"

"No." A smile pulled at her lips. "But thanks for saying so."

Ric started walking again with her hand nestled in his. It felt so natural as though they were always this close. All the while, Gia's gaze searched their surroundings. She knew finding little Gin in this seaside city was a long shot, but she couldn't give up.

"My mother shouldn't have been allowed to have a child. She'd even tell you that herself. I was a mistake—one she reminded me about often."

Gia gasped. Not even her own mother ever mentioned in her journals that she thought of Gia as a mistake—even if she had been an unintentional result of an affair.

Not having anything positive to say about Ric's mother, Gia remained silent. This was his tale to tell. She was just here to listen—even though her heart went out to the image in her mind of Ric as a sweet little boy, a young child who didn't get the love he so rightly deserved.

"My mother wanted an easy life, and she was willing to do whatever it took—even sleeping with every man she thought could give her that lifestyle. And I just happened to be the result."

"But your father—"

"Didn't know about me. As I told you before, my mother doesn't even know who he is—if you can believe her."

"And you don't?"

He shrugged. "I think if she does know who it is, she's never going to tell me."

"But why wouldn't she tell you if she knew?"

He shrugged. "The only thing I can surmise is that it would complicate her life—her very cushy life. The man she married when I was young didn't like kids. And that's how I ended up living with my aunt and uncle. Nothing was going to come between my mother and the lifestyle she thought she deserved."

"I'm sorry. I can't even imagine what that must have been like for you." She squeezed his hand tighter.

"After my aunt died, my uncle still hung in there—never giving up on me. I could tell that he wasn't thrilled to be a single parent, but he never pushed me out the door."

Ric stopped and turned to her. The sun's last lingering rays shrouded him in light. As she stood there looking at him, she saw him completely different now. And she knew why. That reinforced wall around him had come down. He let her see a vulnerable side to him that she never would have thought existed. And that made him even more attractive than ever before.

And then they were gravitating toward each other. She wasn't sure who moved first. Was it her? Or was it him? Either way, their lips met in the middle. Oh, did they meet. It was as though the stars in the sky had lit up just for them. Or maybe it was sparks of desire lighting up the evening.

There was no hesitation as his tongue delved into her

mouth. A moan swelled deep in her throat. He tasted sweet like wine. And she was already intoxicated by his touch.

She knew exactly where this passionate kiss would lead them. And in that instant, she didn't care about the right or wrong of it. She wanted to live in the moment. And that was a first for her.

In Ric's arms she was content—no, not content, exhilarated with the here and now. She wasn't worried about the past. And she wasn't anxious for the future and the answers she might find. Right now, in this moment, she had everything she could possibly want—and a little more.

She leaned into Ric. His muscular chest pressed against her soft curves. Could he feel the pounding of her heart? Did he know how he made her feel—

Buzz. Buzz.

The vibration of his phone in his pants pocket tingled her leg. It was like a wake-up call. This wasn't supposed to be happening. Not now. They had Gin to find.

Gia pulled away from him. She couldn't quite meet his gaze. The guilt of losing herself in the moment was too great for her.

"I'm sorry," Ric said. "I should get this. It might be news about Gin."

Gia nodded. She hoped it was good news.

Ric checked the caller ID and then pressed the phone to his ear. "Marta, have you heard anything?" Silence ensued. "Where?" More silence. "Thanks. We'll check it out."

There was news. Gia's heart filled with hope. "What is it?"

"The puppy has been spotted, at least they think it's Gin, near the south shore."

"Really?" When Ric nodded, her mind started racing. "That's so far away."

"I sent them a photo of him. We'll know soon."

Gia retraced her steps. Her strides quick. Short. All the while, she was thinking. Where would Gin go? Someplace familiar?

Ric's phone dinged with a message. He frowned. "It wasn't him."

"I know where he went."

What happened back there?

As Ric maneuvered his car toward his uncle's villa, he replayed the scene on the beach. What in the world had gotten into him to open up about his past? He never spoke of that time.

It wasn't so much the pain of his mother's rejection—because he'd dealt with that long ago, when he told his mother to her face that he never wanted to see her again—but rather it was the vulnerability attached to the memory. Who admitted that their own mother rejected them?

And yet there was something about Gia that made him want to comfort her—even if it meant revealing more of himself than he'd ever meant to. He cared about her. He knew that was a dangerous admission. The women he'd cared for in the past had hurt him deeply.

But Gia wasn't like those other women. She was kind, thoughtful and caring. If he had any doubts about that, they wouldn't be rushing to his uncle's place to find a stray dog that had stolen Gia's heart.

And then the memory of the kiss they'd shared on the beach came to mind. Okay, she was very special. But what happened when she found her biological father?

A frown pulled at his face. He knew the answer. She would leave here. She would return to the beautiful rolling hills of Tuscany and the boutique hotel that she ran. Her whole life was far from here. And everything he'd ever known—ever wanted—was here.

And he wasn't going to fool himself about a long-distance relationship. His assistant had tried that once before she'd met her husband, and it had been nothing but misery and loneliness. No, he wasn't going to subject himself to that.

"We're here!" Gia practically had the car door open before he pulled to a stop in front of his uncle's villa.

She didn't wait for him. She jumped out of the car, calling the dog's name, and running to the back of the house. He was only a few steps behind her.

As much as he wanted to portray that he was strong and didn't get attached to people or things, there was something about Gin that had gotten to him. He didn't know if it was the sadness in the puppy's eyes when he wanted attention or the rapid swish of his tail when they were playing ball, but that dog was special, just like the woman who loved him—loved the dog that is.

And Ric was silently praying there was a reunion tonight. Because he didn't want to think of how crushed Gia was going to be if they went home without Gin. He refused to consider how he'd feel. He would be fine. He was used to people coming and going from his life. Oh, who was he kidding. He was worried. He missed the little guy.

He turned the corner of the house in time to hear, "Gin, there you are."

Gia was headed for the back corner of the garden that was only now partially cleared. What in the world would Gin be doing back there again? Ric would have thought the puppy would never return to the garden.

Gia knelt next to the spot where Ric had originally freed Gin from the wire. "Aw…"

What was she fawning over? The puppy? Ric stepped up behind her and peered over her shoulder. He couldn't believe his eyes. He blinked, but it was still there.

A mirror image of Gin.

There were two of them.

"Where did he come from?" Ric asked.

"It's a she." Gia lifted her head and glanced around the yard that was still very much a work in progress. And then she pointed. "It must have come in and out of the hole in the fence. It's why no one has seen her until now."

Ric looked at Gin. "You didn't tell us you had a sibling." Then he frowned. "Do you think it has a home?"

She shook her head. "Nothing about her appearance says that she has a home. But the vet can check for a chip just to be sure."

"So we're keeping her?" Ric asked, already knowing the answer.

Arff. Arff.

Gia smiled. "Okay, Gin. We'll take her home too." And then realizing she hadn't actually consulted Ric, she glanced over her shoulder at him. "You don't mind, do you?"

His formerly quiet, spotless home was quickly being overrun by one messy but beautiful woman and one— scratch that, now two talkative dogs. Oh, boy!

"No, I don't mind." What was he saying? Of course he minded.

His home was his oasis from the craziness at the office. It was his sanctuary where he regrouped and strategized. And since Gia and Gin came into his life, he didn't know how lonely he'd been.

"Here." Gia held out Gin's red leash. "Can you hold on to him while I try to catch her?"

Ric took the leash. Gin came over to him and sat down without being told. He was a smart little guy. Now they'd see if his sister was smart enough to let Gia get ahold of her. That little dog had no idea what treats were in store for her. If she did, she'd leap into Gia's arms instead of running from her.

It took Gia a little bit, but finally she had her arms around the barking puppy. It was dirty and a bit on the thin side, but other than that she looked okay.

"Let's go home." Gia smiled.

He'd never seen her look happier. Who knew finding not one but two strays could make someone so happy? He supposed they both were rather cute. He smiled. And then he realized that Gia was rubbing off on him.

CHAPTER FOURTEEN

RIC WASN'T THE only one with contacts.

Gia had some of her own.

And so after the disastrous dinner with Mr. Grosso, she'd made a phone call. Her mother's family had been vastly wealthy with old money. With great wealth came numerous contacts, and there was someone who had been in Gia's life as a child. He was more like an honorary uncle.

However, when she'd initially made the phone call to his office, as she didn't have his personal contact information after all these years, she was informed that he was out. So she'd left a message for him.

Today, he'd gotten back to her. He was willing to meet with her and Ric to discuss Ric's program. She hadn't given out any specific details about it, per Ric's prior request, just enough to pique the man's interest. But the catch was that they'd have to meet with him in Rome. Would Ric be agreeable?

She hoped to catch him before he left for work. She rushed out of her bedroom and practically ran into him in the hallway. She came to an abrupt halt on her tiptoes to keep from crashing into him.

His hands immediately wrapped around her waist as though to steady her. As her hands came to rest on his broad shoulders, her heart pounded harder. It was then that time seemed to suspend itself as they stared at each other.

They'd been here before, but it felt like a lifetime ago. She missed him touching her, feeling his lips move over hers. Her gaze dipped to his lips. It'd be so easy to lean forward and press her mouth to his. Every cell in her body longed to do just that.

And then she heard his voice echo in her head: *Can you just give me a little time?*

The memory cooled her mood. She pulled back, breaking the connection between them. She swallowed hard and struggled to regain her composure.

Her gaze didn't quite meet his. "I was just coming to find you."

"Funny. I was looking for you, too. I have news."

Her heart leaped into her throat. Could this be it? Could this be the moment she'd been waiting for what felt like a lifetime to hear?

"Is it my father?"

Ric smiled. "It is. We found him."

"You did?" She didn't wait for his response, she threw herself at Ric, wrapping her arms around his neck. Her body molded to his body as though they were two halves of a whole.

The jolt of awareness that zinged through her body snapped her out of her state of euphoria. And as much as she loved being this close to Ric, it wasn't right. He had to want her—all of her—before they could move in this direction.

She pulled back. "Sorry. I was just so excited. I was beginning to think this day would never come."

"It's okay. You don't have to apologize."

"Where is he? When can I see him?" She glanced down at her scruffy work clothes that she'd been planning to wear to paint the villa. "I can't meet him dressed like this. I have to change."

When she went to turn back to her room, Ric reached out, gently grabbing her arm. "Slow down. He's not here."

She turned back. "Where is he?"

"In Rome."

"Rome?"

Ric nodded. "He's a high-powered business banker."

"Then I need to book a flight—"

"No, you don't. We'll take my private jet."

"Are you sure?"

He nodded. "I already phoned ahead. It will be fueled and waiting for us."

"You're going with me?"

He nodded. "We've been through this whole journey together. I'd like to be there for you when it ends—or begins, depending on how you look at it."

"Thank you." Tears of joy clouded her eyes. She was about to meet her biological father. She was about to have a parent again. "Thank you for everything."

They agreed to leave for the airport in a half hour. It'd give Gia enough time to call her contractor and let him know she'd be away for a while—maybe forever if all worked out like she wanted. And it gave her time to pack.

Ric said that he would ask his housekeeper watch over the dogs. He said it wouldn't be hard, as the housekeeper had a soft spot in her heart for them. Seemed like the furry duo had everyone wrapped around their paws. They were so adorable.

Once Gia reached her room, she grabbed her phone. First, she texted her brother and sister, letting them know that she'd found her father—or rather that Ric had tracked him down. Her siblings sent good wishes, eager to know more about the man.

Next, she texted her family friend, letting him know that a spur of the moment trip was sending them to Rome and asked if they could meet for dinner. Her friend agreed and suggested tonight. She hesitated. Not sure how her first meeting with her biological father would go, she asked her friend if she could let him know later in the day. He agreed.

She couldn't believe it. Her biological father was finally found. Excitement pumped through her veins as she rushed around her room, packing all her stuff—unsure if she'd ever return.

But what if her father didn't want to know her? Fear clutched her heart. As quickly as the horrid thought came to her, she dismissed it. Things had to work out for the best. She needed to find her happy ending.

He was worried.

And he didn't know what to do about it, which was so unlike him. He was usually the man with the answers.

Ric chanced a glance at Gia as their hired car sped down the road toward her meeting with her biological father. She kept clasping and unclasping her hands. She was so excited. She was so certain this was going to be a happy union.

Ric had been down a similar road, not that he'd ever found his father. And that was the point. He'd been so certain if he wanted something bad enough that everything would work out. It hadn't.

And then he realized just because things hadn't worked out for him that it didn't mean they wouldn't for Gia. The truth was that he wanted her to be happy—for her dreams to come true. After all, one of them should have things work out the way they envisioned.

But he still couldn't help but worry that she'd set herself up for a fall. If that happened, he'd be there to catch her. He'd do everything in his power to make sure she was all right.

"Does he know he's meeting with me?" Gia's voice cut through Ric's thoughts.

"My assistant set up the appointment."

"No. What I mean is, does he know he's meeting his daughter for the first time?" Hope twinkled in her eyes.

Ric shook his head. "I thought you'd want to tell him yourself."

Gia paused as though to think it over. "You're right. It's best coming from me. I know it'll be a shock to him. It certainly was to me. But when he has a chance to absorb the information, I'm sure he's going to be as excited as I am."

"I hope so." Ric's gut twisted in a knot. He had a bad feeling about this.

Gia frowned at him. "Relax. It's all going to work out. You just have to believe."

"I'm trying. But maybe you should also be prepared, in case this doesn't play out the way you're envisioning."

Gia's gaze narrowed. Agitation threaded through her voice. "Why are you doing that?"

"Doing what?"

"Trying to ruin this for me?"

"I'm not. I swear. I just don't want to see you get hurt."

At that point the car pulled to a stop in front of a modern office building. The driver opened the rear passenger door for them. When they stepped onto the curb, they saw the man's name right there on the front of the building.

Gia rushed inside. Ric's long, quick strides kept up with her. After checking the directory on the wall, she pressed the button for the elevator.

Ric leaned close to her and whispered, "No matter what, I'm here for you."

She turned to him and smiled. "Thank you. For everything. This is going to be the best day of my life."

Or one of the worst. Ric kept the pessimistic thought to himself. Nothing was going to bring Gia's feet back down to the ground. Her head was filled with dreams of love, laughter and happiness. And he couldn't blame her. He just hoped the man they were about to meet didn't burst her bubble.

CHAPTER FIFTEEN

THE ELEVATOR MOVED so slowly.

And stopped at every floor.

Gia clasped her hands as she gazed at the floor numbers as they went by. Two more to go. Two more floors until she reached her biological father's office. Two more floors until she was able to right a wrong. She wondered what her parents would think of what she was about to do.

She halted her thoughts. She wasn't going to think about them. She wasn't going to think about the way they'd kept this vital information from her for her entire life.

She'd refused to think very much about her parents since she'd learned the truth about her conception. It was better that way. She didn't want to hate them. They had been good parents to her—more like great parents. Or at least she'd thought they'd been. But do great parents keep a secret of this magnitude from their child?

The elevator dinged as it stopped one floor from her destination. They were almost there. Excitement bubbled up inside her. What was she going to say to this man?

She knew this was going to be a shock to her biological father. She shouldn't expect much at first, but she was certain he would quickly come around.

She'd used the time on Ric's private jet to plan out her words. She rehearsed them over and over in her head. She'd perfected them. This was going to work out just fine.

As the elevator moved to her final destination, she chanced a glance at Ric. His stance was rigid, and the muscle in his cheek jumped. He didn't come straight out and say it, but he thought this meeting was a mistake. He thought it was going to go terribly wrong. And she understood where he was coming from. He hadn't had the easiest childhood, and her heart went out to him. But this was different—they were different. It would work out. He'd see.

Because she couldn't afford to consider the alternative. If she let herself consider how wrong this meeting could go, she'd back out. She'd head back to Tuscany and always wonder what might have been. And when she stared in the mirror, she'd always wonder what aspects of herself had been inherited from her biological father.

The elevator stopped one last time, and then the doors swept open. They stepped out on what looked like marble floors. A grand desk with a beautiful receptionist greeted them. Behind the woman, in big bold letters was her biological father's surname. Very impressive. He appeared to do very well for himself.

Gia stepped up to the desk. "Hi. Gia Bartolini to see Mr. Gallo."

The woman glanced down at the computer monitor. "Ah, yes. There you are. It'll be just a moment." She then spoke softly into her headset before returning her attention to Gia. "Mr. Gallo will be just a few minutes. Please have a seat."

"Thank you." Gia turned to find no expense had been spared in the waiting area. She took a seat in one of the burgundy leather chairs.

Ric sat beside her. "It's not too late to change your mind."

"If that's your attempt at a joke, it's not funny."

He didn't respond. Instead, he put his arm over her shoulders and then leaned in close. "You've got this. If he doesn't love you from the start, he's a very foolish man."

Now this was more like it. She turned to him, finding he

was closer than she'd anticipated. "Thank you." She smiled. "Glad to see you're coming around."

Before he could say more, the receptionist interrupted. "You can go back now. It's the last door on the left."

Suddenly her insides melted into a ball of nerves. When she stood, her knees felt weak. She'd been doing so well. Why now? She had to get it together.

Ric stood and looked back at her as though wondering why she hadn't sprung out of the chair and raced down the hallway. She would, if her legs would cooperate.

His gaze met hers. "You've got this."

In his gaze she found strength. She drew on it, calming her rising nerves. She could do this. He presented his arm to her, she was tempted to hold on to him, but she resisted.

"I need to do this on my own." And then she walked ahead of him.

She wasn't sure if Ric was behind her as the carpeting was thick and muffled their footsteps. She thought of glancing back but decided it was best just to focus on her forward momentum, because no matter what she told herself, she was still nervous.

When she reached the closed wooden doors with Gallo's name on it, she paused. She drew in a deep breath and slowly exhaled it. Then she did it again. This was as calm as she was going to get. She raised her arm, folded her fingers and rapped on the door.

"Come in," said a deep male voice.

She realized in that moment it was the very first time she'd heard her biological father speak.

"You have to open the door," Ric whispered from behind her.

Oh, yeah. Right. Here goes nothing. Or everything.

She grasped the doorknob and turned. It was like having an out-of-body experience. For so long now, she'd dreamed about this moment. She wondered what this man would be like. And now it was happening.

She wasn't sure how her legs held her up, but somehow she made it inside the massive office without stumbling or totally falling on her face. The man was standing with his back to her. He had dark hair and was short in stature. She'd never imagined him as short. Not that there was anything wrong with it. It just wasn't how she'd pictured him.

And then he turned. He was clean-shaven. His suit was gray and obviously didn't come off a rack. He wore a blue tie that highlighted his blue eyes—so much like her own. But it was his mouth that drew her attention. He was frowning. Was he frowning at her? Or was that just his general disposition?

"You wanted to see me," Mr. Gallo said, not bothering to offer her a seat. "My assistant said it was a matter of importance, but yet I don't know you and we've never done business, have we?"

Gia's mouth was dry. Her tongue was stuck to the roof of her mouth. She swallowed hard, hoping when she spoke that she didn't betray her anxiety. "No." When he arched a brow, she continued. "We've never met."

"I didn't think so. I don't recognize the name, and I am good with names. I don't have much time so tell me why you insisted on seeing me."

Not exactly the cordial greeting she'd been hoping for, but it would change once she told him who she was. "I am Gia Bartolini. I… I believe you knew my mother, Carla Bartolini." When there was no recognition in his eyes, Gia realized perhaps that wasn't the name her mother had used when she met him. "Or perhaps you knew her as Carla Ferrari."

Still there was no recognition in his eyes. "I don't know

you. And I don't know your mother. Is there a point to this meeting?"

"You're my father."

Oh, no! Had she just blurted it out? By the darkening look on the man's face, she'd say yes, she'd thrown the bombshell into the room.

And he didn't look happy. Not at all. She felt Ric move directly behind her as though to bolster her should she need it. But she could do this. After all, she'd anticipated that her biological father would be shocked at first. Who wouldn't be?

Once she explained, he'd understand. And so she started to explain about her parents dying and discovering the journal—

"Stop." His hand moved through the air as though cutting off her words. "I don't need to hear this. I'm not your father. If you came here for a handout—"

"A handout?" Was he serious? By the line of his brows, he was very serious. "I don't need your money. I have money of my own. I came here so we could get to know each other."

Mr. Gallo shook his head. "I'm not your father—"

"But my mother—"

"And I don't know your mother. Even if I did, that was a long time ago. I have my own family. I'm not looking for any strays."

Gia inhaled a swift breath. Did he just call her a stray? Tears pricked the backs of her eyes, but she refused to let this man—this horrible little man—see them.

"I must have made a mistake," she said, backing toward the door.

"That's more like it," Mr. Gallo said. "Don't come back looking for a handout. I'll see you in court first."

Gia turned and headed for the door. The rest of the way

out of the building was an utter blur. It wasn't until she was in the backseat of the car with Ric pressing a drink of water into her hand that she realized it was over. It was so over.

How could she have been so wrong? How could she be related to someone so cold—so miserable?

He wanted to make this better.

He wanted to stop the pain.

But Ric couldn't do either of those things for Gia. Why did he have to be right this time? He'd have been thrilled to be wrong—for Gia to get her happy ending.

He glanced over at her as she sat close to the door, leaving a huge gap of seat between them. Her face was turned to the window, taking in the sights of the city. He doubted she truly saw any of it.

His heart was breaking for her. She was stuffing all her disappointment and rejection deep down inside. He wanted her to open up to him—to tell him whatever was on her mind—but she'd become unusually quiet.

The best thing he could do for her was to get them home. He grabbed his phone from his pocket and texted his pilot, letting him know to ready the plane for a return trip. In the meantime, he'd just quietly wait for Gia to speak—if she'd let him in.

When the car pulled to a stop in front of their hotel, Ric joined her off to the side of the large glass doors leading to the lobby. Gia stopped there as though lost in her thoughts. It was only then in the bright Italian sunlight that he noticed the ghostly pallor of her face.

He moved in close to her, in case she wanted to lean on him or needed a hug. But he didn't make the first move. He didn't want to do anything that would cause her more stress.

"Don't worry," he said. "I contacted the pilot. He'll have the plane ready to go just as soon as you're ready to leave."

Gia nodded but didn't say a word. He wasn't sure if she really heard him. She was stunned and disappointed. Who could blame her?

She entered the hotel and headed straight for the elevator. On the way up to their suite, her phone dinged. She pulled it from her purse and checked the screen.

She turned to him. "We can't leave. Not before dinner."

Just then the elevator beeped as it reached their floor and the door slid open. All the while, Ric couldn't help but wonder what had changed. Why would she want to stay? There was no way that man had changed his mind about getting to know Gia. It was totally his loss, as she was the most amazing person. Just her smile was enough to brighten up the world—at least, his world.

Ric used his keycard to let them in the suite. "Is there something you need to do before we leave?"

She nodded. "I'd like to meet an old family friend for dinner."

His gaze searched hers. She looked worn out and defeated. "Are you sure that's a good idea? Maybe another time would be better."

She shook her head. "I'm fine. You were right. I shouldn't have gotten my hopes up."

"I'm sorry. I never wanted to be wrong more in my life."

"I know." She sent him a smile, but it never reached her big beautiful eyes. "I'm just going to answer some emails and stuff until dinner."

"But what about lunch?"

She shook her head. "I'm not hungry."

"I'll order extra just in case you change your mind."

She was already walking away, leaving him alone with his thoughts. People seemed to think that having a lot of money could fix all of life's problems, but he'd be the first to attest that it couldn't. If it could, he'd give up his fortune to give Gia the family she wanted.

Being helpless was not a position he was familiar with. Usually there was something he could do—a plan to follow, a person to hire. But in this case, he had no choice but to sit by while Gia dealt with yet another big blow. First, her parents lied to her about her conception, and then that horrible man rejected her without even taking time to know anything about her. Life was not fair.

CHAPTER SIXTEEN

THEIR VISIT TO Rome hadn't worked out for her.

But that didn't mean it couldn't work out for Ric.

Because as disappointed as she was, Gia wanted Ric to find a good home for his program. She wanted his dreams to come to fruition for him, for herself—to reassure herself that sometimes dreams really did come true—and for all of the people it would help.

As they waited at the restaurant table for her friend, who'd texted to let her know he was running a few minutes late, Ric leaned toward her. "We don't have to do this. Not tonight."

"I'm okay." When Ric sent her a disbelieving look, she added, "I don't regret tracking that man down. And I don't regret meeting him."

"Even though he was an insufferable jerk?"

She nodded. "I now understand why my parents felt it was best to keep me from knowing about him. He's not a nice man—not someone I want in my life. And so my parents did what they felt best because..." Her voice cracked with emotion. "Because they both loved me."

"I didn't know them, but from everything you've said and after knowing their amazing daughter, I believe they loved you with all their hearts."

Tears sprang to her eyes. She blinked them away, not wanting to make a show in public. "For the first time since they unexpectedly died, I'm no longer angry with them. I didn't realize until now just how angry I was with them for leaving me. I know the accident wasn't their fault and they in no way wanted to leave, but I was just so angry of being robbed of their presence in my life that I think I projected all that grief and anger into the secret of my conception. It was easier to be angry with them for keeping a secret than to be angry because they died."

Ric reached out, taking his hand in hers. No words were needed. His presence and show of support meant the world to her. If they were seated closer, she'd have leaned her head on his shoulder—

"Sorry, I'm late." The familiar gravelly male voice interrupted the quiet moment.

Gia and Ric withdrew their hands. She noticed the distinct coldness where just moments ago he'd been touching her.

She pasted on her brightest smile, as it was so good to see Vincent D'Angelo again. In a way, it was like having a piece of her parents back because they'd been such good friends with Vincent. In fact, they'd been so close that he was Enzo's godfather.

Vincent rounded the table. "Gia, I'm so sorry." The tall man with a broad chest enveloped her in a warm hug. When he pulled back, he said, "I was out of the country when I heard the news, and it was too late to make it back for the funeral."

"I understand. The flowers you sent were beautiful." She couldn't remember exactly which bouquet was his, but she recalled seeing his name on one of the many arrangements, and they were all stunning. She turned to Ric. "And I'd like to introduce you to m-my…" She stuttered, not sure what title to give Ric as their relationship was so complicated. And so she settled on "Ric Moretti."

Vincent leaned over and shook Ric's extended hand. "It's good to meet you."

Once they were all seated, they ordered pasta and made small talk, allowing the men to get to know each other little.

And then Vincent turned to her. "It's been far too long. You remind me so much of your parents. You have your mother's beautiful looks and your father's easiness. I could always talk to him about anything."

His words were like a balm on her wounded heart. "You really think so?"

"I do. They were so proud of you. Any time I visited with them, they'd fill me in on all your accomplishments. You and your brother and sister were the highlights of their lives."

Gia genuinely smiled as memories of her parents crowded in her mind. They were caring and loving. She'd spent all this time searching for something she'd already had—parents who loved her. No one could replace them or their love.

And they weren't truly gone. They lived on in her heart and her memories. Instead of fighting the memories, she had to welcome them—accepting the pain of loss as well as the happiness found in those memories.

Gia turned to Ric. "Vincent owns a vast shipping company. It always has him on the road." Out of the corner of her eye, she caught Vincent nodding in agreement. "I thought you two could help each other. He could certainly use your program, and he has a stellar reputation in the transportation community. And I might have mentioned your ultimate goal is to use your program to help get supplies to those in need."

"Yes, she did," Vincent said. "I am very interested in hearing more."

Ric glanced at her. His eyes were dark and unreadable. It was as if suddenly a wall had gone up between them. Bu she told herself it was just the surprise she'd sprung on him. Everything would be all right in the end.

Ric was hesitant to reveal much at first, but Vincent just kept talking. No wonder he was so successful at what he did. He could talk most everyone into seeing things his way. And though Ric was hesitant at first, the more Vincent talked, the more Ric talked.

Gia smiled. This was all going to work out.

What had happened?

Gia had planned this without mentioning it to him.

Throughout the dinner, he'd avoided eye contact with her. He felt as though she'd somehow betrayed him, but he'd done his best to hold it all in during the meal—a meal he'd barely tasted.

Ric had promised to meet with Vincent again to go over details of his program and show him what it had done on a small scale for Gia's boutique hotel business. But he wasn't happy about it. Still, he was a businessman first, and this was an opportunity that he just couldn't ignore—even if he wanted to.

Because this was a pity offering.

Gia didn't believe in him enough to think he could pull off this project on his own. It reminded him of his mother.

But in spite of everything, he'd made a success of himself—a self-made man.

Gia didn't get to take that away from him. Sure, he might have had a setback with Mr. Grosso, but he hadn't given up. He had other options. He just hadn't had time to explore them.

On the ride home, Gia tried to make conversation, but he wasn't in the mood to speak, only giving her a nod or one-word answer.

It wasn't until they were in their suite that he turned to her and asked, "What have you done?"

Her eyes widened with surprise. "I… I was helping you."

"I don't need help! I can manage my business fine on my own."

Anger flared in her eyes. "So you can help me, even though I didn't ask you to, but when I return the favor, it's wrong?"

He raked his fingers through his hair. "It's not the same thing."

"What's the matter? Your ego can't accept the help of a woman? Or is it just this particular woman that you won't take help from?"

A tangle of emotions churned within him. "I don't need your help."

"Good. Because I don't need you either. I don't need anyone." She turned and strode away.

He watched her walk away, leaving him alone once more. Loneliness engulfed him. Refusing to go after her, he retreated to his room. His door shut with a loud thud. It was time to go home.

This trip had been an utter disaster. The one person who he thought believed in him had just turned her back on him, like so many others in his life. He was better off on his own.

Gia regretted her words.

As she threw her things in her suitcase, she realized she was acting just like her biological father—whom she wished she'd never met. The man was selfish and self-centered. She wouldn't turn into him.

Her thoughts turned to her brother and sister. She'd left them to pick up the pieces of her life back in Tuscany when she'd dropped everything to go on this journey of self-discovery. Not wanting to be anything like the man she'd met that morning, she knew the time had come to return home as soon as possible.

And though it broke her heart, she realized that Ric wasn't going to make room in his life for her. He'd been putting off telling her since they'd made love. She knew it then, but she'd been hoping she was wrong. Just like she'd been hoping her biological father was someone she'd want to know. She was wrong in both cases. No man could love her.

With a hole in her chest where her heart had once been, she rolled her suitcase into the common room. Ric was there, checking his phone. He glanced up when she entered. "Good. The plane is ready to go."

She shook her head. "I'm not going back with you."

He opened his mouth to say something, but then changed his mind, closing it without saying a word. And that right there said it all. She was doing the right thing—for both of them.

Tears pricked her eyes, but she blinked them away. She would get through this without breaking down. It was for the best. That's what she kept telling herself. But there was nothing about this departure that felt like it was for the best.

Returning to Lapri would be just too hard. She needed— they needed—to make a clean break. "I'm returning to Tuscany. Tonight."

"And the puppies?"

She loved them nearly as much as she'd thought she loved Ric. But if she were to take them, Ric would have no one. He'd be alone except for his work. They might not belong together, but that didn't mean she wanted him to be alone.

Whereas when she returned to Tuscany, she had her family. Their importance in her life had gotten overlooked with the revelations of the journal, but it was like the blinders

had been lifted from her eyes. She remembered how much
Enzo and Bianca meant to her. She wouldn't forget again.

"You…you keep them. They are devoted to you."

She didn't know what she expected him to say, but he
said nothing.

She clutched the suitcase. This was it. This was the last
time she would ever see him. And yet she didn't have the
strength, the courage to lift her gaze to his. She knew once
she did that the wall she'd built up, damming up her emotions, would come crumbling down. She would be a wet,
blubbering mess. And that was not how she wanted to end
things.

"Thank you," she said, trying to maintain a level voice.
"I appreciate everything you did for me. As for the villa,
it's nearly done. I'll be in contact with the contractor about
the final details."

Still, Ric said nothing. He was not going to make this
easy for her.

After asking him to forward her other pieces of luggage,
she turned and headed for the door. She didn't know what
she expected—perhaps for Ric to come after her and ask
her to stay. Not that it would be good for either of them.
But he didn't speak. He didn't move. So she just kept going.
Walking right out of his life. And she had never known
such misery.

CHAPTER SEVENTEEN

HOME AT LAST.

Gia didn't know how she'd feel when she returned, but it felt good to walk through the doors of the villa. Because no matter where she went in this world, returning to the Bartolini estate for her was still coming home.

And right now, her broken heart needed the comfort of this place. She didn't know what she'd expected when she left here almost two months ago. She felt like a totally different person but not in a good way.

She felt as though she'd aged ten or twenty years. She was disillusioned, disheartened and wanted to disappear. She'd wanted to avoid the main house, but she needed to grab her keys from the office. She'd left them there for safekeeping.

It was late enough in the evening that she hoped to avoid everyone, including her big brother. She just needed time to think—to settle back into her life…without Ric or the puppies. Another wave of sadness struck her.

She heard some laughter. And then a woman said, "I think your wine is a winner. The best I've ever tasted."

"You don't have to say that." Enzo's voice trailed down the hallway.

"No. I mean it. You were definitely born with a gift to run the vineyard."

When the couple stepped into the kitchen, they came to a halt. The other voice belonged to Sylvie, the wedding planner. And these two looked really comfortable together.

Obviously, Gia had missed more than she'd thought while she was away.

"Hello, Enzo. Sylvie."

Was her brother blushing? Impossible. He didn't blush about anything, but then again, she'd never caught him with someone he was attracted to. Interesting. Very interesting.

"Gia, what are you doing here?" Enzo's voice held a note of irritation.

Was he upset that she was back? Or was he upset because she'd interrupted something? Gia was willing to go with the latter. And as much fun as it'd be to tease her brother about this thing with Sylvie—if there was a thing— she just wasn't up for sibling banter.

She was beat from traveling. She was torn up on the inside from not just the rejection of one man but two. Just the thought of Ric caused the backs of her eyes to sting with unshed tears. She blinked them away.

She swallowed hard, hoping her voice wouldn't give away her turbulent emotions. "I just got back. Sorry to interrupt you two—"

"You didn't interrupt," Sylvie said. "In fact, it's getting late. I should go. It's good to see you back, Gia." And with that Sylvie made a quick departure.

"So, you've decided to return. At last."

Gia halted at the sound of Enzo's voice. Her shoulders lowered with guilt for abandoning the only family she'd ever known to go off on a search for a biological parent who wanted absolutely nothing to do with her—who'd have been just as happy to never know she existed.

She turned to her brother, prepared for his anger. She deserved it. She'd handled things wrong. She'd freaked out knowing she wasn't a Bartolini.

She drew her gaze up to meet his. "I'm sorry, Enzo. I really messed up this time."

To her surprise, there was no anger—no resentment—in his eyes. Only a brotherly love. "I'm just glad you're home. You were missed."

His kindness, understanding and caring crumbled the wall she'd put up to keep her emotions in check, and she rushed forward and he wrapped her in a big bear hug. She couldn't believe she'd run away when she had everything she'd ever need right here. This was her family. She may not have Bartolini blood in her, but that hadn't stopped her father from loving her. She had been his daughter by choice, and that meant the world to her because he didn't have to love her but he did anyway.

Gia pulled back and swiped at her damp cheeks. "I'm sorry. I'll do better."

Enzo searched her eyes. "You don't have to apologize. It wasn't fair what you've had to go through. I just wanted to be there for you."

Fresh tears spilled onto her cheeks. "Have I told you lately that you're the best big brother?"

"No. But it's about time you realized it." He sent her a teasing smile. "I thought you weren't coming back for a few more weeks."

"Things changed." Her thoughts turned to Ric, and the pain in her chest still felt raw. She wasn't ready to talk about him. "I'm going to bed. Good night."

"Night."

"Gia?"

Who was calling her name?

She wasn't ready to wake up. Gia snuggled farther under the downy soft duvet. She struggled to return to her dream—her nice dream—her sexy dream.

Ric was there in her dreams. He'd been smiling at her, laughing with her, flirting with her and kissing her. She

moaned. Where was he now? She searched through the
foggy recesses of her dreams—

"Gia?"

Gia grunted. She didn't want to wake up, she wanted
Ric back.

"Gia, I have coffee."

A whiff of coffee reached her nose. It was a jolt to her
sluggish body. That did it. The dream was over. Like Pav-
lov's dog, her mouth watered at the thought of coffee. What
could she say? She loved the stuff.

And when she opened her eyes, she found the coffee and
voice weren't part of another dream. Bianca stood there
holding two steaming mugs of coffee.

"Hey, sleepyhead. I thought you were going to snooze
the day away."

And then everything came rushing back to her—the
reason she'd returned to Tuscany early. Now she wished
more than anything that she was still sleeping.

"Here." Bianca held the mug out to her. "Maybe this
will help."

Gia shimmied into a propped-up position and gladly
accepted the coffee. She pressed the warm mug to her lips
and practically inhaled the creamy brew.

Once she'd swallowed, her gaze returned to her sister—
her sister who would soon be a bona fide princess. She was
all done up, from her white-and-turquoise-striped skirt and
white blouse to her hair, which was twisted at the back
of her head and pinned up with loose corkscrew curls to
soften the look.

"What are you doing here? Shouldn't you be in Patazonia?" Not giving Bianca a chance to respond, Gia
asked, "And why do you look so fancy this early in the
morning?"

"It's not early. In fact, it's almost lunchtime. And I had

planned to return later this week to help Sylvie, but then Enzo called last night. And, well, I hopped on the jet and here I am."

"On your private jet. Must be nice."

Gia was still wrapping her mind around her sister's life turning into a real-life fairy tale, including the evil mother-in-law. Okay, maybe evil was too strong. But the woman had certainly not made things easy for Bianca. But the queen didn't know her sister like Gia did. Bianca never ever gave up on the people she loved. And she loved Leo with all her heart.

"I'm not here to talk about me. I want to know what's going on with you."

"I can't believe Enzo ratted me out." And then she recalled her run-in with him and Sylvie. "Is there something going on with Enzo and Sylvie?"

"Ah…not that I know of. But I'm not here all that much. Why? What did you see?"

Gia shrugged and then took a sip of coffee. "It's not what I saw as much as a vibe I was getting. But then again, I was really tired last night. Maybe it was nothing."

"I don't know, but what I want to hear about is you and what happened in Lapri."

"I don't want to talk about it." Gia drank more coffee as she avoided her sister's narrowed gaze.

"Don't want to talk about what?" Enzo stood in the doorway of her bedroom.

The gang was all here now, and Gia knew there was no way she'd be able to make it to the shower until she told them everything about her journey to find her biological father. She didn't blame them for being curious. If she was in their shoes, she'd be dying to know what had happened.

And so, with Bianca settled on the other side of the bed

with coffee in hand, and Enzo perched on the end of her bed, Gia drew in a deep breath. She could do this—so long as she didn't mention Ric or the puppies she missed so dearly.

Gia told them about the dead ends she'd faced trying to find her father. And about Ric's friend who was able to glean information from the journal that she couldn't see. Then she came to the tough part of the story—about how her biological father was nothing like she'd imagined. She'd been so wrong about him—about their parents.

"Now I understand why our parents kept the truth from me—from us. They weren't trying to keep us apart, they were trying to shield me from a very selfish man. I don't know if I'd have made the same decision as them, but I hope I never have to find out."

"They loved you." Bianca leaned over and hugged her.

Enzo placed a hand on her lower leg. "We love you, sis. And we'll always be here for you. No matter what. We're Bartolinis, and Bartolinis stick together—through thick and thin."

Tears of love and gratefulness rolled onto Gia's cheeks. "Thanks, guys. You two are the best."

While Gia swiped away the tears, Bianca asked, "So what's the deal with Ric? Did you leave early because you found out your biological father isn't who you thought he'd be? Or did something happen with you and Ric?"

That was Gia's cue to get out of bed. "There's nothing to talk about."

"When she says that—" Bianca looked at Enzo "—it means she left the best part out."

Enzo didn't say anything, but he looked at her with those observant eyes of his.

Gia grabbed some fresh clothes from the closet and headed for the shower. "Just leave it be. Please."

And then she shut the bathroom door. It was the shower that muffled her tears. She'd made such a mess of things. She'd risked her heart not once, but twice and been rejected both times. She was never going to trust a man again. Except Enzo. But he didn't count. He was her big brother.

CHAPTER EIGHTEEN

TIME MARCHED ON.

And he was more miserable with each passing day.

Ric held the leashes of the pups as he walked them to the park where Gia used to take them. Even the dogs weren't themselves since she left. They missed her too.

He'd been telling himself that he didn't need Gia in his life—that he'd be fine on his own. It didn't matter how many times he told himself that though; it didn't make it any truer.

He'd gone back to working long hours. He'd put a hold on the remodel of his uncle's villa. He'd picked up everything that reminded him of her in the apartment and placed it all in her room. He closed the door on it. Out of sight, out of mind. Ha! That just wasn't the case.

He thought of her in the morning when he went to the kitchen and found that she hadn't beat him to the coffee. He thought of her at lunchtime when he thought of sneaking out of the office to surprise her with a picnic lunch at his uncle's villa, where she'd been turning it from a rough stone into the true polished gem it could be. He thought of her when the pups whined at him and he had no clue what they were trying to say, but Gia would know—she had that way with animals and humans alike.

And he thought of her when Vincent D'Angelo had given him a follow-up phone call, wanting to know more about Ric's program. In fact, they'd already met to go over the details. They were even moving into negotiations for the rights to the program.

And though his program was at last going to be sold and open the door to help others, he didn't have a feeling of accomplishment—of fulfillment.

He sat down on a park bench. The pups sat on each side of him. When they used to come to the park with Gia, they'd beg to go play with the other dogs, but not anymore. Nothing was the same for any of them.

They all missed Gia.

And it was his fault.

He'd let his ego get in the way. He was a foolish man. How could he think Gia was doing anything other than what she always did—lending a helping hand? He'd measured her by the standards of the other women who'd passed through his life, and that wasn't fair to Gia.

There was only one thing to do.

Ric looked at the dogs, who sensed something was up and stared back at him. "Who wants to go find Gia?"

A round of barks ensued.

It was unanimous.

Ric pulled his phone from his pocket and called his pilot. They were leaving for Tuscany as fast as Ric could make the necessary arrangements. For the first time since Gia left, he smiled.

He stood. "Okay. Let's go get Gia and beg her to forgive me."

They barked in agreement before pulling on the leashes to go home.

They had packing to do.

Hours later, they'd arrived.

Ric and the two pups walked up to the door of the Bartolini Hotel. It was charming, just like the online photos had portrayed. He expected nothing less after getting to know Gia.

He stepped inside. A tall man was passing through the spacious foyer. He paused and glanced up. "Welcome to the Barto Villa. Can I help you?"

"I was hoping to speak with the woman in charge."

"Do you have a reservation?"

"No. I don't."

"I'm afraid we're fully booked. I can give you the name of another hotel—"

"If I could just speak with Gia."

"She isn't available." The man's dark brows drew together. "Do you know her?"

Isn't available? What did that mean? If she wasn't working, where would she be?

A young woman entered the room. Her attentive gaze moved between him and the man frowning at him. Ric wasn't sure what he'd done to set off the man.

"Can I help you?" the woman asked.

Before Ric could answer, the other man spoke. "He's looking for Gia."

The woman's gaze moved to the dogs before returning to meet his gaze. He couldn't tell what she was thinking. "You're Ric, aren't you?"

So, Gia had told them about him. Interesting. "Yes, I am. If you could just tell Gia I'm here—"

"No." The man crossed his arms over his chest.

"Then tell me where she is and I'll go to her."

"No," the man said again.

This guy certainly didn't like him. So was this guy interested in Gia? Or was he the protective older brother? Ric studied the man. The eyes were similar to Gia's. Ric was willing to bet this was her brother. And if that was her brother—he glanced at the woman with similar colored eyes—she was most likely the sister.

"Why do you want to speak with our sister?" the woman asked.

So he was right.

"What does it matter?" Enzo asked. "He had his chance and he blew it."

Bianca frowned at her brother. "Would you let him speak?"

"Won't matter. I don't care what he has to say. He's not going to hurt Gia again."

A smile tugged at Ric's lips though he resisted the urge. He loved that all along Gia had the family that she'd desired just waiting for her. It may not be the father she'd envisioned, but her brother and sister clearly loved her fiercely. Now he just had to convince them that he was here to fix things.

"I don't want to hurt your sister. I swear." Ric searched for anything that would remove the frown from Enzo's face.

Bianca studied him. "I believe him." And then she approached Ric. He wasn't sure what she was going to do until she knelt to fuss over the dogs. "Aren't you two cuties?"

"I don't believe him." Enzo stood there with his arms crossed, not budging at all.

"Just give me a few minutes to speak with her. If she wants me to leave after hearing what I have to say, I will." Ric really didn't want to have to fight his way past Gia's brother, but he wasn't leaving until he spoke with Gia.

Bianca straightened. She turned to her brother. "Let him talk to her. You tried to stop me from seeing Leo and look how that turned out." She leaned toward Ric. "We're getting married at Christmas."

"Congratulations."

"Thank you. But my big brother, he's a bit overprotective."

Enzo's frown deepened. "Fine. You can talk to her, but you leave when she tells you to."

"Fair enough."

"And I'll take care of these cuties while you talk." Bianca held out her hand for the leashes.

Ric handed them over. "Thank you." He glanced over at Enzo, who still didn't look happy. "Thank you both."

And then Bianca directed him to Gia's house on the property. He just hoped Gia wasn't as stubborn as her big brother. Because she'd stolen his heart, and he couldn't imagine life without her.

CHAPTER NINETEEN

WHEN SOMETHING WAS bothering her mother, she would clean.

Gia decided to follow her mother's example, and she set to work cleaning her one-bedroom house. She should be working at the hotel as Ric's program had once more filled their reservations for the near future and beyond, but her manager, Michael, appeared to have everything under control. And he knew to call her if anything came up.

Gia had stripped her bed that morning. Now her linens were fresh and the bed was made. After cleaning and dusting the bedroom and bathroom, she'd moved into the living room. She'd had to borrow a ladder from the main house to reach the curtains. She hadn't decided if they needed dusting or something more drastic.

Knock. Knock.

"Come in," she called from atop the ladder.

She heard the door open and footsteps. She fully expected it to be her brother or sister. It seemed they were taking turns checking on her. How many times did she need to tell them that she was all right until they believed her?

"Gia?"

That voice. That was Ric's voice. Ric was here?

She spun around. She moved too fast. The old wooden ladder lurched to the side. Her body followed the ladder.

And then Ric was there. He braced the ladder with his arms. She'd rather his arms were around her. As soon as the thought came to her, she dismissed it. She refused to let him see that his nearness got to her.

She lowered herself to the floor before lifting her gaze to meet his. "Ric, you shouldn't be here—"

"We need to talk."

She shook her head. "We said everything that needed to be said back in Rome."

His eyes pleaded with her, pulling at her heartstrings. "Just hear me out."

Her mind said no. She couldn't risk being hurt again. But her heart urged her to listen to him. Torn between the two, she closed her eyes and shook her head, attempting to clear her mind.

"I'm so sorry, Gia." His deep voice was so close. "I was wrong."

What exactly was he saying? For so long she'd been making things up in her head the way she'd wanted them to be, and that had brought her nothing but pain. This time she wasn't going to jump to conclusions. This time she needed Ric to spell everything out to her, clearly and with no gray areas.

She opened her eyes and turned to face him. When his sorrowful gaze met hers, her heart leaped into her throat. How was she supposed to resist him when he looked at her with those sad puppy eyes?

She swallowed hard. "About what?"

"I was wrong to think I didn't need anyone in my life." His gaze searched hers. "I was wrong to accuse you of not believing in me."

His words were what she'd longed to hear. "I've always believed you could do anything you set your mind to. I just wanted to help. I never meant to make you doubt yourself."

"It wasn't you. It was me. I thought I was past those old

insecurities from when I was young, but I guess they're still there lurking in the shadows. Will you forgive me?"

Gia bit back the yes that rushed to the tip of her tongue. She wasn't willing to let him off the hook just yet.

As though he sensed her inner struggle, Ric said, "I need you in my life. I've missed your smile. I've missed your coffee. I've missed our talks. I've missed everything about you."

Gia stared up into Ric's eyes. If she had any doubt about his feelings, they were quickly put to rest as the love was right there for her to see.

She had some of her own explaining to do. "I've been searching for my biological father because I thought he was the only true family I have left." Her voice grew thick with a rush of emotions.

"Gia—"

She shook her head. "Let me finish." She quickly gathered her thoughts and searched for the right words. "I was so hurt when my parents died and then when that journal turned up, taking away what was left of my family. I've never been so lost—so hurt. And then you came along. You didn't try to stop me from finding the truth. Instead, you helped me. You were by my side the whole time. Thank you for that. It meant so much."

"There's not any other place I'd rather have been."

She needed to tell him the rest. It was too important not to say it all.

"But when I found my biological father, it was not what I'd imagined. In fact, it was quite the opposite. I was so devastated that it took me a bit to regain my balance. But I have now, and you know what I figured out?"

Ric stared deep into her eyes. "What?"

"I didn't need him to complete me. My parents didn't tell me about him because they didn't want me to be hurt.

My parents loved me. And I always had a father. He may not have been of the same blood, but that just means his love for me was so great that it superseded any biological connection, and for that I am grateful." Tears of joy and of loss spilled onto her cheeks.

Ric swiped away her tears. "I didn't know your parents, but after getting to know you, I have to believe they were good and loving people. They only wanted the best for you."

"I know that now. I know that I still have my family. I never lost them. My siblings are still there for me and I for them. And my parents are right here." She placed her hands over her heart. "It just took me a bit to realize all of this."

Ric smiled at her. "I'm happy for you."

"And there's one more thing I realized."

"What's that?"

"How much I love you."

Ric's smile broadened, lighting up his eyes. He reached out and drew her to him. "I love you too. You are my family."

More tears spilled onto Gia's face—tears of an overabundance of love. She placed her hands on his firm chest as she lifted up on her tiptoes—

Arff! Arff!

The echo of barks filled the room. They both turned to find two happy puppies running toward them through the open door.

Gia turned to Ric. "You brought them?"

"Of course I did. I wasn't the only one who missed you. And I wasn't taking any chances. If you turned me down, I was going to pull out my secret weapon—puppy kisses." Ric stared into her eyes. "I would do anything for you."

Gia leaned into his arms and their lips met. His touch sent her heart soaring. She would never tire of his kisses—just as she would never get enough of them. How had she gotten so lucky to find Ric? Now that she had him, she was never going to let him go.

Arff! Arff! Arff!

The puppies pawed at their legs, wanting some attention.

Ric and Gia pulled apart to look down at their adorable family. She could hardly believe this was happening. Her life was overflowing with love, from the enduring passionate kind to the furry adorable kind. The puppies fussed to be picked up.

She laughed. "Bringing the puppies for backup definitely would have worked."

They both knelt. Each picked up a puppy and then straightened. As though on cue, Blossom—she'd named the female dog before they'd left for Rome—stretched up and licked Gia's cheek.

"I see you weren't kidding about the puppy kisses."

"I'd never joke about something that important. I just don't know how they got down here," Ric said as he ran a hand down over Gin's back. "I left them with your brother and sister at the hotel."

Someone cleared their throat rather loudly.

"That would be our fault," the familiar female voice said.

Both Gia and Ric focused on the doorway where Bianca and Enzo now stood.

"Hey, guys." Gia smiled. In fact, she couldn't stop smiling.

Bianca smiled back. "I guess we don't have to ask how this is going to work out."

"We came to our senses," Gia said.

"Yes, we did," Ric chimed in with one arm holding Gin while his other arm was around Gia's waist.

The only one not smiling was Enzo. "I suppose this means you'll be going back to Lapri with Ric."

Gia turned a questioning gaze to Ric. "We hadn't talked

about it yet, but there is this beautiful seaside villa that I'd love to finish fixing up." And then a worrisome thought came to her. She met Ric's gaze. "That is, unless you sold it."

He shook his head. "I saw the way you looked at it. I knew it right away, even if I wasn't ready to accept the fact that it would one day be our home."

Gin barked in agreement.

She turned back to Enzo. "Looks like you've won the estate."

Her brother didn't smile.

"Yeah," Bianca chimed in. "You won't have us butting into the business. You can change things to the way you want them."

"But if you want to keep them the same," Gia said, "both Michael and Rosa can take over the hotel aspect."

"And Sylvie is marvelous at planning weddings," Bianca added.

"It just won't be the same," Enzo said.

Who'd have thought their strong, unemotional brother would have a hard time with them both leaving? Gia felt guilty for being so excited about this new direction in her life.

"I'm sorry," Gia said.

"I am too," Bianca said. "We don't mean to leave you all alone here. But we'll be back to visit. Won't we?" Bianca's gaze moved to Gia.

"Yes, we will. In fact, we'll be here so much that you'll get sick of us."

Enzo shook his head. "Don't worry about me. I'll be fine. I just want you two to be happy. It's what our parents would have wanted."

"We want the same thing for you." Gia handed Ric the puppy.

She walked up to Enzo and hugged him. Bianca joined

them. At last the tension was gone and they were back to being themselves.

When they pulled back, Gia returned to Ric's side and took the squirming puppy from him. She turned back to her brother. "What are you going to do with the villa now that it's all yours?"

"I don't know. I'll give it some thought when I fly to Paris. I'm attending a wine competition."

"That sounds exciting." Gia smiled, hoping her brother would do the same.

He did, but it didn't quite reach his eyes.

Enzo was about to head off on his own journey, and she wished him the very best. She knew change came with its own sets of bumps and unexpected turns. She was sure when it was all over, he would be happy to be the sole owner of the estate. Their father would be proud to have Enzo in charge. Somehow, she had the feeling things were going to work out just the way they were supposed to.

She returned to Ric's side. Oh, yes, they were definitely working out just right.

Then Ric leaned over to her and whispered in her ear, "I love you."

"I love you too."

* * * * *

THE TEXAN'S BABY
BOMBSHELL

ALLISON LEIGH

This book is dedicated to the extraordinary
Susan Litman and Marcia Book Adirim.
Your minds are simply fierce!

Prologue

"**I**'m never going to be able to thank you enough for what you're doing for my son." The man raked shaky fingers through hair that already looked well-raked. "I don't know what I'd do if I lost Linus, too."

Adam Fortune didn't know exactly what to say. He and his brother had participated in the recent donor drive just like everyone else in town had. It was a way of showing they were in Rambling Rose to stay. He'd never expected to actually be a match. "Glad to help." What was an overnight stay in a Houston hospital compared to what Eric and Linus Johnson had been going through? Linus was only a baby. "Still can't believe how many possible matches came up during the drive."

"Possibles are only possibles. You're the ideal match. Thank God." Eric's voice was shaky through the surgical mask he wore. He also wore a protective gown and booties over his clothes and shoes. "I'd shake your hand—hell, I'd give you a hug if I could—but they warned me against any contact before I came in here."

Here was Adam's hospital room.

He'd checked in a few hours ago. Every nurse who'd been in to take blood or his temperature or a dozen other things had all said what a wonderful thing he was doing. He'd been getting uncomfortable with all the attention. He was donating bone marrow to help a very sick baby. Not once had it crossed Adam's mind to refuse when he'd been a match.

"I mean, seriously," Eric went on. "Anything you need. *Anything.*"

Adam almost said, "Forget it," but thought better of it. For him, this had taken a week of time out of his life with the lab tests and exams that had been necessary. For Linus, diagnosed with aplastic anemia, it was a matter of survival.

He started to reach for the water on his bedside but remembered the nurse had emptied it. Just in case he forgot himself and took a drink. He was in that period of no food and no drink before surgery. "That news crew who was following me around last week get in touch with you, too?"

Eric nodded. "Talked to them on the phone. Linus's medical team has had us basically sequestered the past few weeks while he gets prepped for today. Last thing I wanted to do is interviews, but if the story gets someone else to join a donor registry or do a drive like you folks in Rambling Rose did, it's the least I can do. I can remember when the town was barely a dot on the map. Grown a lot in the last year. Otherwise, I couldn't say I would have expected the drive to yield enough results to matter. Yet," his voice cracked slightly. He cleared his throat. "It's still astonishing," he managed.

He paced across Adam's room and looked out the window. "Life's full of twists. First, I find my son way out there in Rambling Rose after his mother wrote—" He broke off, not finishing that thought. "But then I find the man who's going to save his life lives there, too? What were the odds?"

Adam had no response for that. He knew the man was raising Linus on his own. Even though Adam had only moved to Texas a couple months earlier, he'd still heard the story about the newborn who'd been abandoned at the pediatric center in Rambling Rose. Seemed like more than a "twist" to him. He wasn't sure how he'd have reacted in Eric's shoes.

Almost as if Eric heard his thoughts, he turned and pinned his solemn gaze on Adam. "We were engaged, you know. Linus's mother and me." He made a sound. "I don't know why I'm telling you all this. I don't talk about it much."

Adam had just met the guy. By tomorrow, Adam's bone marrow would be doing its thing inside Linus. It would be something that connected them for life. Nevertheless, he wasn't necessarily comfortable hearing Eric's confidences.

But people had to pour out their guts sometimes. He'd learned that in college when he'd tended bar. "Easier talking about the past than worrying about the future," he hazarded. Just because Adam was a good match for Linus didn't guarantee the transplant would be successful. Only time would tell that.

"Maybe." Eric paced to the opened door. Beyond the room, the nurses' station was busy with staff coming and going. "If she'd only just told me she was pregnant in the beginning instead of disappearing like she did." He exhaled roughly and paced back to the window once more. "It's a mistake to think people don't keep secrets from each other. Even when you love someone. And I was certain she loved me, too."

Familiar story.

Adam made a commiserating sound. The minute hand on the wall clock ticked audibly. Less than two hours to the procedure. He'd be back in Rambling Rose tomorrow morning. Back to perfecting the IPA he'd been experimenting with for the last month.

"We'd set the wedding date. Was going to be a week before Christmas. We'd picked a place." Eric suddenly sent Adam a look. "You know what a hassle that all is?"

Adam shrugged. "Never married."

"If you ever decide to, go to the courthouse. A lot simpler." Eric tugged at the gown tied around him. "Then last summer, not even a month after we'd finally gotten that settled, she tells me she needs more time. More space."

Also familiar words. "I've been on the receiving end of that conversation," Adam admitted. "More than once."

Eric gave a sympathetic wince above the white mask covering his mouth. "Blows."

Adam smiled humorlessly. "From the same girl."

Eric whistled. Or as much a whistle as the mask allowed. "Damn."

"Tell me about it." Adam shifted on the bed. The whole reason he'd left Buffalo was to get away from the memories there. Rambling Rose had simply been a convenient escape.

"I realized something was bothering her—deeply— but she wasn't telling me what. When I look back, I can see there were signs of it."

"She hasn't tried contacting you at all?"

"Just one letter that her parents passed on to me. That's how I learned she was pregnant. But since then?" The other man's expression darkened. "I've learned a lot of things," he said cryptically, "but not what happened to her. If she were able to contact me, she would have. I'm sure of that much. She can't have been thinking straight when she left Linus. She wasn't irresponsible. If I could have her back—" He broke off and paced again.

Adam felt for the guy. "I don't know that many people in your position who would be so forgiving."

"It's hard to forget a woman like her," Eric said, his voice grim. "Not that I didn't try at first. But that only lasted a few months, and then I started looking for her. Retracing her steps. She was in Virginia with her parents last fall. From what it sounds like, she left them just as abruptly as she left me. A disagreement or something, I'm sure, though her parents didn't say that when we spoke on the phone. But I know they didn't get along. She hadn't even been sure she wanted them at our wedding. When I told them she was missing, they weren't even alarmed. Said she'd probably gone to Europe. That was her usual style."

He made a rough sound. "They knew she'd left me, so it's pretty likely they weren't telling me everything they knew. It was weeks later when I received a box in the mail from them. Stuff that she'd left behind when she visited them." He shook his head slightly. "The letter she wrote to me was in her things. She'd never mailed it. Didn't even finish it, but the truth was still there. What I thought was the truth, anyway. She was pregnant. I don't know how her parents didn't realize, but like I said—it's a mistake to think people don't keep secrets."

Adam frowned. "Do they know about Linus? His condition?"

Eric looked away. He shook his head. "I lost her," he muttered. "I wasn't going to chance a fight with them over my son, particularly after finally finding him. And yeah," he added flatly, "I know that makes me sound like a first-class bastard."

"I think it makes you sound like a dad," Adam said quietly.

Eric's shoulders lowered. He rolled his head around and squeezed the back of his neck. "Maybe." He raked his hair. "You said forgiveness, but the truth is I wasn't exactly happy when she put on the brakes. I'm not stupid. I suspected there was someone else but then when I learned about Linus?" His hands rose, a volume of helplessness. "I realize now I shouldn't have let her go so easily last summer. She'd always kept her own apartment, so it wasn't as though she didn't have anywhere to go. But then in July, she quit her job at the art museum." He shook his head again. "Laurel loved that job. She *was* the art museum."

Adam went still.

Everything went still.

Even the minute hand on the clock on the wall seemed to cease its tick.

"I'm rambling." Eric paced back to the doorway, looking out. "Clock is crawling."

"You said *Laurel* quit her job. At the art museum. Here in Houston."

"Yeah. That's how we met. Through the museum."

Adam's sense of doom made it hard to breathe. How many Laurels could there be working at art museums in Houston? "You're not talking about Laurel *Hudson*, are you?"

The other man's shoulders stiffened under the gown tied behind his neck.

And Adam knew. Even before Eric turned to give him a sharp look. He knew.

There was a frown on Eric's face visible above the mask. "Yes. Laurel Hudson. You knew her?"

It took Adam a while to get the words out. But even though it did, he could see realization dawning in the other man's eyes. "I knew her," Adam said hoarsely.

More than that, he'd loved her, too.

Chapter One

"Mr. Fortune?"

Adam shot out of the thinly padded waiting room chair so fast that it bounced against the pale green wall behind him.

Nobody noticed or cared. He'd been the only one occupying the sparsely furnished waiting room of Seattle's Fresh Pine Rehabilitation at eight o'clock in the evening.

The clinic director had an apologetic smile on her comfortably lined face. "I'm sorry you had to wait, Mr. Fortune." Her handshake was firm and brief. "I'm Dr. Granger."

"Call me Adam." Ever since he'd received the call from Dr. Mariel Granger three days ago, it had been a toss-up which emotion had rocked him most.

Relief. Impatience. Pain.

Now, so very close to Laurel, impatience definitely had the upper hand. But expressing it with Dr. Granger wasn't going to solve anything.

If not for her persistence in reaching him, no one would have known that Laurel was even alive.

Despite the mess waiting in Texas, the fact that she *was* alive took precedence.

Fortunately oblivious to his thoughts, the director gestured toward the doorway behind her. "When the guard called me, I turned right around and drove back. My office is this way. Seattle traffic, you know. I'm guessing your flight was delayed?" She glanced up at him as they headed along the wide corridor. It was carpeted so their footsteps were silent.

"In Denver," he said. "Mechanical problems." All of the doors they passed were closed. Hiding whether it was offices or patient rooms on the other side.

The notion that Laurel was behind one of the doors made his mouth dry and his chest ache.

"Here we are." Dr. Granger turned into the opened doorway of a cramped office and took one of the chairs situated in front of the desk. She gestured to the second.

His molars clenched, but he lowered himself into the chair.

Something in her eyes flickered as she watched him. "Are you still experiencing pain?"

He almost laughed. Pain? Which kind? "Hoped it didn't show."

She smiled knowingly. "I've been a donor, myself. Give yourself time. Those little aches will pass. Bone marrow donation is entirely rewarding even without finding yourself the subject of a national news story the way you did." She patted his arm in a way that reminded him of his mother. "But, if not for that story, we still wouldn't know Lisa's—sorry, it's hard to break the habit—*Laurel's* identity. It's anyone's guess how long it would have taken for her to show some improvement if she hadn't reacted to your face on the news last week."

He eyed her closely. "Has she remembered anything—" He broke off, because Dr. Granger was already shaking her head, her forehead knitting.

"I'm sorry. Not beyond knowing you were familiar to her for some reason. But it was enough of a reason for me to reach out to you the way I did. Learning that you recognized her in return? I can't tell you how helpful you've already been, particularly when no other family has stepped forward in all this time. You must have been good friends. College, you said?"

"Yes." He didn't elaborate, quashing the stab of guilt he felt. He hadn't told Dr. Granger about Laurel's parents. Nelson and Sylvia Hudson were still ensconced in the Virginia plantation home where Laurel had grown up. Eric had confirmed it.

And, despite the strained situation, he'd agreed with Adam. Bringing her parents into things just now was the quickest way to lose track of Laurel. Again.

"It's still very good of you to agree to come in person." The doctor was smiling knowingly at him. "Particularly so soon after your procedure. If I'd been your physician, I would have advised against traveling so soon."

In fact the doctor in charge of the harvesting procedure had. Adam didn't figure he needed to confirm Dr. Granger's words, though.

She'd reached over her desk to slide a file across the obviously fake wood surface. Fresh Pine Rehabilitation had been caring for Laurel for two months now—ever since she'd been released from the hospital. But the facility was by no means a luxury establishment.

If Nelson and Sylvia had had anything to do with it, their daughter would be in a much more elite setting and much closer to their home than all the way across the country. He'd met them once. Nearly a decade ago when they'd come to Buffalo for Laurel's college graduation.

To say they had been unimpressed by him was an understatement. They figured their only child deserved a lot more than an out-of-work auto engineer's son who'd been working his way through college waiting tables and tending bar at a blue-collar joint.

Someone like Eric Johnson. Who owned and operated his own nationwide trucking company and who had financial resources to spare. Who turned out to be a lot more honorable than Adam feared he, himself, could have been if their situations were reversed.

"It's also very generous of you to pay for her continuing care." Dr. Granger's voice dragged his attention back to the here and now.

"You haven't told her about that."

"Of course not." She opened the file to a typewritten form. "This is the financial responsibility form I mentioned when we talked last. You'll want to read it over and check the box there at the bottom. You're not the only benefactor who chooses to remain anonymous."

Benefactor. It wasn't a term he'd ever earned before. He didn't feel much like one now, either, considering the rest of the things he could have told Dr. Granger and hadn't.

"Regardless of the financial arrangements, I wouldn't be able to discuss her case with you if she hadn't granted her permission. I managed to keep her here for two extra weeks even though she no longer qualifies for free care, but I was at a point where that choice was being taken out of my hands. Since we're a nonprofit, the requirements are regrettably strict for patients with no other means. That news story of yours seemed heaven-sent."

She'd said all of this when they'd spoken on the phone. And still nothing felt heaven-sent to him.

Since the day of the transplant, he'd been circling a drain to hell.

"As I mentioned, Laurel's physical injuries are healed, though she's still regaining her strength. The frequency of her panic attacks has lessened. I know we've become a haven for her, which is good for a time, but not for her long-term well-being. I would like to have seen her showing more interest in life outside our walls by now." She hesitated for a moment. "I didn't tell you earlier, but now that you're here—"

He braced himself, not liking the way she was fiddling with the file. "Tell me what?"

The doctor sighed, concern clear on her face. "After Laurel's accident, her trauma surgeons realized that she'd recently given birth." She didn't seem to notice the flinch he couldn't quite hide. "As recently as a week or two before her accident." She shook her head. "After she was brought out of the coma and her amnesia became apparent, a decision was made not to tell her. This all occurred before she joined us here at Fresh Pine. I believe we've established enough trust by now that she would have told me if she'd regained that memory. There could be a correlation between the resolution of her pregnancy and the panic attacks. Postpartum disorders can be so tricky to diagnose, even under more usual circumstances." She sighed again.

Adam stared down at his hands. There was no reason for her to connect Laurel's baby with the one who'd needed a bone marrow transplant. Laurel had been languishing in a coma when Linus was diagnosed with aplastic anemia. She'd have no way of knowing about it at all. And certainly no way of knowing the truth about that baby's real father.

"She had the baby." His jaw felt so rigid it was hard to get out the words. "But she gave him up."

Dr. Granger looked confused. "I must have misunderstood when you told me you knew Laurel in college. I thought you meant you hadn't been in touch since then."

"We've…kept up." The statement was almost laughable.

"Does she have a boyfriend, then? A husband, maybe?"

"No."

She blinked a little at his abrupt answer. "I see. Well, I appreciate you telling me about her giving up the baby. Knowing will be helpful as we go forward in her therapy. I hope one day she'll fully understand what a good friend she has in—"

She broke off when he plucked a pen out of the plastic holder and began writing in his credit card number on the form. As he scrawled his signature at the bottom, he didn't dwell on how seriously Fresh Pine's fees would eat into his savings. Savings that he'd been building for the last decade, thinking that one day he'd make something of himself.

Looking slightly uncomfortable, as if she might have divined his thoughts, the director rose. "Why don't we go see her?"

His neck was so tight it was a wonder he could nod. He stood as well, and followed her out of the office.

"I should have asked already," she said over her shoulder. "Do you know how the transplant went?"

The question jarred more than she would ever know. "The procedure went well."

"Engraftment takes time, I know. Meanwhile, everyone is on tenterhooks waiting for complications to set in. Everything was done in Houston, wasn't it?" She didn't wait to see his nod. "Excellent facilities. They'll do everything they can to ensure a successful outcome. Did you meet the father? Some recipients and their families never meet their donors. I always think it's nice when they can."

He made a sound that she probably took as agreement.

There hadn't been anything nice about meeting Eric Johnson. Not from the moment Adam realized Eric was the man Laurel had planned to marry. Or the moment when Eric realized that Adam had been the "someone else" for Laurel.

He'd gone into that surgical suite believing Laurel was dead. And despite the next shock he'd gotten after he'd come out of the surgical suite—a shock that still had him reeling—for three of the longest days of his life, he'd grieved. Grieved her.

And then Dr. Granger had called.

And instead of Eric, it was Adam who was here now.

While Eric stayed with Linus. Even though he'd already figured out he wasn't the baby's biological father. He just hadn't known—until the day of the transplant—who was.

Dr. Granger stopped in the doorway of a spacious room outfitted with mismatched furniture. No matter how well he'd steeled his heart, when he caught sight of Laurel sitting off by herself next to a window, his efforts turned out to be useless.

Dr. Granger had texted him a picture of Laurel when she'd called him in that "do you know this woman" kind of way. She'd had no way of knowing how she'd turned his world on end. How he'd already had his world turned on end by then. But seeing Laurel now, alive and in the flesh—

His heart hammered hard in his chest.

The only difference between now and how he'd felt the first time he'd ever seen her—sitting under a tree on campus with a sketchpad on her raised knees—was that now there was a dull ache in his lower back from the marrow harvest and his splitting head felt like it wanted to pop off his neck.

"Laurel."

He wasn't even aware that he'd whispered her name until Dr. Granger patted his arm in that motherly way again. "She's expecting you. Just go cautiously. She knows you're familiar to her but she doesn't know why."

It was a needless reminder. Dr. Granger had been very clear about Laurel's condition before he'd decided to come to Seattle in person. Five months ago, she'd been in a serious car accident. She'd been kept in a medically induced coma for nearly three months during her recovery. And when she'd emerged, though her broken bones had healed, she'd had no memory of the accident, or the events that had come before, or even her own name.

"You're sure this is a good idea?"

Dr. Granger gave him an encouraging smile. "Your presence may trigger more memories. Then again, it might not. That's the thing about retrograde amnesia. We just don't have all the answers."

He grimaced. "Great."

"I know it's a strange situation."

But she didn't know just exactly how strange.

"I'll be in my office if you need me."

Adam was pretty sure the only thing he needed was his head examined.

Laurel Hudson had already broken his heart twice in one lifetime. He was fully expecting a third. But how could he have refused to come? When it came to her, it was what he'd always done.

Eric Johnson's picture had been on that same news

story that Laurel had seen. But it wasn't Eric's face that had gotten a response from her.

It had been Adam's.

Lecturing himself not to read too much into that had become an hourly task. It didn't take a genius—which he wasn't—to know that the other man was doing the same damn thing.

He entered the room, passing a sulky-looking teenager tapping away at a computer and a couple he figured were her parents who were staring at the blaring television. He stepped around a table where an old couple worked on a puzzle, and crossed the room toward Laurel. The sun was setting, casting glittering light over her hair. It was straight and a rich, shining, variegated brown. Like the colors of an aged oak barrel.

He'd told her that once. Her aquamarine eyes had widened. Then filled with sparkling laughter. She'd leaned across the table in the student union where they were supposed to be studying for exams—hers in art history, his in industrial engineering—and kissed him.

He'd been falling for her from the very first. But that kiss had sealed the deal for him.

Now that glossy oak-barrel hair slid over her shoulder as Laurel's head turned and she looked his way.

His step faltered.

Her eyes were the same stunning shade of blue they'd always been. Her perfectly heart-shaped face was pale and delicate-looking even with the pink scar on her forehead between her eyebrows.

Eyebrows that pulled together as their eyes met.

Remember me.

Remember us.

The words—unwanted and unexpected—pulsed through him, drowning out the splitting headache and the aching back and the impatience, the relief and the pain.

Then she blinked those incredible eyes of hers and he realized there was a flush on her cheeks and she was chewing at the corner of her lips. In contrast to her delicate features, her lips were just as full and pouty as they'd always been.

Kissing them had been an adventure in and of itself.

He shoved the pointless memory out of his head and then had to shove his hands in the pockets of his jeans because they were actually shaking.

"Hi." Puny first word to say to the woman who'd made a wreck out of him.

Still seated, she looked up at him. "Hi." She sounded breathless. "It's…it's Adam, right?"

The pain sitting in the pit of his stomach then had nothing to do with anything except her. He yanked his right hand from his pocket and held it out. "Adam Fortune."

She looked uncertain, then slowly settled her hand into his.

Unlike Dr. Granger's firm, brief clasp, Laurel's touch felt chilled and tentative. And it lingered. "I'm Lisa."

God help him. He was not strong enough for this.

He dragged an unoccupied chair away from the puzzle table, flipped it around near Laurel and sat, straddling it. He folded his arms atop the chairback and tried to smile. He had no way of knowing if it looked as forced as it felt. "How are you feeling?"

She wore a thin sweater buttoned up to her neck, and the shoulder she shrugged looked pointed beneath the pink knit. "Aside from being the resident amnesiac?"

He waited and she shrugged again, her full, pouty lips compressing. "Physically, they tell me I'm fine. Mostly." She waved her fingers slightly. "Except for the fact that I still don't even recognize my own name." Her blue eyes fastened on his. "Seeing you on the news last week—" She broke off and snatched up a black pencil from where it had been sitting on the window ledge. She rolled it between her obviously anxious fingers. "It felt almost like seeing a ghost. Why do I know you?"

He'd prepared himself for this, too, thanks to the clinic director. Didn't make answering any easier. "We were friends—" his fingers dug into his forearms where they were folded on the chair back "—a long time ago. At UB."

Her lips had softened again. "New York," she murmured softly. "Buffalo."

His pulse jerked around. He cleared his throat. "Yeah."

"How long ago?"

Since they'd met? Or since she'd broken his heart the first time around? He went for the former. "Ten years."

"Hmm." She shook her head slightly and her gaze was suddenly far, far away. "All that mud. Oozefest."

He started slightly. Oozefest was the giant volleyball tournament held every spring at the University of Buffalo. In the mud. Students played in it. Alumni played. And last May, so had Laurel. On a team made up of old friends. Adam and some of his buddies had made up another team.

He hadn't heard from her in more than a year. He'd had no idea that she was even in the country, much less in Buffalo, until he'd found himself with only a volley-ball net and a pit of mud up to his calves between them. And after the game had come dinner. Then drinks.

Then her hotel room…

"I was washing mud from places nobody should ever have mud." She was suddenly back in the present, her gaze delving into his. "Did we— Sorry. This is embarrassing. Did we date?"

His fingers dug again. "A few times." Understatement of the decade.

She moistened her lips. Right above the buttoned-up neck of her sweater, the hollow of her long, slender throat worked. "Was it…serious?"

It had been for him. At the time, he'd thought it had been for her, too. For two years, they'd been together. But in the end, she'd chosen to keep her parents happy. Which meant *not* being serious about him.

"Not really," he lied. He barely waited a beat and shrugged. Casually. Dismissively. "We were college kids. We had different goals. Took different paths." All of which was true. All of which he'd thought he'd come to terms with in the years that followed. Years when there could be months and months that passed without a word from her. Months and months when he'd dated other women, when he told himself Laurel was in the past.

Then he'd get a call from her from wherever she was in Europe at the time, or a message that she wanted to talk. Needed advice. Needed to vent her frustration over a boss or a job or her parents, and he'd feel himself getting sucked in all over again and it would take months and months again before he could put her out of his mind.

And then he'd run into her last year at Oozefest. In person. And he'd faced the fact that no amount of time would ever be enough to get Laurel Hudson out from under his skin.

He looked down at her lap. "You're sketching."

She brushed a fingertip over the pencil lines covering the white page of the thick sketchpad. "Initially, it was Dr. Granger's idea. Then I—" Her gaze flicked toward him then skipped away again. "I realized it was something I'd always done. I'm not very good at it, though."

He disagreed. He'd always disagreed, telling her that she was an artist at heart, regardless of her parents' opinion otherwise. "The first time we met, you were sketching."

She looked disbelieving. "Was I?"

He dragged his finger in a cross over his chest then held up his palm. "Honest."

Her lips smiled slightly. But it was the smile that lit her eyes that made him ache inside. Laurel's eyes had always been dead giveaways. She couldn't lie to save her soul. Everything she'd felt—good or bad, happy or sad—had always showed in her blue, blue eyes.

And he could see the truth now in those eyes that she really did *not* remember him.

He'd had no reason to doubt it, but there was no denying it. Not when it was right there, smack in front of his face. Same way the truth had been smack in front of him last May when she'd disappeared after their night together. Sneaking out while he'd slept.

She'd left a note. Telling him it never should have happened. That it had been a mistake.

He hadn't understood just how big a mistake until he'd gone to Texas a month later, ostensibly to attend the wedding of his half uncle.

The wedding had just been an excuse for Adam. He hadn't cared in the least about Gerald Robinson's wedding. He was an uncle Adam hadn't even known existed. But Texas was where Laurel had settled. And a detour from Paseo to Houston was worth it if he finally managed to convince Laurel they belonged together.

What she convinced him of, however, was that they did not. Because this time, when someone else had proposed marriage to her, she'd accepted.

"I think I studied art." Laurel's voice was so painfully cautious it managed to penetrate his grim memories.

"Art history." His answer was so abrupt she looked startled.

He'd have to work on that.

He cleared his throat again and gestured at her sketchbook. "Always thought it was *your* art that'd end up in history."

She nibbled her lip, looking disbelieving. He could

have told her she'd worked at art museums around the world. That most recently, she'd been a curator in Houston. That she'd spent an unforgettable night in Adam's arms despite her way too tardy admission that she'd been involved with someone else.

"The paths," she said, once more interrupting his descent back into that particular snake pit. "I suppose we lost track of each other?"

People who walked through actual minefields had always had his admiration. He imagined he felt a hint of empathy for them now. "After you graduated, you went to Europe on a fellowship."

"I did?" She tugged at the sleeve of the thin sweater, pulling it against her slender wrist even though it was already pulled down as far as it looked meant to go. "I don't feel like I'm that adventurous."

She had dreaded going. She'd only applied for the fellowship because of pressure from her parents. She'd never expected that she'd get it. When she had, her parents had been insistent that she take it.

And whether or not they'd "gotten along," she'd always done what Sylvia and Nelson Hudson expected.

"You must have liked it." His voice sounded flatter than he'd intended. "You stayed longer than the fellowship lasted." Long enough for him to get the message that she wasn't coming back. At least, not to him.

"What about your path?" Her fingers moved from her sleeve to the dog-eared corner of the thick sketching paper, folding it back and forth. "Are you married? Kids?"

The vise around his throat tightened another notch.

"Never married." He pushed himself off the chair and swung it back around to the puzzle table, only to notice that the elderly couple had gone. So had the sullen teenager and her parents.

The television was silent. The flat screen black.

He looked back at Laurel. "Have you decided what you want to do when you leave here?"

"You mean when they kick me out because they can't afford to keep me any longer than they already have?"

"They're not kicking you out."

"How do you know?"

"Dr. Granger told me she's made arrangements." It was at least a partial truth.

She didn't look any less troubled. "I can't stay here forever, though. I assume I have a life I should be getting back to." She pushed the pencil behind her ear, reminding him sharply of days gone by that ought to have dimmed in his memory, and tugged at the bottom of her sleeve again. "Only nobody from that life's come looking for me."

His molars clenched again. He thought of the man who, despite everything, was keeping vigil beside Linus in a Houston hospital. "Not for lack of trying."

She shot him a quick look. "What do you mean?"

"Your fiancé." His voice was brusque. He couldn't help it. "Eric Johnson. He looked for you."

Her brows pulled together. "I'm engaged? How do you know that? And if he looked for me, why isn't he here now?"

He looked at the ceiling, head splitting, back aching,

and wished his heart were empty. "Oh, sweetheart," he sighed. "That is a long, convoluted story." He took a deep breath and looked down at her. The window beside her was darkened. The sun had set. "We can talk about it tomorrow."

Her eyes widened. "You're coming back?"

When it came to Laurel Hudson, it seemed he'd never change. "Yeah." His voice was gruff. "I'm coming back."

Chapter Two

"Well?" Kane's voice was demanding. "You saw her?"

Adam pressed the speaker button on his cell phone and tossed it down on the bed in his motel room while he practically ripped off the cap of the pain relievers he'd bought at the convenience store across the street from Fresh Pine.

"I saw her." He downed two of the pills dry and yanked his shirttails out of his jeans as he crossed the room to the window. It overlooked a parking lot full of work trucks and middle-class cars. The economy rental he'd gotten from the airport was indistinguishable among them.

He pulled the beige curtains closed and punched the Colder button on the air-conditioning unit beneath the window.

"And?"

She didn't have any miraculous recovery at the sight of me. He looked back at the phone as if he were looking at his brother. "And nothing," he said aloud.

"Bull."

He pressed the heels of his palms against his closed eyes and gingerly lowered himself onto the bed beside the phone until he lay flat. The bag of food he'd picked up at the deli next to the motel was sitting by the bolted-down television where he'd left it. His stomach felt hollow, but the effort to get up and retrieve the food didn't seem worth it.

"She has amnesia," he said to the phone and the room at large. "She doesn't actually remember me. My face was just familiar to her for some reason."

"A five-month-old reason," Kane said flatly. "Whether or not her conscious self knows why, something deeper knows she made a baby with you last year. Maybe it's karma for her claiming that baby was someone else's."

Adam winced. Kane spoke about the baby with more ease than Adam could. "More like I'm familiar from college days," he corrected flatly. He didn't want to believe Laurel had deliberately lied about the baby's father, but at the moment, it was more than a little difficult.

"She remembers me from college. It's long-term memory." That was what Dr. Granger believed, at any rate. "What happened last year is too new." As were her actions five months ago, when she'd left her—*their*—newborn son.

Call it what it was. Abandoned.

He wished he could shut the voice in his head up. Even Eric had told him not to think of it in those terms. Yes, Laurel had left her son. But she'd left him in a safe environment, and at a pediatric center, no less, and it was something that they all needed to remember.

His lips twisted. It didn't make anything better.

It was just more proof that Eric was the better man. Legally, he'd been declared the baby's father. He could have kept the truth to himself. But he hadn't. Not once he'd learned that Adam was in the picture.

Kane was on a roll, too. "Except she doesn't recall her parents?" His voice was hard. Sarcastic. "Or her own name? Seems to me those are pretty long-term memories, too."

Adam changed the subject. "Any word about the birth certificate?" Just because Eric had figured out Adam was the baby's father, it didn't mean the Great State of Texas had caught up with that fact. There were rules about who could request official birth records—much less get one man's name off and another on—and for now, Adam didn't meet the requirements.

Which meant involving the official people who could.

"Not yet," Kane said. "Eric had a letter from the missing mama saying *he* was Linus's father and a crappy DNA test that confirmed it well enough for a judge to give him custody back in February. Then he got that second DNA test done after the donor drive a few months ago that conclusively said otherwise. And now all those tests they ran on you before the trans-

plant? It was a short step from HLA markers and whatever to a DNA test. Hell, you've got DNA tests to spare
at this point. It's no wonder the social worker Eric had
back in February is saying that it'll take a few days to
untangle all the legalities."

"It's *been* a few days."

"Don't bite off my head, bro. I'll call her again tomorrow and check on it if you want."

"I want." His voice was terse.

His brother waited a beat. "Have you talked to the
hospital?"

Adam had called the hospital on his way to the motel
from Fresh Pine. He'd spoken to Angelica, who was the
main nurse assigned to Linus, and dissuaded her from
transferring his call to Linus's hospital room.

Since he'd met Eric, there'd already been too many
conversations. He preferred putting off the next one as
long as he could.

Eric was the man Laurel had planned to marry. That
was reason enough to resent him.

He was also the man who had, for months, truly believed Linus was his son. Laurel had hurt him, too, unintentionally or not. They had that in common.

And *that* was something else Adam didn't want to
think about.

The only logical reason for any of it was that Laurel
must have wanted Eric to be her child's father. Maybe
she'd suspected that he wasn't, and *that* was why she'd
disappeared.

"So far, Linus is doing well," he told Kane, focusing
his mind with an effort. "If everything continues that

way, he'll be released in a few weeks once they know he's producing new blood cells."

"And then?"

Adam pinched the bridge of his nose. "And then I bring him home."

The silence from the phone was loud with all of the things neither one of them said.

Like how was Adam supposed to take care of an infant? Much less one with aplastic anemia?

When Eric had claimed Linus in February and taken him home to Houston, he'd hired a full-time nanny. He could afford it, thanks to owning his own company.

Adam, on the other hand, was a restaurant manager. His paycheck was dependent upon actually *being* there to do the managing. Provisions was already a success, but the restaurant was still new and no one was sure whether the town of Rambling Rose would be able to sustain it over the long haul.

And he was well aware that he'd never be more than a manager there despite the fact that it was owned and operated by his cousins, Ashley, Nicole and Megan.

They were all Fortunes, it was true. But they'd only discovered the fact that they were related in the last year. And the sisters were the money behind the restaurant.

Where Adam had gotten a homemade cake from his folks to celebrate his college graduation, his triplet cousins had received a couple hundred thousand dollars apiece from theirs.

Such was the difference between his father, Gary Fortune, and their father, David Fortune.

Adam brought a lot of work experience to Provisions, but he'd never have the stake in the restaurant that the girls did. He didn't want one, either, because his goal lay elsewhere.

But now, he had a son he needed to provide for and he'd just committed to spending several thousand dollars a month for his son's mother's care.

A mother who didn't remember either one of them.

"Yo. Bro." Kane's voice broke into his churning thoughts. "You pass out on me or something?"

He thumbed off the speaker button and held the phone to his ear. "I'm here."

His brother's tone sobered. "How was it seeing her?"

Miraculous.

Hard as hell.

Adam stretched, trying to find a more comfortable position. "Surreal," he finally answered.

"You spend the past year thinking she's in Houston, married to some other guy by now, participate in a donor drive for a baby you think you have no connection to and find out that you're not just a good match, but you're *the* match and then learn that the baby's mama is none other than the loved-and-lost Laurel? The very woman whose complete disappearance from the planet had her fiancé convinced she'd met some untimely end?" Kane let out a laugh short on humor. "Surreal barely begins to cover it. You're in Land of Oz territory."

Adam muttered an oath. "You're not helping."

"Sure she's not faking it?"

"For God's sake!"

"Just playing devil's advocate," Kane defended.

"She's not faking amnesia," he said flatly.

When Kane spoke again, his tone was neutral. "When're you coming back?"

"Tomorrow night. Last flight out."

"How's the back feeling?"

"Don't ask."

"Should've listened to the doctors. They advised you it was too soon to travel."

"Yeah, well, they don't exactly know everything that's happened, do they?"

"They know you spent a night in the hospital five days ago," Kane returned just as sharply.

"My supper's getting cold," Adam said abruptly. Since it was a cold deli sandwich, it was more likely getting warm, sitting on the cheap dresser next to the television. "You can save the lectures until I get home. Better yet, just save 'em from here on out."

"You might convince me to save them, but what about the rest of the family? It's only a matter of time before Mom is on the plane from New York to meet the new grandbaby."

He couldn't afford to let himself think that far ahead. Laurel was recovering. Dr. Granger said the odds of her never regaining her memory were slim, though she might never remember the trauma of her accident. But even if she didn't regain the rest, they couldn't keep the truth from her forever.

She had a child. Whether or not she returned to Eric, Adam couldn't believe she wouldn't want her son with her, regardless of what had motivated her five months ago.

"Not if Dad can talk Mom out of coming," he told Kane. It was a lot easier to think about the tensions in their father's family than in his own. "We might have talked him into coming to Texas last summer, but he said then that he'd never come back."

"That's because he's got a bug up his ass about money. Bad enough to find out he's one of Julius Fortune's illegitimate sons. Learning you're the half brother of the guy who started up Robinson Tech? Gerald Robinson's so rich he probably owns half of Texas. And David's no slouch, either, with those video games he designed. Toss in the others—what have we got? Real estate moguls and financial wizards? But you know Dad. He's got more pride than Midas had money."

When Gary Fortune's job, along with thousands of others in the auto industry, had been cut years ago, he'd never seemed to spring back. But even before then, their family had always been short on money. Adam would say that having six kids tended to cause that, but David Fortune's passel of yours, mine and ours was even larger.

It wasn't enough for Gary to begrudge Gerald his fortune, though. He seemed to feel the same way about David even though David hadn't known anything more about Julius or Gary and Gerald than Gary had known about them.

Adam had no problem with Gerald or his new wife, who'd seemed pretty down-to-earth when he'd met them a year ago for their wedding. He knew David and the other newly discovered uncles were all married. Didn't know or care if their wives worked or not. His own mother, Catherine, did. And the fact that she'd had to contribute to the family coffers had just seemed to add to their dad's simmering bitterness. That was Adam's take on it, anyway.

"Dad's bitter because he doesn't have what all the rest of Julius's sons seem to have," Adam said bluntly.

"Yeah, too true," Kane said. "Anyway, you want some good news?"

Adam gave a half snort, half groan. "I don't know. Do I?" He'd had enough news lately to last a lifetime.

"Callum is ready to submit the revised plans for the hotel to the town council. He ran them by the mayor and she thinks it might actually get approved this time."

That was a surprise. "Callum's finally satisfied?" Callum was the eldest son of David and brother not only to Ashley and her sisters but to Dillon and Steven, who were the other owners of Fortune Brothers Construction—the driving force behind all of the new projects that Rambling Rose had seen in the last year.

A real estate developer and contractor, Callum had also been at Gerald and Deborah's wedding last year. Callum had talked then about the possibilities awaiting in Rambling Rose. And what better way to put Julius's past in the past for all of them than to share those opportunities with Gary's side of the family, too?

Adam's dad had flatly refused to discuss it. He hadn't wanted to attend the wedding in the first place. Hadn't wanted to drive all the way from Buffalo to Paseo—a tiny town he'd considered a zit on the back end of a boar. But either curiosity or jealousy had gotten the better of him.

When it came to the opportunities that Callum talked about? Nothing doing. Gary said they were from Buffalo and from Buffalo they'd remain.

His attitude hadn't stopped Callum, though. He'd been more than willing to bring Adam and Kane into the fold regardless of their father's attitude. Rambling Rose was a not-so-sleepy little town with a great location midway between Austin and Houston, with the burgeoning plan to offer newcomers more affordable land around their mini-mansions than in its larger neighboring cities. And then all of those mini-mansion-dwellers would need newer and fancier places to shop and eat and pamper themselves. They'd need space for their satellite law firms and country clubs and luxury resort living.

In time, there'd be plenty of opportunity for all of the Fortunes if they just took the chance.

Callum had promptly relocated from Florida to Rambling Rose and began turning those opportunities into reality.

It had taken longer for Kane and Adam to move there. They'd both had jobs to get out of first. Jobs they didn't really care about but were committed to doing. Adam had just wanted to get away from Buffalo. It was Kane who'd really been ready for the new challenges. He'd been the one who'd been arguing for weeks now that Callum's plans for an expansive luxury resort needed to be scaled back. Maybe it was because he and Adam came from modest means, but Kane had recognized the growing animosity among the core residents of Rambling Rose toward the wealthy newcomers.

Most of all when it came to the fancy hotel Callum and his brothers had originally planned. Not even Steven's recent marriage to the mayor had gotten the elaborate project past the red tape in which it had been mired. Finally, the plans had been revised entirely from a luxury hotel to a property more in keeping with the town's personality.

"Congratulations," Adam said. "Some progress finally." His brother had a wealth of patience that Adam didn't, but even Kane had limits.

"The only thing we're missing in town is a brewery," Kane said pointedly.

Adam's head throbbed. He wasn't getting into that argument again. A craft brewery cost money. More money than he'd managed to save so far. And way more now that he'd signed Dr. Granger's paperwork.

He wasn't going to worry about that when he had more important things to worry about—like a son he hadn't known he had until a few days ago. A son he hadn't even been able to see except through a window because of the strict protocol surrounding his transplant.

"Sandwich's getting cold," he said again. "I'll talk to you when I get back." Before Kane could say anything else, he ended the call and wearily tossed the phone aside.

He lay there for a while, listening to the click and whirr of the air conditioner beneath the window.

But when Laurel's aquamarine eyes and luscious lips swam into his mind, he rolled off the bed.

He finished pulling off his shirt, pitched it into a corner and went into the bathroom.

The room was dinky, with barely enough space to turn around between the toilet and the shower stall. But the water in the shower ran good and hot, even though he stood beneath the spray for a small eternity until his muscles finally began to relax and his brain finally mastered the art of keeping Laurel out of it.

At least for the moment.

Her breath caught in her chest, and gasping, Lisa sat bolt upright in her narrow bed.

Her heart pounded hard. Not like it used to after she'd had a good run. This was more like she was running from the devil looming inches behind her.

She pressed her shaking fingers to her sweaty forehead. Even though she knew it wasn't actually the scar that ached, she explored the ridge of tissue as though it did.

She forced herself to breathe deeply. Evenly. Waiting for the feeling of dread, of doom, to abate and for her churning stomach to calm.

The last time this happened, when she'd been in the common room working a puzzle with Mr. Grabinski during the evening news, it had taken twenty minutes and Dr. Granger had stuck a needle in her arm and ordered bed rest for a day. Only later, when Lisa was calmer, was she able to convince the doctor that she'd recognized the man in the news story.

She exhaled shakily, bending forward until her head touched her raised knees.

She was making progress, she supposed, when seventeen minutes later, she collapsed onto her pillows again, her racing heart finally slowing.

Then realization hit.

She'd been a runner. She could remember standing on a platform with other girls. The track team. The Laurel Grove Middle School Marauders girls' track team. The name of the school was quite clear in her mind. Why wasn't it clear as being her own name, too?

Laurel. She whispered the name into the dark. It felt as meaningless as the name *Lisa* had when she'd chosen it two months ago.

Not true. The nurses called you Lisa first.

"Better than Jane Doe," one of them—Selena—had told her cheerfully as she'd fastened a delicate gold chain with a tiny *L* around her neck. She'd held up a mirror so that Lisa could see herself.

She'd still had stitches in her forehead, courtesy of the plastic surgery to minimize the facial scar. The stitches had looked like a tiny zipper running straight down between her eyebrows.

The gold chain was a far preferable sight.

The emergency room staff had saved the necklace for her. Everything else she'd possessed—comprised only of the clothes on her broken body—had been cut off her by the team keeping her alive those first hours after she'd been extricated from the mangle of metal that had once been a car.

Against everyone's advice, she'd insisted on seeing the pictures from the accident.

A three-car pileup near the northern border of Washington State. Not even the blinding snowstorm had been enough to douse the inferno that had turned the vehicles into hideous twists of metal and ash.

Lisa's had been in the center of the mess.

Fresh Pine Rehabilitation had a computer in the common room. She might not be able to remember her name, but she'd remembered how to search the internet. Four and a half months after the accident that had changed her life, Lisa had finally read the full account of the crash.

A middle-aged salesman on his way from Vancouver had been in the first car. He'd fallen asleep at the wheel, veered into her lane, hitting her head-on. Then the third vehicle—an old pickup truck that predated airbags and was driven by a local farmer—had smashed into Lisa from behind, unable to stop because of the icy road.

She'd survived only because she'd been thrown clear by way of her car's side window. And for the first several days, even that had been questionable.

The news stories she'd found spoke about her "walking away" from the accident. But of course, she hadn't walked anywhere. Not at first.

No matter how many accounts she'd read, none of the facts extended to the details of her condition. Everything else—the fact that the car and everything in it had been destroyed by fire—had been detailed time and time again. But none had mentioned the small problem when, having emerged from her coma-cocoon three months later, Lisa could walk and talk, dress herself and function in all the usual ways but she couldn't recognize her own face in the mirror.

She didn't know where she came from. Didn't know who she came from.

She didn't know where she belonged and was desperately afraid she'd belonged...nowhere.

There were tears on her face.

Stop dwelling.

She sniffed hard. "Right," she answered the voice in her head. She swiped away the tears with the corner of her sheet and then pushed out of bed.

Despite the fact that Fresh Pine served individuals without healthcare insurance or other financial means, all of the rooms were private. They were small, yes. But each possessed a comfortable bed, a side chair for visitors—until today, Lisa had never had any—and its own bathroom with a shower stall.

She'd gotten used to the shower, though somewhere in her mind she knew she really preferred a deep bath with bubbles up to her chin.

Of course, that might just be a fantasy that she'd adopted as a memory. How was she to know when she didn't even know her own name?

She blinked under the bright light when she flicked on the bathroom light and squinted at her reflection in the mirror over the plain white sink.

"Laurel." The name bounced against the white tiles. Her eyes were light blue and they peered into themselves as if she could see into the blankness inside her mind.

The effort was no more successful now than it had

been any other time when she'd stood just like this, trying to divine the secrets trapped in her brain.

The various experts who'd examined and poked and
prodded her over the last two months were all agreed.
The trauma of her accident followed by months of coma
was at the root of her amnesia. Since the moment she'd
regained consciousness in a hospital bed surrounded
by strangers, she could remember everything that occurred.

In that regard, her memory was perfectly intact.

She remembered the scrambled eggs she'd had for
breakfast that morning. The bagel from yesterday. She
knew that Mrs. Grabinski visited Mr. Grabinski every
day at exactly 4:00 p.m. and that she brought a new
puzzle for them to work on every third day.

Lisa knew all sorts of things that were entirely useless when it came to remembering the things that came
"BA." Before Accident. Like why Adam Fortune's
handsome face plucked a visceral chord inside her.

The porcelain sink felt cool against her fingers
where she gripped it hard. She closed her eyes against
her reflection.

It took no effort to conjure his image.

He had deep, dark brown hair. Short, but thick. And
it sprang with a slight wave away from his forehead.
He had the kind of slashing, masculine brows and a
squared off, faintly clefted chin that graced some movie
actors with timeless appeal.

She'd filled an entire sketchbook with his face before she'd ever seen him on the news.

Was it serious?

He'd shrugged off her question about their past relationship. His eyes—such a dark brown that the pupils were indistinguishable from the irises—had met hers head-on. She hadn't had the sense that he'd been lying.

And yet—

She opened her eyes and looked at herself again. It didn't matter if he'd been lying or not. Because of him, she knew who she really was. *That* was what she needed to focus on.

"You're not Lisa Jane Doe," she reminded herself firmly. "You're Laurel Hudson. Get used to it."

Then she turned away from the mirror. She rubbed the center of her chest as if she could rub away the hollow sensation inside. Because it was easy to tell herself not to be distracted by Adam Fortune. And another matter entirely to actually succeed at it.

Adam was the epitome of tall, dark and broad-shouldered. He had a face that was definitely memorable.

Surely no more memorable than the faces of her own parents, though.

So why would she remember *him*? Someone from nearly ten years past? Why couldn't she remember why she'd been driving in a snowstorm in upstate Washington? Why couldn't she remember the fiancé that Adam had said she had? Was this Eric person the devil she ran from in her nightmares?

She thumped her fists none too lightly against the sides of her head as she padded through the dark room to the bed. She threw the tangled bedclothes back so they hit the floor and the thin pillow followed. Then she lay down and stared blindly up at the ceiling.

The plain sheet covering the mattress beneath her felt vaguely scratchy against her arms and legs.

Mother would never have approved. Nothing but one hundred percent Egyptian cotton would do.

Her mother was dead. Laurel felt certain of it.

But, like the whole bath thing, perhaps it was simply an idea that she'd adopted as truth.

She exhaled deeply, working through the relaxation exercises that her physical therapist had taught her to help combat the sleeplessness she suffered most nights. It was either master the techniques or resort to the prescription drugs she'd been refusing for the last month.

And she had no intention of going back to those.

So she breathed in and counted. She breathed out and counted. She flexed muscles and released and flexed again. Working up and down her body, one muscle at a time, until she thought she'd go mad.

And, like most nights, she didn't begin to doze off again until thin light shined around the edges of the faded window curtains.

Only when her mind was in that infinitesimally narrow space between sleep and wakefulness, did the thought slip inside.

He'd been the first boy she'd ever loved.

Chapter Three

He brought donuts.

Not just for Laurel but for everyone. Patients, staff and even the security guard who sat next to the front door to make sure that everyone who came calling had a proper reason to do so.

Personally, Laurel believed the guards were really there to make sure none of the patients got out when they weren't supposed to.

At the sight—and smell—of fresh donuts, everyone from guard to Grabinski gathered around the two boxes that Adam set out on the table in the common room.

"Like watching a shark attack," Laurel said, standing to one side as everyone else swarmed around the boxes. She looked up at Adam, who was standing by her side.

Even with her shoes on—white canvas sneakers

with yellow smiley faces provided by a local women's shelter—Adam stood at least a half foot taller. He wore blue jeans—the same as the evening before—and another button-down shirt. This one was Prussian blue. Yesterday's had been slate.

And he hadn't shaved. The dark whiskers didn't manage at all to blur his perfectly sculpted square jaw.

"People like donuts," he said easily. His deep brown eyes skimmed over her face. "You always did."

Pleasure flowed through her, swift and sweet. "I did?"

His smile was very faint. "Why do you think I brought them? Deep-fried puffs of heaven, I think you called them." He gestured toward the swarm. "Are you going to get in there or not? There was a maple bar with your name on it when I walked in the door but now I'm not so sure."

She realized she was tugging at the sleeve of her long-sleeved blouse and made herself stop as she worked her way to the table and the heavenly puffs.

One box was totally empty. But there was, indeed, an oblong donut glistening with a caramel-colored glaze still remaining in the second.

She snatched it from the box only moments before Mr. Grabinski did. Considering he already had a pink-frosted donut dangling on one finger and a chocolate-frosted one on another, she didn't feel particularly guilty.

Feeling more than a little triumphant, she took a napkin and moved back to Adam's side.

"Cheers." She lifted the donut in a little toast before she sank her teeth into the end of it.

The sweetness exploded on her taste buds, the maple flavor strong and pure. "Almost as good as Howie's Food Truck in Larkin Square."

She felt Adam tense. "You remember Larkin Square?"

"Not really. The name just came to me." She ducked her head, sucking maple icing off the side of her thumb. "Sorry."

He stepped in front of her and, when she didn't look up at him, tucked a long finger beneath her chin.

Her breath got hung up in a hidden spot she'd never discovered during her nightly breathe-and-count sessions. His warm finger urged her chin upward, but her eyes only lifted as far as his masculine chin because meeting his dark, dark eyes just then seemed like the most dangerous thing she could do in this world.

Why did she remember him?

"Don't be sorry for having memories," he said quietly.

She couldn't help herself. She chanced a quick glance higher. Right up to those eyes. Heat flushed over her. For no earthly reason at all.

"It happens like that," she admitted thoughtlessly. "Words come out without even thinking about them and then I realize afterward what they mean."

"Yeah, well." The corners of his lips lifted slightly and his finger fell away from that spot just beneath her chin. "You always did have the habit of speaking first and regretting later."

"Oh," she managed faintly. She still felt warm. From her face to her toes.

His gaze dropped to the donut that she held between her fingers. "You also used to devour a donut like that in about thirty seconds flat."

"Mother thought donuts were déclassé."

His faint smile turned sardonic. "I'll bet."

She started to ask him if he'd known her parents but Dr. Granger came into the room, holding a coffee urn aloft.

"Here we are," the director said brightly as she sidled between her patients to set the urn on the table. Lesley, one of the day nurses, followed close behind her with disposable coffee cups. "If we're going to have donuts, we must also have coffee."

Since Laurel didn't drink coffee, she hung back. Adam, on the other hand, took a coffee from Dr. Granger. But if he'd eaten one of his treats, he'd done it before he'd arrived at Fresh Pine.

He drank his coffee black and unsweetened, she noticed. Maybe he didn't like sweet things in general.

"Want to go for a walk?"

She stared, surprised, then looked from him to the windows overlooking the back of the building. "The garden outside is pretty nice, but it's not exactly large enough to accommodate a *walk*."

"Not in the garden. Dr. Granger said we could take a spin around the neighborhood. If you're feeling up to it, that is."

She couldn't have been more surprised if he'd announced they were taking a spin around the horn of

Africa. But along with the surprise came a warningly unsteady thump in her heart and a faint agitation in her stomach.

You are not *going to have a panic attack. Not now.*

She polished off the remainder of her donut, though it suddenly tasted like cardboard, and nodded wordlessly.

He smiled slightly in a way she decided looked a little forced. "I'll let Dr. Granger know."

She nodded again. The donut churned inside her.

While he went over to Dr. Granger, she moved to the rear window and looked out on the blooming azalea plants.

Her eyes traced the edges of the delicate petals. She imagined painting them. Watercolors would be best. Melting the magenta in the centers, drawing outward to the faint blush of the outer ruffles.

Her stomach twisted even harder and she inhaled deeply. Exhaled slowly.

It was only ten o'clock in the morning. The sky was clear. Perfect for a leisurely spin.

She could do this.

She *would* do this.

She turned away from the window only to find Adam right behind her. She bounced off his chest and his hands closed around her shoulders, steadying her. "Sorry about that."

She was both relieved and regretful when his hands dropped away from her. "Shall we?"

She nodded jerkily and preceded him from the common room, aiming blindly down the corridor for the lobby.

"D'you want a sweater? You used to get cold at the drop of a hat."

Her mind felt blank in a totally non-amnesia way. "My room is upstairs." She didn't know what on earth was motivating her. "Do you want to see it?"

His eyebrows pulled together a fraction. "Probably better for me to wait for you in the lobby."

Her cheeks felt hot. She wasn't inviting him in for coffee after a date. Which she didn't drink anyway. And which they weren't doing anyway. "I—I'll be right back."

"No rush." The words were easy. The turbulent look in his eyes was not.

She raced up the stairs, rushing regardless of what he'd said. In her room, she nearly tripped over the bedding that was still bunched up on the floor. Those patients physically unable to make their beds had help from the nurses and aides. In her case, now that she was able, she was expected to make her own.

"Later," she muttered and snatched her cardigan from the hook near the window. She pitched the bedding back onto the mattress and hurried out to the stairs, nearly sliding down them in her hurry.

She was breathless when she reached the lobby.

Adam was standing there talking with Jerry.

The security guard's smile was wider than Adam's as he buzzed the lock for the door. "Perfect morning for a walk," he said as they left. "You kids enjoy."

The words stayed with her as she went outside with Adam.

You kids enjoy.

They seemed to echo around inside her head. Achingly familiar without knowing exactly why.

Story of her life for the past two months.

Then she forgot about it when she realized she was actually standing out on the front sidewalk alongside a quiet road. She didn't have a brace on her leg anymore. She would even be able to walk around the block without having to stop every fifty yards to catch her breath.

She was aware of the look Adam sent her. "I haven't been out here before. Not once since I came to Fresh Pine." She took in the modest houses lining the street in one direction and the schoolyard in the other. Across the street, a woman pushing a stroller was entering a worn-looking convenience store.

"How does it feel?"

"Terrifying." The truth escaped and her cheeks got hot. "Probably sounds silly."

But he wasn't smiling. Not even that faint half smile that was about all he'd shown so far. "What terrifies you?"

"I don't know." She chewed the inside of her cheek. "Nothing." She forced herself to move. To put one foot in front of the other.

He fell into step beside her. She knew he was walking slower than usual. To keep pace with her.

She watched the ground in front of them. Fat, round seedpods from the trees lining the road littered the sidewalk. "I have a calendar hanging in my room. Otherwise I'd have no sense of it being June."

"You're pretty insulated inside Fresh Pine. Probably natural for it to feel scary leaving it."

Natural, perhaps. But she still felt silly having admitted it.

She tucked her hair behind her ears and picked up her speed a bit. Again, he kept easy pace beside her.

"My father used to get annoyed with my mother because she didn't walk as fast as he did."

"You remember them?"

She kicked a pod. Deliberately this time. "I remember some things."

"Their names?" His question sounded neutral. When she glanced up at him, he was looking across the street.

"No."

"Do you want to know their names?"

She didn't even have to think about it. "No." She'd reached the seedpod again and kicked it once more. A little harder. It bounced off the sidewalk and into the street just in time for a slow-moving car to roll over it. "My mother's gone anyway. That I'm sure of."

He made a sound. "If you can't remember their names, I wouldn't be so sure."

"Did you know them? When we were not being serious?"

"I met them when we graduated. That was it." He closed his hand lightly around her elbow when they reached the corner and directed her to follow the sidewalk around the bend.

She shivered when his touch fell away again. She

made a point of buttoning up her cardigan even though she wasn't cold.

"I'm sure they're worried about you," he said after they'd walked a while further in silence. Past more houses, larger and more neatly maintained than the other side of the block. The green yards were tidily mown and flower beds beamed with brilliant color.

Her stomach was starting to roll again. There were more seedpods on the sidewalk. She angled her foot toward a particularly fat one and stepped down on it, feeling it snap and pop beneath the sole of her shoe. "I told you—"

He lifted his hand. "Relax. You're a grown woman. It's your decision whether you want to contact your parents or not."

She made a sound that even she didn't know how to interpret. She spotted another fat pod and stepped on it, too.

He looked amused suddenly. "You look about ten years old doing that."

She darted in front of him to smash a third pod. "It's amazingly satisfying. You know. Like popping bubble wrap."

His lips quirked. "If you say so."

She smiled and they continued on in silence. There was more traffic on this street, and no more trees. Down the long block to the corner, a grocery store seemed to be doing a brisk business if the number of cars pulling in and out of the parking lot was anything to go by.

She fiddled with the bottom button on her cardigan. Undoing it. Then buttoning it again.

"What's churning around inside that mind?"

She started guiltily. "What?"

"If you have questions, ask them."

She made a face. "I have so many questions I don't know where to begin."

His only comment was the scrape of his boot on the cement as they walked.

She chewed the inside of her cheek again and watched the ground some more. "Why did you come to see me?"

His pace slowed. He didn't answer immediately.

She stopped altogether and watched him take several more steps ahead of her. "Did Dr. Granger ask you to?"

He stopped then, too, and she could see the tension in his shoulders beneath the blue shirt. He turned around to face her. "At first, she just wanted me to identify you, if I could."

"And then?"

"Then she said she wished there was more time. But you were being released soon and she was concerned that it was premature."

She tugged at the button again, not liking his words. "So you just decided to come and see the ol' ex-girlfriend even though it's been nearly ten years?"

He pushed his fingers into his front pockets, which only succeeded in making his broad shoulders look even wider. "Dr. Granger and I talked on the phone twice," he allowed finally.

She peered at him. She'd had the impression he'd been ready to say something else. "About me."

His eyes were dark and watchful. "Who else? You knew I was familiar from the news story. She speculated that a longer…exposure…might prompt even more memories. And I know she explained this to you, too, or you wouldn't have agreed to let her talk about your health with me."

"You said I have a fiancé. And how'd you even know about him if our paths went different ways?"

"Because the world is a damn small place sometimes," he muttered. "I told you it was complicated."

"You told me it was convoluted," she corrected.

"That, too." He pulled his hands out of his pockets and looked around them. "There. We'll go there and sit down." He pointed to a small building crouched on the opposite corner between a two-story house and a gas station. A rustic sign stuck in the grass in front said Coffee, simply enough.

She didn't want to sit. She wanted to break through the veil draped across her mind. But she nodded, and when they reached the corner, he took her elbow before crossing the street.

Was he old-fashioned? Or did he think she was incapable of staying safely within the crosswalk?

Regardless, his touch left her discomfited. Tingly. Vaguely edgy.

When they reached the curb again, he let her go.

She couldn't decide if she was relieved or not.

He pulled open the door to the small building and waited for her to go inside.

It was crowded nearly wall-to-wall with customers. The line moved quickly, though, and it wasn't until Adam was at the counter giving his order to a scowling young barista with chin-length hair colored in fuchsia, violet and cobalt stripes that Laurel realized she hadn't told him she didn't want coffee.

She stepped to one side when someone else left. At least a dozen people stood between her near the entrance and Adam at the counter. The din inside the crowded space was significant. Laurel couldn't hear what the barista was saying, but she could clearly see that the girl was no longer scowling, but laughing up at Adam with a distinctly flirty air.

Why wouldn't she? Adam was far and away the best looking man there. And the way he was smiling back at the girl…

Laurel crossed her arms and looked away.

She stepped aside again as another customer departed.

It was only a matter of minutes before Adam was carrying two covered cups to Laurel. He held one out to her.

Feeling disgruntled, she didn't take it. "Sorry. I didn't get to tell you that I don't drink coffee."

Rather than look annoyed, he quirked his lips in a smile. "It's iced hibiscus tea with a shot of ginger syrup. Which you used to love as much as maple-glazed donuts."

The smile was arresting. If Laurel had been the barista, she supposed she'd have been entranced, too.

"Just not together." She knew she sounded moody but couldn't seem to help herself.

Had she been the jealous sort?

She didn't want to think she had been.

She took the cold cup from him, careful to keep her fingers from touching his, and took a sip. It was, indeed, a perfect combination of sweet, spicy and tart.

Then she noticed the printing on the side of his cup. Even partially hidden by his long fingers, Laurel could see it was a phone number.

"It's crowded in here," he said. "Trinity said there are a couple of tables outside that nobody uses regularly."

She pushed open the door herself a little harder than necessary. She didn't look at him as they swished through the strip of overgrown grass between the building and the neighboring house. At the back, there was a patch of pavement where a beat-up delivery truck was parked next to several garbage bins. And next to that were two wooden picnic tables with benches.

They were just as beat-up as the truck. She could see why the customers preferred to crowd inside over sitting in this dreary setting.

It's not Larkin Square, that's for sure.

The thought flashed through her mind. It was the second time. "What *is* Larkin Square?"

He set his cup on one of the weathered tables. "A public space in Buffalo. Was a downturned industrial area until it was revitalized. Kind of like Ramb—" He broke off and cleared his throat. "Instead of empty factory buildings there are businesses and shops," he went on, making her wonder what it was he'd stopped himself from saying. "It's a popular place." He sat down on the bench, straddling it. "Back in college I worked at a restaurant there called The Yard."

When we weren't serious. She set her cup several inches from his and pulled out the other bench, sitting properly on it. "Is that why I keep remembering it?"

His shoulders moved. He lifted his coffee cup. "Who knows? Maybe."

She tapped her own cup with her index fingers. Then she shook her head. "You're lying."

Chapter Four

"You're lying."

Laurel's words scraped over Adam's conscience.

But what should he tell her?

That Larkin Square had been "their" place? That they'd had their first date there when they'd danced under the stars while a local band played "Just My Imagination"? That they'd eaten donuts at Howie's Food Truck every weekend? That he'd gone down on one knee and proposed to her there the day after they'd graduated from college? A proposal she'd refused because she was headed to Europe, after all.

Or that, last year, after running into each other at Oozefest, they'd gone to dinner at the restaurant where he'd once worked? And after that, he'd taken her back to her hotel room. Only he hadn't left until morning.

He took another gulp of coffee and was grateful for the way it singed its way down his throat.

"We ate a lot of donuts there," he finally said.

She stared back at him with eyes that were bluer than the sky over their heads. Then her lips compressed slightly and she turned her focus to her hibiscus tea.

He wanted to swear a blue streak.

Instead, he pulled out his cell phone and made a few swipes on the screen until he had an internet connection. A few more swipes and he'd found a picture of Larkin Square. Crowds of people gathered on the green grass fronting the brick buildings. Some were spread out on picnic blankets. Some occupied colorful chairs. Even more were lined up at the food trucks and vendor carts. If there had been a Ferris wheel, it would have looked like a carnival.

Feeling like he was playing with fire, he turned the phone so she could see the screen. "That's Larkin Square," he said abruptly.

Her fingers brushed his as she slowly took the phone and held it closer. "It looks like a happy place," she said eventually. Her voice was soft.

He felt as if someone had tied a knot around his throat and was twisting it tighter. "It was." By some miracle, he managed not to croak the words. Aside from the dinky apartment they'd shared their senior year—managing to do so without her parents ever discovering that she wasn't actually occupying the expensive one that she hated and they'd been paying for—and their entire college campus and basically the whole city, it was also the site of his worst pain.

Until he'd discovered that, against astronomical odds, she was the mother of a baby he'd simply tried to help.

His baby.

He rubbed the pain between his eyebrows and took another gulp of pistol-hot coffee. He didn't really appreciate the fact that it was also delicious. Though it did explain the crowd lining up inside what otherwise looked like a hole in the wall.

"Are you going to call her?"

"Who?" he asked.

She set the phone down on the table between them and tapped the side of her tea. "Trinity. I'm assuming that's her number she wrote on your cup."

He hadn't even noticed. He set down the coffee. Grabbed his phone and stuck it in his pocket again. "I've never called the numbers that women leave for me to find."

Her eyebrows rose. "So it's a usual occurrence, then?"

The vise was still around his throat, only now he could feel his skin burning, too. "Not usual." That wasn't strictly true, either. Back in Buffalo at the bar he'd tended three nights a week in addition to his daytime gig working as a city employee, there'd been a running bet among his coworkers over how many women—or men—would leave a hopeful phone number for Adam to find each week.

"If you know I have a fiancé, why isn't he here instead of you?"

Because Adam was a selfish man.

She'd responded to *his* picture. If Adam had suggested switching places with Eric, he figured the other man would have agreed. Adam could be with Linus. Eric could be with Laurel.

She leaned across the table and closed her fingers around his forearm. "And how *do* you even know I have a fiancé?" Her grip tightened. "Is he the one I'm running from?"

Adam froze. The only point of heat that existed in that moment came from the indent of her fingertips digging into his forearm. "Running?" Was that what this had all been about? She was afraid of Eric? Maybe so afraid that she'd been on her way out of the country for Canada when her accident occurred? "Are you afraid?"

She moistened her lips. Her eyes were wide and suddenly shined with tears. "I don't—I don't know. I have dreams—nightmares, really—and these, um—" she swallowed visibly "—p-panic attacks."

Her fingers twisted in his and he realized he'd closed his hand around hers.

She swallowed visibly. "Why would I have panic attacks? Did I before?"

Cold sweat was collecting between his shoulder blades. His life felt twisted up with Eric's because of Laurel and the baby. But what did he *really* know about the other guy? They'd spent only a handful of hours in each other's company.

Just long enough for both of their worlds to crash and burn.

"Panic attacks?" He shook his head. "Not that I

knew about." If she did have cause to fear Eric, Adam would tear him apart with his bare hands.

The man would cease to exist.

He knew that deep down in his bones. Whatever price he had to pay would be worth it.

And Linus? What about Linus?

Swearing inwardly, he pushed off the bench. No matter what happened with Laurel, he was a father. He couldn't afford to pay *any* sort of price.

He raked his shaking fingers through his hair, trying to rein in his racing mind.

Despite the volatile relationship she'd had with her parents—her mother most particularly—the only thing Laurel had ever tried to keep from them was *him*. It wouldn't matter that he'd made arrangements for Laurel to have more time at Fresh Pine. Once Sylvia and Nelson learned where she was, learned what had happened to her, they'd whisk her back into the protective cocoon they'd always tried to keep around her.

He exhaled. Laurel's expression was pinched. Her shoulders hunched. "You would have told your parents if you were afraid of Eric." The words felt raw. He knew why *he* didn't embrace their presence. But it would explain why Eric hadn't, either. "They live in Virginia. Dr. Granger can call—"

"No!" She sprang off the bench just as abruptly as he had and knocked into her hibiscus tea, sending the cup and contents flying. "I told you. My mother's dead. And my father—" She broke off, shaking her head so fiercely that her hair flung across her face.

"What about him?"

She threw out her arms again. "I don't know," she cried, sudden tears glittering in her eyes. "I don't know! Do you know what this is like? You know more about my life than I do! And…and I'm sure I don't even matter after all these years. You're just here because Dr. Granger prevailed upon you and you felt sorry or someth—"

"Stop." In two strides he'd rounded the table between them and closed his hands around her face. "Stop. Of course you matter."

She shook her head, staring up at him with those great blue tear-filled eyes. "I'm alone," she said hoarsely.

He closed his arms around her shaking body, pulling her against his chest. "You're not alone," he said against her hair. The scent was different—flowery instead of lemony—but the feel was as silky as it had always been. "I promise you're not alone."

Her hands came around him, too, fingertips digging through his shirt against his spine. "Tell me something about you," she begged. "Something I should still know."

That he'd loved her from the first moment he saw her?

That no matter what happened between them or how great the distance was or how many times she broke his heart, he was afraid he'd go to his grave still loving her?

He swiftly buried that.

"Like what?"

She lifted her head suddenly, shaking back her hair.

He was exactly six inches taller than her. She'd always fit perfectly against him. And when her head was tilted like it was now, he needed only to dip his head to capture those lips. To forget everything but the taste of her. To remind himself that every woman he'd known since her had only ever been a pale imitation.

"Like when were you born?"

He dragged his thoughts back from that bridge. "Three months before you."

"That's not—"

"Thirty-one years ago."

"You're being deliberately obtuse."

"No, I'm just glad to see some fire in your eyes."

Her face started to crumple again and he groaned. "Don't cry. I never can stand to see you cry."

"I'm so sorry you're inconvenienced!"

Despite everything, he let out half a laugh. It was always that way. Just when she seemed as fragile as glass, she'd about-face. "What am I going to do with you, Laurel Hudson?"

Her hands clutched at his spine. She was breathing hard. "Take me home with you?"

His brain went slack. He thought maybe he'd said "What?" in a dumbfounded way but he couldn't be sure.

Laurel was pushing away from him and tucking her hair behind her ears. Both hands. Both ears. Obviously nervous.

She wasn't the only one.

He shoved his hands into his front pockets. Both hands. Both pockets.

"You said you're not married," she said quickly. "I s'pose you have a girlfriend, though. N-not that I'm suggesting—"

"I don't," he interrupted. "But I still can't take you with me to Rambling Rose." He'd deliberately avoided saying the town's name. But now it was too late and he braced himself for some reaction.

But none came. Her lush lips had merely rounded into a silent "Oh."

"Laurel—" He broke off, because he was damned if he knew how to handle this. Damned if he said nothing. Damned if he said too much.

Then she tucked her hair again even though it was still tucked. "I'm sorry. Don't pay any attention to that. I know it's a wild idea. I can't help it. I feel more than a little bit out of control, I guess."

He bit off an oath. "You're not."

"Easy for you to say. You can remember what happened BA." She caught his look. "Before Accident." Then she wiped her cheeks and turned away.

She walked over to pick up the cup she'd knocked off the table. She carried it to one of the garbage bins and dumped it inside. Then she dusted her hands together and when she turned back toward him, her shoulders were visibly firmed. "I'm ready to go back to Fresh Pine." She walked past him, her feet kicking through the overgrown grass.

God help him. He really was not strong enough for this.

He lobbed his own cup into the trash. "I hate avocados," he said abruptly. "And bananas."

She stopped. Looked back at him.

"You love 'em," he continued. "Almost as much as you love peanut butter. Always kept trying to convince me I ought to love them, too. But I don't. Tasteless mush, as far as I'm concerned."

"You're insane. Guacamole? Banana pudding? Not together, obviously. But still. Double nirvana!"

"Not the first time I've heard you say that. I still hate them both."

She rocked on the heels of her smiley-faced tennis shoes. "What else?"

"I broke my arm when I was seven, trying to rig up a pulley system between my second-floor bedroom and the house next door so my best friend and I could get across to see each other without going downstairs past our parents."

Her eyebrows rose. "Inventive."

"Not really. Didn't dawn on me that a steel cable would be pretty noticeable as soon as someone looked *up*."

"I broke my arm, too." She held up her right arm. "So they told me when they brought me out of the coma, anyway. What else?"

And her left leg, he thought grimly.

"I have four brothers and one sister. All younger than me." He held up his hand. "And before you ask, no, you don't have any siblings."

"I know." She wrinkled her nose. "I don't know how or why I know, but I know."

"And you're going to have to trust me when I say that you can't come home with me to Rambling Rose."

Her lashes dipped. She kicked the toe of her shoe through the grass. "I told you to forget I asked. It's too much of an imposition. I get it—"

"—not without knowing what you'll be facing when you get there."

Her lashes flew up. Her lips were rounded again. Silently. "I don't understand," she finally said.

"I know you don't." He held out his hand, sending a silent apology to Dr. Granger. "Come here. Sit down again."

Her forehead knit. "You're making me worried."

"I'm sorry." He should drop it now. Dr. Granger was the expert when it came to Laurel's health. He wasn't an expert in anything when it came to her. Except being the one she always walked away from.

But it was too late because she was already retracing her steps back to the picnic table.

This time when she sat down on the bench it was with her back to the table. As if she knew instinctively that there was no way he could sit. Not when he had to say what he had to say.

And how the hell was he supposed to say any of it?

Kane was the one with the gift of words. Adam was just the logical one.

And where was that logic now? Out the window, the way it always was where Laurel was concerned.

He pulled his phone out again.

"Who're you calling?"

"Nobody." He swiped the screen again. The image of Larkin Square disappeared, to be replaced with two tiny ones. Of him. Of Eric. The only reason their story had ended up in the media at all was because a news station out of Houston had been doing a public service series on organ and blood donation. Learning that an entire town had conducted a donor drive on behalf of one little baby had dovetailed right into their series.

It had been a small annoyance during the week before the transplant. A news crew followed Adam for a few hours at Provisions and poked around town. At the time, Callum had said it would be good publicity for the town as a whole. How it portrayed Rambling Rose as a community where people should want to live. Rambling Rose people cared. Just Like Adam and Kane, newcomers themselves, had joined the people lining up at a wellness spa called Paz two months ago to have their cheeks swabbed.

The three-minute news story had aired the night of Linus's transplant. Adam hadn't even seen it at the time because he'd been in a hospital room himself, mired in the dregs of anesthesia and nightmares of Laurel being dead.

In fact, he hadn't even watched the piece on the internet until Dr. Granger had contacted him three days later.

He stepped over to Laurel and handed her the phone as the video began playing on the screen.

And now, in Constance Silberman's continuing series, Doing Good Helping Others, *she heads to Rambling Rose, Texas, where the citizens of this small town recently participated in a donor drive—*

Laurel's thumb grazed the screen, pausing the video. She looked up at Adam, her eyes searching his. "I've seen this." She looked vaguely embarrassed. "Several times, actually. The computer in the common room—"

He'd seen the computer for himself. He didn't know

why it hadn't occurred to him that she might have done her own internet search. "And *nothing* about it was familiar except me? You're sure?"

Her brows pulled together. Without answering, she glanced at the phone again and resumed the video. The anchor continued.

—inspired by a five-month-old infant suffering from aplastic anemia, a condition where one's body fails to produce enough new blood cells—

Adam felt Laurel's glance, though she didn't pause the playback as the reporter took over the story from the anchorman and began spouting off statistics and courses of treatments.

—the greatest gift, of course, is the gift of life. And in the town of Rambling Rose, that's exactly what we found. A perfectly suited bone marrow match for the very child who'd inspired the drive in the first place.

Adam knew there was a brief collage of shots of him at that point—at Provisions talking to one of the waitstaff, striding through the busy kitchen as if he were ready to pitch in there even though he'd get his hands chopped off by Nicole if he ever tried such a thing, and then walking down Main Street before the images changed to the exterior of the Rambling Rose Pediatric Center.

I spoke to Dr. Parker Green, the chief physician at the local pediatric center who first diagnosed our young patient's condition. Dr. Green, is this the first time you've seen the locals rally around an issue like this?

He rubbed his hand down his face while Dr. Green assured Constance Silberman that it wasn't and began recounting tales of Rambling Rose's history. The reporter skillfully stopped the doctor from going on too long, though, redirecting him when he started talking about how the pediatric center had been built on the original site of the Fortune's Foundling Hospital.

Clearly, Rambling Rose is a very special place. It's no wonder that it's ranked one of the fastest growing towns in Texas. And nobody can be more grateful for the New York transplant named Adam Fortune who is donating his bone marrow than the single father of the tiny boy who'll be receiving it the day this story is scheduled to air.

Adam dropped his hand, watching Laurel's face. But she showed no reaction to the image of Eric Johnson that appeared on the screen.

Because of the strict precautions being taken to ensure that his child is not exposed to any contagions at this critical juncture, I wasn't able to meet personally with Eric Johnson. But he did speak with me by phone. And when I asked him what it meant to find a donor match for his son, he had this to say. That the donor was the most important person he'd never met.

Laurel looked up and extended the phone toward Adam. "You donated bone marrow. I knew that because of this news story." She wagged the phone slightly. "What am I missing?"

Adam silenced the phone. "You didn't pay attention. That father. His name was Eric Johnson." His jaw was tight. "*Your* Eric Johnson."

It seemed to sink in then and she stared at him. It

was a full minute before she blinked. "But he has a baby."

It didn't take him a full minute, but it took long enough. "Yes." The effort to push out just that one word made his chest ache.

"And I'm engaged to him." Her gaze flickered. "To be married."

He ground his molars together. "Until you...put on the brakes and told him you needed space." Adam had come to the conclusion she'd done that because she'd been carrying his baby. But now, he had to wonder if fear of Eric had been the motivator.

She barely seemed to hear him. "It said he's a single father." She was pulling so hard on her sweater sleeve it had stretched right over her hand. Only her fingertips showed. And those fingertips were visibly digging into her thigh. "Where's the baby's mother?"

His head ached deep behind his eyes. He slowly took a step toward her. His voice, when he finally marshalled the strength, was hoarse. "I'm looking at her."

Chapter Five

Laurel was barely aware of walking back to Fresh Pine.

I'm looking at her.

It wasn't possible. How could it be? How could she have had a baby that she couldn't remember having?

How can you look in a mirror and not know your own name?

When they reached the entrance to the clinic, Jerry buzzed them in.

She wasn't even able to wonder about Adam at that point. He was just an old boyfriend. Caught in the middle of the mess that was her life.

What other sins had she blocked out of her mind?

Without stopping, she walked straight through the lobby to the stairs and up to her room, climbing onto the bed and curling into a ball before pulling the tangle of blankets up to her chin.

They weren't enough to stop her shivering.

She wasn't sure she'd ever stop shivering.

I'm looking at her.

She closed her eyes. But the image of Adam's expression was burned on the backs of her eyelids.

She opened them again. Stared blindly at the calendar hanging on her wall.

She heard the soft knocking on her door and ignored it.

If her fiancé was at the root of her panic attacks, why would she ever leave their baby alone with him? What kind of a person was she?

A distinctive creak told her someone had opened her door. It took too much energy to turn and see by whom. "Leave me alone." Her voice sounded as dull as her soul clearly was.

"If I could do that, I wouldn't be here in Seattle."

Her eyes suddenly burned. She turned her head and silently watched Adam round her bed. When he sat on the side of it, the mattress dipped, making her roll toward him until her balled up knees were stopped by his back.

He winced slightly and shifted away from the contact. "I'm sorry." The sigh he gave sounded like it came all the way from the bottom of his boots. "I shouldn't have told you like that."

Her stomach rolled. "How else should you have? Why didn't anyone else tell me?" The baby was five months old. Her accident had been five months ago. In all the patching and suturing, was she supposed to believe that none of those doctors or nurses had noticed that she'd recently given birth?

He tugged at the jumbled blankets and smoothed them out, gently tucking them once more beneath her chin. Then his hand moved away. "Until a couple months ago, you weren't in any condition *to* be told."

"It's no excuse," she said thickly. "Maybe if they'd told me, I'd have *remembered*. Dr Granger—"

"Has your best interests at heart." His dark eyes were solemn.

Tears burned her eyes. "Did I know he was sick when I left?" She pushed herself up onto her elbows. "Did I just dump him off on his father to deal with? Am I that callous?" Fresh horror hit. She grasped his arm. "What about the transplant? Did it work?" The questions seemed to be jumping out of her, one on top of the other.

"It's too soon to know if it'll work," he said quietly. "But his doctors are optimistic. It'll take a few weeks to be sure Linus is producing new blood cells the way he should be."

Her fingers relaxed. "That's what we named him?" Of all the names she could have imagined choosing, Linus was not one of them. "Like the comic character? Charlie Brown's best friend with the blanket? Linus like that?"

He looked away and began adjusting her blankets again. "Yeah."

She rubbed her wet cheeks. "His father must have

named him." Then she cringed because she sounded as callous as her mother would have sounded.

She pushed aside the tidy blankets and then pushed aside Adam—which was about as easy as moving the side of a mountain—and rolled off the bed. She yanked open the old-fashioned wardrobe and pulled out the canvas bag she'd used when she'd moved from the hospital to Fresh Pine. It wasn't large. The size of a shopping bag, really. But all of her present possessions—four days' worth of clothes before a laundry session was necessary—would still fit.

"What're you doing?"

"I have to see him."

"Eric? Or Linus?"

She frowned, hesitating for a moment. Waiting for that sense of panic.

But it didn't come and she finished tucking a folded pair of blue jeans into the bottom of the canvas bag. "Linus. Though even I realize I'll have to see his father, too. *Did* you meet him? After the transplant?"

"Before." His voice was short.

"What did you think of him?"

He didn't answer right away. "There wasn't a lot of time to think. But I will tell you that no matter what went on between the two of you, I don't believe he'd harm Linus. He's too devoted."

"Whereas I was on a highway heading to Canada," she said harshly. "Don't suppose he happened to tell you why that was?"

His silence was answer enough. She grabbed the T-shirts stacked on the middle shelf and flicked a look toward Adam. *"What?"* She thrust the shirts in with the jeans and pointed at him. "What else haven't you told me?"

"Nothing that can't wait." Then he pulled out his cell phone.

"No. No more pictures," she begged. "No more videos." She couldn't take any more today.

"No pictures," he assured. He finished tapping the screen and held the phone to his ear while he paced back and forth in the limited space between her bed and the window. "No video— Hey. Need a favor."

He was obviously addressing the person he'd dialed.

She turned back to the wardrobe and grabbed her underwear, tucking the panties down into the corners of the bag.

"See if you can get another ticket on my flight tonight," Adam was saying behind her. "I'll text you everything you'll need for the reservation."

The space between her shoulder blades tickled and she looked back to see his gaze on her.

The second he realized she was looking at him, he made a point of looking out the window. As if the view of the clinic's small parking lot below was the most interesting thing in the world. "If there're no more seats on mine, then get us both on the first available one tomorrow."

Laurel focused on her own task. She could hear the faint buzz of words coming out of his phone but couldn't make out the words. Except the buzz sounded agitated.

Or maybe she was just projecting.

"Kane, save it for now," Adam spoke again. "You going to help me or not? Yeah. I'll text you her birthday. You'll need it to get the ticket. Thanks."

The wardrobe was empty. The canvas bag bulging. She still made herself wait a moment before she turned around to face him again. "That plane ticket you're talking about. It's for me?"

"Obviously."

She chewed the inside of her cheek. He didn't look exceedingly happy about it. "Thank you. Soon as I… figure out things, I'll pay you back."

He looked pained. "I'm not worried about the money, Laurel. I'm worried about *you*."

"Well, don't be. You've done more than enough for me already. I understand why you came here now."

His head jerked back an inch, his eyebrows lowering warily. "You do?"

"My… Eric…couldn't very well make the trip. Not now with the baby in the hospital. It was very decent of you to come all this way instead."

His lips twisted. "That's me. Decent."

She set the loaded bag on the foot of the bed and went into the bathroom. She plucked her toothbrush from its cup on the countertop, avoiding her reflection in the mirror. Then it occurred to her. "Was Eric at UB, too?" She pulled open the little drawer beneath the sink to grab the rest of her toiletries and went back into the bedroom.

"No. You told me you met him a couple years ago."

"Oh." She pushed her handful into the pocket

stitched on one side of the canvas bag. Then she peered at Adam. "When did I tell *you* that?"

He twitched the window curtains and looked out the window again. "We ran into each other last year. Spent a little time catching up."

There were still things he wasn't telling her. She could see that so clearly on his face. She squinted, her artist's eye imagining him ten years younger. "Strange, isn't it? You ending up in Rambling Rose. Being a match for—"

"It's a small world," he said, cutting her off.

"I was thinking more along the lines of fate."

His lips twisted. "I don't believe in fate. People make their own choices in life."

Her chest tightened. "My choices seem to be about heading away from the ones who should matter most."

He looked ready to say something, then gestured at the stuffed bag. "You're not going to fit anything else in there."

"I don't have anything else except my sketch pad and pencils. They're in the common room."

He'd frowned, looking pained all over again. "Go on and get them. I need to speak with Dr. Granger. She's going to want to check you out before letting you leave with me."

"I'm an adult. More or less competent if you don't count the absence of all memories BA. If I want to leave, I can leave."

"Then humor me," he said flatly. "Let her be the doctor."

"Fine, but I'm still getting on a plane with you."

* * *

Kane succeeded in getting another ticket on Adam's original flight back to Houston.

The problem, though, was that Laurel had no form of identification. So even though she had a ticket, she wouldn't be able to board the plane.

Adam felt like a dunce when Dr. Granger pointed that out to him after he went down to her office on the main floor and informed her of the change in plans.

"It's not an insurmountable problem," she said in the face of his consternation. "If you know where she was born, you'll be able to get a copy of her birth certificate. From there, it's a matter of obtaining copies of the rest of her identification. Driver's license. Maybe even a passport. It'll just take some time."

Exactly, Adam thought. Time.

Ashley had been understanding about the time he'd taken off work lately. First to get through the rest of the donor screening after he'd been chosen as the most viable possibility. The times he'd had to drive to Houston for more tests. And then for the bone marrow harvest itself. And now this trip to Seattle.

Regardless of the mess between him and Laurel, and Laurel and Eric, and Eric and the baby, Adam needed to get back to work.

And Laurel needed to see her son.

Their son.

Flying was the quickest. He briefly considered contacting Eric to see if he had any copies of Lauren's identification conveniently lying around.

Adam wasn't proud of it, but he tossed out the idea

just as fast. Knew he would have done so even if Laurel hadn't wondered if she'd been running from Johnson.

"If we drove, we could be in Boise tonight," he said.

"Drive to Texas?" Dr. Granger looked alarmed. "It has to be close to two thousand miles!"

Slightly more than twenty-two hundred. He wisely kept that to himself.

"It'll take you days," the director emphasized, as if he didn't grasp the point.

"Then it'll take us days," Laurel said from the doorway behind Adam. She was holding her sketch pad against her chest with a fistful of pencils clutched in her hand.

Dr. Granger half rose from her seat. "Lisa—"

"It's Laurel." She lifted her chin. "And I know you're concerned, Dr. Granger. But this is something that I have to do."

Dr. Granger slowly sat back down. She watched Laurel closely. "Sit in a car for hours on end?" She shook her head. "I really have to advise against it. What's behind this sudden rush? You still need physical therapy and—"

"Nothing's behind it," Laurel said a little defensively. "I'll find a way to get PT in Texas. One way or another I'm going to get back everything that's trapped in here." She tapped her forehead. "I'm going to get back my life. Once I'm settled, you can forward my records."

"Settled where?"

"I don't know," Laurel said. "But I'll figure it out. I was going to have to move to a shelter when I left here anyway until I got a job, and I imagine there are—"

"I'll see to it," Adam interrupted abruptly. He ignored the looks from both women. "She's not going to be homeless."

"There you go," Laurel said as if the matter was settled, even though nothing really was settled at all beyond that moment.

The doctor opened her mouth, looking ready to protest, but then she leaned back in her chair. "Well." She looked from Laurel's face to Adam's. "Of course I have no authority to stop you." She plucked a pen from her plastic cup and pointed it at Adam. "This isn't the best of plans for you either, young man." She shook her head—whether at them or at herself he couldn't tell—and scribbled something on a small pad. She tore off the sheet and handed it across to Adam.

It was a prescription pad with the doctor's information preprinted on it. Yet it wasn't a prescription she'd written out, but a phone number.

"That's my personal cell phone," she said, her gaze pinning Adam's. "If you need me for anything, and I mean anything, you can reach me twenty-four seven at that number."

He nodded and stuffed the paper in his pocket. "Thank you."

"I'll make sure the charges are refunded on your credit card." As if she'd decided to embrace their departure, she planted her hands on her desktop and stood. Adam shoved to his feet, too. "Stop by the kitchen before you leave," she ordered as she rounded her desk and paused in front of Laurel. "Lunch is nearly over but you might still be in time to get a plate from Maria.

The least you can do is set off with a decent meal in your stomachs."

Laurel looked bewildered. "That's it?"

Dr. Granger smiled gently. "I'd tell you to stay in touch, but it's been my experience that patients who recover enough to leave on their own steam generally don't."

Laurel looked like she was about to cry. "I don't know what to say. 'Thank you for everything' doesn't seem to be enough." She hugged the director. "I'm going to miss you."

"And we'll miss you, too." Dr. Granger patted her back and sniffed before stepping away and leading them out of her cramped office. "Fortunately, I have a meeting to get to, so there's no time to wallow. I am going to call you, Adam," she warned, as she shooed them in the direction of the kitchen while she went in the other. "To make certain you're taking proper care of things. I expect you to answer."

"Always," he said seriously. "You're the only reason I have her back."

The director smiled and sniffed again and turned on her heel.

Even though he said the words, he knew they weren't exactly true. For now, he was the one person Laurel vaguely recalled BA. Before Accident.

What would happen when she remembered everything else?

When she got her life back?

When she remembered Linus? Not that she had been the one to give the baby that name.

Until five days ago, Adam hadn't had any reason to wonder what actual name the baby's mother had bestowed on him when he'd been born.

"You're frowning," Laurel said. "Are you changing your mind before we've even begun our road trip?"

"No. Just wondering. Why didn't you tell Dr. Granger about the baby?"

"Because I didn't want to give her another reason to talk me out of going."

He wasn't sure that would have been the result, but he hadn't been exactly forthright with the director, either.

"So if you haven't changed your mind," she said, smiling gamely even though he could see the uncertainty in her eyes, "let's get moving." She tugged his sleeve. "Lunch on Saturdays is always fish and chips. If we want to get any, we'll need to beat Mr. Grabinski before he has a chance to have his third helping."

Two hours and a helping of fish and chips later, they were finally on their way.

The plane tickets were canceled.

Laurel had shared hugs and goodbyes with every person at Fresh Pine—employee and patient.

The car rental agency had traded in the light gray minuscule economy car for a light gray slightly less minuscule economy car. They'd even provided a map highlighting the best route to get out of Seattle.

And since Adam had checked out of his motel that morning before he'd brought the maple donuts, it was at least one less thing that had needed doing.

"That morning" seemed a lot longer ago than mere hours.

He glanced at Laurel sitting in the passenger seat beside him.

Her window was rolled down a few inches and her hair blew lightly around her shoulders. Her hands were folded together in her lap. But the nail beds were white because of the ferocity of her grip.

"You want to change your mind?"

She gave him a quick look. "No." She looked away. "No," she said more firmly. Less defensively. She stopped clenching her hands and rubbed her palms down her thighs.

"You could have waited until we sorted out your identification so you could fly."

She shook her head. "Who knows how long that'd take? At least this way, I feel like I'm *doing* something. Linus needs his mother. If I let him down again—" She broke off and caught her blowing hair in her hand, looking out the window at the city they were leaving behind. "I can't stay here and just wait, sitting on my thumbs wondering about questions that don't seem to have an answer. Even if there is a part of me saying it would be the safest thing to do."

He shifted in the seat. He'd pushed it back as far as it would go to give himself more leg room, but he'd become accustomed to driving a truck since moving to Rambling Rose. The car felt particularly small with Laurel sitting next to him, so close that his arm brushed hers whenever he rested it on the narrow console between them. "The answers'll come. When they're ready."

"You sound very properly coached by Dr. Granger."

He smiled despite himself.

And she did, too.

"So," she said after he'd navigated to the freeway that was crawling with traffic even on a Saturday afternoon, "how long *will* it take for us to get there?"

Too long. "Is this your version of Are We There Yet?"

She gave him an offended look that wasn't very convincing considering the smile still in her eyes. "I'm not a whiner." She frowned. "Am I?"

She had been many things. But a whiner wasn't one of them. "Not that I recall. We'll know if that's changed about five hours from now and you're sick of sitting in this car with me."

"I'm not going to get sick of that." She reached out and began fiddling with the radio buttons. "I *will* get sick of listening to sports talk, though. We need music. Do you have a preference?"

"Yeah. Sports."

She made a face.

"You liked sports well enough," he told her. "Participating, anyway. Track. Volleyball."

"Sure, but not for hours and hours on end. And definitely not *golf*. About as exciting as waiting for a pot to boil."

And yet, golf lessons had been something Sylvia and Nelson had insisted upon. They were members of the country club, after all, and they couldn't very well have a daughter who didn't excel at golf. And tennis. She'd even had cotillion lessons.

"You think you ever learned, then, to actually boil something? Maybe, say, *water*?"

She made a sound in her throat that—far as Adam had ever determined—only a disgusted woman could make. "Are you suggesting I can't cook?"

He couldn't help smiling. "Unless you learned somewhere along the way, I'm saying it outright. The only thing I ever saw you use an oven for was to dry socks. And then you set off every smoke alarm in—" he barely caught himself from saying *our* "—in the apartment."

She stopped fiddling when she found a station playing the Temptations and adjusted the volume slightly. "I'll have you know, I make a mean chicken piccata."

He changed lanes to get around the SUV. Even with her memory impaired, she'd chosen classic Motown.

At least it wasn't "Just My Imagination."

"Are you sure about that?"

"Yes, I'm sure. I'll even prove it one day. I learned from the owner of a little trattoria in Tuscany who—" She broke off and thumped her palm lightly against her forehead. "This is maddening. Why can I suddenly recall something like that, but I can't remember my own flesh and bl—"

He reached over the console and closed his hand over hers. She'd clenched them together again. "Stop."

"But—"

"Stop." He squeezed her hands. They were so slender he could enclose both in one hand. Dr. Granger must have told him a dozen times not to allow her to push herself too hard too fast. "Give yourself a break. You'll get there."

She was silent for a long while. Long enough for him to work his way around a semi, an SUV and a cherry-red Corvette. Then her fingers twitched against his palm. "What if I don't?" she asked in a small voice.

Then maybe he'd have a chance.

The fact that he thought it at all shamed him.

"Where's that confidence you showed Dr. Granger?" He put his hand back on the steering wheel. "Not remembering everything about your past won't stop you from having a future."

Her shoulders rose and fell with the huge sigh she gave. "I should be grateful that Linus is so young," she said after a while. Her head was resting against the seat back, her focus on the window beside her. "He won't remember anything about me abandoning him with his father."

Adam's hands tightened around the steering wheel.

Four days, he figured. They had at least thirty-five hours on the road ahead of them. He could drive faster, longer. Do it in three days. But four would be better for her. Less taxing. It would still mean eight hours on the road every day.

So four days. Four days to figure out how he was going to tell her that she hadn't left Linus with either the father who'd claimed him or the father who'd made him.

Everyone in Rambling Rose knew the truth about what she'd done.

Which meant he couldn't let her get there without making sure she knew that truth, too.

Chapter Six

"Is it bigger than a bread box?"

"Yes."

"Is it smaller than a—" Laurel tapped her finger against her lips, thinking.

It was their third round of Twenty Questions. So far, he was two games ahead of her. They'd been driving nearly four hours now, stopping once at a rest area on the side of the road to eat the sandwiches that Maria had sent with them. Laurel had been more grateful for the chance to get out of the car and stretch her legs than she had been for the food.

There was no way she was going to admit it, though. Not after telling him she wasn't a whiner. Against the journey still ahead of them, a few hours in the car was nothing.

"Did you fall asleep over there again?"

"No, I'm not asleep." She'd only dozed off for a few minutes before they'd started playing the guessing game. "I was thinking."

His chuckle was barely audible.

"Could it fit in the front seat of this car?"

This time, the chuckle was a little louder. "Pretty sure nothing else could fit in the front seat of this car besides us. But yes."

She looked out the window. They'd already crossed the border into Oregon. Five states yet to go. She'd toed off her shoes and propped her bare feet on the dashboard. "Is it something everybody owns?"

"Nope."

She wiggled her foot. He'd stumped her on Benjamin Franklin, and then on Niagara Falls. She really didn't want to lose a third time, particularly when it had been her idea to play the game in the first place. Did that mean she had a competitive streak in her somewhere?

You ran in track meets, didn't you?

"Is it something *you* own?"

Even in the dwindling light, she caught the look he gave her.

"Right." Silly question. How would she know what he did or did not own nowadays? Their "not really serious" had been a decade before. "What question was that? My fifth?"

"Yeah, but I'll give you that one." He angled his shoulders against the back of the seat as though he was trying to stretch. "You can ask something else."

"You don't have to drive all the way through the night, you know. Just because I'm anxious to get to—"

"Are you going to ask a question or are you giving up?"

"I don't give up."

But you did. You gave up your own child.

She shifted herself, as if she could mentally stretch herself away from that fact.

All she ended up doing was pressing her arm against his where they both rested on the too-narrow console. She pulled her feet down from the dashboard and sat up straighter, putting a quick end to the warmth of his forearm burning through her cotton sleeve.

Her gaze fell on his cell phone where he'd dumped it in one of the cup holders between them. While they'd navigated their way out of Seattle, it had intoned directions. Now, with only the highway stretching out endlessly before them, it was silent. "Is it something high tech?"

"No. Old tech if anything. Way old."

He was giving her hints, now. He'd probably tired of the game within minutes of agreeing. But she hadn't been able to find a radio station and the sound of the tires on the road hadn't been enough to silence the worries bouncing around inside her head.

Truth was, she was tired, too. Not of the silly little game. But of sitting on her rear end, trying to keep herself from leaning naturally toward him. Of trying to stop herself from letting her arm rest against his, where it kept wanting to go.

"I don't know." She guessed wildly. "The Mona Lisa?"

He was silent for half a second before he gave a laugh. "For a wild-ass guess, that's pretty good. Yes. The thing I was thinking of is the Mona Lisa."

She rolled her eyes. "You're making that up."

"Scout's honor."

"I have the feeling you were never a Boy Scout."

"And you'd be wrong." He stretched again, grimacing a little. "I need to get out of this car for a few minutes." They'd left behind anything approaching traffic two hours ago. He slowed and pulled well off on the shoulder, checked his mirror, then got out of the car.

She watched him walk around to the weedy sage-colored grass on her side of the car. Facing away from her, looking out into the distance ahead.

What he could see was anyone's guess.

He rolled his head around a few times, propped his hands on his lean hips and stood there, looking tall and broad and so strangely alone that her throat got tight.

She blamed it on tiredness. She'd had more activity that day than she'd had since BA.

She rubbed her eyes and tugged at the cuff of her sleeve.

Then he was opening the car door and climbing back inside.

As soon as he was buckled in, they were off once more. "We're stopping at the next town we come to," he said. "Don't care how big or small."

They hadn't seen a road sign for miles. But she wasn't going to argue. Not that he'd asked her opinion. "Okay." She started to reach for the radio dial but made herself stop. She didn't want to annoy him by hunting for something besides static.

But he seemed to recognize her aborted movement. "Go ahead. See if we're close enough to anywhere to actually pick up a signal."

"Where's satellite radio when you need it, right?" She didn't need any second urging and began slowly turning the dial. She'd already learned the usual seek button skimmed right on past the weaker stations. "Feels like that old Chevy you had before you put in a radio." She passed the faintest blip of music and turned the dial back again, trying to capture it. But it was too elusive and she continued hunting. "And then Kane borrowed the car for some reason—"

"He needed wheels so he could go see a girl."

"—and the radio got stolen anyway." A burst of country music suddenly exploded from the speakers. "Yes. Hello." Supremely satisfied with herself, as if she were personally responsible for the reception, she adjusted the volume slightly before sitting back and grinning at him.

He was staring fixedly through the windshield and his long fingers looked tight on the steering wheel.

Her pleasure dimmed. "What?"

He shook his head slightly. The sun was hovering just above the horizon, perfectly etching his strong profile against the gentle rolling hills whizzing past. "It was a good car, radio or no radio. Got me to work on time. School on time."

"And it had more leg room than—" Realization

dawned. She exhaled and closed her eyes. "I've done it again."

"So?"

She looked at him. "So it's unsettling. It reminds me I have no control over my mind."

"Do any of us?" He seemed to deliberately loosen his grip on the wheel. "You remember what color that car was?"

"Something hideous, I think."

The corner of his lips kicked up and a small slashing dimple appeared in his lean cheek.

And all of a sudden, she found it hard to breathe. He really was too beautiful for any man to be. But what made her breathless wasn't the physical perfection of him. It was something else.

Something deeper.

Was it serious?

"Puke green," he said.

"Chartreuse," she corrected. Cobbling her wits together took effort. "A perfectly wonderful color—"

"—except on that car."

She could see it so clearly in her mind. Parked at the curb in front of her... Her what? "Did I live in a dorm?"

"You had your own apartment when we met."

She could feel something about that hovering on the edges. Something she couldn't quite grasp. But the harder she tried, the more elusive it became, making it as unreachable as recalling if *she* had been serious about him, but he hadn't been serious about *her*.

So she thought about the car instead. A much safer

focus. "Did you—" she'd almost said *we* "—take any road trips in that car?"

"Toronto a few times. Finger Lakes. No place further than the Adirondacks."

"No cross-country trips like this, then." Technically, she supposed Seattle to Texas wasn't all the way across the country, but it surely classified as more than halfway.

"Not in that car, that's for sure. This'll be the longest haul for me." He waited a beat. "First long road trip I ever made was last year. Kane and my dad and me. Buffalo to Paseo, Texas."

"I'd say I've never heard of it, but—" She spread her hands.

That dimple peeked out again to express a wealth of wryness. "That's not because of the amnesia. It's a seriously tiny town that most people probably hadn't even heard of until last year."

She twisted in her seat so she could face him more fully. "What happened last year?"

He didn't answer right away. And when he did, she couldn't shake the sense that he'd been on the verge of saying something else. "You know what Robinson Tech is?"

She hadn't forgotten common, everyday things. "Of course." The company name was synonymous with the word "computer." Maybe she'd even had one of its devices with her and lost it in the car accident.

"The founder of that company turned out to be my dad's half brother. Gerald Robinson. He got married in Paseo. Last June." His gaze slid over her briefly before turning back to the road. "Made the news despite his plans to keep it on the down low when his ex tried to kidnap the bride during the wedding."

"Good grief! Was everyone all right?"

"Everyone except his ex-wife. She's in a psychiatric hospital now."

"Not your ordinary wedding excitement." She was less interested in that than she was in what he'd said about "turned out to be." "You didn't know Gerald Robinson was your uncle?"

"Nope. We didn't know. My father didn't know. There are other half-brothers, too, and they didn't know. None of them knew each other existed. Had no clue that their father, Julius, had been sowing his oats when he was married to Gerald's mom."

"Talk about family secrets."

He made a grunt of agreement.

The distinctive shape of a road sign loomed closer. Salt Lake City, Utah. 530 miles.

"Well, that's useful," Laurel commented as they whizzed past the sign. "What about how many miles to somewhere a little closer?"

His thumb was tapping the steering wheel, keeping time with Johnny Cash's "Ring of Fire" on the radio. "There's bound to be another little town soon."

True. They'd been passing them like tiny gemstones spaced out on a very long gold chain.

"What happened to the chartreuse car?"

His thumb paused. "Sold it after graduation."

It made no sense to feel sad about that. But she did. They passed several more mile markers and she caught herself when her head started nodding. She sat up straighter again, mentally shaking off the clinging drowsiness. "You made it up that you were thinking of the Mona Lisa."

"Nope."

She let out a breath. "What on earth even made you think of a painting like that?"

"First game of Twenty Questions we ever played. It was the object you chose."

Disarmed, she couldn't manage a response to save her life. Instead, she just sat there, blinking.

He slowed then and took an exit. The headlights swept over the sign bearing hotel and food symbols.

As if on cue, her stomach rumbled softly. Hollowly. "Did I win that game?"

He stopped at an intersection and turned where the sign indicated. "You always won."

He sounded vaguely disgruntled over that fact and she bit the inside of her cheek to keep from smiling.

He followed the signs, but it was fully dark by the time they reached the small town of Buckingham, which, despite its grand name, seemed to possess only a single street and a handful of buildings.

"Okaaay," he murmured as they passed a gas station-combination-post-office on one block. Then another block that seemed comprised of ancient storefronts, all of which looked abandoned. The third block was more promising, with a tall Eat Here sign blinking next to the road.

He turned into the driveway and the tires crunched

over gravel. She was surprised at the number of motor-cycles and vehicles lined up in the lot.

"It's a promising sign, right?"

He found a space in the rear of the lot between an ancient pickup truck and four Harleys and he turned off the engine. It ticked slightly. "Or it simply means there's no other option." He got out of the car and headed around to open her door while she was still tying her tennis shoes.

"It's dark," he cautioned when she got out beside him. "And if it turns out to be a biker bar, we're leav-ing."

"Wouldn't you protect me?"

"Always."

Her question had been light.

His answer was flat.

Then his hand settled on the small of her back and warmth bloomed inside her, weeding out the sprouts of unease.

They crossed the gravel and went up two wooden steps where a small deck crammed with tables was full of men and women dressed in leather and riding jackets.

She felt every eye following her and Adam.

She also felt him looming even closer to her and the warmth of his body burned through her blouse.

Then the beefiest of the bikers nodded his head once, making his wiry red hair bounce where it jutted from beneath the bandanna. He offered an unexpected smile. "Evenin'. Welcome to Ed's."

She felt Adam relax, but only slightly. He returned

the greeting, though, and she offered a quick smile before he nudged her through the door with "Ed's" painted by hand on the front of it.

The interior of the establishment was much larger than the deck and was just as crowded. But in addition to bikers, there were several families—one even with a baby in a high chair.

Adam's hand fell away from her spine, while she couldn't tear her eyes away from the baby. Wispy blond hair. Toothless smile as he—she was only assuming that based on the baseball-patterned shirt—waved fat little hands around, scattering the bits of food that were on the tray of his high chair.

What did Linus look like? Did he have baby-soft brown hair like hers? Or did he look like his father? Were his eyes blue? Although, weren't all babies' eyes blue at first?

When she'd been carrying her baby, had she bothered to learn those kinds of things? Or had she been planning how to escape from motherhood altogether?

"Hungry?" Adam's voice drifted over her temple.

She had been. She made herself nod anyway.

Then a harried-looking woman in tight jeans and an even tighter T-shirt waved them to the far corner. "Jen'll be with you in a minute."

They'd just wedged themselves into the chairs on either side of a small table when another woman—younger, but flaunting the same taste in clothes—brought them a laminated menu. "I'm Jen. You'll have t' share this menu. Busy tonight because of the military veterans ride." She pulled a well-used notepad out of her back pocket and poised a chewed pencil over it. "We got beer on tap and wine out of a box. No liquor. Fresh lemonade's gone but we got plenty of tea and soda. What'll it be?"

"Water," Laurel ordered.

"What's on tap?"

Jen seemed to sigh a little but reeled off a bunch of names. "All local brews."

"I'll take the porter."

Without a word, she turned on her heel and walked away.

"Pleasant," Laurel murmured wryly.

"Too many patrons. Not enough staff." Adam angled the menu so they could both look at it, though he seemed to spend more time studying the rest of the customers than the food selections.

"That's right." Her eyes strayed to the baby across the room. Beneath the cacophony of the Rolling Stones on the speakers, voices and the clatter of plates, she imagined she could still hear his babbling chatter. She dragged her attention back to the laminated sheet Adam held. "You said you used to work at a restaurant."

"Still do." The waitress returned and plunked a glass of water with an ice cube bobbing in it on the table and handed him an overflowing mug before unloading the rest of her tray on the table next to them. "I just manage one now." He caught her expression. "What?"

"I don't know." She shook her head slightly. "It doesn't sound quite…right."

"I assure you, it is." He let go of the menu and swiped a long finger across the top of his mug, taking a swath of foam along the way. He flicked it onto the floor that didn't look as though it would suffer greatly, then took a drink. "Pretty good." He sipped again. "Actually, really good."

Tension seemed to ease from his wide shoulders as he set the glass on the postage stamp of a table.

The scent of the hamburgers from the adjacent table tempted Laurel's appetite back to life. She quit looking at the few choices for salads and focused on the considerably wider selection of hot sandwiches. "Feel better?"

"Getting out of the car makes things better. A better-than-decent beer doesn't hurt, either. Give it a try. See what you think."

She shook her head. "I don't drink beer."

He looked up. The lighting inside Ed's didn't provide a great deal of illumination and it cast everyone in a reddish glow. "Since when?"

"Since I—" She broke off, vaguely consternated. "You said that on purpose."

He looked amused and turned his attention back to the menu.

She sat back in her chair and folded her arms. "Maybe that's upsetting to me. Pointing out details I should know."

"But you're not upset," he observed smoothly. "Maybe a little aggravated, but not upset."

She narrowed her eyes and snatched up the glass, taking a quick swig. Fully prepared to dislike it.

Fully chagrined to realize she didn't.

His eyebrow peaked slightly when she set the glass back on the table with a thunk. "Told you."

She huffed and crossed her arms again. "When you're able to tell me something really useful about myself—like why I walked away from my own child and the man I was supposedly going to marry—you let me know."

She was fairly certain he wouldn't have answered even if Jen hadn't returned at that moment with her dog-eared notepad and chewed-up pencil.

"What'll it be?" the girl asked wearily. "Meatloaf special's gone."

"Cheeseburger and side salad, please," Laurel told her.

"Cheeseburger," Adam echoed. "Double meat. Medium."

"It all comes out well done here, handsome."

"Fair enough. Fries any good?"

She lifted her shoulder. "They get the job done."

"Fries, then. Who's Ed?"

"Ed Maxwell? He's the guy who brewed that porter." She swept up the menu.

"Tell him thanks. It's good."

She cracked the faintest of smiles. "Tell him yourself. You had to have passed him on your way in here. Big guy. Flaming red hair." She headed away once more.

"You do that," Laurel realized slowly.

"What?"

"Reach through the—" She waved her hand, searching for the word she wanted. "I don't know. The *fog* surrounding people. They respond to you."

He grimaced slightly. "I obviously kept you in

the car too long today. You're imagining things." He pushed out of his chair. "You going to be okay if I leave you alone for a minute?"

She raised her eyebrows. "I think I can manage to sit here by myself while you go to the little boys' room."

His lips kicked up. "While you wait," he said as he pulled out his phone and handed it to her, "find out if there's any Wi-Fi."

She took the phone. "Because?"

"Once we find a place to crash for the night, we need to figure out how far we can get tomorrow without you getting delusional. Password's zero-nine-two-nine."

She watched him make his way through the close-set tables. Then she sighed faintly and picked up his beer to take another sip.

"You want one of your own?" The waitress returned with a basket of rolls that she set on the table.

Laurel started to refuse but then nodded. "Thank you."

"Food'll be up in a few. Hope your sex-on-a-stick boyfriend hasn't taken a powder."

It wasn't worth correcting Jen that Adam wasn't her boyfriend. The rest of her description was all too accurate. "He'll be back."

Jen set two sets of flatware wrapped in paper napkins on the table. "Heard that before." Evidently, the good humor she'd exhibited for Adam was reserved strictly for him.

Laurel held up the phone. "Do you have Wi-Fi here?"

"*Edsplace*. No spaces. Password is *GUEST*. All

caps." She moved to the table behind Adam's chair, where she began scooping up plates.

Laurel swiped her thumb across the phone screen and entered the password. The navigation app he'd used earlier that day leaped to life. She'd barely entered the Wi-Fi information before notifications started popping up on the screen.

All of them from *Ashley*. All of them accompanied by a tiny image of an obviously pretty blonde.

Laurel quickly set the phone back on the table and grabbed one of the rolls from the basket.

Of course it was too much to think that Adam wouldn't have an Ashley in his life. For all she knew, he had a half dozen Ashleys in his life.

Shoving half the roll in her mouth did nothing at all to take away the bitter taste of that thought.

"What're you frowning about?" Adam asked as he angled himself back into his chair.

She flushed and forced down the wad of bread with a gulp of water. "Nothing," she managed.

But he was already looking at his phone and the messages there. Whatever he read had him frowning, though he set the phone aside when the waitress delivered their food.

Then his lips twitched when he saw the second mug that she also set on the table in front of Laurel.

"Just…hush," she told him severely.

He lifted his broad hands peaceably. "Didn't say a word, sweetheart. Not one word."

Chapter Seven

The town of Buckingham, they learned when Adam paid the bill after they'd consumed the unexpectedly delicious burgers, possessed three different places to rest one's head for the night.

Buckingham Palace—pun intended—was located only a block down from Ed's. Since it was the first one they came to, it was the first one Adam pulled into.

The small parking lot that sat in the center of the U-shaped building was filled with motorcycles. "Doesn't look promising." He left her sitting in the car while he went inside to check for available rooms.

He was back in seconds and they trolled slowly down the street again until they came to the second motel—Buckingham Suites.

"I see a theme going." He parked again in front of the entrance and quickly went inside.

She yawned and rested her head against the window beside her.

It felt like days since Adam had showed up at Fresh Pine with a maple donut for her, when it had really been just that morning.

The car door opened again. "Clerk inside says the veterans bike rally has taken up every room in town. She even called the Buckingham B&B for me to double-check." He pulled on his seat belt, looking annoyed. "I should have stopped in Pendleton even though you were sleeping."

"Sorry."

He gave her a look that felt close despite the fact that it was dark and the only illumination came from the gauges on the dashboard and the moth-besieged fixture over the motel office door. "For what? Dozing off in a car on a boring drive?"

She hadn't found it particularly boring. She kept that thought to herself. She closed her eyes again, resting against the window once more. "So we'll sleep in the car on the side of the road."

"Hell we will. We're not sleeping in this tin can."

"Wouldn't be the first time we slept in a car," she murmured. "The rain that time in the Adirondacks?"

"Flooded the tent." His voice was quiet, nearly drowned out by the music on the radio even though it, too, was soft.

She felt his gaze on her even though her eyes were

closed. His hand brushed over her sleeve, so lightly she wondered if she imagined it.

Then she jerked hard when someone knocked on the window next to her. Startled, she straightened and looked out to see the red-haired biker-brewer Ed hunched over like a great curious bear.

She looked toward Adam. "Did you forget to tip the waitress or something?"

He leaned right across her and pressed the button for the window and the evening air rushed in.

Even though she hollowed herself against the seat behind her, she couldn't get away from the press of Adam's shoulder against hers. She didn't know whether to attribute the adrenaline suddenly pumping through her veins to him or to Ed's unexpected appearance.

"Evenin'." Ed propped a hairy-knuckled paw over the edge of the window as soon as it had lowered a few inches. "Saw your car sitting here. 'Spect you folks are looking for a place to bed down. Not much available with the ride going on this weekend."

"So we've discovered," Adam said. "How far is it to the next town?"

"Forty-seven miles if you keep on this road. Sixty if you head back to the highway. But if you're not real picky, my sister's got a couple rooms she rents out when everything's booked up in town. The Captain's Quarters. Ain't nothing fancy, but she's got the essentials. The beds are small but good."

He jerked his head toward the motel behind him. "They won't tell you none about it in there. Both motels're owned by her ex-husband and the B&B's

owned by his ma. No pressure or nothing. Just wanted to let you know."

His paw moved away from the window to gesture toward the road. "Turn right here. Another mile there's a railroad crossing. Turn left at the street after—it's called Six-Mile but there's no sign anyways—and the only place you'll come to is Sis's. Take a look at the room. If it suits, good deal. If it doesn't, you keep going on Six-Mile another forty miles to Buford. Got a chain motel there. Imagine they can set you and your missus up fine if you don't mind another hour driving on a winding road."

Adam's eyes skated over Laurel's face, then turned back toward Ed. "Thanks for the information." His arm brushed against her breasts when he stuck his hand out through the window. "That was a great porter at your restaurant. You supply any other places besides your own?"

Ed chuckled as he shook Adam's hand. "Nah. Too much work."

"If you change your mind, I manage a new restaurant in Texas." Adam's arm brushed against Laurel again when he took a business card from his wallet that he'd tossed on top of the dashboard. "Have a few rotating taps," he told the other man, passing him the card. "Might be interested in adding one of yours."

Looking genuinely surprised, Ed angled the card up to the light over the motel door. "Provisions," he read. "Where's Rambling Rose?"

"Midpoint between Austin and Houston."

"Huh. Well, that's real flattering, but I dunno. Lotta paperwork involved."

"Just keep it in mind," Adam said easily. "Have you been brewing long?"

Ed barked out a loud guffaw. "Son, I been brewing one thing 'r another since I discovered matches." He tucked the card away in his pocket and his eyes skated over Laurel. "Held you up enough now. Whatever you decide to do about bedding down, drive careful. Had us a real bad collision by the tracks a couple nights ago. Neither driver made it. Mighty shame." With a wave, he stepped away from the car and headed for a gigantic lowrider.

Adam straightened, taking that warmth and that weight away from her.

She shivered.

"What do you think?"

"I'm okay with anything you decide." She fingered the edge of her sleeve.

"Bother you hearing about that accident?"

She shook her head. Though the truth was, she was bothered by so many things at the moment she wasn't sure what took precedence. The reminder of her own accident—which she couldn't recall herself; the startlingly vivid image she had of a pouring rainstorm, a leaking tent, and a car with the windows steamed; or the knowledge that Adam's weight against her was achingly, desperately familiar.

"The Captain's Quarters, then." He put the car in gear. "If it's a fleabag, we'll drive to Buford."

She cleared her throat. "Fine."

He turned right out of the parking lot and left the town behind them before they reached the train tracks. Ed had been accurate with his description. If there was any sign marking the intersection that followed the tracks, it was too dark to tell.

It was so dark, in fact, that it felt like they were driving into a void when he turned again. No oncoming cars headed toward them. No flickering light came from houses or farms off in the distance. The headlights swept over the curving road. Not even a white line bisected the center. "Do you get the feeling we're heading into our own horror movie?"

"I get the feeling if the Captain's Quarters doesn't have the lights turned on, we're never going to see it."

She reached into the back seat to retrieve her cardigan and pulled it on.

"You're not actually scared, are you?"

Not of the Captain's Quarter's. "You told me yourself I get cold at the drop of a hat."

"Could be ninety degrees but if a breeze blew, you'd get goose bumps. How you ever survived competing at Oozefest, I'll never know. First year we did it, it was pouring rain on top of it."

"Three layers of everything. Thermals. Socks." And duct tape to keep from losing anything critical—like pants or shirts—along the way. She'd seen both happen. And after the first time she'd participated in the muddy event, she'd learned it was easiest for her outer layer to be something she could dispose of entirely.

The road curved again and a brightly lit two-story house came into view. "Suppose that's it?" She tried not to draw comparisons between it and the *Amityville Horror* house.

"Ed said it was the first place we'd come to."

"There's the turnoff." She pointed. He was already slowing and turned onto the paved drive.

The house was further away than it had seemed at first but when Adam finally rolled to a stop beside it, they could see a separate building situated several yards behind it.

"You coming in or you want to wait?"

She pushed open her car door in answer and climbed out. He joined her and they headed toward the door on the side of the house.

Laurel shivered and stepped closer to Adam, sliding her arm through his. "I know. Evidently on top of everything else, I'm a ninny."

He chuckled softly and pulled his arm away but only to close his hand around hers. Then he knocked on the door.

It opened a second later to a face that looked just like Ed's set atop an equally sturdy woman. "I'm Sis," she greeted in a booming voice. Even her wiry red hair seemed to rattle. "Ed warned me someone might stop by. You're here about my Captain's Quarters, right?"

"Yes, ma'am."

She beamed and stepped out of the door. "Where you folks headin' to?"

"Texas."

"Got a long way to go. I'll show you the room. Only have the one available tonight 'cause of the veterans ride." She walked fast, her long stride eating up the distance to the building behind the house.

It was a long, narrow single story. "Advantage for you, though," she said over her shoulder, "is that the room's at the end of the block so to speak. When all the bikers start rolling in tonight, the noise shouldn't disturb you too much."

They passed four windows. Four doors that each had a plain light fixture hanging atop the sill. Presumably that meant four rooms. At the end of the building, Sis rounded the corner and stopped at the lone door there. It opened without a key and she reached in to turn on a light switch before moving out of their way. "Go on in and take a look. Price for all my rooms is the same. Thirty-nine dollars."

Both Laurel and Adam stopped midstep, giving her a surprised look.

"I know." Sis gave an apologetic shrug. "Had to raise it five bucks last year 'cause of the new roof I needed." Then she gave them a bright smile. "But I got a little buffet breakfast I throw in now, too, to help make up for it. Served on the covered patio at the back of the house starting at 6:00 a.m."

Gone were the *Amityville Horror* notions. There was something too engaging about the rawboned woman. "Sounds perfect," Laurel said before she could stop herself. She hadn't even looked inside the room yet.

Adam, on the other hand, had one foot in the room and one foot out. "There's only one—"

"I'm tired." She cut him off knowing that he'd been going to say *bed*. But it was time to be practical and she knew instinctively that he'd choose protective over practical. As if they couldn't occupy a single mattress at the same time.

During dinner he'd planned the route for the next day and she knew it would be a long one. The sooner he could get a decent night of sleep, the sooner they could be on their way in the morning. "And I know you're tired, too. But our choices are here, the car or another hour's drive." And she would have bet her right arm that they wouldn't find anywhere else down the road for such a bargain.

He didn't look quite as convinced as she felt but he gave a capitulating shrug and looked at Sis. "We'll take it. Cash okay?"

"Better 'n okay. Just need to take a picture of your driver's license." She waited while he pulled out his wallet. "I sure do miss the days when I could just have folks sign the register. But a person's gotta protect their interests, you know?" She took his license when he extracted it and snapped a picture of it with her cell phone, then handed it back. The two twenty-dollar bills that Adam gave her were folded in half and tucked down the front of her blouse. "I'll be back with your receipt and change."

"Don't worry about it."

Sis frowned. "Dollar's a dollar in this day and age, hon." She handed him a key hanging from a large plastic diamond-shaped ring. "Don't you forget breakfast, either. My brother might be the best brewmaster around these parts, but this ol' gal makes the best cranberry muffins this side of Portland."

With a little wave, she strode off around the corner and disappeared from sight.

Feeling vaguely winded, Laurel looked at Adam. "Did she exhaust you, too?"

His low chuckle rumbled tantalizingly over her nerve endings. He handed her the room key. "Go inside. I'll get the car." A small gravel area clearly meant for parking was on the other side of the cracked cement walkway. What lay beyond the gravel was anyone's guess. The night absorbed the light like a sponge before the gravel ended.

She went inside and pushed the door closed. For $39 a night, she wouldn't have been surprised if they'd have needed to shove a chair under the knob. But in addition to the dead bolt there was a very sturdy-looking safety latch.

The room wasn't large. In fact, it was smaller than small. The entirety of it was visible in one glance, which was probably the reason for the Captain's Quarters moniker.

The giant in the Lilliputian space was definitely the bed.

One side was pushed all the way against the wall. At the foot, there was just enough room to walk between the mattress and the wooden desk topped by a tiny fridge. Above that was an even smaller microwave and a one-cup coffee maker. When she slid out the single desk drawer, it contained a Bible and a bottle opener.

She pushed the drawer closed to continue the exploration.

On the side of the bed not pushed against the wall,

there was slightly more room to reach the recess, which possessed a closet rod on one side and a sink basin on the other. A second recess, separated from the first by the small flat-screen TV mounted on the wall, had a similar footprint. A toilet behind one folding door and across from it, a tub-shower combination behind another folding door. White towels hung from pegs on the bit of wall straight ahead of her. Maybe a foot and a half separated the folding door on the right from the one on the left.

There wasn't an inch of space to spare and the way the bathroom fixtures were separated was a head-scratcher, but Ed hadn't exaggerated about his sister's establishment. The room did possess the essentials.

With nowhere else to look, Laurel finally studied the bed.

A patchwork quilt covered the top and an additional blanket sat folded in the middle of it. At the head, four pillows in white cases were stacked two high beneath a window covered by a plain brown curtain.

Nothing was new. But everything looked and smelled spotlessly clean.

She placed the key on the desk. Then, because she couldn't imagine what might fit inside such a small refrigerator except a takeout container, she opened the door.

Three label-less beer bottles sat inside.

She smiled faintly. She had no doubt the contents had been brewed by Ed. And the beer explained the church key sitting in the drawer next to the Bible.

She heard the car and quickly went into the one cube

of a room to use the toilet. She was just washing her hands in the sink when Adam came in with her canvas tote bag and his overnighter.

He set both on the desk and closed the door.

The sound of the dead bolt and the safety latch snapping into place seemed very loud.

Then his dark gaze landed on her. "Well?"

She realized all of the towels were in the other closet by the shower, but there wasn't enough room for her to get to it with him standing where he was. "Well?"

He looked toward the bed.

She wasn't going to blush. But telling herself that didn't stop her cheeks from feeling warm.

She swiped her wet hands on the seat of her jeans. "This isn't a big deal." She managed the words she'd rehearsed in her mind in a creditably calm tone. "We're adults." He had an Ashley who texted him ten times a day and she had a baby and whatever mess existed between her and the baby's father. "There are plenty of pillows to put between us. Me on one side. You on the other."

"A very proper arrangement." His voice dripped irony.

She pressed her lips together. Her hands still felt wet. "All of the towels are on the other side."

His eyebrows rose but he moved three steps toward the head of the bed. "I see." He held a towel out to her and while she listened to him sliding one door and then the other, she finished drying her hands.

"Weird setup," he said a moment later. "Tight as hell, but it's better than the car."

"That was my thinking." She folded the towel over the edge of the sink then sidled over to sit on the foot of the bed.

Now that she'd seen the shower, she realized she wanted one in the worst way. She pulled the tote onto her lap and rummaged inside it for her toiletries and realized as she did so that her nightgown was still hanging on the bathroom hook at Fresh Pine.

It wasn't that she cared deeply about the nightgown. But it did mean she'd have to wear one of her shirts to sleep in.

"You can take the shower first." His words broke the uncomfortable silence.

She looked over at him. He'd brushed aside the curtain and was looking out the window.

But since it was dark outside and light in, she knew all he would see was the reflection of the room behind him.

Adults, she reminded herself. With nearly a decade between the present and when they had dated.

With a T-shirt clenched in one hand and clean panties balled in the other, she slipped into the shower.

When she pulled the folding door closed, there was barely enough room to turn around and reach the faucet to turn on the water. She should have done it before closing the door.

From beyond the thin, pleated plastic panels, she heard the television. He was flipping channels.

The prosaic noise helped mask the incredible awkwardness she felt.

With some bumping of elbows and knees, she succeeded in undressing, only to realize she still needed the towel. She opened the door just enough to stick out her arm. "Can you hand me the towel again?"

A second later, it was pushed into her palm.

"Thank you." She pulled the door closed again.

She draped her clean shirt and underwear on the wall hook, then turned on the faucet and flipped the lever for the shower, tugging the flowered curtain into place. The tub wasn't very large, but it still looked inviting. And if Adam weren't three feet away on the other side of a wall and a vague excuse for a door, she'd use it.

But he was, so she didn't.

The water quickly turned hot and she got in.

She couldn't keep from groaning a little as the needling spray rained over her.

Two small bottles sat in the soap niche along with a paper-wrapped bar of soap and a plastic-wrapped disposable razor. Nothing was remotely spa quality, but she didn't care. She washed her hair, and then, because the water was still running hot and strong, did it again just for the sheer pleasure of it.

At Fresh Pine, the water had always run lukewarm after three minutes.

But aware of Adam still waiting for his turn, she made herself finish.

She dried off while standing in the tub, and since it offered the most real estate in the confined space, she pulled on her clean shirt and underwear there, too.

She rubbed as much water from her hair as the towel would take, then wrapped it around her shoulders before opening the accordion door.

Cooler air immediately accosted her and she clutched the ends of the towel together in front of her as she took the only step needed to leave the cube. "All yours." She didn't look at him as she scooted to the foot of the bed and pulled her tote onto her lap once again. "You won't have any room to turn around in there unless you're standing in the tub, but the water's good and hot."

He made an indecipherable sound and tossed the remote on the bed.

She pressed the towel to her face when she heard the door closing and let out a long, shaking breath.

Then, because she had no idea how long he would take, she rapidly brushed her teeth at the sink and combed her hair. She left the towel once more draped over the edge of the sink.

She couldn't imagine him wanting to sleep against the wall, so she made the executive decision to take that side of the bed. Chills bumping all over her skin, she flung the quilt toward the wall and left the folded blanket for him, arranged two pillows down the center of the mattress and crawled into the bed.

She'd just arranged the quilt over herself when she heard a loud thump and a louder curse from the shower. "I warned you." Then she turned on her side to face the wall.

The sheets were cold but the quilt was warm and she yawned so hugely her face felt like it could split. With the TV news accompanying the sound of rushing water, she closed her eyes and snuggled into the pillow.

Staying there had definitely been the right choice.

Chapter Eight

Staying here was the stupidest thing he'd ever done.

Adam eyed the quilt-covered bump lying between a dam of pillows and the wall. Laurel was entirely still, but until he turned down the television and heard the faint rasp of her deep breaths, he wasn't entirely convinced she was asleep.

He still didn't know why he'd gone along with her decision to stay here.

It damn sure wasn't the bargain-basement room rate. He wasn't rolling in dough but he could swing a few nights in a chain hotel.

Moving as quietly as he could, he pulled his shaving kit from his duffel and brushed his teeth. He left the electric razor inside the leather pack.

Unlike Laurel, who'd packed the entire contents of

her closet—meager though that was—he'd left Texas with only one change of clothes.

It occurred to him that Sis might have laundry facilities she let her lodgers use, but he wasn't going to go back up to the house to ask her. She was already charging too little for the room, even considering its quirkiness. He'd worked in more than a few hotels over the years. He wasn't sure how she managed to stay in business charging such a low rate.

With Laurel sound asleep, he checked his phone again for new messages. He'd already dealt with Ashley's texts regarding the problem she was having with one of Provisions' new suppliers.

Dealing with a simple enough work problem, though, hadn't done a hell of a lot to keep him distracted from the fact that Laurel had been in the shower. Nude. Flowing water making her limbs slick and—

He grimaced. Pushing away the thought wasn't easy. How many times had she slipped into their shower after he'd gotten home from his shift at The Yard?

Now, here they were in a room that was smaller than the bedroom had been in that tiny apartment they'd shared.

He'd obviously lost his freaking mind.

If he had any sense at all, he'd sleep on the floor. But after hours of driving, his back couldn't handle it.

He didn't have any new messages. He hoped that meant things were more or less stable where Linus was concerned.

He rubbed the back of his neck and turned off the television and the light. The room plunged into unrelieved darkness and he carefully sat on the side of the bed. Every cell in his body was attuned to the woman sleeping on the other side of the pillows.

She didn't so much as twitch.

He slowly eased himself down. His feet hung off the end of the bed and his shoulder hit the pillow she'd set in the middle. It felt like he'd landed in some screwball scene from one of the old black-and-white movies his mom loved.

He reached up and swiped the curtain aside. Moonlight shafted brightly through the window, but it was better than trying to sleep with a curtain that was exactly the right length to hit him on his nose.

He closed his eyes. He was tired down in his bones. He supposed it could still be the lingering effect of the bone marrow harvest. But far more likely the reason was the woman sleeping next to him.

He lifted his arm above his head, trying to find more room for himself, but his knuckles hit the wall and Laurel murmured something indecipherable. Beyond the reach of the stupid pillows, he felt her foot graze his calf.

She'd always started out bundled in a ball. And she'd always ended up sprawled all over him. Silky hair splaying over his chest. Silky legs tangled with his.

There weren't many days back then that they hadn't begun by making love.

He curled his fingers into a fist as his body stirred.

He really wasn't strong enough for this.

Swearing under his breath, he kicked the folded blanket off the side of the bed and followed it.

Yeah. Driving back to Texas had been a really brilliant idea.

* * *

The wall got in the way of her elbow and Laurel opened her eyes.

Sunlight streamed through the window above her head.

She couldn't believe it. She'd actually slept the entire night through. Not one nightmare. Not one gut-wrenching attack of pure panic that kept her awake for hours and hours and hours.

The other side of the bed was silent. The pillows she'd arranged in the middle of the bed were still there, though slightly askew now.

She lifted her head to peek over them, but the stretch of smooth white sheet only confirmed what she already knew.

Adam wasn't there.

Both of the accordion doors were open. Spaces beyond unoccupied. Nor was he standing in the other alcove at the sink.

He'd probably gone to sample Sis's cranberry muffins.

Which was a relief. They could avoid more of the awkwardness of the night before.

She unwound the quilt from her legs and rolled across the mattress, sliding off the bed.

But her feet didn't encounter the expected floor, and she jumped back, screeching instinctively. "What on—"

Adam sat up, blinking blearily. "What's wrong?"

His dark hair was rumpled and spiked and boyishly endearing.

But that was the only thing about him that was boyish.

From the dark blur of whiskers that didn't do a lick to soften his chiseled jaw to the very, *very* bare torso, he was nothing but all man.

She quickly looked away but still felt as if the sight would be seared on her brain for life. Particularly the long fingers he'd spread over the hard abdomen that she'd nearly trod upon.

She took refuge in tartness. "What on earth are you doing down there?"

"I *was* sleeping," he muttered and planted one hand on the mattress to lever himself upward. But he stopped abruptly and sank back down, looking even more disgruntled. He clawed his fingers through his hair and raked his palm down his face. When he looked up again, his dark eyes were more alert. "What time is it?"

"How would I know?"

"I see you're still sweetness and light when you first roll out of bed in the morning."

She opened her mouth to deny it, but nothing came out. Mostly because her addled brain realized the implication behind his words. "What do you know about my mood when I first roll out of bed? You said we weren't serious."

His dark eyes were suddenly shuttered. "That's right." He rolled to his feet, the blanket bunched in front of him. "If you were on the way to the bathroom, get to it."

She flushed and nearly obeyed. But she wanted to remember her life. Which meant facing questions she was afraid of asking. And the sooner, the better. "We slept together, didn't we?"

His lips compressed as though he didn't want to answer. And she was more convinced than ever that "not serious" had been on his part, alone.

"Often?" she prodded.

A noise from outside the window drew his attention and he yanked on the curtain, sending the hooks careening back across the window. "You want a number?"

Her stomach dipped and swayed. Cowardice toppled her spurt of bravery. She shook her head and looked away, sliding rapidly off the bed.

But she didn't make the two steps required before reaching the paltry privacy of an accordion door, because as soon as her feet hit the ground, Adam swore and caught her hand.

The jagged scar he was staring at wound from her inner wrist, over her forearm and up to her elbow. It was red and ugly. How could he be anything but repulsed?

She yanked her hand free and shut herself into the toilet room.

She was shaking.

"Laurel."

She slapped her hand against the door, holding it firm. "Leave me alone."

"Laurel—"

"I said leave me alone!" She could hear the tears in her voice as surely as they burned her eyes.

He was silent. But she knew he was standing on the

other side of the plastic door. Imagined she could feel the very beat of his heart.

He'd been nothing but kind to her. While she felt barely in control of her life.

"Ten minutes," he said quietly and she felt him walk away.

She heard rustling.

The slide of the dead bolt on the room's door.

And then silence. Real silence.

Tension drained out of her, leaving her feeling dizzy and weak.

Moving as slowly as if she were a hundred years old, she used the toilet and stepped across the square of carpet to close herself in with the shower. She reached out to turn on the faucet, her eyes on her left arm.

It might have been her right arm she'd broken in the accident. But it was the left that had been torn to pieces by jagged metal.

She should have worn a long-sleeved blouse to sleep in. He'd never have seen it, then. *She* didn't like seeing the scar and she lived with it.

She undressed, then stepped into the tub, turning her face up to the water. This time, though, the needle-like spray felt punishing. Cold.

When she stepped out, she realized she'd once again forgotten the towel.

Naturally.

She pulled open the accordion and stepped out.

Adam was sitting, fully dressed, on the bed. He extended the towel he was holding.

Mortified right to her marrow in her bones, she

snatched it away and whipped it around her torso. "So much for ten minutes!"

"It's been twenty," he said quietly.

"And it's still despicable." She grabbed her clothes and brushed past his knees, turning into the sink area. In the cold light of day, the floorplan felt even more ridiculous. "You could have turned your back at least."

"I could have."

She grabbed her toothbrush and toothpaste, her teeth set on edge all the more by his calm agreement.

"You were forever forgetting your towel when we lived together."

Mint-scented green gel spurted all over the white sink.

She slowly looked up at her reflection in the mirror. She opened her mouth to say something but closed it again because her brain had gone blank.

"We were seniors in college."

She realized she'd squeezed the tube in her hand right in half. Swallowing, she fit the cap in place with shaking fingers. "And a-after college?"

"I told you."

"Separate paths," she whispered. When she'd taken a fellowship in Europe. An idea that felt so deeply foreign to her that she couldn't even fathom it. She thought of the sketch pad filled with his image. "Was I in love with you?" The words were out before she thought to stop them.

"No."

The frown between her eyebrows paralleled her scar.

She finally looked away from her reflection and over her shoulder to meet his eyes.

Then what an utter fool she'd been.

He shifted and lifted the paper plate that she hadn't even noticed sitting beside him on the bed. "Sis didn't exaggerate about them."

She noticed the fat muffin studded with crimson cranberries.

She turned so she could reach for the plate with her right hand rather than her left and something in his eyes flickered. "You don't have to hide your scars from me, Laurel."

Her fingers curled and she pulled back. "They're ugly."

"Nothing about you has ever been ugly. Not back then. And not now." He set the plate down on the bed again and nodded toward a cup on the desk. "There wasn't any hibiscus tea, but I brought you what Sis did have." He rose and picked up his overnighter. "I'm putting this in the car. When you're ready, we'll go back and have something more substantial than a muffin. We have a long road ahead of us."

He left, closing the door again quietly behind him.

That long road, she knew, was made of a lot more than simple miles.

They crossed from Oregon into Idaho by midmorning and stopped for lunch a few hours after that at a restaurant overlooking the Snake River in Twin Falls.

Neither one of them brought up what had occurred in the Captain's Quarters.

Instead, they talked about the passing landscape, which was, admittedly, something to talk about. They talked about the weather and what both of them recalled from school about the Oregon Trail.

And the more they circled around what happened that morning before cranberry muffins and homemade sausage and fluffy scrambled eggs and Sis pressing Adam's receipt and his one dollar of change into Laurel's hand before they left, the more it hung in Laurel's mind.

The weekend traffic was heavy when they reached Salt Lake City, Utah. And even though Adam had planned to make it further south of the city before they quit for the night, he pulled off the road and into a hotel while the city's freeways were still packed with traffic.

The hotel had several stories and several wings and a near-empty parking lot.

She knew there wouldn't be any need this time to head down the road in search of alternate lodgings.

He went inside the characterless entrance and returned with a map of the facility and a key card tucked inside a small envelope. "Fourth floor." He handed both to her. "Other end of the right wing."

She folded the map in half, sharpening the crease while he moved the car to a parking spot near the grassy strip separating the parking lot from a chain fence overlooking the freeway below.

He pulled their bags from the back seat and they headed for the glass door at the end of the wing. She slid the key into the security lock and heard it release just when Adam's cell phone rang.

He glanced at it as he pulled open the door. "Head on up. I need to get this."

She nodded and went inside.

"Hey, Ashley," she heard him answer as the door swung closed again.

She chewed the inside of her cheek and forced her feet to continue along the carpeted hallway. She followed the signs to the elevator and went up to the fourth floor. When she unfolded the little envelope, she saw the room number was written on the inside flap and she followed more signs along another carpeted hallway.

The room was at the very end and she realized the lot where they'd parked was right below. Adam was walking slowly along the grassy strip, the phone at his ear.

Her child wasn't the only one waiting in Texas.

He had an Ashley waiting there, too.

She sighed, stuck the key in the door lock, and went inside the room. The door swung closed behind her with a soft *snick*.

Tastefully furnished in neutral colors with two queen-size beds, the room was three times the size of the Captain's Quarters and had none of its character.

Feeling adrift, she dropped the keycard on the dresser and rubbed her arms. Despite her cardigan she was chilled.

When she heard the knock on the door, she swiftly pulled it open.

"Here." Adam handed her her canvas bag. "There's a restaurant downstairs when you're feeling hungry for supper."

"Okay." Her voice sounded faint even to her own

ears. She opened the door wider, stepping back so he could enter, but he held up his hand.

He was holding another little envelope with a key card inside. "I'm next door," he said.

It should have been relief that pumped through her stomach, then. "Okay," she said, even fainter than before.

He gave her a close look. "I figured you'd prefer some privacy."

She made herself nod.

He took a step back, one foot still in the room, one foot out. "There's a connecting door."

She automatically looked and saw there was, indeed, a locked door on the side of the room next to the closet.

Again, she made herself nod.

She knew she had to be imagining what seemed to be hesitancy on his part to actually leave the room.

"I'll be fine," she said more forcefully. She gestured toward the bathroom where all of the fixtures were conveniently located in one space. "Big bathtub. Can't wait."

His gaze shifted to the side, as if confirming the fact that there was, indeed, a big bathtub. "Knock on the door when you're ready to eat."

She hugged her arms again and nodded.

Finally seeming satisfied, he removed his foot from her doorway and it swung closed, leaving her alone.

Her shoulders sagged.

She turned and looked at the two beds. The connecting door.

"You should be glad, Laurel."

Why wasn't she?

She reached up to the thermostat on the wall and turned the temperature up several notches.

Then she sat down on the bed closest to it.

She bounced slightly. Stood and turned around to sit on the second.

It was identical to the first.

And despite the long hours in the car, the many miles they'd traveled that day, she wasn't the least bit inclined to rest. The television held no interest, though she made a stab by flipping through every station it offered. And the big bathtub most certainly could wait until later.

She got up again and tucked the key card in her back pocket and left the room. She was proud of the way her footsteps barely slowed when she passed the room next to hers. Not so proud of the gnawing thought that he was probably on the phone again to his pretty blonde Ashley.

When she'd taken the elevator earlier, she'd seen the signs pointing out the direction of the pool, the fitness center and the guest laundry. She bypassed them all for the complimentary business center.

Once inside, she was alone with the three computers situated against each wall.

She sat at the first one and made a small sound when she noticed the Robinson Tech insignia on the monitor. The screen leaped to vibrant life when she touched the mouse, and she opened the internet browser and began typing.

She wasn't sure exactly what she hoped to find.

She searched *Rambling Rose, Texas*, and found a

simple municipal website featuring a photo of a very attractive woman. Ellie Hernandez Fortune. Mayor.

Good for you, Ellie.

She poked the mouse and the mayor's image disappeared. She skimmed a few blog posts about activities around town. An ice cream social at a medical center. Something called Mariana's Market featuring live music and a new food truck. She even read through the notice of an upcoming town council meeting.

She tucked her hands between her knees, staring blindly at the screen while her pulse ramped up. She hadn't come down here to look up Rambling Rose. Pretending otherwise was just more cowardice.

She swallowed hard and set her hands back on the keyboard. She added more terms to her search and hit the mouse again. The results were so immediate that she snatched her hands away and stared at the picture of Eric Johnson. A much larger picture of him than the one that had been in the video.

A link to an article titled "Museum Benefactor and Business Owner Shows Philanthropic Side" accompanied the image.

She warily probed the nervousness tightening her chest but decided it was no worse now than it had been when she sat down at the computer.

His hair was brown. Shades and shades lighter than Adam's. Lighter than her own, really. Less Van Dyke brown, more raw umber. His eyes were gray and seemed to have a cool shrewdness to them.

He was a business owner, she reasoned. Shouldn't a business owner be shrewd?

She touched the mouse again, opening up the link beneath the headline. She expected an article about his philanthropy. She ended up at the website for his trucking company named JLI.

She started to close the browser but stopped. She'd been engaged to marry the man. He was the father of her child. She tucked her hands between her knees again and made herself read more but after ten minutes, she felt like her eyes were crossing. Logistics and supply chains and warehouse solutions were about as interesting as watching mud dry.

She closed the JLI site and then, feeling like she was sneaking into places she didn't belong, she typed *Adam Fortune.* Then *Provisions.*

She ended up with a bunch of results for someone's obituary in Florida.

She added the word *Ashley*, which didn't change the results in the least.

She sighed and propped her elbow on the table next to the keyboard. Then she typed in *Constance Silberman Doing Good* and the familiar video bloomed to life. But she couldn't make it all the way through the video.

Not anymore. Not knowing that she was the baby's mother. Was it her fault he'd gotten sick?

Delete, delete, delete.

She ferociously jabbed the key repeatedly until all of her search words disappeared, leaving her back at the Rambling Rose municipal site.

She clicked on the ice cream social link and recognized the doctor in the picture as the same one from the Silberman video. Below the announcement for the social was a stream of comments that updated even as she read through a few.

Another chance for me to make a glutton of myself, one person posted, with a smiley face after it. Can't wait!

Smiling slightly, Laurel scrolled further down the screen.

And then her smile died.

Chapter Nine

Adam knocked on the connecting door again. And for the third time, he got no answer at all.

He'd given her an hour since the second knock. In case she was in the bathtub.

But even if she were, he'd never known her to soak in bubbles that long. Because she got too pruny, she'd always said.

He knocked more sharply, trying to curtail the gnawing inside him. "Laurel."

Still nothing. When he pressed his ear against the connecting door, the only thing he could hear was the mumbling drone of the television.

He shouldn't have left her alone. He should have sucked it up and given some excuse about needing to share a room again, no matter how many more sleepless nights he added onto his life as a result.

He palmed his room key and left the room. He went to her door and pounded to no avail, then wheeled around and strode down the hall and around the corner, nearly plowing into the housekeeping cart that sat there.

Seizing the opportunity, he glanced into the room next to the cart and spotted the uniformed girl inside.

"Excuse me." When she looked up with a start from the pillow she was fluffing, he managed a friendly smile. "Sorry to startle you." He jerked his head. "I locked myself out of my room. You wouldn't by chance be able to let me in?"

She was shaking her head before he even finished. "You'll have to go to registration to get another key."

One part of him was glad she wasn't going to be so easily talked into opening up a guest room. But another part was aggravated. All he wanted to do was verify in the most expedient way possible whether Laurel was in her room.

If she were, and was refusing to respond for some reason, that was problem enough. If she weren't, then he needed to find her. He wasn't going to let her disappear on him again.

"Look." He offered a chagrined laugh. "You don't even have to let me in. Just look inside and tell me—" he thought fast "—if I left my cell phone sitting on the bed."

She returned to the heavily loaded cart and reached up to the top of the folded towels stacked higher than her head and when she did, he realized she was pregnant.

He raised his hand, oath-like. "I'll stand at the end of the hall in full view of the security cameras. It's just—well, the thing is my girlfriend went into labor a few hours ago in Texas and I haven't been thinking straight since." He spread his palms. "I just want to know if the phone's there or if I forgot it at the meeting I was at. She'll be calling me, you know?" He waited a beat. "Please?"

Her lips compressed. But he could tell by the way her shoulders softened that she was going to do it even before she nodded.

"Room four-three-two," he told her quickly.

She tucked her hands into the patch pockets of her uniform tunic and quickly headed around the corner.

He followed until he stood in the middle of the adjoining corridors where experience told him the security camera would be focused. When she reached the end of the hallway and glanced back at him once more, he spread his hands. "Staying right here," he promised.

She knocked on Laurel's door, waited a moment for some response and then used her passkey to enter. She emerged a second later, pulling the door closed behind her. She shook her head at him as she approached.

"No phone on the bed," she told him.

And obviously no Laurel, either, he concluded. "Thanks." He took the corner in a hurry, aiming for the elevator. The maid headed the same way, pushing the cumbersome cart.

Laurel had no money. No identification. If she left the hotel, how far could she get?

His gut churned with the possibilities, and none of them was good.

He'd go straight to the security office. He'd paid for both rooms. The same security cameras that might have captured Laurel leaving the hotel were the ones that had seen them entering together. He figured his chances were about even whether they'd be helpful to him.

"Is it your first?"

The housekeeper's question interrupted the plan he was mapping out inside his head and he glanced back at her.

He thought of Linus. The baby who had Adam's bone marrow flowing in his system. Who also had Adam's DNA at his core. The baby he'd never even held or touched.

"Yeah." His voice sounded gruff.

"Everything'll be fine," she told him kindly, coming abreast with him. She patted the small mound at her waist. "My second."

"Congratulations." He could see the elevator now. Right beside a door with the word Housekeeping printed on a small oval plaque.

"It ought to get easier." She sounded breathless. "But my husband is as much a wreck this time as he was the first."

Adam hadn't had an opportunity to be a wreck the first time. He knew there wouldn't be an opportunity to be a wreck the second time, either.

He heard the soft ping of an arriving elevator. "Are you headed there?" He pointed to the Housekeeping door.

"Yes."

He closed his hand over the cart.

"Sir, there's no need—"

"I owe you." He pushed the cart close enough to the door that all she'd have to do was nudge it through once she'd unlocked it. "Thanks for checking the room," he told her just as the elevator doors began sliding open.

A slender virago shot out of the car before he reached it, and Laurel nearly skidded to a halt on the carpet when she spotted him. *"You!"*

That first jolt of pure relief he felt nosedived into abject alarm. Her features were twisted as she hovered there on the balls of her smiley-faced tennis shoes. He started to reach for her. "Laurel, sweetheart, what's—"

She suddenly launched herself at him and shoved him so hard, he nearly fell back.

He heard the housekeeper's gasp.

"Why didn't you tell me!" Laurel's voice was high. Thick with tears. She raised her hands again and he caught her wrists before she could unleash the second attack. "You should have told me the truth about the baby!"

Then she suddenly crumpled against him, crying against his chest.

The kindness in the housekeeper's face had disappeared. She gave him a searing look as she wheeled her cart through the door. "Two-timer. Shame on you," she hissed before the door closed between them.

Adam carefully wrapped his arms around Laurel's heaving shoulders.

Her hands were fists between them. "I didn't

l-leave him with his fa-ather," she hiccupped. "I just *left* h-h-him!"

He closed his eyes, swearing inside.

He should have told her. But he'd still had three days left to figure out how.

"Why?" She took no notice as he began backtracking along the hallway, trying to get her to walk with him, but her feet only dragged. He swung her into his arms and carried her swiftly back to his room.

"Why did I do such a h-horrible thing?" Her face was buried against his neck and she pounded her fist on his back.

If pounding on him made her feel better, he'd take it. "We'll figure it out," he said huskily, though he had no idea how. He had to set her down long enough to unlock his room, which first entailed unwrapping her fisted arms. Not an easy task when she was clinging so tightly. "Come on, sweetheart—"

"Figure out what?" She was beyond logic, her breath a constant wheeze as she cried and swung out wildly again. "That I'm a monster?"

He caught her wrists before she hurt herself and shoved open the door with his foot, carrying her around the waist to get her inside. "You're not a monster."

"What else is a mother who abandons her own child?"

"A woman who obviously believed she had no other choice." The door swung closed behind them, latching hard. "And you didn't abandon him. You left him at a place you trusted to keep him safe." He cautiously set her free. "How did you find out?"

"So you knew. You really knew." Her eyes were ravaged. She was trembling wildly and she wrapped her arms around herself, backing all the way across the room to the window overlooking the freeway. "And you said *nothing*!"

He raked his fingers through his hair. He'd never done well with feeling helpless. He wanted to slam his fist into something. He wanted to find a way to take away her pain and there wasn't one damn thing he could do to make that happen. "Laurel." He kept his voice steady. "How did you find—"

"The internet," she practically screamed.

They both jerked when someone pounded on the door. "Mr. Fortune, please open the door immediately or we'll enter without your help."

Laurel covered her face with her hands, sinking down into a ball right there against the wall next to the window. She'd gone from screaming to crying, and great wrenching sobs shook her too-narrow shoulders, ripping right through Adam's soul.

He jerked the door open. "What the hell—"

A hotel security guard and a female police officer stood on the other side. "Please move aside, sir," the officer said brusquely. Her hand rested on her her billy club.

He backed away. "What—"

"A disturbance was reported." The guard's tone was flat. He stepped in front of Adam, as if he intended to block him if necessary. "Ma'am," he called above Laurel's sobs, "are you all right?"

"Does she look all right?" Adam asked between his

teeth. He was a foot taller than the guard. He could have easily pushed him out of the way, but knew he'd only exacerbate the situation if he did. "She's upset. She's had a shock."

The officer was approaching Laurel.

"Let's move out into the hallway, sir."

"You don't understand—"

"*You* don't understand," the guard returned, looking combative. "Hallway. Now."

Muttering an oath, Adam moved into the doorway. One foot in the hall, one foot not. "This is as far as I go, buddy. I'm not leaving her."

The police officer was crouched next to Laurel now. Whatever she was saying was too low for Adam to hear.

"Yeah, I've seen your type," the guard said. "Think you can keep a woman against her will—"

"I'm not keeping her against her will!"

"We'll see about that, won't we?"

The police officer had risen again and was crossing the room toward them. "She says she's here voluntarily, but she has no identification."

"Right, because she—"

"Sir, you'd best keep your mouth shut," the guard cut him off pugnaciously. "And of course she's gonna say that. She's been terrorized—"

"She has *not* been terrorized," Adam said through his teeth. "Not by me."

"You'd say that, wouldn't you?"

"For the love of—" Adam reached for his wallet and the guard slammed his arm across Adam's chest, pinning him back against the door of the room.

"Now's not the time for sudden moves," the guard warned.

The door handle dug painfully into Adam's back. "And now's not the time for you to be enjoying your job so much," he warned in return.

Laurel was no longer crying hysterically. Her head was buried in her arms, resting on her raised knees. If she was aware of what was happening in the doorway of the hotel room, she wasn't showing it.

He looked toward the police officer, hoping for more reason from her than the guard. "Her name is Laurel Hudson," he said evenly. "She doesn't have identification because it was destroyed in an accident nearly six months ago."

The guard snorted disbelievingly. "Who're you trying to kid?"

Adam ignored him and the damn handle digging into his back and kept his focus on the police officer. "Her doctor's name is Mariel Granger," he said steadily. "She'll confirm what I'm telling you. She's in Seattle, at Fresh Pine Rehabilitation, and her phone number is in my wallet. Which is in my back pocket if Rambo here will back off an inch."

The guard pressed his forearm even harder against Adam's chest. "Sounds like more bull if you ask me."

"I'm not," the police officer said curtly. She gestured. "Let him go, Frankie."

"But—"

"Frankie." The officer's voice sharpened.

Frankie didn't bother masking his reluctance. He

dug his elbow into Adam's sternum one last time before he finally stepped back.

"Take your duties real seriously," Adam muttered.

"When it comes to scumbags who take advantage of women," the guard agreed, sneering.

Adam ignored him and yanked out his wallet to extract his driver's license and the paper that Dr. Granger had given him. "Here." He extended them toward the police officer. "Talk to her yourself."

The officer took both. "If you wouldn't mind waiting outside the room, Mr. Fortune—"

"I do mind." He shoved the guard away and probably took too much pleasure from the way the guy stumbled slightly. He stepped around the police officer to crouch in front of Laurel. "Sweetheart."

She lifted her head. Her eyes were swollen and red, her hair dangling over her face.

His hand shook slightly as he gently slid the strands out of her eyes. "Come on, baby. You don't really want to sit here on the floor, do you? Be mad at me if you have to. I should have told you. I was going to. I just—" His throat was tight. "I didn't know the right words. I'm sorry."

She pressed her hand to her chest. "My heart—" she drew in a harsh, stuttering breath "—is breaking."

So is mine.

He sat on the floor, his feet on either side of hers. He took her hands in his. "It'll get better, Laurel. I promise."

Her raw eyes searched his. "How?"

"Because Linus is going to be fine." He had to believe it. "He's going to grow up tall and strong and one day give you a hell of a time but he's always going to love his mother."

"Mr. Fortune." The police officer stopped next to them, extending his driver's license and the prescription paper. "I'm sorry for the misunderstanding. I spoke with Dr. Granger. She requested that you phone her as soon as possible."

He barely spared the officer a look. "Thank you." He dropped the license and paper on the carpet next to him. *Now get out.* It took all of his self-control not to say it aloud.

Didn't matter, though, because she walked to the door. "Come on, Frankie."

"I'm not satisfied."

"I *am.* Come on." The door closed on them while they were still arguing.

"Do you really believe he will love me?" There was such longing in her shaking words that he hurt inside.

He brushed another lock of hair away from her face. He cupped her wet cheek. "I'm sure of it." He rubbed his thumb over the trail of tears. "How could he not?"

Three hours later, Adam finally remembered to call Dr. Granger. Explaining the situation to her meant confessing a few more details than he'd offered in Seattle. Namely the way that Laurel had actually given up her child.

The connecting doors were open between his room and Laurel's. He stood in the doorway between, his cell phone at his ear while the doctor talked.

Laurel was lying on the bed closest to the window. She was fully dressed but had still piled the covers up to her chin.

Adam couldn't tell if she was asleep or not.

He figured not was more likely.

"It's unfortunate that Laurel discovered something like that the way she did," Dr. Granger was saying. She'd already given him what-for for not having been more forthright before. "Given the situation, I wouldn't classify her reaction as entirely excessive. As long as she doesn't exhibit increased signs of anxiety or depression, I think you should continue with your plans. The alternative would be to return to Seattle. Not here at Fresh Pine—the need for our services is too high and we've already filled her place here—but the shelter we'd found for her might be able to still accommodate—"

"She'd never agree." Adam knew that much.

"As sudden as it was, Laurel now seems highly motivated to regain her life," Dr. Granger said. "Or, at the very least, to find a new place for herself within that life. Progress rarely occurs without growing pains. But it is still progress."

Adam was hard-pressed to classify what had happened as progress. Nightmarish, more like. What would Laurel do when she learned the truth about everything else?

"Nevertheless, it's important not to place too much pressure on her."

"Easy to say," he muttered.

"Not so easy to do," Dr. Granger finished sympathetically. "I can authorize a mild antianxiety—"

"She doesn't want drugs, remember?"

"I was thinking more about you," the doctor said wryly.

He stepped out of the doorway and into his own room, though he left the connecting doors fully open. "Think I'll manage," he told the doctor. "Sorry to disturb you."

"I told you. Call me whenever you need. Laurel is a special girl. She's lucky to have someone who loves her as much as you do."

Adam jerked. "I'm just an old—"

"Friend?" Dr. Granger laughed skeptically. "We should all have old friends who care so deeply," she said before disconnecting.

Adam tossed his phone on the bed and rubbed his face.

Caring about Laurel had never been the problem.

Keeping her had.

Chapter Ten

"Are you sure you've had enough to eat?"

Laurel looked up at Adam. Or rather, she directed her face in his direction.

Actually *looking* at him was proving increasingly difficult since she'd behaved so monstrously the previous evening at the hotel in Utah.

Now they were another several hundred miles down the road at yet another hotel. This time in Durango, Colorado.

But even after sitting beside him in the car for seven hours that day—maybe *because* of those hours spent beside him—she felt more awkward than ever.

He was still waiting for an answer and she glanced at her dinner plate. She'd managed to force down half of the Southwestern salad she'd ordered. "It was a huge salad," she excused.

And she'd ordered it only to keep him from looking at her with that worried expression he'd been wearing for nearly twenty-four hours. If it had been up to her alone, she'd have skipped the meal altogether. He, on the other hand, had demolished a porterhouse and a baked potato with all the fixings.

She glanced toward the entrance of the restaurant to the hotel lobby. "Do you suppose the room is ready yet?"

He finished signing the meal receipt and slid his credit card back into his wallet. "They said it'd be ready by six and it's well after." He pushed his chair back and stood.

She quickly followed suit and they left the restaurant that had grown progressively busier as they'd dined.

While he went to the registration desk, she hung back pretending to study a painting hanging near the imposing staircase.

If she hadn't been right beside him when they'd come into the hotel to get a room, she might not have believed that there was only one room available. But she'd heard the desk clerk herself. Otherwise, she'd have believed Adam had done it deliberately.

He hadn't really let her out of his sight since the night before.

"Think it's museum quality?" Adam asked as he stepped beside her, nodding up at the painting.

"It's good enough for someone to buy and hang over their couch, I suppose."

"I think that's what's called being damned with faint praise."

She shook her head, denying. "I wouldn't know museum quality anyway."

"Yes, you would. You were an art curator."

Startled, she tried to absorb that.

"You deciding if that fits or not?"

She looked at him. "Are you reading my mind?"

"Doesn't take a lot of intuition," he said quietly. "Anyone would feel that way."

She frowned and turned back to the painting for another look. "What I *was* thinking was that this is better than mediocre but not worth an outrageous price like that." She nodded toward the card affixed to the wall next to the rustic frame. "That has two too many zeros. And then I was thinking what a terrific snob that made me seem."

"Maybe you're an art snob, but you're not one otherwise."

It was the most personal words they'd exchanged all day. She let out a mock huff. "I think now I'm being damned with faint praise."

He smiled slightly. "Room's ready. You can head up now. I'll go get the bags from the car."

She stifled a sigh. Another stretch of endless hours with nothing on her mind except her own appalling behavior. Both last night and five months ago. And her increasing confusion over why Adam was helping her the way he was, at all. Their college romance had ended long, long ago. She'd moved on. So had he.

"What's the room number?" she asked him.

"Up the stairs. Two-twelve. Or," he added when she took a step toward the staircase, "we could walk around town for a while. Weather's nice and—"

"Yes," she said so quickly that she felt her face flush.

He gave a single nod and she had the sudden sense that he wasn't all that sure his idea had been a good one. "Okay." He led the way to the entrance and pulled open the oversize timber door.

On the sidewalk, he closed his hand over her elbow.

She was barely able to suppress a shiver. "Don't worry. I'm not going to run off and find some computer for more internet creeping. I've learned enough."

His hold tightened for a moment, then relaxed again. But he didn't release her. "I wasn't worried. Which way do you want to go first?"

Whichever direction she looked, the mountains watched over them. The peaks were verdant with summer growth, and for a moment, she imagined them covered in snow.

Imagined Adam, his hair, longer than it was now, blowing around his head despite the ski goggles.

"We skied once at Holiday Valley." Her fingertips fluttered to the necklace hidden beneath her blouse. "It was Christmastime." Her throat tightened.

This was not imagination. She was certain of it. "The lodge where we stayed had an enormous tree." She could see it in her mind as clearly as if it stood in the middle of the sidewalk in front of them. The fat, shining red globes hanging from the magnificent branches. The hundreds of tiny gold lights that seemed like stars when the lights were low. "It was even larger than the one my parents always had."

She caught the flicker of something in his dark eyes. "Yes." He let go of her elbow and gestured. "Let's go that way first. Maybe I can find a shirt in that souvenir shop. I'm sick of the ones I've been wearing."

She pressed her lips together and fell into step with him. But her mind wasn't on the shops they passed or the other pedestrians or bicyclists, even though they outnumbered the cars on the street.

When Laurel hadn't gone home that year for Christmas, choosing to spend it with Adam, her mother had been livid. Screaming at her over the phone. Then refusing to talk to her at all for weeks and weeks.

Screaming just the same way that Laurel had screamed at Adam the night before.

Her Southwestern salad churned inside her stomach.

"I'm like her."

Until Adam stopped walking, she wasn't even aware that she had done so first. He ignored the people behind them as they parted and flowed around them. "Like who?"

"My mother." Her head swam and she thought for a moment that she might be sick. She looked around blindly, but all she could see were people.

Adam's hands closed over hers. "No. You're not. Look at me."

His touch, his voice, helped center her, and his deep brown gaze seemed to surround her, making the crowds and chaos disappear.

"You are nothing like Sylvia Hudson." His voice was quietly adamant.

"She used to scream at me for nothing at all." Nothing and everything. And if it wasn't screaming, it was silence. Dreadful, weight-of-the-world silence. Designed to ensure Laurel knew exactly how much devastation she was causing her mother.

"I know." His voice was low.

"Sylvia and Nelson," she whispered. "The epitome of culture and refinement. Envy of their friends. Pillars of society. Mother never screamed in public." Laurel couldn't recall everything but she remembered that much. Her mother reserved her screaming for behind closed doors. And she'd have died of pure mortification if a police officer had ever been called to those doors.

Adam looked over her head toward the hotel. "I'll take you back to the room."

"No." She tugged her hands back until he let go. "I don't want coddling." She started to yank on the sleeve of her cardigan and, realizing it, forced her hands down to her side. She took advantage of a brief break in cross traffic and stepped off the curb, hurrying across. "I'd rather walk every mile of this town than sit in a hotel room for hours, fearing what else I've done."

She heard Adam swear, and then he took her arm once more as they crossed the street. Not letting go again until they reached the sidewalk on the other side. "There's nothing for you to fear."

She lifted her brows. "Really? How can I be sure?"

"Because I'm telling you."

"Like you told me how I left my son?" She set off toward the souvenir shop.

"I told you I was sorry for that." She could hear the regret in his deep voice. "I should have figured out a way to—"

"You shouldn't *have* to figure out anything! You're just a nice guy who feels sorry for the old girlfriend with her memories chopped up like Sunday morning hash!" She earned a startled look from the young couple sitting on the bench outside the store and she yanked open the shop door, making the bell hanging over it jingle. She lowered her voice in deference to the other shoppers. "And my treating you as though you're responsible makes me every bit as unreasonable as my mother ever was. Nobody left Linus with strangers but me. *I* did that. Now that I know, you don't have to keep treating me with kid gloves."

"I'm not all that nice." His jaw looked tight. "But until you remember why you left the way you did, the gloves aren't going anywhere."

The shop was lined with aisles packed stem to stern with Durango-themed items. Jackets. Shirts. Baby clothes and dog bowls. She picked up a bowl and waved it at him. "Why am I having this conversation with you at all? You're not the one I've betrayed the most."

She caught the price tag on the ceramic bowl and quickly replaced it far more carefully than she'd removed it. "Don't mind me," she said in the face of Adam's silence. "You just get the added benefit of my venting with the price of admission. Do you still wear an extra large, tall?"

"Yes."

She bent over a display of T-shirts, looking at the sizes. "Don't sound so terse. It's not everyone who can claim the same size they wore ten years ago. I sure can't."

She crouched down and pulled a white shirt with a screen-printed mountain peak from a stack and shook it out for him to see. "Yes? No?"

"Ah...no."

She turned the shirt so she could see the full front. She realized a puff of smoke was superimposed over the mountain outline. Beneath was scrolled "Durango High."

She rolled her eyes, refolding the shirt and setting it back on the stack. Still on her knees—she'd realized all of the "extra" sizes were on the lowest shelves—she moved past several more stacks bearing similar marijuana themes.

"Would you rather he was the one who was here? Or are you still worried you're afraid of him?"

At his question her fingers spasmodically closed on another shirt. "He's where he should be. With the baby. With...Linus."

It was more proof of her failings that she still stumbled over her baby's name. That no matter how many times she thought it, no matter how many times she said it, *Linus* simply didn't seem to fit.

She shook out another shirt—navy blue this time—and held it up for his view.

"I've worn worse."

The town's name was blocked out in bright orange

across the front. She eyed the garment. Then Adam's broad shoulders. "Looks a little small to me."

He took the shirt from her when she stood and balled it in his fist. "It'll be fine," he dismissed. "There are other…people…who could be with Linus. Do you want Eric here or don't you?"

Everything inside her screamed *no!* She ran her palm over the fuzzy knit of a striped scarf. "It would get you off the hook."

His expression tightened.

"Not that you're on any sort of hook to begin with," she added quickly. "No matter what you say, you're just a decent guy who got caught up in all of this. Because the world is too small sometimes." Afraid of seeing the confirmation on his face, she dashed the scarf around her neck and looked in the mirror hanging on the end of the aisle. "Green and yellow stripes. Never were my colors." She reached out to replace the scarf and Adam grabbed her hand.

He pulled her closer. "Just answer the damn question, Laurel. What do you want? Do you want him here instead? Yes or no?"

"No," she whispered, too startled to lie. "I want you here."

His shoulders seemed to relax. "All right, then. Matter closed." He let go of her and walked up the next aisle. "Do you need anything while we're here?"

Her knees felt wobbly. "I'm already in your debt."

His lips tightened again. Her knack for causing that particular look was becoming an art form.

"Pajamas," she admitted hurriedly. "Or a nightshirt. An extra tall Durango High shirt would even do."

He was striding up the aisle, angling past a couple who were quibbling over salt and pepper shakers. She caught up to him where he'd stopped in front of a tiered rack hung with a variety of pajamas. "Choose."

A hand-printed sign was affixed atop the rack showing the price. Even the least expensive pair cost three times what his shirt did. "I'll pay you back. One day."

"For God's sake, Laurel. Just choose. My bank account can handle the excessive burden."

He sounded like he was about at the end of his rope. She blindly pulled a hanger from the rack and pushed it at him. "There."

He glanced at the pink and green flannel pants and hung them back on the rack. "You may not be an extra small anymore, but you're damn sure not an extra large." He swiped through a few more hangers, then extracted another set. "Anything else?"

She shook her head and followed him to the register where a line of customers was already waiting. But even a few minutes gave her time for second thoughts. Flannel pants or not, the pajama top was little more than a spaghetti-strapped camisole.

She tugged at her sleeve.

"Stop worrying."

She dropped her hands to her sides.

So what if the top left her arms bare? He'd already seen the scars. And it wasn't as though she'd be modeling her nightwear for him.

He had an Ashley, after all. Plus—mortifying as it

had been—he'd already seen Laurel naked. He hadn't exactly been overcome with desire.

Her cheeks felt on fire. "I'm going to wait outside." She hurried away before he could protest.

The teenage couple was still sitting on the bench when she went back through the bell-jingling door. She turned her back on them and moved toward the curb.

The door jangled twice more before Adam joined her on the sidewalk, with his purchases inside a paper shopping bag. If he was surprised that she hadn't tried making a break for it, he hid it well. Instead, he pointed up the street. "Look at that. Hot-air balloons. Come on. They don't look too far."

"You can take the trolley." The couple from the bench had obviously overheard and had risen, joining them near the curb. "Should be here any second." The young man jerked his thumb toward the old-fashioned trolley rumbling along the street toward them. "Runs every twenty minutes."

"There's a trolley stop by the balloons. That's where we're heading." As the girl spoke, the trolley glided to a stop in front of them, disgorging several passengers.

Adam looked at her. "What do you say? Walk or ride?"

His warm fingers were still enclosing hers. "Walk." She felt breathless.

The trolley driver was looking at them. "You coming?"

"Maybe on the return trip," Adam told him.

The driver closed the door and the trolley rumbled off again.

A second balloon—this one with red, white and blue chevrons—rose in the air. As they neared, Laurel spotted the ropes tethering the balloons to the ground, as well as the lines of people waiting for a chance to ride.

"Have you ever been up in one?" she asked.

"Yeah." He didn't elaborate, but he let go of her hand when a streak of white-blond hair on stubby legs plowed between them.

"Sorry!" A woman pushing an enormous stroller hurried past. "Abigail, you stop right this minute!"

The tot skidded to a halt but the pure devilment on her face warned it probably wouldn't last long.

Laurel looked up at Adam, seeing the dimple flash in his cheek and she didn't mind so very much then that he'd released her hand.

Even before they reached the park, it was obvious there was some kind of festival going on. In addition to the tethered balloon rides, there were caricaturists set up with their easels and pencils. A table positioned beneath a bright blue tent was occupied by a woman painting flowers on a teenager's cheek. Vendors with pushcarts sold pretzels and hot dogs and huge puffs of pink and blue cotton candy. Two food trucks did an equally brisk business.

And everywhere Laurel looked, she saw couples holding hands. Families with children chasing about.

It was festive and beautiful and still bright before sunset. And it made Laurel ache inside.

The white-blond streak that was little Abigail tore across their path again and they waited while her mother and stroller chased in her wake.

Adam's head bent toward her. "Want an ice cream?"

She looked up at him, ready to shake her head. But the light in his eyes lured a smile from her instead. "How can you possibly want an ice cream after that steak dinner?"

His dimple appeared again and her stomach dipped and swayed. "Ice cream melts, sweetheart. Fills in the cracks."

She couldn't help but smile. "Fine." She waved her hand toward the cart several yards away where an old man wearing a crimson-and-white top hat was scooping ice cream into waffle cones. "Ice cream, then."

He took her hand again as they crossed the green grass.

"Evenin' folks," the man greeted with a broad smile. "What can I getcha?" He had several tubs of different flavors inside his refrigerated cart.

Laurel shook her head. "Nothing for me, thanks."

"Black walnut and pistachio," Adam said.

She tucked her tongue in her cheek. "Because just one nut is never enough?"

"I like what I like." He handed her the paper bag while he pulled out his wallet.

"Man after my own heart," the man said. "Waffle cone or cup?"

"Cone. And she'll have a scoop of that peanut butter ice cream in a cup."

Laurel opened her mouth to protest.

"With chocolate sprinkles," Adam added before she could.

Her stomach actually rumbled. She did love peanut

butter. But she still had to offer some kind of objection. "Maybe I want vanilla."

"When there's peanut butter in the vicinity? Not likely."

He was right, of course. "I don't need sprinkles," she assured dryly when the vendor upended a perfectly round ball of ice cream into a small white cup.

"Every pretty girl needs sprinkles," the man countered, sweeping a scoop of chocolate shavings over the top. "Isn't that right, sir?" He jabbed a small plastic spoon into the scoop and handed it to her with a flourish.

"Every pretty girl does," Adam agreed. He handed over the cash and then took the shopping bag from Laurel again.

She almost regretted that she hadn't insisted on a waffle cone, despite her dislike for them. It would have left one of her hands still free to be held.

But he settled his wide palm on her shoulder, which she quickly realized was even better, despite the shopping bag in his hand bumping against her arm.

They wandered to the far side of the park where even more vendors sold candles and soaps and handmade jewelry. She slowed as a display of gold necklaces caught her eye. They were similar to her *L* necklace, which had her wondering if hers had been handmade, too.

Then they wandered closer to the clearing where the balloons were tethered.

But in her mind, she wasn't seeing the three colorful balloons right in front of her. Instead, it was hundreds and hundreds. Rising up into the air in a spectacular airborne ballet. "I went to the balloon festival once in Albuquerque," she realized aloud. "When I was in high school."

"I know. You told me about it."

She pretended to focus on her ice cream. "I think it was one of the few times everyone was happy together. My parents with each other. My parents with me. Did I tell you that, too?"

His hand tightened on her shoulder. Then he pressed a gentle kiss to her head. "Yeah." His voice was gruff.

A knot formed inside her chest and she suddenly felt like crying. Which she was determined not to do.

Not on a beautiful summer evening when she had peanut butter ice cream in her hand and this man standing beside her.

How many times had Dr. Granger reminded her that her faulty memory needn't rule her present? That, against all odds, she'd survived a horrific accident. She could either disappear into anxiety over what she couldn't yet remember, or she could move forward, living the life she'd been gifted.

She lifted her chin, staring blindly at the balloons. Feeling the warmth of Adam's hand. The lingering sensation of his kiss against her hair.

I could love this man.

The thought filled her. Lifted her. Just as certainly as the hot air lifted the enormous, gently bobbing balloons.

"Want to try?"

She startled, looking up at him. "Ah—"

"Going up." He nodded toward the trio. "There aren't so many people waiting in line now." His gaze seemed to look right into her. "We could take the ride if you're—"

"Yes." She sounded so eager she was almost embarrassed. She tapped her spoon on her ice cream. She hadn't even realized she'd been stirring it into mush. "What about this?"

His eyes crinkled. "What about it?"

"I doubt we'll be able to take ice cream up with us."

"They did." He gestured with his cone at the same couple who'd been sitting on the bench outside the souvenir shop. "But don't worry. I would never make you sacrifice anything that has peanut butter in it."

"I could say the same thing about you and hops. If that ice cream cart would have had beer-flavored ice cream—" she shuddered "—you'd be all over it."

His grin widened. "True." His hand fell away from her shoulder. "I've been working on Ashley to put a boozy float on the menu at Provisions, but so far, no luck."

Her nerves suddenly pinched. *Ashley.*

She focused on her cup, mashing the ice cream even more. "She must miss you a lot." Her voice sounded hollow to her ears and she prayed he wouldn't notice. "Considering how often she texts you."

He bit off the side of his ice cream, reducing the round scoop by nearly half. "Think it's her age," he said after he swallowed. He looked wry. "She's only twenty-three. Why make a two-minute phone call when you can accomplish the same thing in twenty text messages." He grabbed her hand again and set off for the balloons, angling toward the table where a woman was selling the tickets.

Five minutes later, the ticket lady was minding the shopping bag and they were approaching the wicker basket occupied by the balloon pilot—a boy who looked too young to even shave. "If you want that ice cream to stay ice cream, better eat it up quick," he advised. "Gets toasty in here."

Adam took care of the rest of his ice cream in two bites, leaving only what was pushed down inside the waffle cone. He glanced at the contents of Laurel's cup. "You always did stir it around until you turned it into ice cream soup. Go on. Drink it up. I know you want to."

She managed a smile and quickly swallowed down the milkshake-like remainder and tossed the cup in the trash bin before stepping into the wicker basket. It felt alarmingly insubstantial and she nervously latched onto the side. Several fuel tanks were strapped in the interior and she suddenly wondered who in their right mind had ever thought a hot-air balloon seemed like a brilliant idea.

The pilot—"I'm Bobby, nice t' meetcha"—gave a brief safety spiel and asked if either one of them had questions.

Laurel shook her head, mostly because she hadn't really heard a word he'd said in the first place.

And then she felt a fresh rush of heat from the burner above them, and braced herself for God only knew what.

Only there was no yank as they left the ground. No crash as flimsy wicker gave away beneath their feet.

Instead, there was only the simple sense of floating. As easily as a feather drifted on a breeze.

She looked up, up, up, into the balloon. The brilliant colors of the exterior seemed even brighter from the inside. Then she looked out over the side of the basket.

Even though they were leashed to the ground, they still seemed to be rising incredibly high. The tethering ropes grew taut. She knew there was a breeze but couldn't feel even a whisper of it. It was so amazing she actually forgot to clutch the basket like it was her only lifeline.

The entire town and the glittering river that wound around and through it seemed like it had been laid out just for them. "It's so beautiful," she breathed, looking around to find Adam.

He was smiling down at her and her heart stuttered.

She forgot the tethers. Forgot Bobby the balloonist. Forgot everything except Adam.

"We've done this," she realized aloud. Wonder was warming her from the inside out and she touched his chest with her fingertips. "You and I. We've done this before. Only there weren't any ropes tying us to the ground."

He closed his hand over hers, pressing her palm against him until she felt the deep thump of his heartbeat. "Yes." His voice was low. Hushed in the stunningly silent air. "And we've also done this."

Then he lowered his head and pressed his mouth to hers.

Chapter Eleven

Adam felt her quick inhale. The sudden stiffening that was just as suddenly an exhale as Laurel began kissing him back.

It took everything he possessed not to forget where they were. That he couldn't very well pull Laurel into him until everything outside of them, outside of that moment, fell away.

When he finally lifted his head, her aquamarine eyes looked dazed. She lifted her hand and touched his lips, so lightly it could have been nothing but a dream.

"We were celebrating my twenty-first birthday," she whispered. "I brought champagne and we nearly spit it out because it was so dreadful. But you still insisted on finishing it, because it was our first bottle of cham-

pagne together." Her hand lowered and her fingers fluttered to her throat. "You gave me this necklace."

And the next day she'd moved in with him and he'd
started working extra shifts so he could afford to buy
a ring.

A ring she'd never accepted.

He pushed the thought away and looked over her
head, turning her so she was looking out at the beauty
spread out before them. "I think I saw an eagle over
there." He pointed over her shoulder.

"Mmm." She leaned back against him and tugged
at his arm until he lowered it and wrapped it across
her shoulders. And there they stood. Floating above
the treetops.

It was inevitable that such an idyllic moment couldn't
last.

Unlike the two-hour balloon trip he'd scrimped for
months to surprise her with on her birthday, this up-
and-down ride wasn't even fifteen minutes. And it was
Bobby who reminded him of that fact.

"You folks want a picture before we descend?" The
balloonist was looking at them expectantly. "Most people do."

So Adam handed over his cell phone and the kid
held it up, snapping several shots. Then he handed it
back and reached for a line and the balloon immediately began descending.

Adam started to pocket the phone, but it vibrated in
his hand. He glanced at the screen and tensed.

Laurel's expression tightened. "Your girlfriend again?"

He frowned at her as he slid his thumb across the

screen and held it to his ear. "Kane, you heard from the social worker?"

"Not yet. Johnson called. Baby started running a fever this afternoon."

He swore under his breath. He'd spent more time in the last week feeling helpless than ever before in his life and he hated it.

"Where are you, anyway?" Kane asked.

"Colorado. How the hell did Linus get a fever? They've had him nearly hermetically sealed for weeks!"

Laurel's face had paled and she was clutching the side of the basket again as though her life depended on it.

"Adam," Kane's voice was irritatingly reasonable, "all I know is he's got a fever. Doesn't mean he's rejecting the transplant."

"Doesn't mean he isn't," Adam countered flatly.

"I'll drive over to the hospital tonight," Kane told him. "At least to be there."

"Thanks. I'll call the hospital myself, too." Dr. Patel—the guy in charge of the transplant unit at the hospital—and the nurses assigned to Linus would tell Adam anything he needed to know. That fact was only because of Eric's doing, and was just one more reason why Adam's resentment of him made him feel like a crumb.

There was a hard bump as the basket contacted earth again and he gestured for Laurel to climb out. She did so, then clutched her arms around herself as though they'd just spent fifteen minutes in the alpine rather than beneath the hot blasts of the balloon's burner.

"I'll be in touch, Kane." He shoved the phone in his pocket and barely had the presence of mind to remember to tip the pilot before he took Laurel's arm and turned toward the park's exit.

The ticket lady jogged after them and Laurel took the shopping bag they'd both forgotten with a weak thank-you.

"Wait." Adam called the woman when she started back to her ticket table. "What's the fastest way to get back downtown?" He told her the name of their hotel.

"Trolley if you catch it right. Otherwise it's probably just as fast to walk as it would be to wait for a ride share or taxi." She gestured. "Nearest stop is over there by that row of park benches. There's a sign but you can't see it from here because of the trees."

"Thanks." He immediately steered Laurel in the direction of the benches. "We'll wait a couple minutes," he told her. "If it doesn't come, we're hoofing it."

She didn't look inclined to disagree. "What's the reason for the social worker?"

He swallowed the explanation that automatically sprang up. "Transplant stuff," he lied and hoped she was unfamiliar enough with the actual donor process that she wouldn't realize it.

Now was not the time for her to learn that Adam was their son's father.

She'd started chewing on her lip. "Thank you."

He forced himself to slow his pace when he realized she was skipping to keep up. "For what?"

She gaped for a moment. "For keeping up with Linus, obviously." She tugged at her sleeve, then seemed to realize it and stopped. "I'm sure not every donor takes such a keen interest. But you know I'm his mother and…" She trailed off, not finishing.

Just as well. He was practically choking as it was.

Fortunately, he spotted the distinctive red shuttle approaching. "Trolley's nearly to the stop." He looked speculatively from it to the row of benches to her. "Think you can beat it?"

"I wasn't a runner for nothing," she said not so far under her breath that he couldn't hear, and took off like a shot.

He balled the shopping bag in his fist and ran after her.

They made it with barely a second to spare, and then only because the driver saw them coming and pulled to a stop again after he'd already begun pulling away from the benches.

Laurel was breathing very hard as she collapsed into the first seat she came to. She leaned over, hanging her head between her knees while Adam paid their fares. He sat down in the seat opposite her. "Are you all right?"

"I will be." She sat up, looking annoyed. Whether at him for asking or at herself for showing any sort of physical weakness, he couldn't tell. "As soon as I know Linus is all right."

And if he wasn't?

He scrubbed his hand down his face. Giving in to the panic clawing at his gut wasn't going to help. Getting Laurel to the hospital in Houston as quickly as possible would. "We'll get a few hours of sleep and head out early."

"How much further is it to Texas?"

The trolley stopped at a bus stop even though nobody was waiting to board and nobody was waiting to get off. He shoved down his impatience with the trolley driver. "Little over a thousand miles to Houston. Rambling Rose is a little under. We'll get there day after tomorrow."

"If we left now and drove straight through, we'd be there tomorrow."

He shook his head. "It'll be too hard on you."

Her chin set. "Taking it easy on me won't make it better. Not when my son—" Her voice choked off.

The trolley lurched into motion again. In comparison to the balloon, the ride felt as smooth as a bucking horse.

"Fine. We'll stop and take a break every few hours," he said, more to appease his own conscience than to reassure her.

She looked even more put out. "Have to make sure not to overwhelm the woman with the faulty brain?"

He exhaled roughly. "That's not what I meant. And *stop* calling yourself that."

"Or what?" She threw out her hands. "You'll drive off and leave me alone to make my own way? We both know you'll never leave me."

It felt like being cracked with a whip. "Don't push it, sweetheart. Even I have limits."

"The only limit you have is being too good and too protective."

Too good?

He nearly laughed. If he were good at all, he'd have contacted her parents the second he'd hung up the phone after Dr. Granger's first call. He'd have swallowed his pride and asked them for assistance in arranging a flight that Laurel could board without any ID.

Maybe she'd be in Houston right now with her son instead of sitting on this damn trolley that was taking a freaking eternity to get them where they needed to go.

He shoved out of his seat, too restless to sit, and held on to one of the loops hanging from a rod near the roof. He stared out the front windshield, as if he could will the driver to go faster.

Of course, he didn't.

And even though the drive had taken maybe ten minutes when it finally stopped in front of the familiar souvenir shop, it felt like three times that.

Laurel took the bag and they exited quickly, crossing the street to the hotel just as the street lamps began to light up.

He barely noticed.

Albuquerque by midnight, he figured.

Lubbock by dawn.

Houston by early afternoon.

He'd never driven fifteen hours or better at a single stretch, but he was going to now.

They entered the hotel and Adam pulled the keycard from his pocket and handed it to her. "Go up to the room. Take a shower or whatever if you want. Do you need your bag from the car?" Since the room hadn't been ready, they'd left their belongings in the car while they'd gone to the restaurant.

"The parking garage is two blocks away." She patted the shopping bag. "I've got the pj's. I can change into them."

"I'll go fill up on gas, then. We can be on the road in less than an hour."

She plucked the card from his fingers then turned and started up the wide staircase. She paused midway and looked back at him. "Everything is going to be all right, Adam."

He wasn't used to being on the receiving end of reassurance.

Particularly where Laurel Hudson was concerned.

But she wasn't talking about *them*.

She was talking about the baby.

Their baby.

"The gas station isn't far from the parking garage," he said gruffly. "It won't take me long."

"I'll be ready." Then she turned again and headed quickly up the stairs.

Not only was Laurel ready and waiting when Adam returned to the hotel and knocked on the room door, but she'd filled the shopping bag from the souvenir shop with several bottles of water, plastic-wrapped sandwiches, a few pieces of fresh fruit and a large package of cookies.

She'd also obviously showered. Her hair was hanging dark and damp around her shoulders, and she was wearing the new pajamas under her sweater.

She didn't look a day older than she'd been in college.

"I reached the hospital while I was getting gas." He closed the door behind him and couldn't help a double-take at the sight of the spacious suite. When he'd heard "one room available" from the registration clerk, he hadn't asked for details.

Laurel's eyes were wide. "And?"

"His regular nurse was already gone for the day, but the night nurse admitted Linus does have a low fever they're not happy about. They don't think it's a sign of rejection, though. So that's the good thing."

She closed her eyes and her shoulders sagged. "Thank you, God," she whispered. When she looked at him again, her eyes gleamed wetly.

He couldn't take it if she started crying. Not when it was what he'd wanted to do, too, when the nurse had told him. And he hadn't cried even when Laurel told him she was engaged to another man.

He reached in the bag and lifted the cream-filled cookies. "I was only gone thirty minutes. Where'd you manage to get all this?"

Her smile was a little shaky around the edges, but at least it was a smile. "There's a small shop downstairs." She suddenly looked uncertain. "I had to charge it to the room. I hope that's okay." She looked over her shoulder at the luxurious suite. "I figured it would be cheaper than raiding the minibar."

"Surprised you didn't get peanut butter cookies."

"Those are your favorites. If I didn't remember wrong." Her face suddenly colored and she pulled the package out of his hand and stuck it back in the bag.

She tucked her hair behind her ears. "There's a coffee maker if you want me to make you a cup."

"Coffee would be great." He glanced inside the bag again. "Where are the rest of the clothes I bought?"

She set the bag on the table alongside the door. "I laid them out in the bedroom. I figured you'd want to shower and change, too. The shower isn't quite up to Captain's standards," she joked, "but it gets the job done."

"Five minutes and we're out of here." He strode into the bedroom, snatching up the shirt and pack of boxers and socks he'd also grabbed at the souvenir shop while Laurel had been waiting outside.

Despite the situation, he couldn't help smiling when he went into the bathroom. It was bigger than the entire Captain's Quarters room. When he flipped on the shower, hot water shot from four different showerheads, engulfing him in steam.

It would have been a hell of a room, he thought as he grabbed the soap. If they'd have been able to enjoy it.

He toweled off roughly afterward and ripped open the bag with the boxers. They were printed with smiling jalapeño peppers but they were clean. Same thing went for the cannabis-patterned socks. He hitched up his jeans and grabbed the new T-shirt.

The smell of coffee was strong and welcome when he walked out of the bedroom.

"You're right," he said, pulling the T-shirt over his head. "Almost up to the Captain's standards." He pushed his arms through the short sleeves and grimaced as he tugged the tight shirt into place.

"Told you it looked too small." She handed him a disposable coffee cup and picked up the bag of provisions.

"Next time I'll let you choose." He pulled open the suite door.

"Nicest hotel suite I've never stayed in." She paused in the doorway and gave him a twisted smile. "Don't imagine many guests leave wearing pajamas."

"If it weren't for the purple flying pigs on your pants, nobody'd know that's what they are. Do you still have the room key?" She handed it to him and he dropped it in the key drop when they reached the lobby.

He'd left the car parked in front of the hotel in a temporary loading zone.

"Surprised you didn't get a parking ticket," she said once they were on their way. "But you always were lucky like that." She fussed with her wet hair, pulling it over one shoulder and braiding it loosely. "If I parked in front of the apartment building in Buffalo overnight, there was always a ticket under the wiper blade greeting me in the morning. But never when you did it."

He could almost forget that she had amnesia. That she couldn't remember so many other things. So many other critical things. "Luck of the Irish," he dismissed

She made a sound. "You're not Irish. Just lucky."

Not when it came to her.

"That *was* a nice town," she sighed a while later when the city lights were nearly gone in the rearview mirror.

"Maybe you'll get back there one day."

"It wouldn't be the same." She looked over at him

"I could drive, you know. If you get tired. I remember how."

"You don't have a license on you. Car rental agency would probably have an issue with it."

"Only if they knew," she scoffed. "You didn't use to be such a rule follower."

"I didn't use to be a lot of things," he said dryly. "But if I know you, you'll be sleeping in thirty minutes anyway."

"The least I can do is stay awake and keep you company."

It was his turn to scoff. "Whatever you say, sweetheart."

She tsked. "You shouldn't call me that."

He glanced her way.

"Sweetheart," she said as if he were thick. "If I were Ashley, it would seriously annoy me."

"You're not Ashley."

"Tell me about it," she said under her breath.

He told himself he didn't relish the moment. "You don't sign my paycheck."

Aside from the lights on the dash, the inside of the car was dark. He still felt the look she gave him.

"Ashley *owns* Provisions," he said patiently. "She's my boss. And I guarantee she doesn't care how many women I call sweetheart."

"Your *boss.*"

"Along with her two sisters, yes."

"Your boss texts you a lot," she said after a moment.

He chuckled. "She's good at what she does, though. I wasn't sure she would be, at first. Seemed too young to own her own restaurant. But I have to give her props. She's been in the business one way or another since she was in high school. Her sisters, too. They're no slouches. What Ashley still lacks, her fiancé makes up for."

"She's engaged?"

"To a guy named Rodrigo Mendoza. His family has a winery in Austin. And a successful restaurant."

She shifted in her seat. "Tell me more."

"About Rodrigo?"

She huffed. "About Rambling Rose. About your life there."

"Until recently, there hasn't been much to tell."

"How'd you go from studying industrial engineering in New York to managing a restaurant in Texas?" She barely waited a beat. "And don't say it's a long story. We've got nothing but time on our hands here."

"Why do you want to rehash the last decade of my life?"

"If we're talking, you're not falling asleep at the wheel."

Like the guy who'd caused her accident, he realized. Point taken. "Wouldn't you prefer Twenty Questions?"

"As a matter of fact, I would not."

He killed a few minutes sipping the now-lukewarm coffee while he framed an answer. "It's not all that complicated. Or that long of a story," he warned. "I collected a city paycheck that was healthy enough to keep me from starving and I tended bar a few nights a week to save me from boredom." The problem with rehashing the last decade was picking his way around the part she'd played in the decisions he'd made. "I told you about Gerald Robinson. Learning we were related."

"Yes."

"In the process, we learned we had a lot of other relations, too. The number of cousins would—" He shook his head and distilled it down. "It's pretty astonishing. Anyway, last year, when Kane and Dad and I went to Robinson's wedding, I got to talking with some of them—Callum Fortune in particular."

"Oh, I read about him!" Then her tone dimmed a little, obviously recognizing his surprise. "When I was, uh, using the computer in Utah. There was a thing on the municipal website about the hotel he's trying to get approval to build."

"The Hotel Fortune. That's just the latest project." He switched lanes, accelerating past a slow-moving semi. Their rental car didn't offer the height of luxury, but it did have an engine with a respectable amount of pickup. Long as he managed not to score a speeding ticket along the way, he intended to take advantage of it.

"Kane's been working on the plans for the inn, too, since we moved there a couple months ago. He tells me they're finally making some progress. Rodrigo has also teamed up with Fortune Brothers Construction—that's Callum and his brothers' company that'll be building the hotel. It's Callum's baby sisters—Ashley, Megan and Nicole—who own Provisions. I've heard talk that Nicole—she's our sous-chef—will be heading over to the inn's new restaurant as the executive chef. She'll be working with a local woman who has a really loyal clientele they're hoping will follow her."

"Ashley's your cousin, too?"

"I told you. There are lots of cousins. Can't swing a cat in Texas without hitting one of them and particularly in Rambling Rose. My dad and their dad and Gerald didn't know anything about each other, but they've all inherited the same knack for populating the earth. We've all got huge families."

"As big as yours? I remember you telling me there are six of you. And I remember Kane."

"How about the twins?"

She hesitated. "No. Sorry, but I don't—"

"I think you only met them once," he assured. "Brady and Brian. They were still in high school when you and I were toge—when we met. Josh was learning to drive and Arabella was—" he thought a moment "—fourteen."

"The only girl," she murmured. "Driving all of her overprotective big brothers positively mad, no doubt."

He smiled wryly. "Something like that."

"And your parents? Your mom? I feel like she was a teacher or something."

"Not a teacher, but she did work at a school."

"They're well?"

"Mom's good. Dad's the same."

"Same as what?"

He shook his head ruefully. "Doesn't matter. Callum's family is two bigger than ours. And Gerald's— Well, let's just say there are a lot of them from that particular uncle. Legitimate and otherwise from what I've heard."

"I can't imagine what that's like," she murmured. "My parents were only children. I'm an only child."

Was Linus going to grow up as an only child, too? he wondered.

Adam told himself that it didn't matter. As long as Linus *had* a chance to grow up.

He loosened his death grip on the steering wheel. "There were plenty of times growing up when I wished I was an only. Most of Callum's brothers and sisters have landed in Rambling Rose. The only one there who isn't involved that much with the development end of things is Stephanie. She works at the vet clinic." He drummed the steering wheel with his thumb a few times. Hell. Putting it off wouldn't keep Laurel from learning it soon enough and it would be better if it came from him. "She was Linus's foster mom for a while."

Laurel's silence was weighty. Too weighty to think she'd suddenly dozed off in the middle of their conversation.

"Don't know for sure," he added, feeling like he was handling a live explosive, "but I believe she was hoping for a more permanent deal. When… After you—"

"—abandoned him." Her voice shook.

"You left him at the pediatric center." He flexed his fingers again.

"Oh, that makes it all perfectly all right, then."

He ignored the facetiousness. "You left a note in his car seat. It was kind of cryptic."

"Meaning what?"

He flexed his fingers around the wheel again. "The

note said something about him belonging at Fortune's Foundling Hospital."

"Foundling! Like an orphanage?"

"Assume so. It used to stand where the pediatric center is now."

"That doctor talked about that on the news story. So there were Fortunes in Rambling Rose before now who were taking care of babies without a mother."

"You're making me wish I hadn't said anything."

She sighed heavily.

So did he.

They drove in silence again.

He finished the lukewarm coffee. She tossed the empty cup in the back seat and replaced it with one of the water bottles she'd brought. She opened another for herself. "So you were bored in New York." Her words were abrupt, as if the thick silence between them hadn't occurred. "Decided Texas sounded more exciting?"

"Something like that."

"And the restaurant fits the bill?"

Not even remotely. "Provisions isn't the worst gig I've ever had."

"Faint praise," she murmured. "You haven't said anything about brewing."

He gave a surprised jerk. "Brewing?"

"Beer."

"I know what you meant."

She shifted and he could tell she was looking out the side window to hide her yawn. "On my birthday that time, up in the balloon, I remember you said engineering was the smart choice. Good field with lots of potential. But what you really wanted to do was open your own craft brewery. You said there was too much risk, though. More chance of failure than success."

His chest ached. "Anything *else* you remember?"

He felt the weight of her gaze when she shifted again. "I guess you're right," she said instead of answering. "About it being a small world. You being in the right place at the right time to help my son." Her plastic water bottle crinkled softly in her hand. "Who could have predicted that?"

Truer words, he thought.

"Climb in the back seat." Aside from the occasional long-distance truck, there was no traffic to speak of. He wouldn't even need to pull off to the side of the highway first. "You can stretch out and sleep."

"You're not going to sleep. So neither am I." The declaration was somewhat ruined by the yawn that followed.

"Laurel, please. Just—"

"Why did Dr. Granger say she'd refund your credit card?"

It came out of the blue and he frowned at her. "What?"

"In her office the day we left. She said she'd make sure the charges were refunded to your card."

He knew perfectly well what she was referring to. He just didn't know how to answer.

"*You* were the arrangement, weren't you? You were going to pay the fees so that I could stay there. I know how much money that takes. Mrs. Grabinski told me what she has to pay for Mr. Grabinski."

He exhaled loudly. "Does it matter?"

But she wasn't finished with out-of-the blue questions, it seemed. "Do you know what he looks like?"

Linus. Of course she meant Linus.

"Although I guess you wouldn't have any reason to," she answered before he could.

"I saw him at the hospital," he admitted. "Through a window."

"And?" She sounded almost breathless.

"And he's a baby." He wasn't the artist. Nor a man blessed with the gift of words. "He's got a round little head and kind of a pointed chin. Not much hair. One day it'll be the color of an oak barrel, but right now, it's just…wisps of brown. He didn't even really look sick. He had a blue blanket in one hand and was beating the hell out of the floor with the plastic toy in his other."

She undid her safety belt and started clambering over the seat. Her hair slid over his shoulder as she pressed a kiss to his cheek along the way. "Thank you," she whispered.

His cheek burned. "For what?"

"Being you."

Then he heard rustling as she arranged herself in the back seat, followed by the distinctive click of a safety belt.

The rearview mirror told him she was lying down. He figured it wouldn't be long before she was sleeping. The silence that ensued seemed to confirm it.

He lifted the water bottle again and drank. He'd stock up on more caffeine when they hit Albuquerque. He was going to need it. Caffeine and another packet of aspirin. Because his back was killing him again.

"I don't think it was Eric I was afraid of."

Her words were soft. Not at all asleep.

"I think it's just me," she went on huskily. "I think I'm the one I'm afraid of."

He looked in the rearview mirror again. She was still lying out of his sight. "Why do you think that?"

But no answer came.

And he kept driving. The tires inexorably eating away the distance between them and the son she still didn't know was his.

Chapter Twelve

It was the cessation of motion that woke her.

Laurel's eyes felt gritty when she blinked them open. The twisted safety belt was strangling her and she unfastened it and stiffly pushed herself up to a sitting position.

She was alone in the car. And it was dawn, but only just.

A gas pump sat outside her window. Out the other side, pink fingers of light were just creeping along the horizon. She felt around for her shoes, then remembered she'd kicked them off when she'd been sitting in the front seat with Adam.

Adam.

She rummaged through her canvas bag until she found her hairbrush and quickly restored some order.

She still probably looked like she'd been put up wet, but given the limitations, it was the best she could do. She could see that while she'd slept, he'd gotten into more of their provisions. One bruised banana and only half a package of cookies remained.

"Still love your Oreos, I see." The memory of lying on a couch, her head on his lap while she sketched and he studied and demolished cookies was disturbingly bright in her mind.

She grabbed her toothbrush and toothpaste and awkwardly climbed into the front seat again to push her bare feet into the tennis shoes before getting out of the car. The air was dry and cool enough to send chills dancing all over her.

The gas station seemed to be located in the middle of nowhere.

She had no way of knowing what state they were in, much less what town—if there even *was* a town—since the only thing in every direction were wide, flat plains.

She assumed Adam was inside the small building on the other side of the lone pump and headed toward it. Gas stations always had a bathroom. Even ones on an empty road in the middle of nowhere.

The dirt-streaked glass door let out a musical ping when she entered and Adam, standing in front of a gigantic coffee machine, glanced around. His five o'clock shadow had darkened even more. It would only take another day and he'd have a beard. His thick brown hair was rumpled over his forehead and the too-small shirt clung to very, *very* male muscle and sinew.

Her skin suddenly felt one size too small and her cheeks felt five shades too hot.

She held up her toothbrush, desperately trying to banish the alluringly graphic memory of him rising over her. Of his hands and his mouth—

"Bathroom," she squeaked.

Adam jerked his head. "Through the door over there. You want anything to drink? We have another twenty-five miles before we reach Horseback Hollow. We'll stop for breakfast there. Ernie's been telling me there's a good place to stop."

"That's right. The Grill," the clerk—Ernie—advised sagely from his position behind the register. "Place isn't much to look at, but they slap down the best waffles and bacon this side of Vicker's Corners."

"Can't ignore such a rousing recommendation," Adam said, sending her another look. "So?"

She was grateful to her eternal soul that he didn't know what was going on inside her head. She crossed her arms over her chest and shrugged. She'd do better with a cold shower than something to drink. Her nipples were so tight they hurt, and there was a hollow warmth deep inside her that she hadn't experienced in…

"Laurel?"

She gulped. "O-orange juice?" Thankfully, her words didn't sound as strangled as they felt.

"Oh, yeah." The clerk seemed to take it as a question. "I've got all kinds of juice. Far end of the cold case there."

"Great." She didn't dare look at Adam again. "I'll

just, ah, just, ah…be quick." She bolted through the door he'd indicated.

She slammed the door behind her and flipped the lock. The bathroom was unexpectedly clean, scrupulously so. The smell of disinfectant was so strong it was almost overpowering.

She wished she could clean out her mind so thoroughly.

She stood there, back against the door, her hands pressing hard against her aching breasts.

The memories were so vivid. It could have been just yesterday. Or ten minutes ago. Or right now, this very moment.

She lifted the back of her hand to her mouth, stifling the hard, hard breath she drew.

The feel of him. Moving inside her. Filling her.

Oh, the way he tasted her.

Touched her.

Drove her.

There hadn't been an inch of her body that he hadn't explored. An inch of his that she hadn't known.

She wrenched away from the door, her toothbrush and toothpaste clattering in the sink as she slapped the water faucet. She barely had the presence of mind to yank off her sweater so she didn't soak it right through with the water she threw over her face, trying to douse the memories that were flooding her mind. Filling her veins.

Eventually, thankfully, she found some control again.

Though she felt exhausted, like she'd just run a marathon.

She used the toilet. Then back at the sink where her sleep-creased face looked back at her through the water running down the cracked mirror. She used way too many paper towels mopping up. Not just her face and arms, but the floor and the mirror and the sopping front of her thin camisole pajama top.

She should have thought to bring in fresh clothes from her bag. But it was too late now.

She brushed her teeth. Twice. And raked her hair into yet another braid that she had no way to fasten.

Sunlight began slanting through the little window high up on the wall. She'd spent too much time in there. Adam would be wondering what was taking her so long.

She couldn't very well explain, either.

Their relationship was in the past.

Before different paths.

Before life and everything else that had resulted in her leaving her own baby.

Didn't matter that—at the moment—what she and Adam had shared all those years ago felt exquisitely, excruciatingly alive.

She blew out an unsteady breath and reached for her cardigan. The slant of light shined brightly over the scars on her wrist.

Her vision pinpointed and her mind suddenly felt like it was exploding.

She barely had time to reach the toilet before she retched. And retched. And retched.

After, she sank down on the floor, feeling too weak to do anything else.

She didn't know how long she sat there before Adam came looking for her. Just as she'd known he would. Because that was the man he was.

Concern was in his voice as he sharply rattled the locked knob. "Laurel. You in there?"

He didn't deserve any of this. He shouldn't need to come looking for her. To rescue her. She was a grown woman.

It still took everything she possessed to get herself off the floor. To her feet. Her legs felt like unraveling cotton. Her feet felt like blocks of wood.

It took two tries to unlock the door and she pulled it open. "Where else would I be?" She squeezed toothpaste for the third time that morning onto her toothbrush and turned on the faucet again.

"What's wrong?"

Toothbrush in mouth, she shook her head. Tears still managed to squeeze out of her closed eyes. She was a basket case. That was what was wrong. And if he had a lick of sense, he'd stay far away from her.

She held her unraveling braid behind her neck and continued trying to brush the enamel right off her teeth.

Adam finally muttered an oath and took the toothbrush out of her hand. "Laurel."

She leaned over, splashing water on her face all over again. It trickled down her cheeks, her neck, wetting her already damp camisole.

And still the tears burned, but no more so than the realization still charring her mind.

He grabbed her shoulders, forcing her to look at him. His eyebrows were nearly fused over his nose and lines creased his cheek where his dimple usually hid. He slid his hands around her wet face. "What's wrong?"

"She killed herself. My mother. I remember it now." She could no more hold in the thick admission than she could stop her tears. She lifted her wrist between them. Her wrist that was scarred so similarly to her mother's. "She tried the first time when I was in grade school. A-and the second time before I started college. She was so vain you'd think she'd have preferred pills. But it was always her wrists."

"Oh, baby." He pressed his forehead to hers. "I'm sorry. So sorry."

She swallowed hard against another wave of nausea and wrenched away from him. He was comfort. And safety.

And she didn't deserve it.

"I'd visited them last fall. It was the first time in years. I was pregnant but I wasn't really showing much. I intended to tell them, but—" She swallowed hard. "We argued. We always argued. About my friends. My hairstyle, my clothes. You name it. But this time it was my work. Mother was okay if she could brag about me working at some museum in Europe, but she went ballistic when I mentioned a modern gallery in Vancouver that was interested in me. Even though I'd thought I could stay with them for a while, I just…couldn't. If I'd have stayed, I would have lost myself all over again and I walked out the front door and didn't look back." She closed her hands over the sides of the sink and pulled in a shuddering breath. "You know what they say about the third time. When my father called after Christmas to tell me she'd finally succeeded, he made sure to remind me that mother had been upset about Vancouver." She shook her head, even though there was no denying the truth. "Every time." Her throat felt raw. "Every time she tried hurting herself, it was because of me."

"You are *not* at fault." His voice was adamant. Immediate. "I don't know much, Laurel, but I do know that."

She glared at him. "Now every time I see this," she slapped her wrist, "I'll remember!" It was no wonder she'd hated her scars from the very first time she'd seen them.

He grabbed her arm. Tight. Insistent. "Every time I see this," he said, his voice rough, "I'll remember, too. I'll remember that you're still here."

His head ducked and his lips pressed against the inside of her arm. "You're—" he kissed her wrist "—still—" and her hand "—here."

And when he raised his head, his eyes gleamed. He flattened her hand against his chest. His heart was thundering almost as violently as hers.

"You're still here, Laurel. I won't pretend to understand what you're feeling. How to understand what drove your mother. But I do know this. No matter what you think, you're not like her. And you're not responsible for the things she did."

"Why do you even care?" Her voice broke.

"Because I—" He didn't finish. Instead he swore. Loudly and fiercely. It echoed around the tiled, antiseptic-smelling room.

He let go of her and turned his back, head bowed,

hands on his lean, jean-clad hips. Then his shoulders moved, straining the limits of the Durango T-shirt even more. "Because I do."

Then he bent over and picked up her cardigan from the floor where it had fallen. He turned to face her again and held it open for her. "Because I do," he repeated. "Put your arms in."

She swallowed hard, fresh tears threatening all over again, this time owed strictly to him. "I hate crying," she hiccuped.

"I hate you crying, too." Since she hadn't moved, he did, circling behind her, and she felt the soft, familiar safety of her pink sweater being drawn up over her arms. "And never more than when I know there's not one damn thing I can do to make things better for you."

She looked at his face, blurred by tears, but so, so very clear. She swiped her cheeks while he began buttoning her sweater, pushing one button after another through their holes from the bottom up. "You make everything better. I feel like you have always made everything better."

Instead of smiling, though, his lips twisted in a frown. "Laurel, there's something I need to tell—"

"Sorry." Ernie the clerk knocked loudly even though the bathroom door was still open from Adam's entry. "Just wanted to check." He looked awkward, avoiding actually looking in at them. "Getting a line out at the pump, see, and—"

"That's my fault." Laurel wiped her cheeks again and despite her still-clumsy feet, slipped around Adam. "I'm sorry. We'll get out of the way now."

"Some mornings are rougher than others getting going." Ernie's voice followed her through the door.

There were several people now at the coffee machine. She ducked her head and hurried out of the building. The cool air felt even colder thanks to her wet shirt. The thin sweater was no match.

Ernie hadn't exaggerated about the line. Six vehicles waited for a chance at the gas pump.

She sank into the car's back seat and grabbed a shirt from her canvas tote. She'd change in the car, the same way she used to when Adam would pick her up after her last class of the week on their way to Larkin Square. Once there, they'd eat—usually food from one of the ever-present food trucks—and they'd sit on the grass together and study or, just as often, end up dancing to the music from one of the local bands. Then he'd go to his shift at The Yard and she'd take the bus back to their apartment.

Why...*why* had she ever accepted that fellowship that had taken her away from him?

The question wasn't really a question considering she now knew the answer. Along with every other memory about her parents that had exploded in her mind, she'd remembered that.

She'd chosen the fellowship because she'd been afraid of what her mother might do if Laurel chose Adam.

Adam opened the driver's door and his weary eyes skated over her in the back seat.

She held up the fresh shirt in silent explanation.

He handed her the plastic bottle of orange juice that

she'd entirely forgotten about and then slid behind the
wheel and closed the door. A moment later, the engine
rumbled and they were driving away from the pump.

She turned and looked out the back window to see
the line of cars jockeying for fresh positions. "Ernie
needs another gas pump." She turned back around and
Adam's eyes seemed to trap hers in the rearview mirror.

Every memory BA that she'd regained—good and
bad—had been because of him.

"Do you still want to stop in Horseback Hollow?"
he asked her.

"I think we'll have to," she said huskily. "These will
never last you the rest of the way to Houston." She
lifted the nearly empty bag of cookies for him to see
and smiled shakily. "And you hate bananas."

When they reached The Grill in Horseback Hollow—
Ernie hadn't exaggerated about the place not being much
to look at—Adam phoned the hospital while Laurel pe-
rused the restaurant's one-sided menu.

She was calmer than she'd been. Her tears had dried,
her eyes no longer red. She'd changed out of the flying
pig pajama pants and wet camisole into narrow blue
jeans and a white button-down shirt that would have
looked like a man's shirt except for the way it hugged
her slender curves.

Adam figured the only reason she wasn't wearing
that ever-present sweater was because the shirt had
long sleeves.

Not a single scar on her arm showed.

Neither did the gold necklace hanging around her neck. A gold necklace that *he'd* given her.

It had shaken the hell out of him to see it on her back in Seattle.

He was acutely aware of how brittle she was. As if one hit from a strong Texas wind would send her toppling.

If he was certain he was the one meant to catch her, he wouldn't feel as brittle himself as he did.

"Mr. Fortune." The night nurse who was still on duty that early in the morning finally came on the line. "I'm sorry for making you wait. We had a small emergency."

His nerves tightened. "Not Linus—"

"No, no," she assured quickly. "We had a security alarm malfunctioning. Maintenance has been all over up here working on getting it fixed. Linus is sleeping, though. He had a good night. The fever hasn't diminished. But it hasn't worsened, either. His fa—Mr. Johnson, I mean—fed him last evening before leaving for the night and Linus ate very well. Finished his entire bottle for the first time in several days. We don't want to change his diet too much during this stage of his recovery, of course, but he'll certainly be ready for introducing more baby food when it's time for him to come home."

He should know that his son was ready to eat real food. He should know a million and one things, and Adam didn't know any of them.

There was a reason why pregnancies took so long. To give parents an opportunity to get used to the idea of actually *being* a parent.

In Adam's case, there'd been no time at all.

"We tried pureed bananas the other day," the nurse was saying. "Just a taste. Little guy didn't want anything to do with them. But that's common. You'll just try offering them again sometime down the road. Chances are he'll have completely changed his mind about them."

"Not if he's anything like—" He broke off, realizing what he'd been about to say. *Like me.* He cleared his throat. "Any idea when that time to go home might actually be?"

"I'm sorry," she said sympathetically. "It's too soon to speculate on that."

Which he already knew. But he couldn't help asking.

The server—a girl who looked about thirteen—was heading their way with two glasses of water. She set them on the table then went away again when she saw he was on his cell phone.

"His mother and I should be at the hospital sometime this afternoon," he told the nurse.

"Angelica made a note in his chart that you'd be arriving soon. For some reason, I thought it wouldn't be until tomorrow."

He looked at Laurel. She was listening raptly to his side of the conversation, the menu forgotten. "Is she going to be able to see him? And I don't mean with a window separating them."

"That'll be up to Dr. Patel. You know the rules."

He rubbed his hands down his face. The rules that had prevented him from being able to hold Linus were the same rules that could prevent Laurel from doing so, too. "Isn't there a test or something you can run? Something that proves she's not carrying any kind of germ or infection?"

"Dr. Patel—"

"Yeah, I know. Everything's up to Dr. Patel." He shoved his fingers through his hair. The shower he'd grabbed in Durango seemed like it had been days ago. If he weren't consumed with worry over Linus and Laurel and what sort of situation awaited them in Houston, he felt like he could sleep a week straight. "I should have cell service pretty consistently from here on out, so if anything—"

"We'll call you, Mr. Fortune. Please don't worry yourself unnecessarily. Linus needs you to be fit and able. That means you need to take care of yourself, as well."

"You give that same lecture to Mr. Johnson?"

He could hear the smile in her voice. "We give that same lecture to all the families of our patients, Mr. Fortune. Unless you have any other questions, I really should—"

"No. I appreciate your time."

"Of course. We know this is a challenging time. Whatever we can do to help ease the pain of waiting, we'll try to do." She hung up.

"No change, I gather," Laurel concluded quietly.

He pinched his eyes closed. "Not yet." Then he deliberately set aside the phone and tapped the menu. "Well? Anything interesting? Guacamole on toast or something?"

"It's avocado on toast," she corrected wryly, "and

no." She handed him the menu. "I'm sticking with Ernie's recommendation."

After a quick glance down the limited choices, he agreed. "So am I." They gave their orders to the server and Adam leaned back as far as his chair allowed and stretched out his legs.

Laurel, on the other hand, seemed to be making herself as small as humanly possible.

"What're you worrying about? If the maple syrup here is the real thing or not?"

Her aquamarine eyes lifted and the corners of her lips twitched. "I was…" She let out a sudden, noisy breath. "Actually, I was wondering what will happen once we get to Houston."

"Parents can stay twenty-four-seven in the room with their kids."

That fact didn't seem to ease her mind any.

He sat forward again and rested his arms on the table, covering her twisting hands with his. "I don't think Eric usually spends the night there. He's got a business to run, too." He wasn't leaving her alone with the guy, either, until he knew for certain that she didn't fear him for some reason. And if she really didn't, he still didn't want to leave her alone with him.

Yeah, she was still wearing that necklace after all these years, but she'd also told Adam to his face last June that she intended to honor her engagement. She was marrying Eric and what had happened between her and Adam after Oozefest was best forgotten.

Not wanting to think about that fact didn't mean it hadn't happened.

Her fingers moved inside his, dragging him back from the edge of that particular pit. "Are all donors usually granted this sort of access?"

"What do you mean?"

"You know. The way you're able to talk to the doctors and nurses about the patient who received your donation?"

He heard a strange ringing in his ears as his mind went blank. His hands went lax and he sat back in his seat.

"Or is it just because they know—" she moistened her lips and picked up her fork to study it as if it were the most fascinating thing on the planet "—that they know *I'm* with you?"

"Yeah." Like the coward he was, he latched onto the vaguely plausible excuse that she'd conveniently dropped right into his lap. "Yeah. That's it. Probably."

Her expression didn't look any less anxious, though.

"You don't have to stay there at the hospital, though," he assured. "Not if you aren't ready for that. Nobody's going to judge you if you aren't."

She was chewing her lip. "Truth? I don't know what I'm ready for. I don't think I'll know until I actually get there. But—"

It dawned on him, then. What was at the root of the uncertainty clouding her eyes. "You can stay with me."

Her lips parted softly.

"Kane and me," he revised. "We're renting a bungalow not too far from Provisions."

"A bungalow." She'd stopped biting her lip, but had started twirling her fork in her fingers. "Sounds small."

"Two bedrooms." He worked his jaw to one side, trying and failing to loosen it up. "I'll sleep on the couch."

Her lashes lowered.

He felt increasingly cornered. "If you need a place, that is. You might not, once you've seen—"

"Linus."

His pulse pounded in his head for a prolonged moment. "I was thinking of Eric Johnson," he admitted finally and his words seemed to sit like a ticking bomb in the air between them.

"Here we go." The server arrived, cheerfully setting two oversize plates in front of them, each loaded with a steaming, golden brown waffle, a mound of fluffy scrambled eggs and several strips of thick, masterfully cooked bacon.

Despite the situation, Adam's stomach growled.

Laurel heard.

Her expression finally lightened and she smiled slightly as she picked up the small carafe of syrup the server had also brought. "What do you think? Real maple or imitation? Shall we place bets?"

Chapter Thirteen

The syrup was real maple.

And the taste lingered on Laurel's tongue long after they'd left The Grill—and the small town of Horseback Hollow—in the rearview mirror.

Texas was a big state. She knew it would take hours yet before they reached Houston.

She'd already tried sketching. The decaying remnant of what had once been a barn that they passed. Adam's hand and the way his wrist hung over the top of the steering wheel as he drove. The three hot-air balloons in Durango. But the motion of the car meant everything showed the slight vibration of the engine and the constant buffeting of the wind blowing across the plains. She finally replaced her pencils in their box and closed the pad.

"Give up?"

"I only have a few pages of paper left. I don't want to waste them."

"You can get another sketch pad."

She lifted her shoulder, a noncommittal "hmm" in her throat. She didn't know how, when she had no source of income at all. She doubted that the job offer in Vancouver she'd accepted was still waiting after she'd managed to be a no-show thanks to the car accident. She couldn't quite put her finger on *what* had occurred during those days between her father calling to tell Laurel about her mother and the car accident. Not only had she forgotten the baby, but she couldn't even remember her mother's funeral, and there surely must have been one. But it seemed safe to assume the reason she'd been heading north from Seattle during the storm was to get to Vancouver.

"Are you *sure* you don't want me to drive for a while?" They were surrounded by nothing but miles and miles of windblown plains, punctuated occasionally by a windmill or oil pump jack. And the only thing on the car radio again was static.

"You don't have a driver's license on you, remember?"

She sighed loudly. "Details." She lifted her hand, absently pressing against the necklace hidden beneath her shirt. "I wonder how long it will take to get a copy of my birth certificate."

"Too long, if I had to make a guess."

He sounded so cross, she shot him another look. "If

you won't let me drive, then pull over for an hour so you can sleep."

"I'm fine." He flexed his hand on the steering wheel. "It's more complicated than you might think, getting a copy of a birth certificate. That's all."

She frowned and stared out the window.

"My mom still has copies of all of ours," he said after a moment and just left it at that. Like a person who drops a stone in a pond to watch the ripples.

"Subtle," she murmured. "If my mother *had* kept a copy—" She broke off and it took a long moment before she succeeded in forcing back more tears. "My father's not likely to know or care where it would be. The cleaning crew would have a better idea than he would."

"Would it hurt to ask?"

"There's nothing that simple when it comes to Nelson Hudson." Her mother had been manipulative and tragic. On the other hand, her father had simply been demanding. Controlling. He'd wanted the perfect family to hold up to his friends.

What he'd gotten was Sylvia and Laurel.

"You lived in Europe. You had a passport."

"I already thought of that. I would have had it with me if I'd been on my way to Canada. Surely, there is some procedure in place for people to obtain new ID when—"

"—the unthinkable happens," he said gruffly. She realized the car was slowing. And then he pulled off onto the dirt shoulder and stopped altogether. "Okay. You want to drive. I'll give you one hour."

She was too surprised to respond and just stared

at him as he put the car in Park and got out, walking around the front of the car to her side.

He opened her door. "Changed your mind?"

She quickly unfastened her safety belt. She slid out of the car and looked up at him. "What do you think?"

"I think I never could make the smart decisions where you're concerned," he muttered.

She narrowed her eyes. "What's that supposed to mean?"

He waved his hand at her. "Just go on. Before I change my mind."

She gave him another look but then crossed around to the driver's side and got in. She adjusted the seat so she could reach the gas and brake pedals better while he adjusted the passenger seat so he could stretch out his legs better. Then she fussed with the mirrors until they, too, were perfectly positioned.

"Wasting daylight, sweetheart. Or don't you feel as confident now that you're behind the wheel?"

She gave him a tight smile. "Don't be nast— Oh. I see." She pointed her finger into his face. "I see what you're doing."

She put the car in gear and checked the road. It was as empty as it had been when he'd pulled over, and she started accelerating.

She could feel her heart climbing up into her head where it pounded noisily in her ears. Her fingers were so tight it was as if they were trying to strangle the steering wheel. She unwound them, one at a time, flexing them until her knuckles were no longer white.

How many times had she seen Adam do the very same thing?

The wheels bumped off the shoulder as she steered back onto the highway and sped up even more until the speedometer needle was squarely on top of the bright white sixty.

"Speed limit is ten miles faster," he said a while later.

She grimaced. "I know." She managed to edge up five more miles per hour, which made it feel as though she was speeding hell-bent for leather. "Just...don't bother me." At least there were no other cars to be annoyed with her failure to drive at the full speed.

He adjusted the back of his seat so that it was reclining several inches. "One hour," he reminded sternly.

"You're going to sleep anyway."

"No." He crossed his arms over his wide chest and exhaled audibly. "Just giving you a chance to spread your wings."

She was quite afraid that he meant it.

The road ahead was one narrow sweep bisecting closely shorn fields of earth green and flaxen gold. The sky was a big round bowl of pale blue, striped with nearly translucent streaks of white cloud.

"Last summer. You said we ran into each other."

"Hmm."

She glanced at him. His eyes were closed. But there was nothing relaxed about him.

She watched the road again, felt the vibration of the tires. And she hated the fact that—even though the road was bone-dry, the sky clear—she still felt nervous. As if she were riding a bronco that could break out of control at the drop of a hat. She peeled one of her hands away from the steering wheel and tested the reception on the radio. She found one station. The Tejano music was faint but it wasn't riddled with static. She turned up the volume a notch. "Where did we see each other?"

He didn't answer right away. A woman singing in Spanish underscored by bright horns filled the silence but didn't keep it from feeling much too thick. "Does it matter?"

"The fact that you're asking makes me tend to think it does." She could see a semi now in her rearview mirror. Gaining rapidly.

She chewed the inside of her lip, feeling tense until it buffeted the car as it passed them. Only once it was speeding ahead of her, the mud flaps bearing silhouettes of a buxom girl, did she let out a long breath.

"You're doing fine." His eyes were still closed.

"You're supposed to be sleeping."

The corner of his lips lifted slightly. He looked vaguely piratical with his dark whiskers and tumbled hair. She'd never thought she cared for facial hair on men, but there was no denying his dark appeal.

She nudged the vent so the air-conditioning blew more directly at her face.

"In Houston. At the art museum."

She almost thought she'd imagined his words. She glanced at him. "I worked there."

He opened his eyes. "You remember?"

She shook her head and focused on the road again.

"Did we really just run into each other, or did you come to see me?"

"It doesn't matter."

"It feels like it does."

"I came to see you," he said eventually.

"Why?"

He shifted. "Because I was in Texas for Gerald Robinson's wedding. Decided to look you up."

"Just for old times' sake."

"Yup." His voice sounded clipped.

He wasn't telling her everything. She knew it in her soul. Part of her wanted to force the matter. Part of her—the larger part—wanted to pretend she'd never asked. Wanted to rewind the moment altogether. "Was I engaged?"

He shifted again. "You had an enormous diamond on your finger. Two of those bridal magazines sitting on the desk in your office. You were looking at gowns. And flowers, if I remember."

She wished *she* could remember.

"Did I tell you Eric and I were pregnant?"

"No."

No hesitation in *that* answer.

She chewed the inside of her lip for another quarter mile. "Did you meet him then? Eric?"

"I didn't meet him until the day of the transplant."

She tried to make the pieces fit inside her mind. But it felt as fruitless as pounding a square peg into the proverbial round hole. "How could I abandon my own baby, Adam?"

"Pull over."

"What? No! No," she added more calmly. "You're the one who needs to sleep. How long have you been awake now?"

"Too long. Pull over."

Her hands tightened. "I don't want to."

He swore. "Laurel, pull the damn car over."

He hadn't raised his voice. She was pretty sure that if he had, she could have ignored him. But he hadn't.

She slowed and steered onto the shoulder. "If we keep stopping like this, it's going to take forever to get to Houston."

"We'll be there soon enough." He barely waited for the tires to stop before he pushed open the car door and got out. His long legs ate up the ground as he paced, then turned around and strode back to the car. He gestured at her. "Get out."

She put the car in Park, exhaling. Then she got out of the car and walked around to the passenger side, prepared to get in, but he held out his hand. "Wait."

She went on the toes of her smiley-faced tennis shoes. Then back down again. She nervously fingered her necklace just below the buttoned collar. "Okay. I'm waiting."

He shoved his fingers through his hair, then hooked them in his front pockets. "There's no easy way to say this, so I'm just going to—" his lips pressed together "—to lay it out there."

"The more you talk like that, the more I think I have to brace myself," she warned. Half lightly, as if she could force him into agreeing.

"You didn't tell me you were pregnant," he said abruptly. "And you particularly didn't tell me you and *Eric* were pregnant."

"This was a year ago, though. Last June? I had to have been pregnant. The baby was born in January."

"He wasn't due until February."

An SUV roared past and she saw the flash of a face in the window looking their way.

"Is that why he got sick? Because he was early?"

"No."

"Are you *sure*?"

"When we get to Houston, Dr. Patel will give you the same answers he's already given me. It's not likely."

"How do you know when I was due, anyway?" She pressed her finger to the pain that had appeared in the center of her forehead.

"Because I know exactly when he was conceived."

Another SUV zoomed past them. If there were any faces staring their way, Laurel didn't notice. "*I* told you that?"

"You didn't tell me anything."

"Then Eric—"

"He didn't tell me anything, either." He hooked his hand behind his neck as if it were paining him. "I know when Linus was conceived, because I was there. Linus is my son, Laurel. Mine and yours."

She felt the ground tilt. She opened her mouth, but nothing emerged. Her head was roaring.

From somewhere far off, she heard Adam swear.

And after that she heard nothing at all.

* * *

Adam cursed himself to hell and back all over again when Laurel's eyes rolled. He barely managed to catch her before she hit the ground.

Her head lolled against his shoulder when he picked her up and carried her to the car, carefully lowering her onto the rear seat.

He crouched alongside the vehicle, leaning inside. "Come on, baby." His hand shook as he gingerly touched her cheek. "Wake up, sweetheart. We'll figure all of this out, I promise."

She didn't stir. Her face was unearthly pale but she was breathing.

He pressed his forehead against her cool cheek and forced himself to stay calm. His mom had fainted once when he'd been a kid. She'd been pregnant with Arabella. Out cold for several minutes. The longest minutes of his life, until he'd been an adult and had offered a ring and his heart to Laurel Hudson.

He reached across her for the water bottle sitting in the cup holder. It was practically empty but he poured out what was left on a crumpled napkin and pressed it to her forehead. He undid the button at her throat and loosened her collar. The gold *L* on her necklace glinted in the light.

After everything that had happened, why did she still wear the necklace?

"Come on, sweetheart. Come back to me." He wedged himself onto an edge of the seat and lifted her feet. Above the heart, if he remembered his first aid correctly. Considering the panic piercing through him, it was hard to think at all. "I shouldn't have told you." He propped her heels on his shoulder and moved the wet napkin from her forehead over her cheeks. "Not on top of you remembering your mother. I should have waited. I should—"

She stirred and her foot slipped from his grasp, landing hard on his hip. He barely noticed. He cupped her cheek, breathing only slightly easier when he saw the sliver of aquamarine between her long eyelashes.

"What—"

"Shh. You're fine. Everything's going to be fine."

Her expression crumpled. "How can anything ever be fine?"

"I told you. You're *here*."

"Everyone would be better off without me."

"Don't even go there," he warned flatly. "That's the kind of thing your mother used to tell you and you hated it."

Her fine eyebrows tugged together. Color was coming back into her cheeks. "I did hate it," she whispered. She pulled the wet napkin away from her face and grimaced at it before tossing it aside. "I fainted."

"I know."

"I've never fainted in my life."

"Sure about that?"

Her lips twisted and she pulled her legs off his. She pushed herself up until she was sitting. "I can't be sure of anything, can I?"

You can be sure of me.

He didn't say the words, though. Last year at the art museum when he'd seen the diamond, seen the wedding magazines, seen the truth in her eyes, he'd finally faced the truth. Despite everything, despite that night together in New York after the muddy festival, she still hadn't chosen him. Chosen them.

He'd told her he was done. Never again. He wasn't ever again going to be the safety net she'd kept dangling from her fingertips. When she was upset about her mother, when she was struggling against her father's controlling expectations, when she was frustrated with the dullness of the jobs she'd taken in one museum or art gallery after another because what she really wanted to do was create her own art. She could dump it all on the fiancé she hadn't even had the guts to tell Adam about before the two of them had been climbing inside each other's skin barely a month earlier.

Then he'd turned on his heel and walked away.

Now she pushed at him until he got out of the car. She followed. "Let's just get to Houston, please. You can explain everything else you're not saying along the way." She lowered herself into the passenger seat and began adjusting it.

He pushed her door closed. Houston. Where the man whose diamond she *had* been wearing last year was still waiting.

He rounded the car and got in, shoved the seat back as far as it would go, and started driving. Again.

Only this time, he told her the rest.

He told her everything.

Except for the fact that he had never stopped loving her. And that if he were a better man, she'd have never felt so alone and so desperate that she'd believed leaving their child was the only option left.

The wing of the Houston hospital where the transplant unit was located was smaller than Laurel had pictured in her mind.

By the time they'd entered and were standing in a waiting room that bore cartoon characters all over the walls, she was sweating. She could feel beads of it sliding down her spine and her hair kept clinging to her face no matter how many times she tucked it behind her ears.

"Are you sure you're up to this?" He took her hand and squeezed gently. They were waiting for the duck who'd greeted them to come back and grant permission to pass through the castle door. "You look ready to pass out again."

She did feel ready to pass out, but she was loath to admit the obvious.

She could feel the panic coming, but knowing what was happening and being able to stop it were two different things. "I have to—I have to get out of here." Before the horrible, terrible clawing shredded her from the inside out. While his expression was still forming a frown, she bolted out the door and immediately found herself standing in the middle of a city she couldn't remember.

One hand on the stitch in her side, one on the ache in her chest, she searched for a street sign. A building sign. Anything that would help ground her back in something remotely approaching reality.

Intersection. She needed an intersection. She ran again. Skidded to a halt at a corner where dune buggies and chariots crisscrossed in busy confusion along with pedestrians. She read the street signs. They were in French and meant nothing to her.

"Please," she said frantically, "please can you help me?" She stretched her hand toward a man in a gray suit and red tie who swerved away with a look of pure distaste. She whirled again toward another pedestrian. Dark sunglasses perched on her patrician nose. "Do you know where the hospital is?"

Laurel's mother tugged down her sunglasses with scarred wrists. "You have to choose," she screeched.

Laurel gasped, her eyes flying open. But instead of her mother, she stared into Adam's frowning face.

She blinked. She wasn't standing on a strange street corner in Houston. She hadn't run out on her child, yet again.

She let out a shuddering breath. She was with Adam. The *father* of that child.

And they were parked at the curb in front of a small house.

"You were having a bad dream," he said. "You want to talk about it?"

"No." She rubbed her eyes, wishing she could also rub away the dregs of the nightmare. Was it better to have a dream about a panic attack or actually *have* a panic attack?

At least she didn't feel like she was having a heart attack. So maybe that was progress.

"Where are we?"

"My place." He pushed open the car door and climbed out, moving stiffly. "In Rambling Rose."

She looked quickly at the house again.

Then Adam opened her door. "Come on."

His fingers closed warmly around hers as she climbed from the car. But as soon as she was standing beside him, he let go of her again.

She crossed her arms in front of her, tucking away her hands. "I didn't know you wanted to stop in Rambling Rose."

"Only to switch to my truck." He opened the trunk and removed his overnighter and her canvas tote. She wasn't even sure when he'd moved them from the back seat. "I talked to the hospital again while you were sleeping. The fever's gone."

She blinked. "Just…just like that."

"Just like that."

She was relieved. Desperately so. She also felt decidedly off-kilter. "How long did I sleep?"

"Five hours." He strode up the quaint stone walkway to the front door and pushed open the door, waiting for her. "It's too hot to stand out there in the sun."

She ducked her head slightly and went inside.

There was nothing remarkable about the house's interior. The door opened straight into a small living room occupied by a drab couch, a couple of worn chairs and a scarred coffee table that looked straight out of the sixties. "You've mastered the Early First-Apartment style, I see."

"Picked up everything at Mariana's Market." He dropped his overnighter and her tote on the couch. "It was cheap and it gets the job done. Sorry if it doesn't live up to the Hudson standards."

She bit her lip. "That's not what I meant."

"I know." He went through a doorway. "I'm putting on a shirt that fits," he said over his shoulder. "Then we'll get going. There should be cold drinks in the fridge if you want to grab a couple. If not in there, then check the garage. There's a spare fridge out there, too."

She plucked her hairbrush from her tote and dragged it through her tangled hair as she glanced around. Three doorways led from the living room. She assumed the one he'd taken went to the bedrooms. She chose the one in the middle.

Vile orange tile covered the kitchen floor, but it struck her as very clean. Adam always had been a neat-nick. She'd been the one who'd left her clothes tossed around carelessly.

She pushed that memory to the back of her mind and yanked open the small, old-fashioned refrigerator.

Inside, save the label-less brown bottles that she instinctively knew contained beer that Adam had brewed, the metal shelves were nearly empty.

She closed the fridge and opened the door on the opposite side of the room, correctly assuming it led to the garage.

There wasn't anything as ordinary as a vehicle parked inside, though. What Adam hadn't spent on furniture, he'd more than made up for in brewing equipment. Large stainless tanks lined one wall. Supplies were stacked neatly on shelves on the other wall. There were plumbing lines and flow pipes and pumps and electrical equipment, and for a moment she remembered the rudimentary setup he'd had back in New York.

"You find something to drink?" Adam's voice called from inside the house and she quickly wiped away the moisture that had formed at the corners of her eyes. She crossed to the gigantic stainless steel refrigerator on the far wall.

Still no food to speak of, but there were several bottles of vitamin-infused water and a few cans of soda.

"Yes," she called back. She took two waters and went back into the kitchen, closing the door after herself.

He was bent over, looking inside the small refrigerator. The Durango shirt was gone, replaced by a charcoal gray button-down.

"There's nothing much in there."

He shut the door and straightened. "I noticed." He turned to face her and held out his hand for one of the vitamin waters. Along with the fresh shirt, he'd also brushed his hair and it no longer fell engagingly over his forehead. His eyes were hooded, and with that near beard, he almost looked like a stranger.

She chewed the inside of her cheek. There were things that she should say. But what?

"You need your own brewery," she blurted, which wasn't at all what she really wanted to say.

"Yeah, well, maybe one day I'll have enough money to get one. It's going to be an hour to Houston. Bathroom's down the hall if you need it."

"Thanks," she muttered like the gargantuan coward

that she was, and left the kitchen. She went through the doorway he'd used and found the bathroom on the right. Like the kitchen, it was tidy and clean.

She left it that way a minute later.

He was flipping through the mail that was collected on the small table next to the front door. "Ready?"

She shouldered the canvas tote in answer.

His expression seemed to tighten, though she had no idea why, and he ushered her out the front door again, locking it after them.

The big black truck parked at the curb was the destination and she climbed up inside when he opened the door for her. "Nice truck," she murmured, even though she felt distinct regret as she watched the small silvery sedan through the side mirror.

His phone gave a little chime and he glanced at it when he stopped at the corner stop sign. He sighed slightly.

"Ashley?"

"Yeah." He slid the phone into a slot on the fancy console between their seats. "She thinks she's got the flu. I need to stop by the restaurant and take care of a few things that can't wait. Won't take me long."

"Whatever you need to do." She wasn't in any position to dictate the schedule.

He turned at the stop sign and soon they'd left behind the neighborhood of bungalow homes just like his. He drove past a municipal complex. A post office. The buildings grew fancier. Newer. A spa. A Mexican restaurant where cars were overflowing the parking lot.

She suddenly clutched his arm. "Stop. Wait."

He muttered an oath, obviously startled. "What?"

She was staring at the brick building across the street. "There. The pediatric center. I want to go in here." Then she shook herself. "You can drop me off. Pick me up again when you're finished at Provisions."

He turned into the parking lot. But instead of dropping her off, he parked.

"You don't have to go with me."

"You think I'm going to leave you alone? *Here?*" He got out of the truck when she did, and together they went up the wide, shallow steps of the restored building. Adam pulled open the door for her and they went inside.

She looked around. Anxious. Eager.

For a medical clinic, it wasn't the least bit clinic-y. Lots of exposed brick. Wood floors with a gleaming, warm patina. Two women wearing colorful scrubs stood behind a reception desk, and beyond them, Laurel could see a play area.

Adam's fingers grazed her elbow. "Remember being here?"

Her shoulders fell. She'd so hoped. "N-not at all."

She turned to head back to the entrance.

"Adam?"

They both stopped. A white-haired man with an equally white beard was hurrying around the reception desk. He had a broad smile on his face as he clapped Adam on the shoulder. "Haven't had a chance to talk since you had the harvest. How are you?"

"Good." Adam's gaze slanted to Laurel. "This is Dr. Green."

She managed a smile of sorts. "I recognized you from the news story."

The doctor nearly did a double take. "My God," he breathed, the twinkle in his eyes turning to shock. "You're—"

"Laurel Hudson," Adam provided, sounding much calmer than Laurel felt. "Linus's mother."

Chapter Fourteen

Laurel heard twin gasps coming from the women in the scrubs and suddenly wished that she hadn't asked Adam to stop at the pediatric center at all.

Dr. Green recovered more quickly than anyone else. He clasped Laurel's hand in both of his. "My dear. I am so happy to see you. The last time—well, it was quite a muddle, wasn't it? The grand opening going on and you going into labor right there on the steps. And then—"

"Yes," she said quickly, really and truly reluctant to hear his recap of her behavior after that. She couldn't tell if he knew anything about her accident or her memory loss. And she didn't want to know. It was bad enough to think how much gossip she must have caused by abandoning Linus right here, much less so soon after he'd been born. "It's good to see you, too," she lied, then tugged her hand away to tuck it through Adam's arm.

As if he sensed her overwhelming discomfort, Adam closed his hand over hers. "We're on our way to Houston." His words were as smooth as the way he began moving toward the door. "Just wanted to stop in and say thanks for everything you've done for Linus."

"Of course." The doctor's genial voice followed them. "Dr. Patel's reports have been very promising."

Laurel stopped. She looked around Adam's broad shoulder. "They *have*? But Linus had a fever."

Dr. Green's eyes were kind as he approached her again. "Very promising," he assured. "Despite a little fever." He pulled a business card from the pocket of his white coat and slid it into her free hand. "If you ever feel like talking," he said quietly. "About anything."

Her vision blurred. How could anyone who knew what she'd done treat her with any kindness at all? She looked away. "Thank you."

"Dr. Green," one of the women called his name. "Becky's ready for you with Nathaniel in room two."

The doctor nodded. He clapped Adam on the shoulder again before hurrying back toward the reception desk.

Laurel breathed easier once they were outside again. She didn't say anything when they returned to the truck and made a short drive before Adam pulled into a parking lot outside the large building that was obviously Provisions.

"It used to be a grain warehouse," he explained.

There was still a lot of industrial vibe going on, Laurel thought as they entered the building. It was the middle of the afternoon and more than half of the tables inside were occupied. As soon as Adam's presence was noticed, people seemed to come at him from all sides. "Give me a sec," he told them all and escorted Laurel over to the bar where wooden stools sat in perfect alignment.

He pulled one out. "Relax. I'll be back as soon as I can." He turned on his heel and strode across the wood-planked floor, disappearing through a swinging door at the far end.

She'd barely slipped onto the stool when a young man approached from behind the bar. "What can I get you?"

"I don't suppose you have hibiscus tea?"

He smiled. "New on the menu, thanks to Adam. I'll have it for you in two shakes."

"Thank you."

She folded her arms atop the gleaming wood bar top and looked around. The row of black-and-white photography on one wall drew her attention and she wandered over to take a closer look. She wasn't the only one. An older woman was standing in front of one photo in particular. Laurel stopped next to her. "Is that the pediatric center?"

"Back when it was an orphanage." The woman barely glanced at Laurel as she donned a pair of glasses and leaned even closer to the image. "Look at all of those children. They don't look unhappy, though, do they?"

Laurel found it disturbing to look too closely at the dozen or so children, dressed in shapeless dresses and pants that were inches too short. Two of the older kids were holding babies in their arms. All were lined up on the steps of the building that used to be the foundling hospital.

She realized the woman was still looking at her, clearly expecting an answer.

"No," Laurel said, making herself take a second look. "They don't look unhappy." Some more solemn than others, but not unhappy.

"This baby. The one with the blanket." The woman tucked the reading glasses into her bleached blond hair and tapped a suntanned fingertip against the canvas-backed photo. "First time I've seen the photo enlarged like this and I could swear that's my mother. She never told me she was adopted, but what other reason would she be right there at the foundling hospital?" Her laugh was a little brittle. "My wild imagination. Next thing I'll be wondering just what that monogram on her blanket means." She shook her head slightly and gave Laurel another look. "Haven't seen you before." She suddenly stuck out her hand. "I'm Mariana."

Bemused, Laurel shook her hand. "Of the Market?"

The woman gave a loud bark of laughter that was much less brittle this time. "That'd be me." She patted her plump hips. "In the flesh. I remember a time when I knew every face in this town." She lifted her arms, seeming to encompass all that surrounded them. "Now we have places like this and The Shoppes and gated neighborhoods where the rich folks go." She peered at Laurel. "You look like one of them."

There wasn't anything particularly accusatory in her tone, so Laurel had no reason to take offense. "Don't see how," she said wryly. She looked down at her smiley-face tennis shoes that were more grungy now than white and the jeans she'd been allotted from the women's shelter in Seattle. "I'm Laurel, by the way."

"It's not the clothes, sweetie," Mariana said sagely. "It's what's underneath."

"That's even less impressive, I'm afraid."

Mariana barked her laugh again, then spotted a slickly handsome dark-haired man enter the restaurant. "There's my date," she said a little mischievously. "See you around, Laurel." She headed toward the man. "Yoo-hoo, Mr. Dimples," she greeted with a wave.

Laurel looked back at the photograph, focusing on the two babies in particular, as if by doing so, she could force herself to remember leaving her own child. The one that had so taken Mariana's interest had a blanket wrapped loosely around her legs. The corner that dangled had a clear "F" embroidered on the edge. While the other baby had no blanket at all.

Had Laurel left anything personal with Linus? Or had she simply just…left?

"Thinking about taking up photography?"

She startled at the sound of Adam's voice. He was holding out a transparent to-go cup. "Your hibiscus tea."

She took it, unintentionally brushing his fingers with her own. Feeling flustered, she focused on the enlargement once more. "I never had the talent for photography. Whoever did these enlargements did a nice job, though. Very evocative. You can almost feel the effects from the Dust Bowl and the Great Depression from their faces." Feeling self-conscious, she busied herself flipping open the little flap on the cup lid so she could take a drink. "Are you finished already?"

"Yeah."

A young woman with a black apron tied around her trim hips hurried toward them with a twine-handled paper bag in her hand. The name of the restaurant was splashed across the front. "Here's your order, Adam."

"Thanks." He took the bag, not seeming to notice the adoration gleaming from the girl's pretty brown eyes.

"She's half in love with you," Laurel told him once they were in his truck again. "That waitress."

"She'll get over it. Give me one of the sandwiches in there."

"How do you know?" She looked into the bag. "Does it matter which one?"

He slanted her a look that gave her shivers, though she couldn't quite say why. "Because they always do," he said almost inaudibly. Then he cleared his throat. "And yes, it matters," he added almost indignantly. "The one marked No Avocado."

She pulled out the sandwich, unwrapped it and handed it to him along with one of the paper napkins that were also tucked in the bag.

Then she unwrapped her own sandwich. Fat, rich slices of absolutely perfect avocado resting atop grilled chicken sat between two thick slices of aromatic sour-dough bread.

No, she thought. *They don't always get over you.*

She knew that she wouldn't.

"Put on these gowns," the nurse said, handing Adam and Laurel each a plastic-sealed package. They were standing outside the closed door of Linus's hospital room. "Mask on the face. Booties on the shoes. No gloves, but you'll need to wash your hands at the sink there." She gestured toward the sink nearby. "Use the soap that's provided. You can use the lounge behind the desk here to get gowned up if you want."

Adam was aware of Laurel's increasing pallor as Angelica reeled off the instructions.

"Usually, we wouldn't need all of this," the nurse went on. "Every room in the transplant unit is equipped with specialized air-filtration systems that minimize patient risk of contracting infections. But after Linus's fever, Dr. Patel has ordered stricter measures."

"How, uh, how long can we stay with him?"

"As long as you want," Angelica assured Laurel. "As a general rule, we limit visitors to two at a time, but parents are always allowed. Any other questions?" Her bright eyes moved from Laurel's face to Adam's. "No?" She smiled as she reached for a chart on her desk. "If you need me, just push the call button on the wall over the baby's crib."

Adam pushed his thumb through the thin plastic bag and tore it open. He shook out the gown, and he barely caught the booties before they fell onto the floor. Laurel on the other hand was squeezing the package between her fingers, looking terrified.

He took her arm and led her unresistingly into the nurse's lounge. "Sit down before you pass out again."

"I'm not going to pass out." But she did sit before she finally tore open her package. "He doesn't know me," she whispered.

"He doesn't know me, either." Adam sat down and worked the booties over his shoes, then stood up again and shoved his arms into the sleeves of the gown. It was exactly the same style that Eric had worn the day of the transplant.

He calculated. It had only been nine days ago.

"What if we scare him, dressed up in these things?" She shook the pale blue mask at him.

"We're not going to know until we go in." He tied the back of the gown behind his neck and then looped the mask over his ears. "We've spent the last three and a half days getting here, Laurel."

"I know. I know you're right." Looking more determined, she shook out her own gown and pulled it on. "At least I've made it further than I did in my nightmare," she muttered as she pushed aside her hair to tie the back of the gown. "And there's a comforting absence of nurses who look like ducks." She leaned down to work the booties over her shoes. When she straightened, there was more color in the cheeks that she then hid behind her mask.

"Ducks?"

"Don't even ask." Above the gauzy blue mask, her

eyes were impossibly wide. "Nightmares are weird things."

They left the lounge and stopped at the sink, where she folded up the too-long sleeves of the gown and thoroughly washed her hands and wrists.

He did the same while she dried off with the towels that popped up from a dispenser on the wall.

And then it was time.

The curtain had been drawn across the window that looked into the room. The heavy wide door was slightly ajar and Adam pushed it open with his elbow, waiting for Laurel to enter first.

Her eyes clung to his for a long moment, then she pressed her hand into his and went inside.

They both went stock-still at the sight of the other man standing next to the crib. Even gowned up the same way they were, he was still recognizable.

At least to Adam.

Eric Johnson's eyes met his for a brief moment, then dropped to their clasped hands. He looked away. "He's sleeping," he said quietly and reached into the crib for a moment. "Angelica said you expected to get here today. I thought I'd be gone by the time—" He broke off and looked at them again. "I know when it's my cue to leave."

He passed them out into the hall, hesitating briefly in front of Laurel.

Adam felt her hand trembling in his. He covered her shoulder with his other.

Eric tugged the mask down his chin. His twisted smile was humorless and full of regret.

"It didn't last very long, but I like to think I was a good father." He reached under his gown and emerged with an envelope. "Margaret Malloy's still getting the birth certificate worked out. The social worker," he added for Laurel's benefit.

"Her letter's in here explaining the DNA mess. Turns out there's a whale of a difference between a 99 percent likelihood of paternity backed up by enough personal statements to convince a judge, and a 99.99 percent likelihood that doesn't have to be backed by anything at all except the science." He held out the envelope and Adam took it with fingers that felt numb. "I'd say I'll see you around, but I figure that's nothing any one of us wants to hear. So..." He leaned over and brushed a quick kiss against Laurel's masked cheek. "Goodbye, Laurel." Then he walked away.

Laurel suddenly pulled away from Adam and went through the doorway after him. "Eric, wait."

Adam closed his eyes. The last bit of suspicion he'd been holding on to of Laurel having reason to fear Eric circled down the drain.

He'd known it.

Hadn't he known this would happen all along?

So why did it still feel like he'd been kicked in the kidneys?

A soft whimper from the crib made him open his eyes.

He looked over to see Linus—his son—pushing his padded butt up in the air. He was wearing a stretchy one-piece thing patterned in sailboats that covered him from neck to toes and his brown tufts of hair stood out at all sorts of odd angles.

Adam swallowed hard. His eyes were burning. Whether because of Linus or because of Laurel, he didn't know.

Didn't much care right at that particular moment in time.

He dropped the envelope on the counter next to the doorway before slowly lifting the baby from the crib. Instead of fussing, though, Linus just kicked his feet, clearly excited to be escaping.

He was taller than Adam had expected. And far, far lighter. Which just served to remind him how delicate life could be. "Hey there, buddy."

Linus eyed him curiously, then reached out to hook his fingers on the mask.

"Yeah," Adam said huskily, "I don't like it, either." He held him closer. Linus smelled sweet. Like babies always did. "This is all pretty confusing, isn't it? Even for us grownups."

Linus wriggled. He grabbed unsuccessfully at the mask again, showing off a dimple as he grinned.

Adam caught the baby's fist and kissed it through his mask. "Can I tell you a secret?"

Linus chortled and promptly sank his pink sharpish gums around Adam's knuckle.

He pressed his lips to the little round head. "You've got your mama's eyes."

Outside the room, Eric stopped and stared incredulously at Laurel. "You remember me?"

She pulled off her mask, shaking her head as she studied his face, searching for some smidgeon of familiarity. But the only reason he didn't look like a total stranger was because she'd watched the news video so many times now. "I'm sorry. I... I don't."

He looked pained. "Then why come after me?"

"Because I feel like I need to...to apologize. At least."

His lips twisted. "For what? Breaking up with me? Having someone else's baby even though you told me in a letter that *I* was going to be a father?"

She started. "What letter?"

"It was in your overnight bag. The one you left behind at your folks' place last year. Maybe they felt sorry for me or something, but they sent it to me before Christmas." He rubbed his face tiredly. "Maybe things weren't perfect with us, but you could have told me the truth, Laurel, instead of running off and nearly getting yourself killed. I can't even tell you what a roller coaster the past few months have been."

She probed her mind, trying to remember ever writing a letter to Eric. But she couldn't even remember *him*.

She spread her hands. "If things weren't perfect, why did you want to marry me?"

"I've asked myself that a hundred times," he said wearily. "I'm thirty-five years old. It was time to settle down. And we were good together. I had my business. You had the art museum. We had the same tastes. We enjoyed each other's company. It made sense." He shook his head. "I thought it made sense, anyway. If you'd told me the truth about the baby, we still could have made things work."

"The letter." The base of her head throbbed. "I actually wrote, 'Dear Eric—'"

He made a sound. "'My only love,'" he said gruffly. "'I wish I were braver. I wish I deserved you. I don't know how to tell you that we made a baby together—'" His lips twisted and he looked over her head toward Linus's room. "Foolish of me to assume the letter was meant for me. I realize otherwise now. But you had at one time agreed to be my wife."

"I'm sorry," she said again, feeling helpless.

"Story of my life," he murmured.

"You deserve more," she said suddenly. "Everyone should deserve more than a relationship that just makes sense." She spread her hands. "I hope you find that, Eric. If for no other reason than that you were there for Linus when I wasn't."

He sighed heavily. "I was fine before you, you know. I'll be fine after you. But Linus—" He shook his head. "That's gonna take longer than I want to think about right now."

"I know it's not a perfect solution, but you don't have to disappear from his life."

"I appreciate the sentiment, Laurel. Maybe one day. But for right now, I'm too old to pretend that I don't know it's long past the time to leave the party."

And with that, he turned and walked away.

She stood there in the hall even after he'd disappeared, trying to put a name to the feeling inside her.

Angelica walked past, carrying a plastic bucket filled with medical supplies. "Everything okay?"

"I have no idea," Laurel admitted rawly.

Angelica smiled gently. "You don't have to be afraid. Just go in there and hold your baby," she advised. "Everything else will either fall into place or won't. But you'll have your baby in your arms."

The nurse was right. Everything else would either fall into place or it wouldn't. Laurel could either worry about the past or she could start making her future.

She donned the mask once more and rewashed and dried her hands, and this time when she walked into the hospital room, she held her shoulders straight.

Adam was sitting in the rocking chair she hadn't even noticed the first time. Linus was on his lap, bouncing and wobbling and garbling sweet, sweet baby sounds.

She was tired of the tears that came so easily and too often, but she could no more stop them now than she could stop the earth from turning.

She held out her arms.

Adam stood and settled Linus into them.

"He's so perfect." She pressed her cheek to the baby's, and let out a bubbling sob. "I'm so sorry, baby. I'm so…so…sorry. I promise I won't ever leave you again."

"I'm very glad to hear that," a man said from the doorway. "I'm sorry to interrupt your homecoming. Do you mind?"

"Of course not," Adam said abruptly. "Laurel, this is Dr. Patel."

She quickly swiped her cheeks as he entered, pulling

his own mask into place. He was a head shorter than Laurel and slender as a reed, with a handshake that managed to be both comforting and authoritative. "Dr. Rama Patel," he told her in a slightly British accent.

"Laurel Hudson," she murmured. It was a wrench to let go of Linus with one arm for even as little time as it took to shake the doctor's hand and when she did, Linus managed to grasp her mask and pull it aside. "I'm sorry he doesn't want to cooperate where the masks are concerned." She hastily straightened it.

"Babies like to see a person's full face. Can't blame them for that." He touched his own mask. "These should soon be unnecessary, too."

"Thank you for taking care of him."

"This is my work," he said, a smile in his eyes. He pressed his hands together, almost prayerlike. "I understand you've had a long journey."

Laurel looked toward Adam. "An incomplete one, still." She cradled Linus with both arms once more. He'd moved from playing with her mask to yanking on her hair. "Until we know he's going to be okay."

"A few more days of testing," Dr. Patel said. "Then we will be more certain of it." He patted the baby's back. "Meanwhile, I'm sure you're aware that we encourage mom and dad to stay here." He spread his palms, encompassing the spacious room. "The bench there pulls out into a bed. It's not a five-star resort, of course, but it serves the purpose fairly well."

He gave Adam a wry glance. "It may be a few inches too short in your case. We also have a laundry area where you can take care of your personal needs, and a family kitchen. You can bring in your own food. Have meals together if you wish. Linus has no dietary restrictions. In all regards beside the obvious, he should be treated as a typical infant of his age."

He lifted the chart that had been sitting on the counter and pulled a gold pen from his lapel pocket. "The more normal Linus's life remains, the better off he'll be." His pen scratched across the page as he spoke. "And of course if you aren't able to stay overnight, we'll take excellent care of him until the day that you're finally able to take him home." He closed the chart with a soft snap. "Do you have any questions?"

She shook her head. "Thank you."

"The nurses will check on him regularly," he said. "If his temp stays normal by this evening, I think it'll be safe for you to discontinue the gowns and mask." Then he bowed his head slightly and left. He pulled the door closed after him.

Laurel looked over at Adam. "I'm staying."

"Figured as much." He pushed off the rocking chair and started for the door.

She felt a quick bolt of panic. "Where are you going?"

"To get your stuff from the truck."

"Oh, right." She felt foolish then. "Thanks."

He pulled open the door and left.

The room felt suddenly very large and very empty without him.

She pressed her cheek against Linus's forehead and scooped a plastic ball out of the crib before she sat down in the rocking chair.

"That's your daddy," she whispered. The ball was really just a brightly colored hollow shell with dozens of holes for inquisitive little fingers to latch onto. She waggled it in front of Linus. He grabbed it and eagerly tried to fit it into his mouth—a hopeless endeavor considering its size. "He's pretty amazing," she whispered, "but you're going to find that out for yourself before long. He'll never ever let you down."

Linus smiled toothlessly and pitched the ball at her face.

She caught it with a little laugh.

And then she cradled him to her and cried.

Chapter Fifteen

Laurel was lying on the floor with Linus when Adam returned to the room, and even though he could tell she'd been crying, her eyes were brilliant. "He can roll over!"

"That's great." He set her tote on the bench that could turn into a bed. A bed that, for all he knew, she'd be sharing with Eric.

He cordoned off that thought and pulled out his wallet and extracted his credit card and several bills of cash.

She looked confused. "What's that for?"

"In case you need anything for Linus. I doubt Eric'll let him go without anything, but he's *my* son." He set it all on the bench next to the tote. "I'll come back tomorrow when I can."

She looked even more bewildered. "But you...you're *leaving*?"

"Laurel, I can't stay here with you and him."

"But we need you!"

"It's been a long day. On top of several long days. The only thing you *need* to do is focus on Linus."

"I...see." But she clearly didn't. "What about you? What do you need to focus on?"

Not losing his mind entirely. But that was like closing the coop after the screaming banshees had already escaped. "You want a laundry list?" He held up his hand. "The rental car needs to be turned in. Provisions doesn't have a manager on site right now with me here and Ashley out sick. I've got to figure out the medical insurance mess to make sure everything going on here continues going on here. I need to let Dr. Granger know you're safe and get a damn book or something so I don't feel like a complete ass when it comes to knowing when my *son* is ready to start eating real food!"

Her jaw had dropped. She suddenly reached down and scooped up Linus and plopped him in Adam's arms. "Shut up, Adam. Just shut up and hold your son. You don't have to be the one who always fixes everything all the time. Sometimes—like right now—you can just *be*." She pushed at him and he was so surprised by her vehemence that he actually let her.

He felt the edge of the chair against his legs and sat.

She propped her hands on her hips and he realized then that she hadn't rolled down her sleeves after using the sink outside the room and the scars on her inner arm stood out, vivid and pink.

"It's going to get too crowded in here."

"This is bigger than the Captain's Quarters," she said irritably. "Stop hunting for excuses to leave. Your place is here. With Linus."

"But not with you."

She flinched. "Well, at least we have that clear." She raked her hair from her face and grabbed her tote, clutching it as if it contained her life's worth. Which, aside from the baby on Adam's lap, it did.

"This room has its own bathroom," she said. "I'm going to take a shower and then I'm going to find the laundry facility that Dr. Patel mentioned and wash my clothes. And you and Linus will have this place all to yourselves while I do. And that's the best I can do right now to give you your space. Once the baby's well enough to go home, I'll figure out the next step. Shocking though it might be, I *am* actually capable of figuring some things out on my own!"

Linus's face screwed up in an expression very similar to his mother's and he let out a loud wail.

"Now look what you've done!"

"Me?" Adam stood, jiggling the baby, which didn't do the least bit of good to soothe either one of them. "You're the one yelling." He looked to the doorway, expecting to see Eric rushing through it at any moment. "He's not used to either one of us."

"Babies are resilient." She lifted Linus out of Adam's arms. "He'll adjust."

"How do you know?"

"I don't know!" She carried Linus around the room

in a rocking, swaying sort of way that had as little effect as Adam's jiggling. "I read it somewhere!"

Listening to the baby cry was almost as hard to bear as Laurel's tears. "Just go get him," he said roughly.

"Get *who*? Dr. Patel? I don't think he—"

"Eric!" Adam swore when Laurel just stared at him like he'd grown another head. He crossed the room in a couple strides and threw open the door, fully expecting to see the other man in the hallway, waiting.

But the only person in the hall was a white-haired woman pushing an oversize rack of meal trays.

The wail from inside the room was nearly as loud outside the room. Adam reentered and closed the door. Laurel was still walking Linus around the room. "Where is Eric?"

"How would I know? Gone home? Gone to his office?"

Adam propped his fists on his hips. "Why the hell isn't he here?"

"Why the hell should he be?"

God save him. "Because you went after him!"

Laurel stopped, midstep. "To tell him I was sorry. Not to ask him to stay."

Linus hiccupped into silence. He'd found his thumb and dropped his head onto Laurel's shoulder.

"You were going to marry him."

"And as I've had pointed out to me more than once, I backed out!" She exhaled audibly and pressed her cheek against Linus's head. "I wasn't in love with Eric. Not the way I should have been."

"You don't remember, though."

"I don't need to," she said tiredly. "If I'd been in love with him the way I—" She broke off and carried Linus over to the changing table and laid him atop the padded surface. "I wouldn't have slept with you if everything had been right between Eric and me. I might not remember everything, but that's one thing I am absolutely certain about."

She fumbled with Linus's stretchy outfit, finally managing to extract his legs so she could change his diaper. "No wonder you were wailing," she crooned. "All wet like this."

Considering she hadn't been hands-on with Linus since he'd been a couple weeks old, she changed his diaper with impressive speed. Then she was maneuvering his legs back into the sleeper and she picked him up from the changing table.

Adam lifted the baby out of her arms. "Go and take your shower," he said gruffly.

"You're going to stay, then?"

He grabbed the soft blanket hanging over the side of the crib and the colorful ball from the floor, and sat down in the rocking chair. "For now."

When Laurel came out of the bathroom twenty minutes later, Adam was still holding Linus on his lap in the rocker, face mask askew.

And both of them were sound asleep.

She pressed her hand against the ache in her chest and just stood there, watching them and memorizing the precious sight.

Then she heard the soft, distinctive ping from Adam's phone where it was sitting on the counter near the door and she finally moved again. She lightly brushed her fingers through Linus's wispy-soft hair. Then she slipped the empty baby bottle from Adam's lax fingers and leaned over and lightly brushed her lips over his before adjusting his mask and then her own.

He didn't stir a muscle.

She straightened and quietly gathered up the tote and pocketed some of the cash. She also picked up Adam's phone and slipped out of the room, pulling the smoothly heavy door closed after her. She pulled off her mask again, pressing her lips together for a moment, savoring the lingering warmth she'd felt from his.

There were two nurses at their station, laughing over something, and they pointed the way to the laundry when Laurel asked. It was empty when she got there and she dumped every piece of clothing save the T-shirt and shorts she was wearing into the machine. There wasn't a charge for it, though there was a collection kitty next to the industrial-sized containers of supplies. She pushed a crumpled bill through the slot in the kitty and with the washing machine clicking and whirring busily through its cycle, she swiped the screen on Adam's phone and an image of the two of them from the balloon in Durango appeared, stealing her breath for a long moment.

Was it a random coincidence? Or did it mean something more?

She entered his password then pressed the call icon, and the image was replaced by the keypad. She started to press the first number, but then she hesitated, struggling against the spurt of nerves that felt way too familiar and way too old.

But if she wanted to prove to herself once and for all that she *was* as capable as she'd claimed, she needed to start somewhere.

She still felt vaguely nauseated as she dialed the number that had been the same for her entire life.

It rang precisely four times before the line was picked up. "Yes?"

In her mind's eye, she saw him sitting at his desk in his ubiquitous gray suit and red tie.

She straightened her shoulders as if he were able to see her standing in the middle of the small laundry room, wearing second-hand clothes. "Hello, Father. It's Laurel."

The room was cool, dark and silent when Adam opened his eyes. He was disoriented for half a second, his tired mind tripping through states and motels and hotels and miles spent on the road.

But the weight of the baby stretched across his lap, and the prickles in his numb arm rapidly grounded him. It wasn't entirely dark in the room. Not once his eyes adjusted.

He could see the shapes of the furniture. The darker rectangle of the opened bathroom door. And no slender shape of a woman at all.

He edged carefully off the rocking chair and gingerly moved to the crib. Moving at a sloth's pace for fear he'd wake the baby, he leaned over and settled him in the center of the crib. And then he waited even longer before pulling his hands from beneath Linus's warm head and diaper-padded butt.

By the time he finally straightened, his back ached from the awkward position. He arched, rotated his arms and shoulders and neck, but he still felt like a hot metal poker was jabbing him in the middle of his spine.

He carefully pulled open the room door, wincing at the loudness of the latch, and stepped into the cornea-searing brightness on the other side.

He didn't close the door all the way. He was afraid he wouldn't hear Linus if he woke.

The nurses' station was unoccupied but the commercial-sized coffee urn located against the back wall was hot and full. He tugged the mask off one ear while he filled one of the disposable cups nearly to the brim. The clock on the wall told him it was still early. Not even eight o'clock.

Which meant he'd slept in that chair for close to three hours.

He flipped open the pink bakery box sitting next to the coffee machine but the two lone muffins inside looked as though they'd been there for days.

He dropped the cover back down and followed the signs to the play area, where two kids in pajamas were playing video games and a grandmotherly woman sat nearby, her knitting needles clicking softly and flashing in the light.

The kitchen area had two refrigerators and three long tables, picnic style. At the end of one, a man stared morosely into the plate of food in front of him.

Adam backed out unnoticed.

The laundry was next to the kitchen. But Laurel wasn't there, either.

He didn't want to feel alarmed. But that didn't stop it. He went back to the kitchen. "Excuse me." The guy looked up. "Have you seen a slender woman?" He held his hand up. "This tall? Long brown hair. Prettiest blue eyes you've ever seen?"

The man shook his head and turned back to surveying his plate again.

Adam repeated the question to the knitter and the two gamers with the same result.

He left his coffee sitting on the raised ledge surrounding the nurses' station. All of the patient rooms were positioned like spokes on a wheel with the nurses in the center. He strode the entire circuit but still didn't find Laurel.

On the white board hanging outside of Linus's room, Angelica's name had been replaced by the night nurse's. Penny. He didn't know if he needed to wash up again before re-entering the room, so he did it anyway and pulled his mask back in place. Then he went back into the room, leaving the door open so he could see without turning on the light.

The chart was still sitting on the counter beside the door, along with the envelope that Eric had left. But Adam's phone was gone and he was sure he'd left it there.

So she had his phone.

And every room in the transplant unit had a wired landline. He snatched it up and dialed his cell phone number. It went straight to voice mail.

Either she was talking on the phone or the battery was dead.

He went back to the playroom where he'd noticed a computer and pulled out the chair. Another white-board on the wall beside the monitor gave the name of the Wi-Fi and the password of the day. Soon, he'd accessed his phone account and he breathed easier at the sight of the bright red pin sitting squarely at the address of the hospital.

He propped his elbow on the table and exhaled. She was still on the property, then.

Somewhere.

He exited his account and returned to Linus's room. A dim line of light circled the ceiling and Penny the nurse was there, smoothing out a sheet on the mattress topping the bench that was now twice the size it had been earlier. She wasn't wearing a mask. "You can lose the mask now," she said when he asked. "Dr. Patel is satisfied they're no longer needed. You can also bring your own bedding if you want," she said softly. "Fits a full-size sheet. Just make sure everything is freshly laundered before you bring it into the unit." Her shoes squeaked slightly as she crossed the room. "I've put in an order for housekeeping to bring another set of towels, too. Knowing them, it'll probably be midnight before they show up, though. The door has a lock if you— Oh, hello." She smiled when Laurel appeared in the doorway. "I was just saying the door has a lock if you want to make sure nobody interrupts your sleep at night."

Adam peered at Laurel, but the ambient light was

too dim to read her expression above the mask she was wearing.

"Medical staff can override the lock," Penny was still talking, "but unless there's an emergency, we generally try to give everyone some uninterrupted privacy at night." She patted the cabinet hanging on the wall next to the door. "Extra formula and bottles for Linus are in here. He usually wants one around three, but don't worry if he sleeps through."

"Angelica told me earlier," Adam said.

"Perfect. Use the call button if you need anything." She clipped her pen onto her lanyard and squeaked out of the room. A moment later, she'd slipped into the room next door, leaving Adam and Laurel alone.

"Hope you don't mind." She held up his phone before setting it on top of the medical chart.

"No." Though he was mighty curious about whoever she'd called.

Her canvas tote was looped over her shoulder and she unloaded the clothes inside into one of the drawers built into the wall near the crib. Then she looked down at Linus and lightly covered his legs with the edge of the blue blanket.

"How's the mattress?" she asked in a low whisper.

"Didn't try it." Adam hadn't planned to spend the night. There was too much to take care of at Provisions in the morning. And the rental car. And the insurance. He literally had a dozen tasks that needed handling.

Laurel slipped around him and sat experimentally on the corner of the mattress. "More comfortable than it looks." She patted the space beside her. "Give it a try."

"If I do, I'm not going to want to get back up."

"You of all people have earned some sleep. More than you got in the rocking chair."

"I wasn't thinking about sleep."

She gave him a quick look before her lashes swept down again. "Give it a try," she said again. Even more softly.

The words sank through him. Tempting. "Not a good idea."

"Because...?"

"Because we're both too raw after the last few days." He walked over to her and closed his hands around her face, tilting it upward. Her pale blue eyes seemed to glimmer in the dim light. "Because it's been more than a year since I've touched you and when I do, I don't want it to be in a hospital room with our baby sleeping two feet away. But even more, because I'm not sure I can survive another dose of Laurel Hudson."

Her eyes were solemn. "I'm that poisonous?"

"Ah, sweetheart." He leaned over and deliberately pulled off her mask to press his mouth lightly, lingeringly, against hers. It would take nothing, nothing at all and his tenuous hold on practicality would scatter like dandelion fluff. "You're that addictive." He dropped the mask in her lap.

Then he moved to the crib and leaned over the side to kiss his son's soft cheek. "Take care of Mommy," he whispered.

Then he straightened and scooped up his phone before reaching for the door. "I'll be back tomorrow."

"Adam?"

His hand tightened on the door handle. He looked back at her.

"What's going to happen to us when Linus is ready to come home?"

"I don't know," he said honestly. "But we'll figure it out. All right?"

Her fingers were pressed against her throat. She nodded. "All right."

He pushed down on the door handle.

"Adam."

He steeled himself yet again. "Yeah?"

"I wish I had said yes."

There was no pretending he didn't know what she meant.

But a lot of years and a lot of words had happened since then.

With the knot in his throat nearly strangling him, he pushed open the door and he left.

Chapter Sixteen

Adam turned off the truck engine in front of the clay-tile-roofed house and looked at Laurel, sitting on the seat beside him. "Here we are."

Laurel exhaled audibly. Her eyes skipped to his and then away. Ever since they'd left the hospital in Houston that afternoon for what he dearly hoped was the last time, she'd grown increasingly quiet. More quiet than Linus was being in the back seat, at any rate.

Sprung from the hospital with Dr. Patel's and all of the nursing staff's heartfelt blessing, Linus had jabbered and chortled and played with the raucously noisy toy his uncle Kane had given him the entire way.

"You're sure about this? About staying here?" He spread his fingers, taking in the house in front of the truck. "Just because Callum offered the place doesn't mean we had to take him up on it." Adam hadn't even agreed to his cousin's offer until Callum had accepted Adam's insistence on paying monthly rent for the place. Family or not, Adam didn't take charity. "You and Linus could have it all to yourself if you'd be more comfortable."

She gave him a look as she unsnapped her safety belt and pushed open her door. "Don't start that again. Linus should have *both* of his parents with him. We agreed on that a week ago."

A week ago, he'd figured they'd be returning to the bungalow where Kane's presence would help keep Adam from forgetting that they weren't just any regular family. But that was before Callum's brilliant idea that they move into the empty guesthouse situated on the grounds of the Fame and Fortune Ranch he'd purchased nearly a year ago.

"Yeah, but if you change your mind, all you have to do is say so."

"Have *you* changed your mind?"

"No."

"Then stop harping on it!" She hopped out of the truck and closed the door a little harder than necessary before she opened the rear door and began unbuckling Linus from his car seat.

Adam got out, too, and lifted his duffel and the small suitcase that had replaced her canvas tote bag from the truck bed, and they headed toward the front door. "Kane should have dropped off the crib and the rest of the boxes of baby gear by now." He'd have liked to refuse the stuff Eric had sent to the bungalow on a JLI truck a few days ago, but Linus shouldn't have to suffer just because his father was churlish.

Laurel's head was like a swivel as she took in their surroundings. "When you said this wasn't a working ranch, I didn't expect to see so many horses." She rubbed her nose against Linus's. "Want to learn how to ride, sweet pea? I was a year old when I was put on the back of my first horse."

"Let's put a pin in that for now," Adam suggested as he pushed open the front door for her. "We haven't even gotten used to his starting to crawl."

Her eyes sparkled humorously as she carried Linus inside. "City boy. I bet I could get you to like horses, given the opportunity—" She stopped so abruptly Adam bumped into her from behind. She jumped as if she'd been scorched and crossed the furnished great room to stand in front of the tall windows overlooking an open range. When she gave him a quick look, her cheeks looked red. "It's lovely here."

It was.

But he was thinking more about the sight of her standing in front of the tall windows than the leather furniture and the fresh flowers that had welcomed them.

Callum had said the place was furnished. Adam should have realized his cousin hadn't meant it was furnished with items similar to what he and Kane had picked up from Mariana's Market.

"You're going to put a million fingerprints on these windows," she was telling Linus as she carried him through the house, obviously intent on exploring the new digs.

Adam dumped the bags on the couch and went the other direction, just to give himself an opportunity to breathe easier. For the last week and a half, he'd been preparing for the time when Linus would be ready to leave the hospital. When Adam wouldn't be seeing the baby and Laurel for just the few hours that he'd managed each day, traveling back and forth between Rambling Rose and Provisions and the hospital in Houston.

Now that the day had arrived, instead of thinking how lucky they were where Linus's recovery was concerned, all he could think about was the fact that there were real beds in this house and no nurses working on the other side of the hospital room door.

A bucket of daisies sat on the table in the breakfast nook, too, and when Adam opened the fridge in the kitchen, he found it had been stocked with fresh food.

Between Callum and his wife, Becky, they hadn't missed a trick. If Adam and Laurel had *really* been a family, the guesthouse would seem like a dream come true. Instead, he was feeling more caged than when they'd been crammed into a rental car driving across the country together.

"The boxes are here," Laurel's voice called to him from the other side of the house. "Kane put them in the nursery."

He exhaled. Avoiding Laurel wasn't going to solve anything. Particularly now that they were under their "own" roof. He went into the living area and grabbed her suitcase and cursed under his breath when the sketchbook tucked in the pocket on the side slid out and fell on the floor.

He leaned over and grabbed it but stopped when he saw the sketch of Linus.

He set down the suitcase and paged backward through the book. It was the same one she'd used back in Seattle and he felt bad that he hadn't thought to make sure she'd gotten a new one. She'd sketched flowers. And Jerry the security guard's face. Dr. Granger, with a chewed pen tucked in her gray hair.

Then he turned another page and saw his own face.

And another page. And another sketch of him. Like the doodling a teenage girl might do, they were small sketches, large sketches, partial sketches. They covered page after page after page until he reached the front cover of the book.

He exhaled. Told himself it meant nothing and he pushed the book back into the pocket again. More firmly so it wouldn't fall out again.

The nursery was easy enough to find, thanks to the crib. The boxes stacked beneath the window were still sealed. Sooner or later, they'd have to deal with unpacking all of the stuff Eric had bought when Linus had been his. Aside from those items, though, the room was empty.

Next to the nursery was a bathroom, and beyond that was another bedroom with a rustic four-poster bed. Laurel had plucked a sunflower from the collection filling a milk jar that sat on the windowsill and was waving it in front of Linus. "I'll take this room," she said when Adam entered. "It's closer to the nursery."

He set the suitcase on the rocking chair angled into a corner.

"Have you seen the other bedroom?"

He shook his head and dragged his attention away from her bed and went to find the third bedroom.

It sat on the opposite side of the house and was obviously meant to be the master suite. It had a similar sweep of windows as the living area did and its own bathroom complete with a claw-foot tub.

"Not the Captain's Quarters, that's for sure," Laurel said behind him.

He tried to rid the image he'd conjured of Laurel neck deep in that tub, but it was too busy tattooing itself on the inside of his eyelids in much the same way she'd sketched images of him. "Yeah."

She moved Linus from one hip to her other. Her eyes studied Adam too closely. "You all right?"

He stepped around them, needing escape. "Going to bring in the rest of the stuff from the truck."

Fortunately for him, it took most of the day to get settled. Mostly because they were interrupted almost hourly by one Fortune cousin or another stopping by to see how they were coming along. Callum invited them up to the main house for dinner and Adam was just opening his mouth to accept when Laurel plopped Linus on his lap.

"That's a wonderful offer," she'd told Callum, "but could we take a rain check?" She'd smiled ruefully. "It's just been a long day and—"

"No problem," Callum had said. "Don't forget there's always someone around up at the house if you need help with the baby or anything." Then, sending Adam a knowing look, he'd left, too.

While Laurel clanged pots in the kitchen—which *had* to be for effect, Adam figured—he gave Linus his bath. It was something he'd gotten used to in the last ten days traveling back and forth to the hospital in Houston. He'd give Linus a bath while Laurel disappeared for the hour.

The event always ended with Adam dripping wet, and that evening was no exception. But he'd learned to doff his shirt before the ritual, so at least he still had a dry shirt to put on afterward. With Linus wrapped in a diaper and a towel, he carried him into the kitchen. "I can have something delivered from Prov—" He broke off at the sight of Laurel whisking a pan sauce together in the cast-iron skillet.

"Chicken piccata," she said airily. "I *told* you."

He had to admit the chicken cutlets looked perfectly golden and the lemony sauce she was tending in the pan made his mouth water. The rest of the kitchen, however, looked like a bomb had gone off.

"Mommy's a messy cook," he told Linus, not remotely capable of hiding a smile. Adam was pretty sure he'd never felt more content than he did at that moment.

After dinner, Laurel prepared a bottle for Linus and disappeared down the hall. He went into the kitchen and stared at the mess for a moment before he mentally rolled up his sleeves and started to work.

The dishwasher was nearly loaded when he heard a soft sound coming from one of the baby monitors that he'd spent ninety minutes that afternoon moving from one place to another until she was satisfied.

This one didn't have a video monitor, but it did have an excellent speaker, and he notched up the volume at the sound of Laurel's distinctly off-key voice singing, "Just My Imagination."

He turned the volume off and rubbed his shaking hand down his face. The beard that had started growing on the trip from Seattle was full now. He dropped his hand and started opening one kitchen drawer after another until he found what he needed.

He went into the bathroom attached to his bedroom and eyed his reflection in the mirror over the sink. Then he lifted the scissors he'd found and began clipping away at the beard.

He was sitting on the wedge of deck behind the house watching the sunset when Laurel sat down beside him nearly an hour later.

"Linus asleep?"

"If he wakes up before morning again, I'm taking Becky's advice to feed him more before he—" She broke off. "You shaved!"

He was glad for the dim light because he could feel a hot tide rising up his throat. "Been known to happen now and then," he dismissed. "What's with the envelope?"

"Oh." She flipped the envelope as if she'd forgotten she was holding it. She dropped it on his lap. "A surprise."

Frowning, he tore it open and a slick driver's license fell into his hand. Even without good light, he was able to identify the picture of Laurel on the front. "You didn't step outside the hospital until today. How did you get—"

"I called my father," she said diffidently.

If she'd said she'd called Jesus himself, Adam couldn't have been more stunned.

"That first day at the hospital," she added, seeming to feel a need to fill his stupefied silence. "You fell asleep in the chair holding Linus and—" She lifted her shoulder. "I called my father. He put his lawyer on it and that was delivered to me yesterday."

"Why didn't you say something before?"

"I don't know. Less than a month ago I was calling myself Lisa Jane Doe." She lifted her shoulder a second time. "Now I have back my own name. I have some legal ID and some of my memories. And the most perfect son I could ever imagine. It's…a lot."

She'd also stopped covering up the scars on her arm. The sleeveless blouse she wore was one of several that Becky and Stephanie had gathered and sent with him to the hospital after learning Laurel only had a few items of her own.

"Is it too much?"

"You know that feeling you get when you're afraid to breathe because you might burst the beautiful bubble that you've somehow managed to form?"

"Your life isn't a fragile bubble, Laurel."

"That's what Dr. Green says, too."

"Dr. Green?" He stared at her. "When have you been talking to him?"

"Every day, actually. While I left you alone to give

Linus his bath, I was participating in a support group of his via teleconference." She cupped her hands around the edge of the deck beneath them and her long hair slid over her shoulders. "I know he's a pediatrician, but he gave me his card that one day and—" She broke off for a moment. "He's just been very nice. He said I wasn't the only mom he's met who's dealt with postpartum issues. Between him and Dr. Granger, at least I have a reason why I…left my baby. I had what's called postpartum panic disorder."

His throat tightened. "Sweetheart, you never needed a diagnosis."

"*I* needed it. So I can stop hating myself and maybe start forgiving myself. That's what a lot of the other moms in the group say, too." She angled her head, sliding a look his way. "Maybe if I hadn't been dealing with the news about my mother and Eric and—"

"Me."

Her lashes lowered. "And you," she conceded.

His chest ached. "Why didn't you tell me about all this before now?"

She shook her head, a bittersweet smile on her face. "You're no more to blame for my actions than I am for my mother's. And I didn't tell you before because it was something *I* needed to do. For *me*." She shrugged her shoulders a bit. "But we're here now and I didn't want you to think I was keeping secrets."

"Laurel—"

"Don't look at me like that," she said swiftly. Huskily. "This isn't something I want us crying over. If I hadn't had the accident, maybe I'd have come to my senses and returned straightaway to Linus. But I have to accept the fact that I may never know." She picked up the driver's license where it had fallen onto the deck and slid it into her pocket. "But no matter what, you can stop feeling like you need to be responsible for me. I may not have all my cheese squarely back on my cracker yet, but I'm not fragile."

He forced a wry smile. "Trust me, sweetheart. Nobody who makes that much of a mess in the kitchen is fragile."

She raised one eyebrow. "If you don't want me to make a mess, *you* do the cooking. You always used to, anyway."

They'd spent more hours together getting from Seattle to Texas than some people spent together after months of dating. He still wasn't used to the way she sometimes mentioned their past as if she'd never lost her memory at all.

"When you talked to your dad, how was he doing?" He felt cautious bringing it up. "After what happened with your mom?"

"He didn't tell me again that it was my fault." She plucked the fringed hem of her denim shorts. "And he helped me get my license. So progress is progress, I guess."

Adam figured Nelson was still Nelson. "He start insisting yet that you go back to Virginia?"

She exhaled softly. "He called the hospital every single day, trying to whittle me down. But I'm not going."

"He'll come here. You prepared to stand up to him when you're face-to-face?"

"I'm not twenty-two anymore," she said quietly. "I have a child of my own. A…family…of my own. And if my father behaves, maybe I'll let him be a part of it." She pushed herself to her bare feet. "Are you going to be out here for a while yet?"

He looked away from the racehorse-lean legs six inches away from his face. "Why?"

"Because you have a claw-foot tub in your bathroom and Becky—it had to be her, same as the flowers—left a beautiful jar full of bath salts for me."

No matter what happened, Laurel was still Laurel. He waved his hand. "Go."

She didn't dart off, though. "There's room for two, you know. And just to be clear," she said, crouching next to him and drawing her finger along his freshly shaved cheek, "I'm not talking about Linus."

Then she straightened and padded silently into the house.

Adam fell back on the wooden deck until he was staring up at the darkening sky and thumped his head. Once. Twice. Then he gave in and rolled to his feet.

He went inside the house. Checked on Linus. He was sleeping, sprawled on his back and taking up as much of the crib as he could take. He pulled the nursery door nearly closed.

He went into the bedroom. He could hear the water running. She hadn't closed the bathroom door and he stopped in the doorway.

Her aquamarine gaze met his and she let the blouse in her fingers fall to the floor. The only thing she still wore was the necklace he'd given her all those years ago. He could see her pulse beating in her long, lovely throat, making the gold L glint in the light.

From the day he'd met her, he'd wanted her. "Be very sure, Laurel."

She held out her left hand toward him. The scars no less red now than they'd been the first time he'd seen them. "I'm sure."

The water gushed from the tap, plunging through the center of the frothing bubbles. He reached over and turned it off. And then he took Laurel's hand. He kissed her palm. Her wrist. The inside of her elbow. He kissed the too-narrow point of her shoulder and the pulse beating beneath the necklace he'd given her. His hands shook as he clasped them around her face and he pressed his lips to the scar on her forehead.

When he lifted his head again, her eyes glittered with unshed tears.

"Don't cry. I told you, I can't take it when you cry."

She slid her arm around his neck, pulling him back to her. Her lips—those soft, full lips—grazed against his. "Then take me, Adam." She slid her fingers through his and pressed them to her breast. "Take my heart. It's only ever belonged to you."

He pulled her closer, sweeping his hand down the elegant line of her spine, the indent of her waist, the swell of her hip. A last bit of sanity intruded. "I don't have any protection."

"I don't need protection from you."

He laughed, growled, caught between aching need and frustration. "And that resulted in the little guy sleeping on the other side of the house, if you remember."

She'd managed to unfasten his shirt without him even noticing, and her hair grazed his chin as she kissed his throat. Her fingers drifted down his chest and reached his belt. "Is that regret?"

He trapped her hand. "Never."

Her eyes met his. "Then I don't see the problem." She slid her hand free and set to work on his belt. Everything inside him short-circuited when her hand closed around him.

By some small miracle, he managed not to trip over his own clothes as he lifted her against him. They didn't even make it all the way to the bed before her legs were wrapped around him and he was buried inside her. And when he felt her tightening, felt that quaking and the sound of her gasps filling his ear with some of the sweetest music he'd ever heard, he finally let himself go.

He woke with a start, hours later and stared into darkness.

His arms were empty. So was the rest of the bed.

He pulled on his jeans and left the room.

Linus was still sleeping when he checked.

The four-poster bed in the other bedroom was untouched.

He rasped his hand down his chest, not wanting to feel alarmed, though he did, particularly when he didn't find Laurel anywhere in the house.

Soon, he'd turned on every light in the house except Linus's room. He called the guard at the gatehouse,

ven though he couldn't imagine Laurel walking all
hat way on foot. His truck was where he'd parked it.

He was on the verge of calling Callum when he
eard a noise outside and he bolted out the door, nearly
ollapsing with relief at the sight of her walking toward
he house wearing only the button-down shirt she'd
ulled off him hours earlier. "What the hell, Laurel?"

She stepped up onto the deck and her face looked
avaged. "I remember, Adam. I remember *all* of it."

He stared. His hands fisted. "All—"

"Seeing you last May." Her voice sounded raw. "In-
iting you up to my hotel room even though I knew I
houldn't. You sh-showing up at my office in Houston
month later. And the look on your face when I told
ou I was engaged—" She swiped her wet cheek and
rushed past him, going inside.

He realized she'd been barefoot when he saw the
lick of blood on the kitchen tile.

He grabbed a towel and shoved it under the faucet
or half a second before following her. She was sitting
n the edge of the four-poster, staring at her hands.

He knelt down and lifted her foot. "Don't ever wan-
er off barefoot again," he said quietly. He carefully
viped the dirt and blood away from her heel.

"Why are you doing this?"

"Because you're bleeding."

She sucked in a thick, sobbing breath. "I called it off
ith Eric before I realized I was pregnant."

"Laurel." His jaw was rigid. "It's three-freaking-
'clock in the morning. I don't really want to hear about

the guy." He folded the towel to a clean corner and pressed it against the cut on her foot.

But she didn't listen. "He was a good man."

Adam dropped the towel and rose. "I just said didn't—"

"He was." Her throat worked as she faced him down, her aquamarine eyes flooding. "He just wasn't…you. And I knew," she said as she swiped her cheek, "I knew after the things you said to me in June, I knew you'd never forgive me. So I didn't tell you about the baby either. I don't know how many times I started writing you a letter to tell you the truth, but I never had the guts to finish. I did so many things wrong. I went to see my parents and that was a disaster—"

"Laurel, don't. You don't have to do this—"

"But I do! I was having nightmares about the baby. About being my mother's daughter. My father had just told me about her death. He was refusing to even have a funeral and I was too pregnant to fly to Virginia, anyway. I stopped in Rambling Rose just because you mentioned it last year when you came to the museum. I never expected to go into labor at the pediatric center dedication. Everyone there was so nice to me, though. They got me into an ambulance. I barely made it to San Antonio before Larkin was born."

Adam jerked. "Larkin."

Another tear slid down her cheek. "That's what I named him." She spread her palms. "He was in the NICU for days. I stayed in a hotel near the hospital. My father stopped taking my calls. And then it was time for Larkin to leave the hospital and—" She broke off

I don't remember leaving him at Dr. Green's office. don't remember how I even got to Seattle. Or the accident or any of it. I just remember I was so afraid of urting someone else I loved—"

"Stop." He knelt in front of her again, closing his ands around hers. "What matters is you're here now. .nd Linus—*Larkin.* God." He pressed his forehead gainst her hands until he could speak again. He looked t her. "You're both here and everything is going to e okay."

"But you'll never love me like you used to."

"There's nothing past tense when it comes to loving ou." He cupped her face. "Don't you get that by now? m never going to stop loving you. If you hurt, I hurt. ` you cry—" He hauled in a shaky breath. "Eric told ie he thought you were dead. Otherwise he'd have lo- ated you. They were the worst three days of my life. *nything* can be fixed as long as you're safe. I've loved ou since the day I met you and I'll love you until the ay I die. But I swear to God, Laurel, if you ever feel overwhelmed again and don't just *tell* me—" His oice broke.

She was staring at him, wonder filling her eyes. You *are* my safe place, Adam. You always have been. ve never deserved you. But I've always loved you. Iy only love." She brushed her thumb over his cheek. I told you that first night at the hospital that I wished d said yes. You didn't say anything. I thought that eant…" Her eyes flooded again. "I thought you didn't el the same."

"You can make up for it by saying yes now."

Her throat worked. "You still want to marry me?"

"Every day of my life, sweetheart." He brushed he tangled hair away from her face. "I don't have a rin at the moment to make this more official, but will yo please, *finally*, marry me?"

She smiled through her tears.

And she said yes.

Epilogue

"*Do you think she is ever going to let someone else hold him?*"

Adam glanced over to where his parents were sitting on one side of Provisions. The restaurant might have been closed for their private dinner, but it was packed fuller than it had ever been, what with all of the guests arriving for the wedding that was being held the following afternoon.

And it was true. Now that Caroline Fortune finally had a grandbaby to hold in her arms, she didn't look like she was going to let Larkin loose any time soon. Not even to Nelson Hudson, who'd been hovering around her for a while now. If he noticed the speculative looks he'd been receiving from Mariana, who was helping out on the serving crew that evening, he didn't show it.

"I don't know," he murmured, pressing his lip against Laurel's cheek. "I wouldn't take bets on any thing right now, since I never figured my father wou step foot in Texas again or believed your dad wou show up and give his blessing."

"I guess it's true that a grandbaby can move mou tains." Laurel smiled and rested her hand on his thig It was entirely distracting, that hand. Particularly whe there wasn't a thing he could do about it when they we surrounded by what seemed a hundred Fortune fami members. He honestly couldn't even say where they a were coming from. Their wedding guest list had som how gotten completely out of control. Probably wh they deserved, having left a lot of those details in th hands of Ashley, Megan and Nicole this past month

The wedding itself was supposed to be a simp affair—to be held outside at the Fame and Fortur Ranch with a barbecue to follow as a reception. A Adam really cared about was having his family ther They had all come down from New York, even h brothers, Brady, Brian and Josh, and his sister, Arabell And his dad seemed to be on good behavior for onc

Somehow, though, the affair was turning out to l a little larger than they'd anticipated. But Adam did really care if the entire state of Texas showed up. H only cared that Laurel was finally going to be his wit

He caught her hand as it drifted a little higher his thigh. "Behave yourself," he warned with a chok laugh.

She smiled angelically. "It's so much more fun whe I don't."

Heat was rising up his spine and he grabbed the cold beer sitting on the table in front of them. He'd perfected the IPA, finally. There'd even be enough for the wedding reception.

Along with the champagne, of course.

Nelson had arrived with a crate of Cristal. As if that were enough to make up for everything.

Laurel had just shrugged. Her father was her father. She'd invited him to their wedding, and he'd come.

It was enough.

"We can have fun tomorrow," Adam promised.

Laurel's eyes danced. They were having one night—their wedding night—on their own. Caroline and Gary would stay at the guest house to take care of Larkin. But then Adam and Laurel were picking up their son and taking him on their honeymoon with them.

Larkin was doing magnificently since his bone-marrow transplant two months ago, but it would be a long time before either one of them were ready to leave him for any length of time. Certainly not for the week that they'd be spending in Oregon.

Laurel wanted to paint the coastline.

Adam wanted to make love to his wife. And maybe to convince Ed Maxwell to share some of that porter of his with Provisions. At least until Adam's brewery was truly up and running.

So far it was still a bunch of architectural drawings and dreams.

Laurel leaned against him and her glossy oak-barrel hair slid over his arm. "What're you smiling about?"

He looked down into her aquamarine eyes. "Dreams."

She lifted her eyebrows slightly.

"They do come true." He slid his fingers through hers and lifted her hand to kiss it. "You and Larkin are all the proof I'll ever need."

* * * * *

COMING SOON!

We really hope you enjoyed reading this book.
If you're looking for more romance, be sure to
head to the shops when new books are
available on

Thursday 11th June

To see which titles are coming soon, please visit

millsandboon.co.uk/nextmonth

MILLS & BOON

Coming next month

CINDERELLA'S NEW YORK FLING
Cara Colter

The sales assistant, Meredith, swept up all the clothes and left them.

"I feel like Cinderella," Jessica said, sinking into the chair beside him. The dress hitched up on a slender leg. He tried not to look. Failing in that, he tried not to be obvious about looking.

"But it's just about midnight. The glass slipper falls off and I see what it all costs. I probably can't even afford one thing from here."

Jamie looked at his watch so she wouldn't see the pleasure in his eyes that he was going to play a part in her fairytale.

Not the prince part, of course. Though something about seeing her in all those clothes could tempt any man to play that role, even one as cynical about fairytales as him.

Meredith came back. She held out a piece of paper to Jessica.

Jessica took it, looked at it, and blinked. "Oh," she said. "It's so much less than I expected. Still, I don't need two skirts. So, I should probably take out the pencil-line one and keep the navy slacks."

Meredith snatched the paper back from her. "I forgot to add our preferred customer discount."

Jessica took back the paper with the adjusted price. Her mouth fell open with shocked surprise.

"Alright," she cried, beaming, "I'll take it all!"

As Meredith handled the transaction – giving the one

bill to Jessica and putting the real amount on Jamie's credit card, Jamie realized this was probably the most duplicitous thing he had ever done. But Jessica was absolutely radiant.

"I'll pay you back, of course. The insurance representative said I'll have some money by this afternoon."

How could something feel both so very wrong and so very right at the same time?

When they left the store, Jessica was wearing the brand new sundress. Jamie couldn't help but notice that, in a city where no one paid any attention to anyone else, Jessica was receiving subtle – and deeply appreciative glances – from the men of New York.

A man on a construction site whistled at her. Jamie threw him a warning glance, and then noticed Jessica was blushing as though she had been propositioned.

How could he turn her over to an assistant when it was so complicated? Jessica now looked like a sophisticated woman of the world. But she was the furthest thing from that. He couldn't just cast her out on her own. A still small voice, somewhere in the region of his heart, whispered to him, *admit it, pal, you don't want to*.

Continue reading
CINDERELLA'S NEW YORK FLING
Cara Colter

Available next month
www.millsandboon.co.uk

LET'S TALK
Romance

For exclusive extracts, competitions
and special offers, find us online:

- facebook.com/millsandboon
- @MillsandBoon
- @MillsandBoonUK

Get in touch on 01413 063232

For all the latest titles coming soon, visit
millsandboon.co.uk/nextmonth

JOIN THE
MILLS & BOON
BOOKCLUB

* **FREE** delivery direct to your door

* **EXCLUSIVE** offers every month

* **EXCITING** rewards programme

50% OFF
YOUR FIRST
PARCEL

Join today at
Millsandboon.co.uk/Bookclub

MILLS & BOON

HISTORICAL

Awaken the romance of the past

Escape with historical heroes from time gone by. Whether your passion is for wicked Regency Rakes, muscled Viking warriors or rugged Highlanders, indulge your fantasies and awaken the romance of the past.

MILLS & BOON
MEDICAL
Pulse-Racing Passion

Set your pulse racing with dedicated, delectable doctors in the high-pressure world of medicine, where emotions run high and passion, comfort and love are the best medicine.

GET YOUR ROMANCE FIX!

MILLS & BOON
blog

Get the latest romance news, exclusive author
interviews, story extracts and much more!

JOIN US ON SOCIAL MEDIA!

Stay up to date with our latest releases, author news and gossip, special offers and discounts, and all the behind-the-scenes action from Mills & Boon...

 millsandboon

 millsandboonuk

 millsandboon

night just be true love...

7/10/20